After the Lie

Also by Kerry Fisher

The School Gate Survival Guide
The Island Escape

After the Lie

KERRY FISHER

bookouture

Published by Bookouture - an imprint of StoryFire Ltd.
23 Sussex Road, Ickenham, UB10 8PN, United Kingdom
www.bookouture.com

ISBN: 978-1-78681-110-3
eBook ISBN: 978-1-910751-80-0

For my mum, and all the other mothers out there,
trying to do their best.

PROLOGUE

In June 1982, I was thirteen. Pre-internet. Pre-Facebook. Pre-Twitter. We were oblivious to the *#proudparents* of four-year-olds who'd swum five metres for a duckling certificate. We had no idea how many people were eating perfect poached eggs for breakfast. We certainly didn't know that our neighbour down the road 'loved her husband to the moon and back – twice'. And we didn't have the pressure of capturing the one nanosecond that the whole family was happy against a sunny backdrop of turquoise sea, so that everyone else could feel a grumbling sense of dissatisfaction with their own lives.

1982 didn't seem different to any other year. At weekends, I'd disappear off on my bike with a couple of jam sandwiches, a bottle of squash and a warning from my mother to 'Mind what you're up to' before reappearing at teatime hours later. When it was rainy, I'd lie on my bed taping Kool & The Gang off the radio with the microphone jammed up against the speaker, desperately trying to get a version of *Get Down On It* that didn't have the DJ talking over the beginning or someone shouting 'Dinnertime!' in the middle. When it was hot, I'd sunbathe on the Norfolk dunes slathered in baby oil, flicking through *Smash Hits* and plotting how to buy and wear a mini skirt without my mother finding out. The perennial arguments still raged on: why I couldn't have my ears pierced, why we couldn't have a video recorder, why I still had to go to church every Sunday.

The one thing my mother and I weren't at loggerheads about was how often I needed to cycle to the library after school to find new reference books for a particularly onerous history project.

Or at least, that's what I told her.

And that little lie made the big difference. It led to the ten minutes I could never get back, never undo. Like smashing your iPhone, leaving your bag on the bus, driving into a bollard in a car park – but with consequences that money couldn't fix. That sick feeling of self-loathing that all of this could have been avoided if you'd just slowed down, taken your time, *thought things through.* Or as my sixteen-year-old son would say now, 'Not been such a dickhead'.

But in those glorious ten minutes, I didn't even realise I was making a mistake.

Let alone one I could never leave behind.

If the internet had existed back then, I'd have dreaded logging onto Facebook. No doubt my classmates would have been retweeting and WTFing until their fingers fell off.

But in 1982, the only thing that went viral in my little Norfolk village was glandular fever. I wouldn't have expected to get away completely unscathed, of course. I would have braced myself for shocked disapproval from the milkman, an abrupt halt to conversation in the greengrocer's or some knowing looks from the neighbours. Worst case scenario, I'd have skulked past the bus shelter, ignoring the jeers from the boys sharing stolen Benson & Hedges and swigging Bacardi filched from their parents' cocktail cabinets.

No, for a mistake to go viral in the '80s, you needed a deputy headmaster for a dad. A dad who adored his daughter and ended up in prison. To make sure it haunted you forever, you needed a Catholic mother to fall on her rosary beads and declare that 'all that business' should never be spoken about again.

Ever.

CHAPTER ONE

Birthday presents terrify me. Nothing shows up the chasm between who you are and who everyone else would like you to be more than what they 'saw and thought of you'. And what anyone thought of me never quite matched what I thought of myself.

By far the most dread-inducing present was the flourish of a gift from my mother, delivered in recycled paper carefully smoothed out and reused. Nothing screamed 'this is the person I wish you were' more than the parade of diaries, drawer dividers and polo-necked sweaters delivered to me over the decades. But this year, on my forty-third birthday, she'd surpassed herself. She sat with her hands folded in her lap, expectation scaffolding her face. She nodded at the box on the table. 'Go on then. Open it.'

I picked at the Sellotape, taking care not to tear the paper. A gold cross necklace. I only wore silver. And I never wore crosses. Never. Of all the ways I'd tried to make amends over the last thirty years, giving in to my mother's rampant Catholicism had remained a glittering exception. No conversation was complete without a variation on 'God knows what's in your heart' – which was really my mother's shorthand for 'God will get you back'.

A great bubble of resentment surged up. An image of flinging the necklace into the patch of nettles at the bottom of the garden rushed through my mind.

'That's lovely, thank you.'

'Put it on, darling. Come here, I'll do it up for you.'

I sat down with my back towards her – a straight back in order not to cop the 'You're becoming so round-shouldered' speech. As she clicked the necklace around my neck with a satisfied 'Perfect', I resisted the urge to leap up, throw open my kitchen cupboards and fling out the Wedgwood tea service she'd bought me 'for best'. To sweep my Christmas present of fussy cut glass tumblers to the floor. To hurl around the collection of jugs she'd infiltrated into my home over the years in the hope that my children would stop their 'uncouth' dumping of plastic milk cartons on the table.

'Go and look in the mirror.'

I walked out to the downstairs cloakroom and peered at myself in the mirror, amazed that my face looked smooth and neutral rather than like a ball of dough in the proving stage. I touched the cross. Not quite as hideous as the Pope Francis thimble, Pope John Paul II commemorative plate or the absolute *pièce de résistance*, the china Popemobile complete with waving pontiff. I could have made a fortune if I'd allowed the kids to put it all on eBay, but I kept it as an insurance against the day when she'd ask, 'Now what happened to…?'

I knew Mark would tease me and say, 'Why didn't she have done with it and buy you a hairshirt?' All our married life, he'd kept out of the tangled dynamics that passed for a relationship between my mother and me. He'd reluctantly agreed to have Jamie and Izzy baptised, but put his foot down about a full-blown Catholic upbringing. 'I'm not having the kids indoctrinated with guilt, blame and shame in the name of religion.'

It was the one time I'd been forced to stand up to my mother when she got her needle stuck on when they were going to be confirmed. I'd fudged it by saying we'd let them decide when they were old enough. Now they were teenagers and refusing even to go to church, my mother was on a mission. But so far, neither of them appeared the slightest bit worried about going to hell.

I walked back in, concentrating on a light, sunny step.

'So, what are you doing for the rest of the day?' my mother asked, in a tone that suggested she'd been the highlight.

'I've just been elected chairwoman of the fundraising committee at school. They want a new rugby clubhouse, so I need to go to a meeting about that.' Even I could see that as birthdays went, it was rather short on celebration.

I was prepared for a little dig of 'Hasn't Mark planned anything special for you?' but instead my mother burst out with an animated 'Really, darling? You should have said earlier. You have done well.'

My mother wasn't given to over-the-top praise. Any praise, in fact. But she was teetering right on the edge of a squeak of approval at my 'news', which was proof indeed that my bar for success was not so much low as buried. Hallelujah for climbing up another rung on the redeeming scale. I usually managed to haul myself up a notch about every five years. There was nothing she liked more than a crumb of evidence that Lydia Rushford, miscreant offspring of Arthur and Dorothy Southport, was no longer the social pariah of yesteryear.

She grabbed my hand and squeezed it. The softness of her skin surprised me.

I waited.

My mother selected a tone several decibels below the one she'd used to congratulate me. 'It's wonderful how you've moved on from all that…you know…'

I stared at her. In our family, no one *moved on*. The passage of time had covered the worst wounds with a scattering of normality. But like watchful crows gathered on a garden fence, our conflicting resentments were always waiting to swoop down for a vicious peck. Just before I took my dad's arm to walk down the aisle to marry Mark, my mother clutched my hand and whispered, 'It hasn't turned out so badly, considering…' My first born, Jamie, had barely taken a breath in the world before she murmured, 'We'll keep an eye on this one, we don't want history repeating itself…'

Too flipping right about that. Whatever mistakes Jamie made, I wouldn't cling to them like a koala to a eucalyptus for three decades.

Unfortunately, I now had my mother's full attention. 'What will you have to do on this committee, dear?'

The full horrors of what it would entail eluded me. Despite my mother's delight, being voted chairwoman wasn't a question of 'doing well'. In any half-accurate poll, I reckoned there would be a one in two chance of people opting to clean the sports hall loos rather than chair a school committee.

Personally, I would have happily put on the Marigolds and got scrubbing. I was cringing at the thought of sitting in front of the headmaster, discussing the merits of a hog roast over a quiz evening. I should have refused immediately when the class über-rep, Melanie, had put my name forward at the coffee morning. The enthusiastic endorsements from the others had paralysed me. It seemed easier to get the spotlight off me if I agreed than to explain why the very word – *headmaster* – made me want to hide behind the bike sheds and start smoking for the first time in my life.

When I tried to discuss my misgivings with my mother, she might as well have stuck her fingers in her ears and tra-la-la'd. 'You spend your life fiddling about with balloons and coffee in that wedding business of yours, don't you? You'll be perfect.'

After all these years, it was astonishing that my mother could still engender a little frisson of fury every time she talked about my career. 'That business of mine' often took care of the exorbitant school fees, plus the running of the whole Rushford household whenever Mark's kitchen business was in a slump. But unlike my doctor brother who saved lives, my job keeping bride and groom calm with precision event planning was a little frippery – a small step up from origami and pom-pom making.

'I'm not centre stage at work. No one is watching me. I'm just creeping about behind the scenes, straightening bows and making sure there are enough wine glasses.'

But nothing would derail my mother from her cock-a-hoopness that her daughter had reached the pinnacle of social acceptability. Who could blame her? After the miracle of snagging a husband in the first place, I'd spent nearly two decades airbrushing myself into a perfect wife. Just enough small talk, Boden and discreet pearl earrings to pass through life, slipping under the radar, as unremarkable as a mid-range estate car. No wonder Melanie had peered at all the mothers scrabbling down the hallway, FitFlops flapping at the mere mention of 'volunteers needed' and thought, 'Where's Lydia? She can organise baskets of almond favours and rose petals on tables. A couple of quizzes and a raffle should be well within her grasp.'

As a measure of my mother letting her hair down in wild celebration, she sawed another slice off the birthday Battenberg, saying, 'I shouldn't really,' and mumbling, 'Accolades like that don't come along every day.' If I'd just kept my mouth shut, I wouldn't have to endure months of my mother wanting to know the minutiae of every tedious meeting. Or worse, grilling me on my social connections: had I met any lawyers, doctors or dentists? Whether or not they were nice, decent people didn't even feature. And now her interrogations were spreading down the generations with 'innocent' enquiries whenever she clapped eyes on my children –

'Izzy, so who are you friendly with now? Hannah? Isn't her mother the one with a stud in her nose? I wouldn't bother with her. Don't you see anything of the little girl whose father's a surgeon in London, what's she called, Alexandra?' – followed by Izzy disappearing upstairs with the insolent stomp of a thirteen-year-old.

If Jamie wasn't quick enough to evaporate at the same time, the focus would switch to him. 'I hope you're going to join the

orchestra? It's a very good way to get to know the right people.'
Which was enough to make him sever a few fingers so he'd never
have to pick up his saxophone again. Luckily, at sixteen, Jamie
had mastered the art of the grunt that could be construed as a
'yes' or a 'no'.

As usual, my mother heard what she wanted to hear.

Eventually the conversation came full circle, a rainbow of
Battenberg crumbs flying out of my mother's mouth as she made
the point – again – that 'after all that business' I'd been lucky to
end up with a husband and family.

After thirty years, the only reply that allowed us to grind along
without bloodshed was 'Another piece of cake?'

CHAPTER TWO

Unlike my mother, Mark had been more put-out than proud that I was head honcho of the fundraising committee. 'Couldn't they find someone who doesn't work to do it? Surely one of the Eastington House mothers could take a break from making quinoa and pomegranate salads to push around their plates?'

The fact that Mark even knew what quinoa was made me laugh. 'Get you, MasterChef. I know. It was just really hard to say no.'

Mark stabbed at his phone and sighed. 'I hope you're not taking on too much. I don't want you keeling over with exhaustion. And frankly, I need your fundraising skills a bit more than Eastington House's posh and privileged. I've no doubt those kids can go on to lead fulfilling lives without underfloor heating in their changing rooms. I could really do with a hand chasing up kitchen leads before Christmas. The order book is completely empty for November.'

'I don't suppose it will be very onerous, so perhaps I could do some follow-ups for you in the evenings. The main event is the hog roast in October to raise money for the new clubhouse.'

'I'd much rather have a few grand a year off the fees than a swanky new bar. I'd be quite happy to sit on a camping chair under a gazebo.'

Yet again, I wished I'd stood up to my mother when she'd done her whole 'private school or die' as soon as I'd had kids. By the time I'd packed Jamie off to Eastington House kindergarten aged three – in his cap, for god's sake – I was still deluded enough to think I could build some bridges with her. Instead, I'd just signed us up for a lifetime of tightening our belts, which made my poor husband feel as though he'd let me down.

If only he knew the truth about me.

About all of us.

I heaved a sigh of relief as Mark picked up his laptop and started packing his briefcase for work. I had to squeeze in a meeting with my fellow fundraisers before racing off to a consultation with a woman who'd sounded more funereal than bridal. Black tulips, black jelly babies and black candles. The idea of standing my ground with the bossy women on the committee was stressing me enough without having to persuade a client that caves, crypts and dungeons were not suitable wedding venues.

The front door clicking shut, for me, was right up there with a baby's laugh and the first cup of tea after the school run. The moment of the day when I could just be myself. The self that no one knew. The person who wanted to shake my mother by her scrawny shoulders when she banged on about the right way to behave, the right circle of friends, the right connections. The wife who wanted to make plans for the future without fearing the past. The mother who wanted to encourage her children to live expansively, joyously, to cultivate a healthy immunity to what 'everyone' thinks.

About anything.

Instead, I checked my make-up and took my navy blazer from the coat cupboard. I tried to ignore the whimpering of our black Labrador, Mabel, who had just realised that a walk was not on the immediate agenda.

Despite arriving at the café twenty minutes early, Melanie was already sitting in the far corner. I paused on the threshold, recoiling from a one-to-one spotlight with the woman whose opinions came at you with all the finesse of a prop forward: 'We shouldn't allow alcohol at school social evenings. One father was sick in the flowerbed that had been specially planted to look like the school crest last year'; 'The school really needs to serve plain water, not fruit juice, at sports matches because of the risk of tooth enamel erosion.'

And if that wasn't bad enough, Melanie also seemed to have a secret hotline to the exam results of every child in her son's year, with a special terminal illness announcement voice for anyone with less than fifty-five per cent in Maths. As it was the start of a new term, she'd no doubt be up till midnight trying to crack the teacher's streaming code. It would only be a matter of time before she worked out that the duffers were languishing in the Rhododendron set, with the brainy ones beavering away in the Apple Blossom group.

Although Melanie was scribbling in a notebook, she appeared to have little antennae on the top of her head that swivelled round the second my foot creaked on the step. 'Lydia. Lovely to see you.' She untucked herself from the armchair in a graceful movement, her black trousers swishing to attention above her ballerina pumps. 'Come and sit down.'

'I'll just get a coffee.'

'I thought we'd do one big round when everyone gets here, to save wasting time. There are a few things I'd like to discuss with you first, without the others.'

It seemed a bit childish to get into a big hoo-ha over the cappuccino timings, even though I hated giving into Melanie's little power play. I pulled out a chair.

Melanie crossed her legs and tapped her pen on her notebook. 'Now, the main project this year is the new rugby clubhouse. It's going to be your job to keep the form reps involved and force them to push the other parents to help out. You'll have to be a bit dictatorial, otherwise nothing will happen.'

I told myself that I made life-changing weddings happen all the time, without ever needing to draw on my inner dictator.

Quiet efficiency and polite requests had worked well enough so far.

Melanie stared at me. 'You'll have to accept that not everyone is going to like you. As I'm sure you know, I've ruffled a few feathers, but that comes with the job.'

I couldn't even tell the dog off without kissing her head and giving her a biscuit afterwards.

'We need to raise at least twenty thousand pounds. There's a parent who's joined the school this year who's very interested in photography. He's going to take photos at various sports matches, which he will then print and sell at other events. He's coming along this morning so you can meet him.'

'Don't we need permission from the parents to take photos?'

Melanie twittered her fingers airily as though I was obstructing her brilliant ideas. 'You'll have to get permissions signed. The sports staff can send them out to the parents.'

Oh dear. That would mean talking to Mr O'Ryan who called all the pupils 'Boooooy!' and frothed at the mouth whenever Eastington House was losing.

Before I could sink any further under my burden of duties, a few other women came clacking in. Melanie pointed them into seats, cutting across chatter about the new Italian restaurant. She whistled up a waitress and dispatched her to get coffee. 'White Americano okay for everyone?'

I dared to disrupt Melanie's call to action with a request for soya milk, earning me an irritable glance as though I'd started discussing a complicated order for a triple decker sandwich, hold the mayo, no tomato.

Melanie tapped her clipboard for silence. She turned to Fleur, an ex-model and Pied Piper for the dads at any school event. 'Right. Fleur, your job is to source some shawls, scarves and shrugs we can sell at the Christmas fair. Do you think some of your connections in the rag trade would be happy to donate?'

Fleur raised her eyebrows and smoothed her glossy hair behind her ear. 'Fashion designers, do you mean, Melanie? I'm sure a few of my friends will be able to oblige.'

'Good.' Melanie ploughed on. 'Terri, could your husband offer some complimentary tickets to… What is it he does? Bingo evenings?' Melanie managed to say the word 'Bingo' in the manner of someone who'd just bitten into a maggot-ridden nectarine.

Terri cackled with laughter and slapped Melanie's knee as though she'd cracked a great joke. Melanie made a big show of struggling not to spill her coffee. 'Come on, Mel, don't be naughty, you know he owns casinos now. You should come down sometime. Get you on the blackjack tables. Free drinks when you're gambling. I'll sort out some freebies for you. You'll have to stick his name at the top of the programme though – he likes a bit of a fanfare.'

At that moment, a stocky man strode up to the table. Melanie leapt to her feet, running her fingers through her hair and straightening the neckline of her T-shirt. 'Sean! You found our little gathering. Come on in. He'll make a great addition, won't he, ladies? We could do with a bit of male insight.'

I looked up at the object of her adulation and blinked hard, feeling the world quiver slightly. While Terri launched in with a hundred questions about what year his kids were in and where he was living, I excused myself to the loo, aware of my feet skittering on the wooden floor like the dog when she was trying to escape the Hoover.

Why would it be him, here, now?

CHAPTER THREE

I lowered the loo lid and sat down. I couldn't be sure. There was no sign that he'd recognised me. He probably didn't see me in the worshipful fog surrounding him. I hadn't seen the man in thirty years. I hadn't forgotten about him – how could I? – but I'd stored him away in the understairs cupboard of my mind, to remain there undiscovered until I died, with any luck. Last I'd heard he was living in America, some big-shot estate agent for the rich and famous. Why would he turn up in a Surrey backwater? Sean was a pretty common name. It didn't have to be Sean McAllister. I re-applied my lipstick and prayed that it was any other Sean: Sean Smith, Sean Connery, Shaun the flaming sheep.

My body seemed to think it was him, though. Every time I tried to bring his face to mind and compare the chunky adolescent with today's broad-shouldered man, my stomach suffered from air turbulence. If it was him, his hair wasn't as dark as I recalled. But maybe, like me, he had plenty of grey. I hauled myself up and leant on the sink. My hands were shaking so much I was rattling the taps. I had to go back out there. I'd brave a few more of Melanie's diktats, then I'd make an excuse to disappear.

I opened the door and pretended I was stepping into a meeting with a new client, steeling myself to look smiling, confident and capable. I hovered at the side of the room, staring straight at the back of the man who'd blown my life apart so many years ago. Was it him? I didn't remember his hair being that wavy. I strained my ears. There was a deep timbre to his voice. Was that a slightly

American inflection? Or Irish? Mark always teased me about my inability to distinguish a Brummie from a Liverpudlian. I consoled myself that if Sean wanted to ingratiate himself with the great and good of Eastington House, he wouldn't be in a hurry to tell the story either. Too many of the women out there had teenage girls themselves.

I slunk towards the group, undecided whether I was going to introduce myself or just slip in quietly. Melanie made the decision for me. 'Sean. This is our new chairwoman – the very capable Lydia Rushford.'

Hallelujah for my parents' decision to call me by my middle name when we moved away after everything that had happened. For the millionth time I thanked my lucky stars that I'd married Mark. Right now, the fact that he was kind and honourable was a bonus. Having his surname, totally different from my original name was the real prize. Sally Southport sounded like a weathergirl on the TV to me now.

Sean stood up. If it was him, he'd ended up quite tall, well over six foot. I remembered him as a thickset bulldozer on the rugby field, steaming through the opposition, stubby legs powering away. I'd loved watching him play. Saturday was my favourite day of the week, when I was allowed to linger on the edge of the 'in' crowd. When I stopped being the deputy headmaster's daughter and became one of the rugby girlfriends.

My hand shook a little in his firm grasp. 'Lydia, lovely to meet you.' Had he lingered on 'Lydia'? Put a little bit of emphasis on 'meet'? Would he even recognise me now, with my blonde highlighted bob rather than the long brown hair I used to have? I'd been stick-thin then as well. I was what my mother would call 'solid' now. Certainly not the thirteen-year-old girl with the jutting hip bones of adolescence. Mark chivalrously called me 'hourglass', which would have worked if I'd been three inches taller.

I automatic-piloted, 'Pleased to meet you, too' and sat back in my armchair, unable to concentrate on any of the bulk-buying of jelly snakes as prizes, glow-in-the-dark antlers for the fireworks evening or rigid rules for the contents of the Christmas gift box for the children of Africa.

'Toothpaste, toothbrush – yes. Chocolate, soldiers, anything gun- or sword-shaped – no.' Everything had a life-or-death quality when Melanie spoke, as though slipping in a chocolate button would result in a revolution in Uganda.

Sean caught me staring and winked at me. It was him. That little lopsided grin. His nose didn't seem crooked, though. He leaned back, one foot crossed over his knee. Long-discarded memories shrugged off their dust sheets. I batted them away, picking up my coffee to hide my face but I couldn't take a sip. Everything in me seemed bilious, as though I'd glugged down a two-litre bottle of coke without pausing to breathe. I was making a gulping noise, the way the dog did when she was about to throw up. I put my cup back down and coughed, hoping to release, very quietly, some of the trapped air from my stomach. Instead, a big swell – a hard knot of fright – lodged itself halfway up my oesophagus, threatening to bring my porridge with it. I tried to breathe steadily, my mind catching wafts of Melanie's 'fundamental principles', 'expenses down and income up', 'more volunteers, lighter burden'. I was aware of Sean glancing at me now and again. His eyes were constantly on the move, drinking us all in. Still restless, then.

Would it all come out now, this secret we'd fought so hard to keep? What would they think, these people with their granite-topped kitchens, their husbands in the latest Range Rovers, their children with cellos in wheeled cases? Every time Jamie fouled at rugby, overdid the rough and tumble in the playground, or, god forbid, got into a fight, would there be mutterings of 'From what I hear, it runs in the family'? Or would it be a total non-event, greeted with a shrug before they all went back to watching the *Great British Bake Off.* With my mother's barometer stuck on stormy for all these years, I had no way of working out an accurate public disapproval forecast. Mark would know. But of course, he didn't *know.*

'Lydia. Lydia!' Melanie's sharp voice cut into my fear.

I dragged my eyes up to meet her questioning glance, feeling the beginning of a migraine.

She said, 'You'd better have a separate meeting with Sean, to discuss pricing and publicity. It's going to be a real money-spinner for us. I've seen his pictures; he's an excellent photographer.'

Photographer.

The word bounced off the walls at me.

'I'm sure he is.'

I gathered every last bit of strength, imagined my thigh muscles connecting to my knees and contracting to force myself into a standing position. I grabbed my handbag.

Sean smiled, a man used to a warm welcome wherever he went. 'I'll give you a ring, Lydia, and we can come up with a strategy.'

If he hadn't recognised me, it was just a matter of time. My voice sounded thick, as though I was speaking underwater. 'Okay. Sorry, I have a meeting now, I have to go.'

I raced out into the street, gulping in the urban air of exhaust, Chinese takeaway and fresh bread. I just managed to dash into an alleyway before I lost the battle with the porridge.

CHAPTER FOUR

On days like today, I wished we'd stayed in our little village in Norfolk and let everybody gossip their arses off until they'd found someone else to talk about. I fantasised about telling my mother that I wouldn't go along with her charade any more. That I didn't care that she arranged the flowers at St Joseph's, that Dad had had his application accepted to join the golf club, that she loved telling everyone that her grandchildren went to Eastington House. I just wanted to be who I was, imperfect bloody me, who messed up.

But most of all, I wished I'd told Mark – some of it at least – the first day I met him after he rescued me when my stall collapsed at a wedding show. I wished I'd never allowed the secret to grow, rolling down the generations like a toffee under a sofa, collecting dust, hair and grit as it went.

'I've led a very dull existence,' I said when people asked me about my past. I'd been in Surrey long enough to lose my Norfolk accent, except for the occasional word. Mark knew we'd lived there but I blocked all suggestions about going back to show him where I grew up.

'It's so flat and boring.'

'You'd hate all that seaside town nonsense, amusement arcades and silly souvenir shops.'

'I'm a townie now. All those marshes depress me. It's so bleak.'

In reality, I longed to be under those big open skies again. Yearned to walk for miles and miles on those sandy beaches, picking

up razor shells or crabbing ankle- deep in freezing water. I craved
the sea air, with its taint of dead seal and seaweed. I wanted to
burst through the front door, cheeks whipped by blasts of sand and
winter wind. I'd even run squealing into the Wash in April, just as
we used to, disdainful of the out-of-towners who stood shivering on
the shore, wrapped in their puffy anoraks and suburban attitudes.

Even my mother, who was a great one for snuffing out any
source of fun, never batted an eyelid about me being gone for
hours, as long as I didn't commit the cardinal sins of getting
home after dark and letting my dinner go cold. That freedom
seemed laughable now when I thought of my own kids and their
constant texting about where they were and what time they
needed picking up.

And now I'd missed my moment to come clean. Perhaps if I
hadn't been so *grateful* that someone could see the good in me,
I might have trusted Mark. I could have flopped against him,
maybe heard him say, 'Poor you. You were so young.' Sometimes
I struggled to remember how this Bazooka bubble gum of a lie
had burst and engulfed us all.

I hardly ever cried. It was as though I didn't have the same
amount of moisture in my body as other people. When the
whole room wept at wedding speeches, I stood dry-eyed at the
back, wondering where people found the huge well of emotion
to display. But today I was making up for it.

I needed to talk to Sean. Surely he had as much to lose as me?
What if he just viewed it as a bit of fun, something that happened
so long ago as to merit barely a mention? What if he couldn't
believe it was still governing my life, my family's life, changing
us all forever? Of course, he hadn't lived it the way we had, but
if his lips, those perfect lips, even suggested a smile, I'd have to
be kept away from pitchforks.

I forced myself to take deep breaths until I stopped shaking.
Nearly time to go and meet the bride who was taking the theme

of 'Until death do us part' to extremes. I didn't dare cancel in case I lost the ability to face anyone ever again once I'd stepped off the merry-go-round. Onwards and upwards with eye-whitening drops, foundation and a quick polish of my backbone.

I found the bride's house easily. From the outside, it was a smart executive home, a square of lawn in front, garage to the side. When Clarissa answered the door, I did have to practise 'eyes in', as I instructed the children whenever we walked past a shouting match in the street, a car accident or anyone who was passé enough to be sporting a Mohican. Clarissa had enough nose and lip jewellery to quake in fear at magnetic forces. Beneath the long black hair streaked with pink, she had the sweetest elfin face. I did wonder what her fiancé looked like. How would he kiss her without getting an eye tooth hooked in a hoop? I wondered whether the neighbours shooed their children away in case they were invited in to eat barbecued bat.

She waved an arm tattooed with crossbows and gothic symbols and swept me across the threshold. 'Come in, come in. I'm Clarissa.'

I held out my hand, noticing the inky skulls on her knuckles. She led me into a sitting room that looked like a skeleton might jiggle out from behind the velvet curtains. The walls were black. Two deep purple sofas were suspended from the ceiling by thick rope, dominating the room. Despite my misery, I was still trying to catalogue every little detail, storing it up to make the kids laugh. I didn't want to think about what the bedroom looked like – chains and drapes and spiky things came to mind.

Clarissa indicated one of the swings. 'Have a seat.'

I hesitated. 'Is there anywhere I could sit with the laptop at a table?'

Clarissa smiled. 'We don't have a table.'

I moulded my face into a blank. 'Okay, I'll just balance on the swing.' Nothing like trying to look professional while clinging onto playground equipment.

While we discussed her desire to come down the aisle to *Bat Out of Hell* and the logistics of having her Doberman, Satan, as a bridesmaid, my mind was chasing all sorts of solutions to stop Sean messing up my life for a second time. I needed to warn my parents. I couldn't allow them to bump into him at school over coffee and croissants on French Day. Disappearing abroad was beginning to look very attractive.

'Could you organise a wedding cake with a big skull on top?' Clarissa asked, breaking into my miserable thoughts. 'Would it be hugely expensive? My fiancé is concerned about the finances. He thinks we should just have cupcakes, but I've got my heart set on it. It would be so cool with a little bride and groom sitting in the eye sockets.'

'I do know a clever cake maker but she doesn't come cheap. Of course, if it really matters to you, I can spread the cost about among some other things on the invoice, so your fiancé wouldn't necessarily have to know that it went on the cake.'

Clarissa looked aghast.

'No. That wouldn't be right. I love Mungo so much, we tell each other everything. You can't go into a marriage without total honesty, can you?'

She looked at me with those huge eyes, thick black eyeliner distorting their beauty. Who was I to criticise the stuffed bat spread-eagled on the wall? Who cared if they donned dog collars and ate their supper from bowls on the floor? She was streets ahead of me. Fifteen years younger and generations smarter.

Total honesty was the way to go. But would my own marriage be able to withstand it after eighteen years of half-truths?

CHAPTER FIVE

Most of the time, my mother steered through choppy waters with the air of someone who didn't even break a sweat until the mainsail ripped in half. In the six months leading up to Dad's trial, when he'd been too broken to steady the family ship, my mother had written herself a list and set about ticking it off.

- ✓ *Sell the house.*
- ✓ *Rent a house far away, somewhere that attracts lots of outsiders. London? Surrey? Brighton?*
- ✓ *Find a school for Sally, now to be known as Lydia.*
- ✓ *Find a job.*
- ✓ *Find a solution for Tripod.*

There was no discussion about our dog. My mother wasn't taking any chances. Tripod had lost one leg to a tumour, hence her name, and had one white ear in an otherwise black coat. My father's photograph walking her on the beach had appeared in the papers. Too distinctive. 'Sorry, Sally.'

I'd hardly ever seen my mother cry. She disdained tears. Even when I said goodbye to Tripod, the effort my mother was making not to tell me off for crying penetrated the moment so deeply that afterwards I felt guilty that I hadn't focused on Tripod completely, transmitting how much I loved her. Worrying about whether Tripod knew how much I didn't want to let her go kept me awake for months afterwards. In the event, I needn't have fretted. I learnt much later that my mother had her put down.

'Surely you must have realised no one would have wanted a three-legged mongrel?'

Dad had no problem with me crying. When my mother wasn't there to cotter about 'girls needing to toughen up, to stop expecting to be rescued by a handsome prince', he would hug me and tell me to have a good cry, get it out of my system. He smelt of Extra Strong Mints, which I found comforting. The day after 'all that business', I understood why. I stumbled across him sitting on the dunes, staring across the Wash, smoking. If I'd been able to feel anything other than gut-wrenching fear, I would have been delighted to know that he had his own rebellion going on.

I tried to tell him how sorry I was. I struggled to look at him, pretending instead to watch the seagulls swooping over the inlet.

'We all make mistakes, pet. Unfortunately, sometimes we have to pay a high price to put them right,' he said, taking a deep drag on his cigarette.

Then we sat, the dune grasses whispering around us, while the questions I wanted to ask and the ones I hoped I wouldn't have to answer drifted away on the autumn breeze.

In that moment, I thought the high price would be an apology, maybe a fidgety meeting with Sean's parents with my dad in the unusual position of accepting admonishment rather than dispensing discipline. My understanding of the magnitude of what I'd done, what he'd done, came the following day, after Dad had met with the headmaster. I listened, spying from the stairs, as he spoke to my mother in a voice I struggled to match to my dad's booming, jolly demeanour.

'It's out of their hands now. The police have stepped in. The father wants to prosecute. It's not looking good, Dorothy.'

My mother muttered something sharp that I didn't catch, something that seared a fraction more pain across my dad's face.

Then he said, 'No, absolutely no chance of the headship now when Bill retires. He told me that the governors have already written a joint letter instructing him to advertise for a replacement to start next year.'

My mother rested her hand briefly on his shoulder. She put a lamb chop and potatoes in front of him. 'Well. That's that, then. Always said we shouldn't have been so lax with her. Then none of this would have happened. I expect they'll ask her to leave the church choir now. I didn't have a daughter so that she could become the local legend. We're not going to be able to stay here, you know.'

Even back then, our priorities were polar opposites.

My dad looked as though he was incapable of absorbing another piece of information, but my mother still launched into the plan she had in mind. Through my spy gap, I saw that she was drying her little china teacups and putting them into the glass cabinet, handles turned outwards. At thirteen, I was old enough to wonder how anyone as loving as my father could have chosen someone as cold as my mother. She could have rented herself out as a backup refrigerator for emergencies.

What I didn't realise was that was just the beginning of the recriminations. For the next six months, my mother alternated between buoying up my dad with comforting but terrifying phrases such as 'previous good character' and 'mitigating circumstances' and berating him with questions he couldn't answer: 'Who's going to employ you if you get a criminal record?'

What she never wavered on was that, whatever the outcome of the court case, the Southport family was moving, far away, where Dad wouldn't be *that man* and I wouldn't be *that girl*. Some days she could barely stand to be in the same room as me. Spilling a drink, leaving my shoes in the hall, forgetting to hang up my coat – everything was a trigger for a rant about the disgrace I'd brought on the family, followed by her flouncing out to church.

Then, after all that waiting, dreading and hoping, on a freezing November day, we finally found out our fate.

My mother walked through the door with the news that Dad had gone to prison. 'Three months will pass soon enough. It's what comes next that's the real challenge.'

That evening, we ate fish fingers and chocolate mini-rolls in silence, sitting on the sofa among half-packed boxes. The departure from the rigid routine of eating at the table frightened me. That and my mother telling me that we were never to speak of 'it' again. That no one ever needed to know.

Late that night, when I finally ran out of my own tears, my mother's muffled sobs filled the darkness.

A week later, we locked the door for the last time and walked out of our lives, away from the village where we'd lived in our upside-down house with the kitchen and sitting room upstairs, views stretching over the sands and the quiet punctuated with the fluctuating sound of the tide – close, then far, then close again. Away from Sean. Away from the embarrassed throat-clearing when we walked into the newsagent's, averting our gaze from the headlines in the *Eastern Daily Press*.

Away from Sally and towards Lydia.

I didn't realise I would have to become someone else entirely. Not for the first time, I envied my brother, Michael, who'd thrown himself into university life up in Edinburgh. The suggestion of a scandal appeared to be all that was needed for the Perfect First Born to remain north of the border until Dad came out of prison and the furore at my old school in Norfolk faded into relative oblivion. My mother greeted any enquiries about my brother with the wrinkled brow of someone who feels their children's pain. 'Honestly, what with studying for his degree – he's specialising in neurology, you know – there's no time to be wasted on visits to us. Utterly dedicated, he is, that boy. Dedicated.'

For me, it was the ultimate proof that you wouldn't want to be the fat girl marooned on a boat with Michael when the food was running out. He was going to be a 'Doc-Tor' and no family crisis was going to interfere with that. Maybe it was the selfishness of youth, maybe he had simply sucked up too many of my mother's mean-spirited chromosomes, but while Dad was in prison and Mum was conducting a cross-country relocation, he proved himself so self-centred, it was surprising that he didn't turn in circles when he walked. He visited not once, not twice, but never.

And now, after a thirty-year interval, I had another crisis to bring to the family door. My mother was never the source of comfort, but she was often the font of solutions.

Unpalatable ones.

I phoned to explain that Sean McAllister had turned up as a parent at her grandchildren's school. Within fifteen minutes, she'd barged into my kitchen. 'Are you sure, Lydia?'

'Yes.'

'How did that scoundrel end up here?'

I wished she could articulate the words 'fucking bastard'. The whole 'Sherlock Holmes chasing down a bounder' language made me feel as though we were in a 1970s sitcom, though god knows, I'd never felt less like laughing. I told her what I knew.

'It'll break your father. He can't know. He's never been quite right since, you know…' For a fraction of a second, my mother sagged. Then straightened.

A rush of weariness washed over me. 'How can we keep it a secret? What about Mark?'

My mother frowned. 'Sean's not likely to tell anyone, is he? I think I'll have a word with him.'

It was safe to say that all the peace envoys to the Middle East had no redundancy worries on my mother's account. Even as a teenager, Sean McAllister had a lively disregard for authority.

Backed into a corner by my mother's rules and rants, he might just blurt it out to spite us all. With bells on.

I put up my hand to stop her. 'Let me deal with it. Hopefully he'll see that it's not in anybody's interest for it all to come to light now, after so many years. He's a professional man. He won't want people to know about it either. Especially while he's so busy arse-licking at the school.'

'Lydia! Could you kindly not…?'

'Sorry. But it is true.' I wondered if a Guinness World Record existed for the ability to split hairs at times of crisis.

She rested her chin on her hands, unconsciously pulling at her wrinkled skin with her thumbs, then smoothing it back into place. 'We should tell your brother. He might have a good idea.'

'No. Michael is well out of it, now he's up in Oxford.' I couldn't bear a second-hand interpretation of my brother's supercilious comments. Especially if he came up with the same suggestions as me, which my mother would suddenly see as glitteringly original rather than ridiculous.

I tried to divert her. 'Realistically, except for the local gossip factor of "Did you know Lydia Rushford's dad was in prison? And them so respectable…", who is going to be the slightest bit interested in what a seventy-five-year-old man did years ago?'

It was futile. Respectability was the pinnacle of petticoats as far as my mother was concerned. Then, of course, there was the small matter of Mark, who could be forgiven for being ever so slightly pissed off that no one had thought to slip the words 'your future father-in-law has been in prison', into any prenuptial conversation, never mind the rest.

My mother smoothed her cardigan. 'I moved heaven and earth so we could start again. I wanted people to remember that you played the piano beautifully. That you had the most school merits for Latin. That you sang like an angel.'

I wasn't sure if I was imagining the tremor in my mother's voice. I could feel my own body go weak, powerless to force back the memories that were breaking free, dragging me back to 1982, to an afternoon I had blanked out in the intervening years.

It was my first day back from holiday after a tedious week caravanning in Cromer with my parents. The last Sunday of the May half-term, the roadside fluttering with red admirals and cabbage whites, the sunshine carrying the promise of a summer heatwave.

But instead of disappearing to the beach like I'd told my mother, I'd pedalled over to Sean's.

His parents were just on their way out to a beach barbecue. His mother, Margie, was holding a bottle of Cinzano, vivacious and vibrant in a tiered broderie anglaise skirt, her long curly hair held back in a bright pink scarf.

'Come on in, lovely to see you. You've caught the sun this week.'

Sean's dad, Stuart, grunted a hello, his gut hanging over a pair of shorts too tight for his stocky legs. As the door closed behind us, Sean and I stood opposite each other, slightly awkward now the whole of his house was our unfettered domain. But it wasn't long before he held out his hand to me.

'Let's go upstairs and listen to some music.'

With Yazoo blasting out of the cassette player, we tumbled onto his unmade bed, with no pretence at conversation, just snogging, urgent and intense, Sean's hands everywhere, unbuttoning and unhooking. The heat of the day mingled with the heat of our bodies pressing through our thin shorts and T-shirts. As our clothes gradually fell to the floor, Sean lifted his head. His hands were still working their way down to a place that left me shocked and ashamed of my own desire.

'It's my birthday tomorrow. I know what I'd like as a present.' He kissed my breasts, before hauling himself off the bed. 'Back in a mo.'

I lay there for a few minutes, with the sunlight bouncing off the pillar-box red wall opposite the bed, giving everything a pinkish tint. My mother would never have agreed to me painting my room that colour. I took in the posters of the Athena tennis girl, the World Cup football squad, the England flag. The rag rug on the floor, now littered with my bra and my rose-patterned pants.

Sean reappeared, clutching a Polaroid camera. 'Give me a birthday present to remember. Then you'll always be with me, even when you're not here. When I'm missing you.'

He loved me. This was the proof. I wanted him to have something special from me, something that would seal our relationship, underline the fact that this wasn't some silly crush on someone who lived in a poster on my wall like Simon Le Bon. This was a proper full-blown love affair with a real person.

Who'd chosen me.

He lay down on the bed again, the camera next to his pillow, his lips on mine, his hand between my legs. I squirmed against him, knowing that I shouldn't be doing this but not wanting to stop.

He put his mouth close to my ear. 'Go on, you're beautiful.' He reached for the camera.

'You won't show anyone, will you?'

'Don't be silly. I'm keeping you all to myself.'

I nodded, smug in the knowledge that this secret act would bind him to me, stop him moving onto one of the blonde girls in the cool crowd, prevent me from plunging out of the sunshine that Sean shone onto me.

A week later, we spent our lunch hour in the far corner of the playing fields, shielded from view by a cluster of oak trees. I lay on my back in the cool grass. Sean's face kept appearing above me, his eyes trapping me there, his lips searching out mine. The bell in the distance signalled the end of break, dragging us out of our world and into the real one. As we got up, brushing the grass from our uniforms, he pulled out the Polaroids we'd taken. 'You look gorgeous. Sexy. Keep them right here. Next to my heart,' he said, tapping his chest. 'Best birthday present ever.'

Sean had the flippant delivery of the super-confident that kept me on my guard in case I took him seriously when he was joking. I glanced back towards school. They weren't photos to examine in broad daylight, outside the cosy cocoon of his room. He flicked through them. 'This is my favourite.' I looked down at Sean's hands cupping my breasts, embarrassed by how small they looked in the photo.

He gathered them up, pursing his lips and patting his pocket. 'Where's the last one? We took six, didn't we?'

'Do you think you've dropped it?' I tried to sound nonchalant, but my voice was already thin with fright.

'Nah. Should think it's in my bag somewhere. I only put them in my blazer at lunch.'

'No one else has seen them, have they?'

A flicker of a frown passed over Sean's face. Then he shrugged and kissed my nose. 'Course not. I'm not sharing you with anyone.'

I wanted to run back to school, to have him empty out his bag, to reassure me that our secret was safe. But he'd already made a couple of 'Well, you're only thirteen' comments when I'd been shocked at things he'd done with his friends – drinking on the dunes, nicking sweets from Woolworths, banging the machines in the amusement arcades to make the coins rattle out. I didn't dare say anything more and turned my attention to not being late for Maths with the terrifying Mr Ashcombe. I was trying to hurry without Sean noticing. He was hell-bent on dawdling back, blasé, even though he was in my dad's French class straight after lunch. In the end, the fear of Mr Ashcombe shouting at me in front of everyone was too strong. I needed to fetch my books from my locker, so I raced on ahead.

When I emerged back out into the playground, my dad was disappearing into his class as the second bell rang for the start of lessons. So he wouldn't catch me cutting it fine to get to class on time, I hung back behind a pillar a few yards away. I watched him open his textbook, then pick up something inside it and study it closely. I was just about to duck past when Sean strolled round the corner.

He winked as he opened the classroom door. 'Back to mine after school, yeah?'

I nodded, a little shiver of anticipation running through me.

Then it all happened so quickly. A great roar of fury from inside. Sean flying out with Dad chasing after him, clutching something in his hand. Dad reaching Sean. Thrusting something square at him. A photo. The one Sean couldn't find. The last one, when we'd been confident and carried away. When we'd stopped laughing when the self-timer went off. When we'd worked out how to balance the camera on a pile of LPs and tilt it at an angle so the picture got our whole bodies in. Where Sean had one hand on my breast and another spreading my legs.

The only photo where you could see *everything*.

There was a pause. Then Dad's cufflinks glittering in the May sunshine, the tie with the school crest flapping back over his shoulder, the crack as he drove his fist into Sean's face. Sean grunting and buckling over. Dad's foot, clad in a highly polished shoe, making contact with Sean's ribs. A shout. Mr Shaw, our pale Geography teacher, scattering papers as he ran. Sean on the floor, curled up, hands covering his head. Mr Shaw's thin fingers clawing onto Dad's arm.

The disbelief on Dad's face.

On everybody's.

Even now, my feeling of terror could reignite, like trick candles on a birthday cake.

My mother's voice took on a rasping harshness. 'I didn't want you to be forever etched in people's minds as the girl who was stupid enough to let *a boy* photograph her private parts.' She managed to say '*a boy*' as though I'd run into the street and jiggled an array of body parts at the first male clutching a Polaroid camera.

After all these years, I still didn't know how to seal her words in. If ever the phrase 'to have your say' took on a human form, I was quite sure it would look like my mother, knotting scarves with precision and terrifying clothes into hanging without creases.

And she was off, as ferocious and determined as the mothers in the egg-and-spoon race on sports day. 'I can't believe you trusted him not to show the photos to his friends. What did you think he was going to do with them?'

Treasure them as a memento of how much I loved him, not boast about them to Nigel Graves, the captain of the rugby team and all-round alpha male.

I could feel my throat ache with the strain of not shouting. I managed to say, quite calmly, 'We've been through this. Hundreds of times. If I could live my life over again, of course, I wouldn't have done it, but I can't change what happened.'

My mother was ripping up little shreds of doily.

I took a sip of tea. 'Obviously it was naïve to think it would never catch up with us. I'll tackle Sean. In the meantime, don't come down to the school, at least not with Dad.' I got up and put my hand on her shoulder. She shrugged me off. 'Try not to get in a conversation with Sean if you see him.'

'I don't think he'll recognise me. He only saw me once or twice. You always went to his, remember?'

And frankly, *why* wouldn't I have done? Sean's mum, Margie, had made me so welcome with her relaxed ways, her 'Staying for tea?' No one stayed for tea at my house without a good month's notice and my mother huffing and puffing about what hard work it was catering for extra guests. I loved going to Sean's house where we could walk out of the bottom of the garden, over the dunes and onto the beach. Where we'd spent hours, skimming pebbles on the water, daring each other to paddle in the creek on freezing February days. Sometimes Sean would drop the rugby player bravado and make a little heart out of cockles, a razor shell for an arrow. Those six months were the happiest of my life. Even the cool girls squiggled along to make room for me on the bench in the dining hall. No wonder I'd been drawn to Sean and his cosy house, with its piles of magazines, plates of cakes and yes, damn it, that big bedroom of his where his mother seemed not to care that we emerged rumpled, smudged and flushed.

Thankfully, before my mother could really hit her stride, Jamie strolled through the door, flicking his dark fringe out of his eyes with the studied cool-dudeness of a sixteen-year-old.

'Hello, Grandma. Didn't know you were going to be here.'

Jamie sounded as though he'd been promised a bacon sandwich, then opened the fridge to find a spinach and watercress salad. In turn, my mother was finding it difficult to smile as she was too busy making a mental list of things she didn't like about my son's appearance. Top button undone, tie too far down, dark curly hair in need of a good cut, blazer sleeves rolled up and, new for today, a rip in his trouser knee. Eventually, she managed to crinkle her lips into an upward motion. 'Jamie. I just popped in. Must be going anyway.'

I got up to help him lug in his school paraphernalia – his kitbag, boot bag and rucksack – all as heavy as a small wardrobe. Impulsively, I planted a little kiss on the nape of his neck and he squirmed away.

'Mum! Off!' He batted me away, eyes glued to his phone as though the world was a bonfire of information he needed to contain.

He was lucky I hadn't scooped him into a full-blown body hug. I was desperate to cuddle him close, to make certain that if this precarious house of cards blew down, whirling debris and detritus around every corner of our lives, that he knew that I loved him. That I hadn't set out to be a rubbish mother, the subject of derision at the school gates.

Izzy slammed through the door, her long blonde hair coming loose from her ponytail and her skirt rolled up way too high.

'Hi, Grandma.'

My mother found anything other than 'Hello' repellent unless it was on a Scrabble board. A small cloud scudded across her features. Izzy ignored her and ran over to whisper something in my ear. I could almost hear the squeak of my mother's disapproving eyebrow.

'Izzy, don't whisper. It's rude,' I said, without conviction.

She giggled and looked over at Jamie. 'I know who fancies Jamie.'

Right on cue, his phone beeped. He glanced down. A smile, secret and satisfied, flicked across his face before he narrowed his eyes at Izzy. 'Yeah, right. Who's gonna tell you anything?'

'I heard her talking about you in the lunch queue.'

'Shut up, dickhead.'

'Jamie! Do not speak to your sister like that.' I was clinging onto the hope that my mother might still be rooted in Famous Five land and think 'dick' was short for Richard.

Jamie marched off to the fridge. My mother gazed after him. I felt my teeth clench as I waited for the 'He needs a proper meal, young people think eating's a movable feast' conversation. My mother shuddered so dramatically that her necklace rattled as Jamie swigged directly out of the milk carton.

'So anything happen today at school?' I'd show my mother that we were a happy, chatty family.

'No.'

'Did you play rugby?'

'Yeah.'

Honestly. If my mother sucked her face in any more she'd look like she'd swallowed her teeth. I willed Jamie to be a bit bloody cooperative.

'Did you score any tries?'

'Yeah.' Suddenly Jamie perked up. 'There was a dad taking photos. He said I'd played really well. He's really cool. I think he got one of me sprinting to the touchline. Can we buy it?'

'No!'

The momentary connection faded away like a dodgy Wi-Fi signal.

'All right. Calm down, Kermit. Just asking.'

'Sorry. You're right. Let me think about it.'

I glanced at my mother. Her eyebrows shot up.

The secret contaminated another generation.

CHAPTER SIX

Over the next week, the idea of emigrating consumed me. Somewhere vast. Not somewhere like Britain where sixty million inhabitants trapped in a mere 94,000 square miles led to people you never wanted to see again strolling into your life and turning it upside down. I Googled Canada, America, steppes of Outer Mongolia. Then more sensibly, Northumberland, Cornwall and Pembrokeshire.

Mark laughed and asked me if I was having a midlife crisis as I listed the benefits of starting somewhere new and isolated. 'Never saw you as a rural tree-hugger type. You never even want to take me to Norfolk for a weekend. Go and rent a caravan somewhere for a week if you need a change of scene.'

My sudden desire to live in the middle of a moor wasn't at the top of Mark's priority list anyway. Since a shop that fitted new kitchen unit fronts had opened in the high street, Mark was spending a lot of evenings adding up columns of ever-diminishing figures over and over again, then doodling diamonds on the corner of his notebook. We could have lived worry-free in a house my mother wouldn't have approved of, with the kids at a school she would have disdained. But I'd adopted her priorities for so long as part of the post-apocalypse appeasement process, Mark would think I was lying if I tried to convince him otherwise.

I was working harder than ever. In-between sourcing a skull-shaped wedding favour basket to hold Liquorice Allsorts, I dodged email communications from Melanie, asking me to contact Sean to sort out the photography. I kept fobbing her off with my work commitments. I refused to go to the school at all, not even to pick up the kids when it was raining. I was still waiting for the magical day when I would wake up with the determination to confront Sean. More often than not, I spent nights blinking into the darkness. Many times, I wanted to shake Mark awake, whisper my worries into his chest, have him shrug and say, 'That was all so long ago. It's okay now.'

But it could never really be okay. Every time Dad sank into one of his dark depressions was a reminder of that.

A memory I didn't know I still had squeezed out. A little image of Mark lifting my chin shortly before we got married, staring into my eyes and saying, 'You're so self-contained, Lyddie. What secrets are you keeping from me?' He said it with a smile, but I caught a note of genuine enquiry.

I'd squirmed from his gaze, batting him away with 'Me? What secrets would someone like me have? Reading thrillers is about as exciting as I get.' Then I kissed him until he wasn't thinking about my secrets, and the racing in my heart dissipated in his solid embrace.

Would he remember that? Would he care? Would he forgive me? I just didn't know.

The more I tried to second-guess Mark's reaction, the more I could only imagine domestic Armageddon, the dividing of marital assets. I found it hard to envisage him accepting the news without an accompanying sea change. Far easier to conjure up a picture of me ensconced in a single bed, without the warmth Mark radiated, without him sleepily pushing away the freezing feet I tried to tuck under his calves.

Fortunately, Mark was preoccupied with his business and seemed oblivious to the effort it was costing me to carry on as usual. Living with a little jump of apprehension became my new normal. Every time the phone went, or Mark said, 'I bumped into...', or 'Guess who I met today?', my heart fizzed as though life as we knew it was about to be ripped away.

Tomorrow. Tomorrow I would phone Sean and ask to meet him.

Today I'd agreed to help Mark in the shop with a woman who had several rental properties requiring kitchen modernisation.

'I really need this contract. And you, darling wife, are much better at winning their trust than me. Your ability to flog a solid oak butcher's block is just one of your many qualities.'

During the fifteen-minute drive to the shop, we hatched a cunning plan on how to reel the woman in. 'Let's offer her a free spice rack if she goes for solid oak. Get her to go for the Corian work surfaces. The margins are higher on them.'

By the time she arrived, it was all I could do not to pounce on her the second she walked through the door, shouting, 'We really need this! Please.'

Instead of flinging myself on her, we shook hands.

'Katya Sandstead. Hello.'

There was something so Meg Ryan-ish about her that I did a double-take. A pointed little elfin face and a purple woolly dress over black snakeskin-print leggings. I sat her down and made notes on what she wanted: a refit for her own kitchen, plus two refurbishments of houses she and her husband rented out.

I gave her the tour of the showroom. I pointed out a steam oven. 'This is top of the range, but it depends how high-end you want to go.'

'My husband targets corporate rentals, so nothing too cheap.'

I began to relax as she started asking about the length of installation and whether penalty clauses were written into the contract. Within minutes, she had notched herself up into the serious punter category. Mark drew up a time frame, enough work to keep him going for the next three months. He was struggling to rein in his grin as he pulled out samples of wood and swapped colours around.

Katya tapped the pale oak. 'I really like that. It will be you installing it, won't it? My husband wants the main man on the job, though it will be me overseeing the work.'

Mark's eyes almost did a cartoon character cash register 'ker-ching'. 'We've just installed that oak in the headmaster's kitchen at Eastington House. Looks absolutely gorgeous. Contemporary but clean.'

Katya grinned. 'My daughter is at Eastington House. Perhaps I'll ask him if I can go and have a little look.'

I leapt on the Eastington House association. First rule of selling: create a bond. 'Our children are there too. Which year?'

'Eleanor has just started in Year Eleven. Not an ideal time to change schools, but we've just moved back from the States.'

'My son is in that year. I'll have to ask him if he knows an Eleanor Sandstead.'

'I kept my maiden name. So damn old by the time I got married, I couldn't be bothered to adopt a new surname. My daughter's surname is McAllister. Have you come across her?'

CHAPTER SEVEN

Mark opened a bottle of Châteauneuf in celebration of the prospect of refurbishing three kitchens. 'Cheers. Might be a bit premature, but I'm pretty sure we'll get something out of the McAllisters. I hope she goes for the wine fridge. There's a nice mark-up on that. Sounds like the husband is worth a bob or two.'

I couldn't even hear the name McAllister without wanting to smash things. Mark was jovial, lighthearted, talking about how we might even be able to afford to take the kids skiing the following Easter.

'Let's see what happens. I got the impression that it's the husband who has the final say on the finances. If they're renting out the properties, they might decide to go to that new store and just do the cupboard fronts, rather than spend so much money on completely new kitchens.'

Mark stared at me. 'Jesus, Lyddie, you're a ray of sunshine. Thanks for your confidence in me. This is the biggest opportunity to come my way this year. I'm going to do everything I can to pull this off.'

I had so many emotions rushing to triumph – guilt, anger, frustration – that I didn't know which one to latch onto. My head pounded from the effort of having a discussion with someone who only knew half the story. I was groping around for an impossible response: an apology that wouldn't encourage him to pursue work with the McAllisters.

Jamie and Izzy chose that moment to start fighting over who needed the iPad most 'for homework'.

Izzy blew a raspberry at Jamie. 'You're not even going to do homework on it. I need to find out what caused the French Revolution. You just want to go on Facebook. And message your girlfriend. Twit-twoooo.'

'Shut up. I haven't got a girlfriend. I'm working on a Biology project with one of the girls in my class and I need to discuss something with her. You just want to post a load of selfies of you pouting on Snapchat and talk about your spots with your friends.'

My brain was simultaneously processing the fact that Izzy had Snapchat – which I had expressly forbidden – and the fact that Jamie had mentioned Izzy's spots, the one thing guaranteed to tap into her temper. Before I could react, Jamie tugged the iPad out of Izzy's hand. She tried to snatch it back and it backflipped into the air, crashing down onto the kitchen tiles with an unmistakable smash.

Izzy screamed and burst into tears.

Without thinking, I swiped Jamie round the back of the head, a proper old-fashioned clout to make his eyes reverberate in their sockets, patented by my mum, circa 1980. He spun round. 'Owww! For god's sake, Mum.'

Mark frowned at me as though I'd suddenly appeared wearing a Ku Klux Klan suit. I'd taken ages to get pregnant with Jamie. For the first few years of his life, I'd been ridiculously overprotective. Mark would say I still was. So there'd been absolutely no question of us being parents who smacked. Apart from the occasional firm grasp of a wrist during a supermarket tantrum, I'd only ever smoothed hair away from the kids' troubled faces and rubbed Deep Heat into aching muscles.

I wanted to take Jamie's bewildered face between my hands and tell him that my sudden transformation into a parent who belts first and talks later was nothing to do with the iPad. Instead, a torrent of blame gushed out. 'What do you bloody expect? I'm trying to have a conversation with Dad and you two are bickering over the flaming iPad so that I can't hear myself think. And then you're all surprised when I get to the end of my tether.'

I looked round the table at them. Both of the children were staring at me as though a T. rex had suddenly rattled to life in the corner of the kitchen. With the contrariness of teenagers, Izzy united with Jamie, a sullen sibling gang against the madness of the mother. The effort Mark was making not to undermine me had brought colour to his cheeks. He was standing rubbing the back of Jamie's head. Somehow the soothing gesture of Mark's hand ruffling Jamie's hair up and down lit the dynamite under me.

I turned on Mark. 'Stop fucking looking at me like I'm the bad guy. You're the one who's always banging on about how the kids take everything for granted and now you're standing there going, "No matter, it's only an iPad." Right. Only an iPad that costs six hundred bloody pounds.'

I never said anything worse than 'shit' and now I felt as though I'd like to see how many swear words I knew. In multiple languages. I approached, then backed away from the C-word. That really would be the ultimate in hurling myself off the cliff.

'It's okay for all of you. There's you, Jamie, with your nose in your phone barely looking up to speak and when you do, you manage to grunt at me as though I'm just here to facilitate clean pants and porridge. Then you, Izzy, thinking the world's ground to a halt because your hair isn't flicking the right way, and you, Mark, with your nose so far up Katya McAllister's backside that I'll be lucky if you pop out again before Christmas.'

Mark put his wine glass down, his face full of confusion that a celebration had ended up with me rampaging about the kitchen barking about random grievances. A great swell of fury rose in my chest. 'So tonight I'm going on bloody strike. I'm going out. Get your own sodding dinner. Let's see if anyone other than me is capable of picking up a bloody oven glove. You can all sit there on your screens. Go on, fill your boots having conversations with people you don't even know rather than communicating with each other. Though you might find the iPad a bit slower than usual.'

No one said anything. I snatched up my handbag, longing for Mark to hold me tight until all the fright, the shock at my own behaviour, drained away. Izzy shrank down onto a chair, looking young and uncertain. Jamie was caught in that unhappy state between tears and anger. When the children behaved badly, I always left a door open so they could find their way back with minimum humiliation. For myself, however, I'd sealed it as tight as Tupperware.

I slammed out of the house and slid into my Mini. I drove to the address Katya had given on the kitchen sample forms. I knew what the house would be like. A modern executive home with zero character, LED downlighters, study with built-in computer desk, en suite to every bedroom.

I drove past the house. Blinds, not curtains. Very clinical. The opposite of my house, where toddler drawings were still stuck on the fridge a decade later. I pulled over at the end of the cul-de-sac and held my breath, trying to stop the tears. I couldn't live like this. I wanted to storm up to the front door and hammer on it until the perfect paint cracked. Or bellow obscenities through the letterbox. I wanted to give Katya, that charming wife of his, the A-Z of everything he'd done. Watch her face shift from annoyance at being disturbed to disbelief. Most of all, I wanted to see him squirm, back away, hands up in defeat, deliberating over whether to come clean or to take the 'that woman is deranged' defence. His turn to be uncomfortable now.

All that deceit, hiding, humiliation was bursting out of the cage I'd trapped it in and roaring to be heard. I opened the car door. Izzy's hairbrush fell out of the door pocket. I picked it up from the gutter, a knotty tangle of blonde hair stuck in its bristles.

Could I really bear Izzy's friends whispering to each other, the form teacher approaching me 'to have a quick word, as she'd heard that there'd been a tricky situation with Eleanor's dad'?

Especially as I'd been to a seminar they'd held at school on the dangers of social media a fortnight ago. I didn't want to be the school example of 'look what happened even without the internet – think how much worse it could be for you.'

I'd gone along out of a smug curiosity, given that my rules were quite strict – no TVs, computers, iPads or phones in bedrooms ever. I'd left a gibbering wreck after three different teachers gave examples of things that had happened at the school on Facebook, Snapchat and a hundred other sites that I'd never even heard of. The key message had been the importance of impressing on children the fact that any photo on the internet was there *forever*. I'd whirled home and started reading the riot act about privacy settings, acceptable photos and personal information. My kids adopted the face I used for my own mother whenever she tried to text on her mobile. No doubt they then hurried off to increase security on all things electronic but only so that *I* couldn't see what they were up to.

I fastened my seatbelt again. The image that I'd been clinging onto of marching up to Sean and having my say faded away. I couldn't be the mother that everyone talked about. I'd been that daughter.

My role as a mother was to have prim little conversations with other earnest parents about the benefits of learning the saxophone – improved confidence, increased connections between all the synapses – without once blurting out that Jamie's sole motivation was that he thought it was the instrument most likely to get him a shag when he was older: 'Who could resist me serenading them with *If You Leave Me Now*?'

I leaned back on the headrest. I needed to make Sean my friend. Or at least make him think he was. My stomach tightened into a hard marble of hate. If I wanted to get him on my side, I'd need to be patient. I'd waited three decades. It was surprising how ill-prepared I was now. I must have thought I'd never meet him, or anyone from my class or village again. Deluded.

I reached for my phone.

He answered immediately.

'Is that Sean?'

'Speaking.'

'Hello, it's Lydia Rushford, the new chair of the fundraising committee. Melanie asked me to call you. Have I called at a convenient time? Not too late?' Just a delay of thirty years and I was nit-picking about the sacred and self-imposed rule of not calling anyone after eight-thirty.

He greeted me as though I was the person he was most looking forward to speaking to. It made me want to lean on the horn and bellow, 'You do know you put my dad in prison, don't you?'

'I wondered if you had any time to meet to discuss the photography you had in mind?' I rasped out the word photography, my throat constricting, as though I'd swallowed a lump of dry bread.

'Sure.' Very American. 'When were you thinking, Lydia?'

Again. Had I imagined the small hesitation, the slight drawing-out of Lydia?

I stuck to my script. 'As soon as possible, really. I know Melanie wanted the permission letters sent out no later than next week.'

'Is tomorrow any good? I'm free first thing. We could meet for coffee at the Art Café?'

'Sure.' I had never said 'sure' in my life. I had no idea why I was starting now. 'Nine-thirty?'

'Yes, looking forward to it.' A little pause. 'Lydia.'

'Me too.' A hiccup of bile rose in my throat.

We said goodbye. I drove home with the odd feeling that I'd jumped without knowing whether my parachute would open.

CHAPTER EIGHT

Sean had chosen the squidgy armchairs in the corner, under an oil painting of bright purple lips. As soon as I walked in, he jumped up. 'Lydia, hello. What can I get you?'

'I'll get it, thank you.'

'No, let me, honestly, my pleasure.'

Social niceties would have worked better several decades ago but a coffee shop with the slogan 'Peace, love and great coffee' didn't seem the correct location to start a manners revolution.

'Americano with soya milk, please.'

I still wasn't sure whether he knew it was me. I tried to sit nonchalantly but was having difficulty encouraging my body into anything other than a straight-backed schoolmistress sort of pose.

How was I going to broach the subject if he didn't? Was I really going to sit there and talk fundraising? I did a quick scan of the café to see if there were any other mothers I knew, sitting there ready to record and repeat the conversation if it all turned nasty.

Sean returned with a tray of coffee, looking as though he'd slept on scented lavender pillows with nothing more concerning than *The Times* crossword to solve. I, on the other hand, was carrying the rawness of an argument that had see-sawed until the early hours as Mark struggled to understand why I'd suddenly lashed out after sixteen years of strict adherence to rational, hands-to-yourself-whatever-the-provocation parenting. Unable to find a small explanation that didn't drag in a huge one, I'd gone on the attack.

Mark had stayed calm as I'd become more hysterical. 'I'm worried about you. You've been so bad-tempered and snappy lately. Do you think you need to go and see someone?'

I'd considered telling him the truth. But the truth was so unwieldy now, a great avalanche of omissions ready to thunder through so many people's lives, sweeping away everything we took for granted. How could I explain now that the slapping scene over the broken iPad was just the tip of an ancient iceberg blundering through the family sea? I couldn't find the words to start that discussion.

I took my coffee from Sean.

He sat. I sipped. A toddler running away from his mother stuck his tongue out at me. I pulled a face back, delaying the moment, now it was here. Sean was still good-looking. Still assumed he was top of the tree and everyone else was blessed to bask in his shade. He bent over to bring out a folder from his briefcase. I liked folders. Papers. Plans. Organising. Certainty.

When he looked up again, I spoke, my voice coming out in a funny squeak. 'Do you know who I am?'

He stirred his coffee and laughed. 'Off with his head! Of course I know who you are. I knew as soon as I saw you. Like the blonde. Wasn't convinced you'd want me greeting you like a long-lost friend the other day, though.'

I really thought I might slap him. He looked delighted to see me as though I was some classmate he hadn't seen for an age and we were about to embark on a 'Do you remember?' session about rosy times past. I swallowed.

'So, Sal, how did it all pan out for you in the end? Rumour has it you've done pretty well for yourself, with the event business and all that. Melanie was filling me in.'

'Don't call me Sally. Sally doesn't exist anymore.' I hoped he hadn't been filling in Melanie, in return.

'Bit extreme, wasn't it? Changing your name and moving away? I mean, I know it all got a bit out of hand but I didn't realise you were going to do a Lord Lucan.'

'Sean. It didn't get "out of hand". My dad went to prison. He was never able to teach again. You know, the job that was his whole life? He ended up working as a gardener while my mother got a job as a bookkeeper to keep us afloat.'

I shook my head to dislodge the image of my dad sitting blankfaced in his armchair in the weeks after he came out of prison. My mother urging him to change out of his pyjamas, go for a walk, play golf. Cajoling, coaxing and then shouting. Shouting so loud that I'd hide in my room, my ear pressed against the radio on full volume, trying to drown out her voice.

I could have sworn one of Sean's shoulders raised a couple of centimetres in a shrug.

'It was a bit of a mess, wasn't it? To be fair though, a bloke with an unpredictable temper like that shouldn't really be teaching kids, should he?'

His words acted as a screwdriver jabbed into an already seeping, weeping wound. I breathed out slowly. 'My dad wouldn't hurt a fly and you know it. He had never behaved like that before or since.'

Some of the bravado slipped. 'Yeah. I know. I liked your dad. I did feel bad about what happened.'

'Bad' didn't even begin to cover it. 'Nice of you to press charges.' I never knew bitterness had a taste before. I could feel it, souring my saliva, scorching down my oesophagus.

'Come on. You know my dad. He was a tough old boy, brought up to protect his own. He didn't care much for school, anyway. He always liked a pop at authority. I was just a kid. I didn't know which way was up, back then. Thought the old man had all the answers. And your dad did crack one of my ribs and break my nose.' He fingered the slight bump.

I couldn't shake off the feeling that Sean was still viewing it as a prank that went wrong. I tried to follow the advice that Mark often gave to Jamie: 'Focus on the outcome you want. You can't change the past, only the future.'

Before I could speak again, Sean twirled his coffee cup. 'Dad died ten years ago. I never did connect with him properly. We started to get a bit closer when Eleanor was born.'

I wondered what his daughter looked like. Like him? A hint of rebellion and a smile everyone remembered? Or like Katya, elfin and petite?

Sean carried on. 'Dad was much softer with her, light of his life really, like he'd got all the hardness out of him in my childhood. He mellowed as he got older.'

I noticed the Norfolk in his speech. Those soft vowels and country burr.

Social convention demanded that I utter the word, 'Sorry'. But I wasn't sorry. I hoped Sean's grief had ripped him apart. That he'd experienced some of what my father lived every day, the loss of the future that he – we – should have had, that searing, tearing feeling of life changed forever, our permanent low-level fear of him spiralling downwards, unable to get out of bed. I wondered if my mother even told me the half of it.

I put down my mug and plunged in. 'I don't want to discuss what happened with anyone from round here. I'd appreciate it if you didn't either.' There. The request for my future, undisturbed, unchanged, was out there.

The electronic plink-plonk of a baby's toy filled the silence.

This time, an unmistakable shrug. 'No one's really going to be interested in some ancient story of a misspent youth, are they? Everyone's got naked with someone they shouldn't have at one time or another with unpredictable consequences.' He gave me a cheeky grin.

An unbidden image of Sean peeling off my school shirt bounced into my mind. I hoped to god that he wasn't recalling my

Playtex bra and my Woolworths knickers. He did look amused, which, if he wasn't careful, might result in him needing a plot in the cemetery sooner than he'd anticipated. Flutters of emotion were vibrating all the way from my stomach to the base of my throat, as though I was standing on a bridge with heavy lorries thundering underneath.

I dabbed at my lips with my napkin. 'I don't think you have any idea what we went through.' I concentrated on looking Sean straight in the eye. 'So I'd be really grateful if you kept quiet about it. We've made a new start here. I'd like to draw a line under it and not contaminate my children's lives with it. They don't need to know their granddad was in prison. And I definitely don't want a discussion about the photograph.'

Sean laughed. Actually burst out with a chuckle of proper merriment. 'Come on. They're watching all sorts on the computer. I bet teenagers today think a threesome is old hat. I doubt that they're going to be too scandalised at us oldies getting a bit frisky.'

'Frisky' was for lambs gambolling about in spring. It went nowhere near describing the mayhem that had ensued from a few bloody Polaroids. Sean was grinning, as though if he waited for a minute or two, I might develop a sense of humour.

'Sean. Let's be really clear. No one is to know anything about this. Ever. Especially my kids. Or my husband.'

'Mark doesn't know?' He flopped back in his seat. 'Does he think your real name is Lydia?'

'No. He knows that my first name is Sally. He just doesn't know why I don't use it.'

Sean sat shaking his head. 'Jesus. Are we going to pretend we don't know each other at all?'

'Yes please.'

'Better not blurt out that you've got a Mickey Mouse-shaped mole on your left buttock then.'

I blushed until I could feel my eyebrows sweating. At thirteen, my fledgling sexuality had been hammered into a box with a boulder rolled on top. I'd never managed to shake off the idea that I shouldn't actually be doing 'it', even after I was married. So Sean thinking about my left buttock – any buttock – was the quickest way to get me zipping up my handbag. Then I paused.

'Does Katya know about the Polaroid saga?'

'I haven't told her.' Sean looked off into a corner. Despite myself, I felt a little wrinkling of curiosity.

'Why not?'

'Katya has, shall we say, an ability to get rather possessive. I've learnt not to tell her anything about past girlfriends.'

'What, not even teenage-years-before-I-met-you girlfriends?'

'Nope. Leads to grief. As far as she's concerned I was all but a virgin when we got together.'

I bet there was a bit more of a story to that, which, I was ashamed to admit, I wouldn't have minded hearing.

Sean leaned forward, smiling up at me under his lashes. 'Plus, of course, you have blossomed into rather a gorgeous swan, so that wouldn't help matters.'

I was just pondering the fact that the English language lacked a word for the reluctant pleasure experienced when someone you hate admits to finding you attractive, when Sean said, 'Of course, I didn't expect to live in the same town as you.'

'Join the club.'

Sean cracked his knuckles. 'We could just bite the bullet, come clean and have done with it. Might be easier in the long term. At least tell them we knew each other at school years ago. If not the rest.' He rolled his eyes. 'Katya might take a bit of time to get used to the idea of a woman from my past popping up. You might not get the starring role as her new best friend.'

Fright made me slop my coffee. 'No! No. We can't do that. You can't say anything. This involves my whole family, my mum and dad as well. It will just lead to more questions about my childhood, more discussions about why we left Norfolk. It will all come out. Mark wouldn't ever trust me again.'

Sean put his hand up. 'Give it some thought. I'm very happy to talk to Mark with you if that would help, though I suggest you leave Katya to me.'

'Sean. Listen to me. You're not going to be having any cosy little chats with my husband. You can't say anything to anyone.'

And there it was. That flare of rebellion, of defiance, across his face. A memory of my dad telling him to get his hair cut for school, to get it off his collar, flashed into my mind. The next day he'd turned up with a ponytail.

'Sal. You can't dictate what I choose to tell my wife.'

I hissed at him. 'Stop calling me Sally.'

He shrugged. 'Come on, I don't think it has to be such a drama.'

'Which just goes to show you have no bloody clue what you did.'

He really didn't.

Frustration made me want to snatch the purple lips off the wall and smash them over his head. I grabbed my bag and scooted out of the door before the whole café was left in no doubt about how much of a drama it was.

CHAPTER NINE

'Why do I have to come and watch Jamie? He never comes to anything I'm in.' Izzy was standing in front of the mirror, dividing her hair into lots of little blonde plaits.

Since I'd slapped Jamie a week ago, I was frightened to get cross with either child. I'd cuddled Jamie to me the day after, apologising over and over until he'd shrugged me off with 'Mum, it's okay. No biggie.' I still felt shaky when I thought about taking my temper out on him. The fact that neither child seemed to be trying very hard to keep the peace, arguing and answering back as usual, gave me hope that they wouldn't wheel out the 'hideous slapping incident' to their psychologists in twenty years' time. In fact, Izzy appeared to have sprouted more opinions than a MORI poll, delivered in such an insolent manner that if I had been a hitting sort of mother, I could have launched into a right old smackfest.

This evening, we had twenty minutes before we had to be at a school concert to watch Jamie playing the sax. Twenty minutes before I might have to face Sean if he was the kind of dad who came to concerts. Maybe Katya too. What if he'd told her? What if it all kicked off during *Fly Me to the Moon*? The little jolts of fear that coursed through me were becoming more and more frequent.

I glanced at my watch. Izzy appeared to be separating each individual hair follicle. 'Come on, love. We really need to go.'

'Won't matter if we're a bit late.'

I wanted to snatch the brush out of her hand and smash the mirror with it. I took a step towards the front door. 'Out. Now.'

I didn't dare make a threat in case I ended up with a mountain of sanctions piled one on top of the other à la 'You've got a computer ban, TV ban, sweet ban and you'll never go to another party until you are eighty-five years old.'

Thankfully, Izzy scuffed out to the car. We drove to school in silence. When we arrived, I got stuck behind the school parent with the biggest Land Rover and smallest parking capability, watching the minutes tick away. Half a lifetime of gear crunching later, Izzy and I slipped into the hall. The lights had already gone down and the orchestra was playing a jaunty *It Don't Mean a Thing (If It Ain't Got That Swing)*.

I peered round for Mark. He couldn't have saved seats more slap-bang in the middle of the hall if he'd used a set square. I whispered to Izzy that we'd stand at the back until the interval at which point she marched to the end of the row and made everyone stand up to let her through. I had no choice but to follow, shuffling along, rolling my eyes and smiling through clenched teeth.

I didn't bother with the smiling when I got as far as Mark. I hissed in his ear, 'For god's sake, I suppose it didn't occur to you to save seats on the end?'

Yet again, he looked at me as though he couldn't quite place who I was.

I wasn't sure who I was.

Certainly not this person who snarled instead of spoke. Perhaps the real me would be unpalatable to everyone. Bits of anger raced around my brain, blowing about like shreds of tissue paper in the wind, leaving me unable to concentrate on the beautiful solo of *Ave Maria* that Melanie's son, Victor, was performing. In fact, seeing Melanie sitting there, conducting with her forefinger and mouthing every word in the next row, made me feel awful that I didn't even know what piece of music Jamie was playing.

By the time he came onto the stage, looking utterly dishevelled even though I had ironed his uniform that very morning, the vicious thumping in my brain had subsided. I caught Mark's eye and smiled. If I'd been a Facebook sort of mother, I'd have posted photos with the hashtags: *#proudmothermoment #sotalented*. I didn't allow myself to notice the slightly out-of-tune toots, the curtailed notes when his breathing was out of sync.

I tried not to be that mother who could see no wrong in her kids, but secretly I thought they were slightly more wonderful than everyone else's. Mark always laughed at me for bringing out the decorations the children had made in kindergarten, balder and less glittery, as each Christmas went by. I hadn't thrown out a creative writing book since Izzy wrote: 'My mum shows she cares for me because she puts my pillows just how they should be.' If we ever moved, I'd need a Pantechnicon just to transport clumpy clay pots.

When I was Jamie's age, I was shrinking away from adults in case they asked too many questions. I was guarded with friends, reluctant to invite them to my house with my mother's constant monitoring of my conversations in case I told them anything too personal – such as 'My dad's been in prison'. She didn't understand that to have a close friend, you needed to reveal more of yourself than a penchant for strawberry bonbons.

So when the children were little, I lost hours of my life to worrying when they were left out of parties, magnifying every conversation I'd had with other mothers in case it was something I'd done. Then Mark would put his arm round me and say, 'They're seven years old. They won't die if they miss out on a bouncy castle.'

Seeing Izzy and Jamie making the most of their teenage years filled me with a peculiar delight and envy. I'd missed out on so much by keeping my head down, spending breaks in the library and weekends reading. I loved that they had a level playing field as a springboard into life. And I wasn't about to spoil it for them.

Once Jamie left the stage, I turned my attention to examining any unfamiliar faces in the choir to see if I could spot Sean's daughter. So odd to think of the maverick boy I'd once loved having responsibility for anything more than a goldfish. I mentally rehearsed how I would introduce Mark to Sean if we bumped into him.

When the lights came up for the interval, Mark nodded towards the adjoining hall. 'Let's get a drink.'

He put his hand on my waist and propelled me forward. I knew I'd been hard to live with recently. We weren't a couple who liked to air our grievances. We tended towards quiet withdrawal, silent elephants lumbering about the room, the deafening hush of non-discussion rather than slamming out of the house in big dramatics. Mark's natural good humour usually ended the stand-off by making me laugh.

Katya bounded over to greet us like a long-lost friend. No edge, no glare. I was safe for the moment.

'Mark, sorry I haven't been in touch, meant to email you to say I twisted the headmaster's arm and he let me look at the kitchen you did for him. Looks fab, so I've discussed it with my husband and we definitely want to go ahead.'

Relief washed over Mark's face. One sentence from Katya smoothed his features and relaxed his shoulders. He looked so happy, it felt traitorous to wish they'd decided to go to B&Q. Sean was going to become a feature in my life whether I liked it or not.

I felt a touch on my arm.

'Hello again, Lydia.' Sean, smiling away, as though our last meeting had been a jolly session of reminiscing about old school mates.

I had to concentrate on lifting my top teeth off my bottom set to squeeze out a greeting.

Katya snapped her head round. She burst out with 'I didn't know you two knew each other.'

Sean turned into a jovial maître d', taking charge of the meet and greet. My stomach was clenched, braced for the 'we go way back' line, but he confined his description to the fundraising committee link. As people walked past, Sean was clapping various men on the back and kissing women on the cheek, with a sense of entitlement radiating from every pore.

Mark discussed kitchens with Katya. I willed him not to be too friendly, too trusting, share too much of our lives. I managed a handful of short chats with people I'd known since the kids were in nursery about an upcoming army camp and the shocking cost of the netball tour to Dubai. I could feel resentment bubbling. Sean had marched onto my turf and in the space of a few weeks was more at ease than we'd managed in a decade. I'd never been quite so delighted to hear the words, 'The beginners' recorder group is about to start.' Bring on the squeaks. But before I could escape, Katya grabbed my arm.

'Sean and I are going to invite a few people from the fundraising committee over for dinner. You'll have to join us with Mark. Can you give us some dates in the next month or so?'

I refrained from telling her that the only weekends we were ever busy were when I had a wedding on. I'd never let anyone get close enough to be included in the dinner party circuit. I was scrabbling about for an excuse, when Mark suddenly came earwigging in. 'We'd love to, wouldn't we, Lydia?'

The response, *No, I'd rather take my mother shoe shopping,* was so loud in my head that I expected everyone to glance down at their feet.

The last thing I needed was Mark and the McAllisters becoming best mates.

CHAPTER TEN

By the end of September, I'd run out of excuses to avoid dinner at the McAllisters'. Mark had been unusually forceful on the subject, seeing it as an opportunity to cement his position as their favourite tradesman. In the end, he just came home and told me that we were going that weekend. There was no way round it. The rest of the week slipped away in a snowball of dread until Saturday evening rolled around.

'You look amazing,' Mark said, as I came downstairs.

Clearly he spent the majority of his life thinking he was married to a badly stuffed sausage. 'Thanks.'

'Have you changed your hair?'

'I've curled it.' And used blusher, eyeliner, hold-your-blubber-in pants and a clever grey dress with ruching that confused the eye about whether the folds were fat or fabric. We were not going to look like a charity case on whom Sean was going to bestow his largesse by ordering a built-in coffee grinder.

Years ago, I'd vowed never to do the whole 'You're not going out in that' scenario on the grounds that my poor dad couldn't pick out a pair of socks without my mother having an opinion on them. Tonight, though, I wanted to change everything Mark was wearing. Top of my hate list were the canvas plimsolls – far too children's PE bag. The tank top was second – only a bloke with an electric guitar and raffish hair curling round the collar could carry that off. Sean always looked so stylish in a casual, Timberlandy sort of way.

I hesitated, then grabbed the car keys. 'I don't want to stay late. I'm really tired.'

'Don't forget that the McAllisters could make a serious difference to my turnover this year. I don't know why you're so anti them. Anyway, you won't even have to talk to them much. There are two other couples going, didn't he say?'

I shrugged. Mark's attempt at making me feel better just multiplied the possibility that someone would take an interest in my life 'before Surrey'. Mark frowned and picked up the bottle of Brunello he'd been given by a grateful client.

I allowed Mark to direct me to Sean's house. I couldn't admit I'd already sat outside it, watching the shadows of his life pass back and forth behind those sterile blinds. As we walked up the drive, I found myself shuffling behind with all the gusto Jamie had demonstrated on a recent trip to the British Museum.

'You'll be the most gorgeous wife there,' Mark said, as we stood on the doorstep. I didn't care about being gorgeous half as much as I cared about being 'there'.

Sean's daughter opened the door. She looked so much like him that my defences locked down as though someone had pressed a panic button. She ushered us in, her dark hair gleaming with the natural shine of someone who is a stranger to the dye bottle. I couldn't take my eyes off her.

Sean bowled out of the sitting room. 'Come in, come in. I see you've already met Eleanor.' He turned to his daughter. 'This is Jamie's mum and dad.'

'I'm in a lot of classes with Jamie. We're working on a project together in Biology.'

My stomach dropped. Blood rushed to my brain and started clattering around like water driving an old mill wheel. That was *her*. The one Jamie always 'had to speak to' about his Biology. Jesus Christ. Flaming Sean McAllister's daughter who looked like she could eat Jamie for breakfast, burping lightly into a napkin, no cutlery required. There was something slightly South American about her, with her dark eyes and full lips, all raunchy samba and swaying hips. She looked far older than fifteen.

'Bet you're streets ahead of him in class. He's such a lazy toad,' I said. 'Don't let him distract you from doing well.' My voice was all stilted, as though I was talking to someone with a poor grasp of English.

Mark threw me a puzzled look. I ignored him.

Eleanor mirrored Mark, screwing up her face as though I'd just coughed garlic over her. 'I don't think he's lazy. He's really clever. Especially at Science and Maths. I try and get into his group when we do experiments because he always understands the instructions.'

God. How I would love to have had the confidence at fifteen to disagree with a parent about their own child.

I deliberately avoided Mark's raised eyebrows. 'Last I heard, he got into trouble for letting the lizards out in the Biology lab. I don't think he's a very good influence on the class.'

'Did he? I didn't know about that.' Eleanor held out her hand for my coat.

Sean was shrugging in a 'boys will be boys' way, but I hoped I'd sown enough seeds of doubt to convince him that my naïve and academic, not-to-be-wasted-on-offspring-of-the-devil son spelt trouble for a teenage girl. Couldn't see Sean letting his beloved daughter go out with a wrong 'un, having been one himself.

On the other hand, if Eleanor had a shred of Sean's rebelliousness, I'd probably described the must-have boy on the block.

Before I could think up any more misdemeanours for Jamie, Katya emerged from the kitchen, wiping her hands on her apron, a tiny wisp in a pale brown sheath dress, like a spun sugar caramel decoration.

'Hello there, come on in. What will you have to drink, Lydia?'

Still no indication that she knew I was anything other than another bog-standard mother from school.

The fear bulging in my throat subsided enough for me to produce a normal-sounding 'A spritzer, please.'

Sean looked at the bottle of red wine Mark handed him and whistled. 'Brunello. Very generous. I'll open that.'

I tried telepathically to encourage Mark to wave it away and say, 'No, you save it for a special occasion.' I couldn't bear the thought of Sean taking the piss afterwards. 'Jesus, did you see his eyes light up when I said I was going to open the Brunello?'

Sean clapped his hands. 'Right, before the others get here, shall we just have a quick run-through of the kitchen?' Mark was immediately in his element. My earlier irritation morphed into pride as Sean nodded agreement at his suggestions. I'd expected Katya to rule the kitchen domain, but it was clear that Sean was the cook in their house.

Katya turned to me. 'Honestly, he puts me to shame. Anything more complicated than a spag bol or fish fingers, I let Sean take over. He's done the beef bourguignon tonight.'

I was astonished that Sean had turned out to be such a family man. Maybe I was more like my mother than I'd thought, freeze-framing everyone into the person they were thirty years ago. Sean stabbed out some notes on his iPad, threw out a few more questions about the various merits of oak over maple, then declared it 'party time'. A candlelit vigil by an open coffin would have appealed more.

Katya handed me a drink as we moved into the sitting room. Along one wall was a collage of photographs. They were all of Katya. She reminded me of the blonde girls in the 'in' group at school. Staring into the camera, sultry bordering on aggressive, head thrown back, every photo exuding sexiness and confidence. I looked away without commenting. By the fireplace was a col-lection of smaller prints of Eleanor: on the beach, hair trailing behind her on a swing, lying in a hammock in a polka-dot bikini, running through a wood in wellies. She looked like a model out of a Gap advert. Difficult to see how Jamie wouldn't fancy her. The thought made me want to choke on my peanuts.

Katya waved her arm at the wall. 'Rogues' gallery. As I'm sure you know by now, Sean loves his photography.'

I felt Sean glance over at me. I searched for a suitable comment. Instead of a nice, anodyne 'He's very good', I said, 'So it seems,' in a tone that suggested I thought it was all crap. Katya frowned. Mark kept sending me meaningful looks. I'd seen the figures for his business. I knew how much this meant to him.

I scratched up some charm. 'Eleanor is very beautiful.'

Katya softened. 'Thank you. It's always hard to judge your own children, isn't it? I can't take the credit for it. She looks a lot like Sean when he was young.'

I nodded, then quickly stopped. The doorbell saved me. The way Katya shot off into the hallway made me realise that she would probably rather be having a mammogram than be stuck with me.

The shrieking, laughing and 'Oh bugger me!' signified Terri's arrival. She came bursting into the sitting room in a stretchy sequinned tunic that made her look like an oversized disco ball. She bowled over to me. 'Lydia! Hello!' and did a funny half-nelson hug/kiss, which ended up with her spilling champagne into her cleavage. 'Oopsy. How are you, anyway? I hear Jamie's doing fantastically well,' she said, patting her chest dry with her hand.

I hoped Sean couldn't hear, given I'd just made out that my studious son was a troublemaker to be avoided at all costs. I shrugged and nodded, groping about for a change of subject.

'Christ, lucky you. You must send him round to teach Ashton a thing or two. He's so bloody lazy, he wouldn't get up if he sat on a scorpion. And Jamie's got such lovely manners. I spoke to him after the swing concert about his sax playing – so polite. You should zoom straight to the top of the marvellous mother charts.'

I felt a sudden urge to cry. If only she knew that the cover-up started in my own childhood now had roots so extensive that it was threatening to burst through the tarmac of my life and bring us all toppling down.

I cleared my throat. 'Ashton's got so much personality though. He's really popular. And he *is* captain of the rugby A-team. Jamie would swap academic success for that accolade any day.'

Terri waved her hand dismissively. 'Being good at rugby isn't going to keep him in the lifestyle he wants. He's going to have to get working them roulette tables for that.' She nodded over to the door where her husband, Gavin, was booming about the merits of his latest Porsche over his previous Mercedes and lowered her voice. 'Either that, or do what I did and marry someone with money.' She giggled, unfettered by any thoughts about how I might find that attitude a bit outdated.

It was impossible not to like Terri, though. She was so honest, teetering on the spot in ridiculously high heels and swearing about how much her feet were hurting. 'I can never walk in my bloody shoes, but I can't resist a pretty sandal. It's because I'm such a short-arse. I'd be looking up people's noses if I didn't wear these. Gav gets proper pissed off with me, but he married the wrong woman if he wanted someone clumping about in Crocs.'

I found myself relaxing as Terri nattered on, telling Katya how Gavin had insisted on completely revamping her kitchen. 'Think he was hoping the grub might improve but I'm a shit cook. Finding the new pantry useful for storing all my new shoes though.' The complete contrast to Melanie, who'd launched into a 'marinade for thirty-six hours or bust' conversation when I'd overheard her accepting Katya's invitation.

And a fashionable ten minutes later, Melanie glided in, her boyish figure encased in a 1950s-style dress, complete with flouncy skirt. She'd even perfected that one foot in front of the other walk that actresses do when they're up for an Oscar. After the briefest greeting, she waved her pashmina at her husband and directed her conversation to the person she considered most important – Katya – leaving Terri and me standing around as though we were groupies at a celebrity book signing. As Melanie launched into the beginner's guide to Eastington House etiquette, Terri gave me the tiniest wink and asked how the fundraising was going.

'We should get Sean to take a photo of you, me and Mel to put on the school website. If the other parents see our friendly fizzogs, we might get some more volunteers. Let's ask him before we get too piddled. Correction: before *I* get too piddled.'

'I don't think my face is going to encourage anyone to help out. Get him to take one of you and Melanie.'

'Don't be silly. You're absolutely gorgeous. You'll get all the dads volunteering. You can be the pin-up girl for the parents. You know, like the Calendar Girls, but with clothes on.' Terri laughed. 'Or maybe we could really hit a recruitment drive and take our kit off.'

I could feel the sweat starting to gather under my armpits. I didn't dare look down in case I had two big dark circles on my dress.

Terri blundered on. 'You'd look lovely behind a strategically placed rugby ball or two. The only thing that would cover up my fat arse would be the bloody marquee.' She dropped her voice, though by most people's standards it was still a bellow. 'A javelin would do for Mel.'

I did have to laugh at that, despite myself.

Thankfully, Sean waved us through to the dining room. Katya said, 'Boy/girl, or boys at one end and girls at the other?' There was a chorus of boy/girl, except from me. I wanted to hide behind Terri's all-encompassing warmth and presence. Her husband, Gavin, called women 'me darling', drank red wine like it was Diet Coke and described everyone who didn't see the world from his extravagant and anarchical point of view as a 'knobhead'.

His huge personality made me feel as though whatever I said, he wouldn't be listening, he'd just be waiting for the opportunity to broadcast his opinions again.

Katya started directing us to seats. Sean next to me. Melanie and Gavin opposite. I couldn't find a way to sit without turning away from Sean. It was going to take more than my left shoulder to protect myself. I shrank into my chair at the prospect of Melanie finding everything I said ill-informed, parochial and unambitious, let alone Gavin mowing me down with his 'You're having me on, woman!' every time I defended the school's draconian rules about pupils' use of the internet or their insistence on students standing up when adults walked into the room. Mark was diagonally opposite me, sending me encouraging wiggles of the eyebrows, which I suppose in long-time married speak meant 'Cheer up and look a bit enthusiastic, this could pay for us to go on holiday next year.'

As for Mark, a group of Morris dancers flapping their handkerchiefs would have been hard pressed to look jollier.

I reined in the sourpuss. I concentrated on complimenting Sean on his cooking and Katya on her lovely home. Melanie insisted on talking Sean through the various teachers – the merits of whom appeared to depend solely on their ability to herd ninety-nine per cent of the students to an A*. His ability to feign interest in things that bored him had improved over the years.

'The thing is, Sean, I know RS isn't terribly important *per se* but everyone who takes it gets an A*, so it's one in the bag. Better an A* in RS, than a B in Geography, don't you think?'

Terri caught my eye and winked. 'Mel, if they don't want to do something like Philosophy at A level, it seems like a right old waste of time to learn all that gubbins about Buddhas and wotnot when they could actually be learning something useful, like where the hell Great Yarmouth is.'

Melanie looked nonplussed. 'Why would you want to know where Great Yarmouth is?'

I had no doubt that if they did a post-mortem on Melanie, the part of her brain responsible for open-mindedness would look like a shred of desiccated coconut, upon which the pathologist would be able to make out the eerie etchings of Surrey, Harvey Nicks and skinny cappuccino.

Sean said, 'Oi! All the best people come from Norfolk. Great Yarmouth was the scene of much flirting at the funfair in my youth.'

A huge roll of fear gripped me again, followed by a memory of Sean and I kissing on the waltzers in the rain, giddy with love and lust. I felt a movement under the table. Had Sean kicked me?

I wanted to shout, 'It is not funny! Stay away from me!' Instead, I smoothed my napkin down and stared at my plate. I didn't dare look up, didn't trust myself to speak. I just prayed Mark wasn't listening to the conversation. The question, 'Where are you from in Norfolk?' could be the beginning of the end. It wouldn't take long for Katya to work out that I grew up in the same village as Sean. My fragile existence was built on successive omissions. I could fall down the gaps at any time. I stuffed another forkful of beef bourguignon into my mouth, then found I couldn't swallow.

When Katya got up to clear the table, I leapt up, grateful for any diversion. I carried the cheesecake back in and started serving. When I reached Mark, he put his hand on my waist and looked up at me. 'All right, my love?'

He was slurring slightly. I hissed a quiet 'I think you've had enough to drink.'

He frowned. 'I'm enjoying myself.'

I had to let it go before I drew the attention of everyone at the table. I sat back down. Terri looked over at me. 'Not having a pud? That's how you stay so slim. I need to skip the sweet stuff. I lost loads of weight a few years ago but it's slowly crept back on.'

'How did you lose the weight?'

'Gavin had an affair with a little tart of a croupier. Sad, deserted wife diet.'

I felt my eyes fling open in surprise. How bloody wonderful to be so relaxed about what people think that you could admit something so personal to someone you hardly knew. She hadn't let her catastrophes define her. She'd owned up to them, bandied them about until they'd lost their power over her.

I smiled at her. 'But he's back now.'

She laughed. 'Yeah. Maybe he needs to bugger off again, then I could lose two stone. I do keep a photo of me on the fridge as a reminder that I did manage it once.'

She leaned over to Sean, taking a huge swig of wine as she did so. 'Here, me and Lydia had a brilliant idea for fundraising. We thought the mums could do a Calendar Girls sort of photo shoot, you know, naked, wrapped up in football nets and shit… What do you think?'

I almost heard the grating of Melanie's buttocks as they ground together. 'That's entirely inappropriate, Terri. It would be a terrible example to the pupils. We can't have mothers at the school making it look acceptable to bare all in public, however well-meaning. We don't want all this "sexting" business coming to Eastington House. It's up to us to impress on them that being naked is something you do in private, not something to photograph and circulate to all and sundry.'

Terri laughed. 'Come on, Mel. Lighten up. It's just a bit of fun. If my ageing knockers raise a bit of cash for the new clubhouse, well, bottoms up!'

I desperately didn't want to side with Melanie but the mere suggestion made me queasy. Sean wasn't going to take any more photos of me ever, clothed or otherwise. I forced a smile. 'I don't think that's going to be something I'd join in with, Terri. I'm not brave enough for a start.'

Sean fidgeted beside me. I kept my back to him. If he dared to make a joke, the pretty little candle emitting its pomegranate scent might get shoved where you didn't usually find fruit.

Mark slurred from his end of the table. 'You'd look amazing. But I don't think I want the blokes I have a beer with in the clubhouse staring at my wife naked. Even if it is for a good cause.'

All the women around the table oohed and aahed, with Terri clapping her hands and declaring, 'Sweeeet!'

I pushed my plate away. The sick feeling that had dogged me since Sean had turned up in my life was back again.

For once I was grateful for Gavin bowling in with his off-colour opinions and drawing the attention of the table. 'You spoilsports. Oldest trick in the book, isn't it? Woman gets her kit off, man shells out money. It's worked for me and Tezza, anyway, hasn't it, doll? I get what I want, she gets a new handbag.'

Terri flapped her napkin at him. 'New shoes, you mean. I've just seen some new Louboutins I've taken a fancy to,' she said, laughing as though he was a naughty schoolboy.

Before Melanie could rise up like a snake about to strike, Sean swirled his wine around his big balloon glass. 'Well, girls, any time you want to strip off, I'm quite happy to oblige. Dirty job and all that.'

Suddenly, there was a big thud as Katya stood up with such force that her chair fell over backwards. 'I don't think you'll be doing that, will you, Sean?' She didn't even try to make a joke of it. Just kicked the chair out of the way, snatched up some plates and clattered off into the kitchen. From the sound of metal crashing onto tiles, she must have been throwing the knives into the dishwasher cutlery basket – and missing.

Sean shrugged. 'Oops. Don't think that was my best idea ever.'

Everyone sat in an embarrassed silence. Terri pulled a 'whoops' face at me. I caught Mark's eye and nodded to the door.

Mark dragged himself to his feet. 'Sean, lovely evening, look forward to pinning down the details. Thanks very much.' He shook Sean's hand and swayed off to the hallway to find his coat. Sean leaned in to peck me on the cheek and murmured, 'Think that answers how she'd react if I tell her about you, me and the Polaroid.'

I glanced around the room to see if anyone was listening but thankfully Gavin was hogging the airwaves with a story about strip poker. I made up for my lack of volume with the force of my hatred.

'Don't you bloody dare.'

I stomped away from him, into the kitchen where Katya was scraping leftovers into the bin. The bird pattern on the plates would be beakless by the time she'd finished.

Her distress tempered my anger. 'I just wanted to say thank you for a lovely evening.' I put my hand on her arm. She flung the knife down and turned towards me. I was ready to placate.

Her voice, when it came, was soft and weary. 'Sorry. I've made a fool of myself. It's complicated.'

'It always is. You don't need to explain. We've had a lovely time. Half of them won't even have noticed, you were so generous with the wine,' I said.

'Thank you. Thank you so much.' She stepped forward to hug me. Her cheeks were burning hot. I steeled myself not to shrink away from her. Katya was so slight, she felt like a little sparrow clinging onto me with its wings. Her misery was palpable. Maybe Sean didn't have the Midas touch I'd imagined all these years.

'I wish I wasn't like this,' she said, as she released me.

'I understand that.'

I really did.

CHAPTER ELEVEN

After the dinner party, I avoided Katya and Sean as much as possible. Now I'd seen the intensity of Katya's jealousy first-hand, as each day went past I became more hopeful that Sean wouldn't race to tell her about us. I was becoming so good at pretending I'd never met Sean before that I was almost convinced by my own lie.

If I saw Katya at school, I did a quick U-turn or waved from a distance if she spotted me. But a couple of weeks later, we had a Surrey moment and bumped into each other over the blueberries in Marks & Spencers.

'Hello there.'

'Lydia. How are you?'

There was something in the flat monotone of her voice that made me look at her more closely. Her skin was blotchy. 'Are you okay?'

She nodded, but big tears were running down her cheeks and blobbing onto the punnets.

I hovered awkwardly. The idea of crying in public, of having someone else witness such a lack of control was so hideous I wanted to throw a blanket over her and bundle her out of the shop. 'Here. Give me your stuff and wait outside. Do you need anything else?'

She shook her head and disappeared. I watched her through the window as I queued for the till, her pale face pinched with unhappiness. Could Sean have told her? I tried to get my breathing back into a steady pattern. She hadn't seemed hostile. Maybe she'd had a row with him. He was pretty fearsome when he was riled. He hadn't lost many fights at school – his dad wouldn't allow him to.

I carried the shopping outside. 'Do you want to talk or do you want to go home and I'll forget I ever saw you?'

'God, I don't know. I'd better go.' Her face crumpled into the perfect Eton mess of misery.

'I'm a good listener.'

Why hadn't I just stuck my head in the rocket salad until she'd gone? But I couldn't have left her weeping into the soft fruits. 'Do you fancy walking the dog with me? We'll head up to the hill. It's usually so wild up there, everyone will think any tears are down to the wind.'

She nodded.

'Come on. I'll drop you back for your car later.'

I drove home and raced in to fetch Mabel, leaving Katya in the car. I didn't want her telling Sean anything about my house, my little sanctuary. Though why it should matter what he knew about my house when he was acquainted with my naked body was warped logic even for me.

Having seen the prospect of someone new to meet and greet, Mabel refused to get into the boot, parking her hairy hound's backside on the drive and refusing to be dislodged. I didn't have the energy for an 'I am the mistress of this house and you will do what I say,' in case she rolled over onto her back and writhed with canine laughter. I let her hop onto the back seat where she resolutely refused to sit down and kept sticking her snout around the headrest into Katya's ear.

'Sorry. She'll settle down in a minute. Mabel!'

Mabel didn't accept admonishments. She thought any telling off using her name was simply a louder way of showering her with affection. With that, she started to squeeze through onto the passenger seat, narrowly missing knocking the gear stick into reverse.

'Mabel! For god's sake.'

Even Katya laughed as Mabel ended up with her head in the footwell and her backside in Katya's face. I tried to push her down when we stopped at traffic lights, imagining the explanation I would give to the police officer when I drove into someone else's boot. 'Sorry, but the dog doesn't like to be left out and she wouldn't sit in the boot, then I got distracted when she farted in my friend's face.'

It probably wouldn't stand up in court.

When we finally made it to the top of the hill, Mabel hopped out and danced around in a circle, barking and dropping her ball at Katya's feet, then jumping up with muddy paws.

'I'm so sorry about your trousers. I would be considered a particularly poor parent if Mabel was a child.'

Katya made all the right noises but she was probably wishing she'd tootled off into a dark corner to cry unhindered.

We walked across the South Downs, with Mabel careering about, sniffing discarded picnic remnants and gobbling up rabbit droppings like they were Maltesers.

'Do you want to tell me what's wrong? Or we can just enjoy the view if you like. That's therapeutic in itself.'

'There's no mystery. It's Sean.'

'Oh.' I didn't know how to encourage – or discourage – any further revelations. I'd never developed the sort of friendships that relied on reciprocal confidences. Although in Katya's case, I already knew so much about her and Sean via Mark that I could have breezed through *Mr & Mrs* if they ever decided to revive it. Luckily, Mabel took it upon herself to steal a squeaky ball from another dog. She was tazzing about over the hill, weaving about madly like a fly sprayed with Raid, then bounding off as soon as the golden retriever looked the slightest bit interested in regaining ownership.

'Sugar. Sorry, Katya. Just a minute.'

The owner was gesticulating at me.

'Just a minute, I'll get it back.' What I really meant was I'd fall in the mud as Mabel squealed past me and watch as she lay down in a puddle before flicking water all over an old lady who was sipping tea from a flask. Finally, I'd have to ask the other owner to grab her. Even then, the evil creature wouldn't relinquish the ball and I had to prise it out of her mouth. The golden retriever owner looked at me pityingly. I would have to kill her if she said it.

'Have you tried dog training classes?'

Fortunately, I didn't have a machete with me. Though as I stood there with a great patch of cowpat on my coat, I could see where she was coming from.

I clipped Mabel onto a lead, which she promptly whirled round to bite, dancing backwards and trying to chew through it as I struggled to stay upright on the slippery mud.

On the upside, Katya had stopped crying and was trying to stifle her laughter. As Mabel succeeded in tugging the lead out of my hand, scooting off with it trailing behind her, I turned back to Katya. 'Now, where were we before I decided to treat you to a display of animal and owner in perfect harmony?'

Katya had obviously decided that she had nothing to lose by being honest with a woman in a cow-shit coat. Within minutes, she'd told me she was always on the back foot with Sean, that she felt she was constantly fighting off other women, especially since he'd come into contact with a new audience at Eastington House.

'He's really attractive, to both men and women. It's his manner as much as his looks. He's so friendly. People warm to him, in a way they don't warm to me.'

I frowned. 'That's not true. You make a great impression on people. You were so hospitable when we came over for dinner. At least you're not up your own bottom like half the women round here.'

'Anyone in mind?'

I could have sworn that Katya sucked her cheeks in and arched her eyebrows in a parody of Melanie but I didn't dare make the comparison in case Katya and Mel were best friends.

'The thing is, if he didn't want to be with you, I don't think he would be. He's quite strong-minded.'

Katya flicked a glance towards me.

'From what I've seen of him, anyway.'

She nodded. 'He is. He won't tell me anything he doesn't want me to know. I can't have an honest conversation with him about the past. He always says that he doesn't remember or that he can't see the point in talking about it. It drives me mad. Makes me feel as though there was someone he really loved, whom he can't have for some reason, so he's making do with me.'

'But you've been with him for – what, twenty-three years, did you say? He's not going to have had many serious relationships before then, is he? Only silly teenage crushes.'

'I don't know. I've always felt that he was keeping something from me, but lately, he's even touchier about the past. I keep thinking back to what his mother said when I first met him. "You be careful with my Sean. He loves deeply. I don't want him getting his heart broken again." Then Sean's father came in and told her she was soft in the head and that Sean was a chip off the old block and knew how to keep a woman toeing the line. But why would she say "again", unless he'd had some great big love affair?'

I could imagine Sean's mum adjusting the scarf that held back her long curly hair. I pictured her rinsing blackberries foraged from the hedgerows before beginning the laborious process that led to the jars of jam I hadn't dared take home. My mother would have gone nuts if she knew I'd been with a boy instead of in the library.

Inexplicably, I felt a surge of jealousy that Katya had also enjoyed Margie's kindness. She'd always been so welcoming. She never scowled at me and said things like 'Why do you always wear black?' Or made me feel that there was a right or wrong answer to questions such as 'Are you interested in going to university?' or 'Do you think you'd like to live in London?', delivered in her soft Norfolk lilt.

I'd grown to trust her. I asked her things I couldn't ask my own mum. She never made me feel ashamed of being me. It still hurt that she hadn't stopped Sean's dad from pressing charges. I'd bumped into her in the Co-op shortly after Dad was arrested. She'd called me pet and said she was sorry. I'd shaken her off and marched out of the supermarket, leaving my basket in the middle of the aisle.

I pulled myself back to the present. 'I don't think you've got anything to worry about. Everyone has little love affairs before they settle down but once you've had kids together, that's such a big deal, it wipes out everything that's gone before.'

'I suppose so.' Katya sounded unconvinced. 'He's definitely cagier about everything since we moved to Surrey. Do you feel you know everything about Mark?'

I ignored the fact that Mabel was dive-bombing crows off the edge of the hill. While I searched for a suitable answer, I realised I'd never dug into Mark's past on the grounds that I didn't want him microscoping into mine. 'I think so, but who knows? If he's hanging onto some little secrets from before he met me, I can't really see the harm in it.'

It was a good job we were walking on a big hill with open skies. Otherwise I might have suffocated under my hypocrisy.

Katya stopped to flick a clod of earth off her shoe. 'When I look at you and Mark, I can see how secure you both are. You tell him off for drinking too much. I heard him get cross with you for saying Jamie is a troublemaker, but there's no big drama about it. You don't start wondering if he'd rather be married to someone else. Whereas the second Sean makes a joke about other women, or questions anything I do with Eleanor, I immediately start imagining that he's either having an affair or he wishes he'd never married me.'

'How could he wish he'd never married you? You're gorgeous. The trouble is, he's not the sort of man you can pin down, is he? No one is ever going to tell him what to do. A combination of having a mother who adores you and a father who dominates you, I suppose.'

Katya swung round to look at me.

I managed not to clap my hand over my mouth. For the first time ever, I was grateful to Mabel for barking after a kite. My gratitude petered out as I saw her snatch a packet of sausage rolls out of the kite man's bag. Thankfully, his eyes were fixed skywards and Katya and I squelched back over the mud without bothering to enlighten him about his pork-free future.

We'd just reached the car when Katya looked at me over the roof. 'When I get home, I'll start tying myself in knots wondering how you knew what his parents were like. Total paranoia.'

I bent down to take Mabel's harness off. I gave myself a second to think. My voice came out high and tight. 'He was talking about his parents at your dinner party. I think you were fetching the pudding.'

'Was he really? He hardly ever mentions his dad. He died when Eleanor was young. There always seemed to be so much tension between them but I didn't really understand why. Just another little mystery surrounding my husband.'

I made a show of struggling to get Mabel into the boot, even though for once in her contrary life, she hopped in without a bribe.

CHAPTER TWELVE

Over the next couple of weeks, my mistake became clear. Katya took my one-off walking kindness as a sign that I'd opened the door to her becoming my best friend. She kept phoning me with suggestions of things to do. I batted her away, claiming that my latest commission, planning a wedding in Italy, was taking up all my time.

My resistance was no match for Katya's fear of her own company. 'Get your diary out. Let's make a plan.'

I couldn't say that I didn't have a free day for the next year. Especially with Mark urging me to keep the McAllisters sweet.

Katya had so much energy for the new and the different. She came up with things I had always wanted to do but that led to the kids finding urgent homework and Mark needing to sort out his toolbox if I ever suggested them. So, when Katya mentioned jazz at Polesden Lacey, an art exhibition in Dorking, the sculpture park at Churt, I found myself agreeing. After every outing, I vowed to disentangle myself from the McAllisters' lives, but then she'd call again, picking just the places I fancied going and I'd promise myself it would be the last time.

As we wandered through the sculpture park, looking at horses made from recycled rubbish and skeletons dancing on the lawn, I couldn't remember the last time I'd spoken to a single person who could name any sculptor other than Henry Moore and Rodin. One of the offshoots of an adolescence spent on my own was that I'd been bored enough to discover hobbies to entertain me.

Encouraged by my father, I had spent an entire summer reading about artists and sculptors. I harboured a little hope that I might follow in their footsteps, all easels and flowing smocks on the South Downs, until my mother crushed that idea with a sharp 'The last thing we need in this family is a starving artist. You get on and study sciences like Michael and get yourself a decent job.'

So art as a career was knocked on the head. All these years later, I was overjoyed to find an outlet for admiring textures and discussing dimensions without Izzy and Jamie practically blowing me away with their yawning. In fact, Katya and I puzzled over how we'd managed to produce children who shared none of our passion.

'Honestly, Eleanor is so like Sean. She likes photography, 'real stuff' as she calls it. Anything abstract or surreal she thinks is a load of old nonsense. But maybe that arty-farty gene brings a measure of fragility with it. At least she isn't full of self-doubt, like me.'

I restrained myself from saying, 'You can say that again, cocky little madam,' and restricted myself to 'Do you think the two are related? I'd love to blame my insecurities on my arty-farty gene.'

Katya turned to me. 'I can't believe you have any insecurities. You always seem so in control to me.'

For some reason, that struck me as ridiculously funny and I laughed until I was in danger of looking like someone you wouldn't want to be alone with among a canopy of trees.

'What's so funny?' Katya sounded slightly offended at my hilarity.

Where to start? It was so tempting to burst out with 'Oh yes, I'm so in control, I've been living a lie for years. Even my own husband doesn't know the truth and guess what? Your husband, who, incidentally, I have kissed hundreds of times, has been at the root of it all. Still want to be my friend? No. Thought not.'

I managed to curtail my laughter by thinking about dying while the children were still young and Mark having to do the periods talk with Izzy. 'It's just that I don't see myself like that at all.'

'But look at you. Mark is always saying how proud he is of you, what a brilliant businesswoman you are. Sean never says things like that about me. He's always telling me how intellectual this or that person is, how he admires so-and-so, how he's met this mum who spotted a gap in the market and set up such-and-such a business. It makes me feel so inadequate.'

I hated discussing Sean, so I kept quiet. Katya waited for a response. 'Have you noticed that he's always praising other women?'

'No. But even if he does, I don't think he means to make you feel bad. His family were self-made and admiring entrepreneurship was just something that was prized when he was growing up.'

Jesus. I really had to stop doing that. 'Or at least, that's the impression I get.'

I blushed into the pause before Katya replied. I pretended to be examining a trio of frogs very closely, running my hands over the pitted bronze.

'I'm not sure he's ever explained that to me in those terms.' Little pin darts of puzzlement and defensiveness studded her voice.

I scrabbled for a recovery. 'Mark told me the other day that they'd had a long discussion about whether the desire to be self-employed stems from your family background. Mark's dad was a self-employed carpenter, and I think Sean's dad worked for himself too, didn't he?'

'He ran his own garage. Sean really rates Mark. He finds so many of the men round here such willy-wagglers – all talk about cars, holiday homes and what bloody bonus they're hoping for.' She carried on. 'Generally he gets on better with women. He finds you fascinating.'

I tried to make a joke. 'Oh yes, that's the first word that springs to his mind, no doubt.'

'He's always really interested in what we've talked about. Usually he finds women's conversation a bit banal.'

Katya's demeanour made me wonder whether there was a body language position known as the half-hedgehog – a semi-defensive stance, prickles at the ready without ascertaining a definite threat.

I tried to deflect her. 'To be fair, you can't blame him for not wanting to listen to eyebrow waxing recommendations or the pros and cons of the Mirena coil.'

It was so unlike me to mention anything to do with sex. And the fact that I had made me blush. I guess Sean and nudity were inextricably linked in my brain.

Luckily, Katya laughed. 'Oh god, I know. Still, I imagine a quick discussion about the Mirena coil is slightly preferable to a breakdown of their child's effort grades versus achievement grades. I don't want to know that their kids have made no effort and still got a bloody A* in Physics.'

It was so easy to bond over a combined dislike of all that was petty, competitive and self-aggrandising. I'd never had a friend I could march straight up to at the kids' school and be confident of an enthusiastic welcome. Over the last few weeks, I hadn't had to hang around at swimming galas and music evenings waiting to be invited into a group. Whenever I appeared, Katya was always waving, ushering me into a little posse, making me look quite the woman about town as she regaled them with our latest trip to the National Portrait Gallery.

For the first time in my life, I appeared to belong without even applying to join the club.

CHAPTER THIRTEEN

In my saner moments, I knew spending time with Katya was like running up to a snarling dog to see if I could cut it as a dog whisperer. As long as we didn't talk about Sean, the habit of pretending everything was normal was so ingrained in me that I'd almost begun to see her as my arty friend with shared interests, rather than a landmine waiting to be trodden on.

Until Mark said, 'I think Eleanor's got a soft spot for Jamie.'

'She'd better not have.'

'Why? She came in when I was fitting the cupboards today and started chatting. She seems to know an awful lot about what position he plays in rugby and which choices he's making for A levels. There was a huge amount of "Jamie doesn't really like our Spanish teacher"; "I might take Jamie's advice and do History in the sixth form."'

I was shaking my head. 'She's far too advanced for him. She'd frighten him to death. I don't think he's interested in girls yet, anyway.'

Mark laughed. 'Don't you believe it. Whenever I go up to bed, he's always texting someone.'

'You never told me that. He's supposed to leave his phone in the kitchen at bedtime.'

'Lydia. He's sixteen. He's going to have a girlfriend at some point. And here's breaking news: he might not tell us when he does.'

With a rush of recognition, I realised all the signs were there – the hours in the shower, the flexing of the muscles every time he walked past the hall mirror, the big cloud of Lynx engulfing us over breakfast. And he couldn't tear his eyes away from that bloody phone. If it was up to me, he'd still have a fifty pence piece Sellotaped into his school bag for emergencies.

God, how I envied Mark. He thought Jamie getting a girlfriend was a bit of fun, a rite of passage. My intellectual self knew that too. But my paranoid self wanted to vet all the girls he came into contact with, until I found a sensible one to make him happy. One who didn't have burgeoning breasts popping out of a T-shirt and a smile to steal his heart.

The thought of Jamie going anywhere near Eleanor made me dizzy. I couldn't let him date someone whose father knew my past when his own dad didn't. As soon as I'd chased everyone off to work and school, I stood hovering by Jamie's computer. There were answers to be had, right there in front of me.

I lifted the laptop lid, pulling a face at the screensaver message of: *I ain't doing shit today – mission accomplished*. I moved the cursor to the password box, then folded my arms. My mother had read my diary when I was about twelve – luckily, endless variations on how much I loved Simon Le Bon and wanted to look like Abba's Agnetha – though I'd still felt humiliated that I couldn't have a single secret thought without my mother intruding. But this, surely, was different? It was for Jamie's own good that I had to stop him getting involved with Eleanor. Before I could talk myself out of it, I quickly typed in 'Absolute Bullshit'. Izzy had told me his password ages ago in the hope of getting him into trouble but subconsciously, I'd known that the day might come when I needed it.

Hello that day.

I logged onto his Facebook account and scrolled down the newsfeed of YouTube videos, which appeared to appeal to the lowest common denominator – a combination of old ladies breaking wind, people dancing at bus stops and dogs pulling over their owners. The appalling language running through the comment sections astonished me – the casual way 'gay', 'fuck' and worse were bandied about by children whose parents were killing themselves to meet the £20,000 fees a year. It was so tempting to print out a sample to shove under my mother's nose when she said, 'I was saying to Joyce, at least at Eastington House, the children are mixing with the right sort of people. Her youngest grandson didn't even get into grammar school.'

It didn't seem to occur to her that Jamie and Izzy might not be considered 'the right sort of people' if it came out that their grandfather had done time for assault.

I couldn't see anything on the newsfeed that suggested Jamie was involved with Eleanor. I clicked on the private messages. I scrolled down, reading various boring exchanges with his friends about the thrill of a new FIFA game, a bit of rugby banter and some utterly banal 'WUU2?' 'Not much'. Plus the truly horrible 'Taking a dump' exchanges that made me want to shout, 'Get off the computer and go and read a book!'

And then there she was, a tiny thumbnail at the top of the list, leaning forward into the camera. The way a hint of cleavage was visible above her vest top made my stomach clench. Little hussy.

I clicked on the message, flicking away a hot burst of shame at my snooping.

'As I said, u can come to mine. Will let u no when parents go out. And DW about the other thing.'

Jamie had replied, 'Good good. Let me no when.'

So. There it was in Facebook technicolour. What the hell was 'the other thing' he shouldn't worry about? I didn't even want to start listing possibilities. It was bad enough that the little minx was scheming to get him round when the coast was clear. The apple doesn't fall far from the bloody tree.

I needed to have a proper discussion with Jamie, rather than one that involved snatches of eye contact over a laptop lid.

Approaching the whole Eleanor debacle without revealing that I was hacking into his computer would be tricky. I wished that I didn't have to go out to a Surrey Business Stars dinner that evening. Mark was keen for me to go as most business came through word of mouth and I could sell kitchens *and* event planning, whereas he was a one-trick pony. I always stayed over at these dinners. I made the best contacts late at night when the wine was flowing and everyone was in an expansive mood.

I phoned Mark. He sounded distracted. I pictured him methodically lining up his spirit level, pencil in hand. 'Are you listening to me? I'm really worried about Jamie.' I started to explain, desperate to impress on him how we couldn't allow this fledgling relationship to happen, even if he was only privy to half the reasons why.

He cut me off. 'As you know, that's a tricky subject to discuss right now.'

I heard Katya's voice in the background. I persisted, warming to the whole Facebook/super-snoop discussion.

'Lydia! I can't believe you went nosing into his computer. I don't think that is on at all. He does deserve some privacy. I know you're concerned about him but you can't do that.'

The qualities I loved most about Mark – his sense of fair play and calmness – were fast shooting to the top of my hate list.

'At least I've found out what's going on. I don't want to be the parent saying, "Sorry, I had no idea that my son was giving your daughter one" when Sean's jumping up and down on our doorstep in nine months' time.'

'Don't be such a drama queen. Just because Jamie is planning to meet up with E—, I mean someone, it doesn't mean that he's up to no good.' I heard him turn away from the phone. 'Yes, one sugar and a little drop of milk, please.'

He came back again. 'I've got to get on. I don't think it's as dire as you are making out. He has to have some freedom. Have a good time tonight and let's talk about this tomorrow.'

The line went dead. I had to unclench my fingers from the receiver. I couldn't seem to get through to Mark at all any more. We used to be so united about the way we brought up the kids. Was I so deranged? Why was I the only one worrying about Jamie? Sometimes I felt that my love for the children was so deep that the roots spread right through my body, whereas Mark's feelings for them were like a scattering of soil on the surface of his skin. The fact that he couldn't understand my fears made me want to – what? Fly at him. Walk out of the door. Scream in his face. How could something so important to me be so irrelevant to him?

I packed. I was glad I didn't have to deal with Mark's bemusement tonight over my pathological interest in the love life of a sixteen-year-old. Jamie couldn't go out with Eleanor. Absolutely not. I should never have become friendly with Katya. I'd made hanging out with the McAllisters seem normal, when, of course, it was insane.

I drove to Guildford, barging my way through the rush-hour traffic. Once I'd checked in at the hotel, I lay on my bed like a petulant teenager, feeling misunderstood and misrepresented. Drama queen, my arse. Mark made more fuss over a broken chisel than I'd made out of changing my whole identity. Tears huddled in a hard mass in my chest. I wouldn't give in to those.

I dragged myself up and put on my long dress. At least I could hide behind the formality of business. I enjoyed being with men from that point of view. They didn't often stray into emotional territory on a first meeting. When my feelings were raw like this, I'd learned to bury them until they started to scab over.

I stood outside the venue, gathering myself to march into the glittering palace of silver and purple. The balloon wholesalers must have made a killing. I glanced round for familiar faces – caterers, florists, marquee people, hoteliers, hairdressers. On the table plan I didn't recognise the names of anyone I was seated with. Apart from one other woman who ran a chain of beauty salons, the rest were men. A waitress offered me some champagne. I took a big gulp. Just what I needed to take the edge off my grump.

I leant against the wall and looked at my watch, hoping that Mark would be supervising Facebook use at home.

'Hello there.' A young man walking past raised his champagne glass to me. 'You look like you'd rather be curled up on the sofa with a good book.'

I laughed because it was so true. 'How did you guess?'

'You seemed deep in thought about something that I don't think was the Surrey Business Stars.'

I bet I'd been talking to myself. The kids always pointed it out and laughed at me. 'I'm not as sociable as some people here. I'm always embarrassed in case they'd rather chat to someone more useful but don't know how to escape me.'

'Useful? Is that how you judge people, by their usefulness?' He sounded serious but his eyes were teasing. 'Might work both ways. Maybe you don't want to waste time with me.'

I relaxed slightly. It was so much easier to talk to complete strangers when I felt like this. 'What do you do?'

'Ha. I like that. You're going to judge my worth by my job. Very male. What do you think I do?'

The Jamie/Eleanor cloud was starting to dissipate slightly. 'Funeral director?'

'No. Do I look that miserable?'

'I was thinking about usefulness.'

He laughed. 'Try again. I am quite useful but you'll never guess.'

I studied him carefully. Dark blond hair but bright blue eyes contrasting against an almost swarthy skin. He looked as though he was ready to find fun in everything. 'I don't know. Lion tamer? Submarine specialist? Aubergine grower?'

'Jesus. I'd love to be inside your brain for a day.' Again, a ripple of great mirth. I could imagine him around a big pine table on Christmas Day, joking over the turkey and wearing a paper hat with aplomb. I bet he didn't spend a moment of his life deliberating over whether the crackers were value for money and whether you could tell that the Yorkshire puds were Aunt Bessie's.

'No, I run a business inspecting hotels.'

'Bet you're popular.'

'I am, actually, because the hotels employ me to check that they comply with all the millions of rules and regulations before they get an official inspection.'

My surprise must have showed.

'You didn't have me down as a box ticker, did you? No one ever does. In my next life, I'm going to be a racing driver.'

He took a step back and pretended to look me up and down. 'So, what about you? Let me guess. You look rather brainy. You hold yourself very well. You're fresh-faced and healthy. Chiropractor? Nutritionist?'

I blushed. I should have been flattered that the first thing that sprang to his mind was 'brainy'. I wanted it to be 'gorgeous'.

He noticed. 'Ha! You're going red. Something embarrassing?'

At that point I wanted to run away in case he started listing sex therapist, Ann Summers consultant or a host of other jobs that would have me squirming.

Luckily, the event compère took to the stage to direct us to our seats and the hubbub in the room quietened to a low buzz.

'Nice to meet you,' I said.

'You're not going to dash off without at least telling me what you do, are you? And do you have a name, elusive one?'

'Lydia. I'm an event planner. Not very exciting.'

'Tomaso. Italian parents. Come and find me later if you don't find anyone more useful to talk to.'

I smiled and walked off in the direction of my table. Several guests were already seated, a motley crew of men with varying amounts of hair. A few nodded to me. I chose the middle seat of the three left empty and sat, staring down at my plate. The beautician woman, Janine, slipped in next to me, all pert little features, matte make-up and elongated eyelashes. I was wishing I'd had my eyebrows waxed when I felt a warm hand on my shoulder. 'Lydia, we meet again so soon. Now you'll have to tell me all about yourself.'

I looked up to see Tomaso. 'That won't take long.'

'You don't know what I want to know yet.'

I pushed my chair back and introduced Tomaso to Janine, fully expecting him to transfer his attention to her. Janine talked across me to discuss a range of male products she'd just started stocking in her Guildford store. He should pop in and try them sometime, maybe have a facial?

The rattling of a spoon on a glass signalled that the chairman of the Surrey Business Stars was about to make the first of his humour-free speeches. Tomaso attracted the attention of the waitress and minutes later, a couple of bottles of wine appeared. He did a 'white or red' shuffle in my direction.

'Just a drop of white. The champagne's already gone to my head. I don't want to be remembered for the wrong reasons.'

Tomaso laughed. 'I *love* the sound of being remembered for the wrong reasons.'

Fortunately, waitresses arriving with our starters brought the chairman's monologue to an end. On the downside, the whole slimy texture and old-bins-in-the-sun smell of the smoked salmon turned my stomach.

Tomaso leaned in. 'Not hungry?'

'I don't eat fish.'

Tomaso picked up the breadbasket and handed it to me. 'Can't have you wasting away. Please let me see if they've got any non-fish alternatives for you.'

'No, I'm fine, honestly.' I really was the dinner companion equivalent of a bag of salad a week past its sell-by date.

Janine spotted an opportunity to turn the conversation back to her. She butted in with a list of one hundred and one reasons to eat fish. 'Salmon is brilliant for your complexion. Tomaso, I guarantee, if you eat it every day, you'll have the skin of a twenty-five-year-old.'

Tomaso turned his bright eyes on her. 'How do you know that I'm not twenty-five? I hope you're not implying that I'm in my thirties?'

Janine laughed. 'You've got one of those ageless faces. Hard to tell how old you are.'

I was surprised how much I wanted to know. I'd learnt to be disinterested in details about other people over the years. I didn't want to encourage curiosity. I had enough trouble adjusting the facts for the people who mattered. I didn't have the energy to weave a story for ones who didn't.

Tomaso held his hands up in surrender. 'I'm thirty-two.'

Janine giggled. 'You're just a youngster. I'm thirty-five.'

I didn't volunteer anything. For me, thirty-two was when Jamie was five and I could still choose his friends for him.

'Hey, Lydia, you've gone serious all of a sudden. Go on, you're going to tell me that you're really seventy-five, aren't you?'

I grinned but didn't respond. I pushed my chair slightly further back so Janine could focus her attention on Tomaso without breathing in my ear. It was just like being back at school on the edge of the swishy blonde girls group. I couldn't fake belonging.

I wasn't going to tell him anything.

CHAPTER FOURTEEN

I sat through the rest of dinner offering just enough comment and eye contact to appear polite. I kept looking at my watch, wondering what time the awards would finish, how long it would be before I could escape back to my bedroom.

We duly clapped the best start-up, best food business, best entrepreneur under thirty. Tomaso caught my eye and mimed dropping off to sleep. I suppressed a smile. Then the lights dimmed, a drum roll sounded and the compère announced the Surrey Business Star of the Year, as voted by customers.

'Lydia Rushford, for her event planning business.'

The spotlight swung round and lit me up. Tomaso nudged me. 'Go on. That's you.'

I couldn't stand up. I sat there blinking in the light as the applause died away. I was aware of the compère squinting out into the audience with a sense of impatience, as though someone had called out a raffle ticket number and no one was making any moves to claim the hamper.

Tomaso got up and pulled me to my feet. He propelled me to the edge of the stage, then shoved me gently up the stairs. The compère shook my hand, gave me a bottle of champagne and turned me to face the camera so the photographer could take our picture. I had to make a conscious effort not to look down. The caption would probably read 'Lydia Rushford: Most Miserable Winner of Surrey Business Star of the Year'.

I bolted off the stage, relieved to see that Tomaso was waiting for me.

'You like the limelight then?'

'Love it.' I handed him the champagne when we sat down.

He glanced at my wedding ring. 'Don't you want to take it home to drink with your husband?'

'No, it's your reward for escorting me. I wouldn't have come if I'd known I'd won an award.'

'Why? I'd bloody love to win something for my business. Shall I open this? You should be celebrating.'

'Feel free. I'm just popping to the loo.'

I blundered into the Ladies and leant against the wall, feeling the coolness of the concrete against my back. The flushed and tousled reflection in the mirror didn't look like me at all. Without the pressure of everyone staring and clapping, it began to sink in. I'd won. Lydia Rushford, prodigal daughter, had made a success of something. Mark would be so proud.

I phoned him to tell him my news but I sensed he wasn't really listening. He sounded distracted and harassed. 'Good. Well done.'

I heard the tap of the computer keyboard.

'Are you working? Are the children there?' I tried to keep the irritation out of my voice.

'I'm just going through some figures. Without the McAllisters, they'd be pretty depressing.'

Piss off with the McAllisters.

'Are the kids all right?'

'I've been trying to help Izzy with her Shakespeare project. You don't know where that book is that we had on the Globe, do you?'

'Have you looked in the bookcase in the sitting room? Otherwise it might be in the attic.' Mark's ability to find anything that wasn't waving a big neon hand was limited.

'We'll have a look. Met anyone interesting?'

'Not yet, but it's still early.' I knew he wanted to know if I'd done some kitchen PR.

He sighed.

'Is everything all right?' I asked.

I heard him shoo Izzy out of the room. 'I need to talk to you about Jamie.'

'What about him?' My mind was running down all the possible avenues of doom.

'I'm worried about how much you obsess about what he's doing. I know you still think of him as your little boy but he is sixteen. He should be allowed to have a girlfriend without you reading his private messages. Let go a bit. He'll never tell us anything again if he realises we're spying on him.'

The great rush of fury I felt at his words made me tighten my grip on the phone in case I hurled it to the ground.

'It's not about letting go. I have a fundamental problem with him hanging around with that conniving little monkey, trying to get him round to her house when she knows the bloody McAllisters are going to be out.'

'What *is* your problem with them?' The anger in Mark's voice surprised me. 'All I can see is two perfectly decent, hard-working people with a daughter that our son happens to have taken a shine to. Plus they are making a significant contribution to our finances.'

I couldn't help myself. 'Oh yes, let's not forget Sean McAllister's great big wallet buying his way into our lives.'

Mark went silent. Then he spoke gently. 'Lyddie. Don't be like this. If I earn a bit more money, you won't have to work so hard.'

'I don't care about working hard. I don't want to be a little housewife, sitting at home, waiting for her husband to bring home the bacon. I love my job. I just don't want to see you arse-licking round the McAllisters, all 'yes sir, no sir', thinking the sun shines out of their backsides when their little slapper of a daughter is leading our son astray.'

Mark cut me short. 'I've got to help Izzy. I'll see you tomorrow.'

I stared at my mobile. That was the second time he'd put the phone down on me in one day.

The brief spark of pride I'd felt about my award was snuffed out. Sean McAllister was like a poisonous gas seeping through my life, contaminating every last thing that was precious to me, however hard I tried to plug the gaps.

I headed back towards my table, irrationally furious that Mark was making judgments about me based on only a fraction of the facts. The music had started. Tomaso and Janine were on the floor, dancing to *Brown Eyed Girl*. Janine was all taut stomach and fluid moves. Tomaso had that confident air of someone who'd captained the A-team. And he could dance. As soon as Tomaso saw me, he beckoned me over. I waved him away.

'Don't tell me. You don't like dancing either.'

There was something in the way he said it that made me want to surpass his expectations of me. 'I'll dance to the next one.' I prayed it wouldn't be something like *Come On Eileen*.

I sat back down, relieved that all the others were on the dance floor. Tomaso had commandeered some champagne flutes. I filled one of them, did a silent cheers to myself and took a gulp as *The Way You Look Tonight* came on and Tomaso arrived at the table.

'I can't dance to that. Too slow.'

'You promised.'

I was someone who watched handbags and drinks, not someone who got close enough to non-husband men to smell their aftershave. But Tomaso wouldn't take no for an answer. 'Jesus, Lydia, you're not going to make me walk back across the dance floor, turned down by the most famous person in the room? The shame of it.'

Tomaso looked spectacularly unconcerned but I took his hand anyway. His skin was soft, much softer than Mark's, which was calloused and dry from working on wood all day.

He pulled me towards him. Close enough that I could feel the warmth emanating from his chest. I couldn't remember the last time I'd danced with a man. Probably with Mark on our wedding day. My arms were rigid on Tomaso's waist.

He leaned forward. 'You don't have to do the robot stance. It's just a dance, you can relax.'

I looked over at Janine, who was swaying away to the music, chatting and giggling with the only other guy under forty on our table. I bet Tomaso was wishing he'd asked her instead. Slow dancing was such an intimate thing to do, so un-British. We spent all that time respecting personal space, saying sorry if we accidentally touched someone's hand, then deliberately put ourselves in a position where we could smell each other's breath. I hoped I wasn't fogging out a big cloud of garlic.

Tomaso was leaning back slightly, watching me and smiling. 'You're a funny woman. I'd be standing on the table, shouting about my business and getting my face splashed all over the place if I'd won the award.'

'That's not really my style.'

'What is your style?'

I longed to be witty, but pedestrian won the day. 'I haven't got a style. I don't like being the centre of attention.'

'Why not?'

Just briefly, for one mad second, I considered telling him.

'It's a long story.'

'When we've finished dancing, you can tell me.'

There was something so cheeky about him, I didn't do my usual haughty silence. 'I might just do that.'

Tomaso looked like a bloke who wouldn't worry about unseemly behaviour captured in a brown-tinged photo thirty years ago. When he was a toddler. Jesus. He probably wasn't even out of nappies when I was busy exploring Sean McAllister. Still, he'd have been part of the Facebook generation in his twenties. He'd probably posted his own pictures of himself, drunk, kissing girls, smoking weed, even. Did people in their thirties call it weed anymore? I wondered if he had a wife or a girlfriend. He didn't have a ring.

He took my hands off his waist, pulled me in closer and spoke into my ear. 'You smell lovely.'

I froze. This wasn't a normal, friendly woman-man conversation. Even my gnat-sized men-on-the-prowl antennae were beginning to quiver. I didn't answer. I waited for my flight mechanism to kick in but it seemed to have flapped off already.

'Thanks.'

He let out a burst of laughter that made me giggle as well. It had to be the champagne.

'What's the opposite of an open book?' He cocked his head on one side, his eyes crinkling up with amusement. 'A closed secret?'

Something in the word 'secret' sparked the essence of a memory. Sean. Sean kissing my neck, telling me the photo of us naked would be his 'delicious secret'.

I forced my brain away from that image. I didn't want the song to finish, though the thought that Mark wouldn't like me dancing with Tomaso was making me acutely aware of where our bodies were touching. Or maybe he wouldn't care? I'd never seen him jealous. I'd never given him cause to be. As the last notes petered out, Tomaso took my hand and led me to the table. Janine caught up with us. 'Got the champagne open?'

I poured her a glass. She was much nearer Tomaso's age. She lifted the glass to us both. 'Here's to success!'

'So, Janine, what beauty treatments do you have for men? You know us Italians like a bit of pampering,' Tomaso said.

She giggled. 'Everything, really. Facials, massages, waxing.'

Tomaso laughed. 'Waxing? No thank you. What do you wax?'

Janine leaned forward and patted Tomaso on the knee. 'Backs and toes are pretty popular. And of course, back, sack and crack. But I don't have to do many of those, thank god.'

Tomaso shuddered theatrically. 'That must be a bit embarrassing.'

'For that particular treatment, I only take men recommended to me by their wives or girlfriends. I don't accept men who just wander in off the street.'

'So if I came in, you'd chase me away with a broom?'

Janine didn't look like she'd even wave a feather duster. More like produce an industrial-strength magnet and suck his belt off. She'd managed not to look at me once during the whole exchange, none of that polite glancing over to include the person supplying the champagne in the conversation. Two could play at that. I filled my glass right to the brim, topped up Tomaso's, then feigned shock that there was only the tiniest dribble left for her.

I took a huge swig to disguise the fact that I had deliberately left her out. Tomaso offered to buy her a drink. I immediately felt petty and silly. 'Let me go to the bar. What would you like, Janine?'

She got up. 'I'll go, I need the loo anyway.'

She tottered off in her fabulous heels. I tucked my feet, clad in sensible sandals, under the chair. Tomaso leaned forward. 'Are you staying at the hotel?'

'Yes, I'll make a move soon.'

'Don't do that. Stay for another half an hour.'

I was sure Janine, at least, considered me a big gooseberry, the dullard in the way of her destiny.

'No, I'm going to get off. Nice to meet you.' I stuck out my hand.

As I stood up, the champagne made me sway and I clutched at his hand for support. Thank god for Granny Grimble shoes.

'You okay? Let me walk you to the lift.'

Tomaso walked close to me. Even though I wasn't looking at him, I could feel his masculinity, right there, solid. The blond hair combined with his dark skin was unusual and people turned to look at him. He introduced me to everyone, making progress across the room slow. My eyes were feeling heavy. My brain seemed to be one step behind my mouth.

In the foyer, the cool air hit me. By the lift, he asked, 'Have you got your key?'

'Somewhere.' I opened my handbag. I scrabbled under the camera, Izzy's hairbrush, Jamie's rugby mouthguard, my diary. In my haste, I managed to dislodge the pile of promotional leaflets Mark had given me, which scattered all over the floor.

Tomaso bent down to pick them up. He looked up at me. 'You should have given these out when I was introducing you to people.'

'I know, I'm hopeless at all this publicity stuff.'

He stood up. Close. Far too close. 'I'll give you some lessons.'

I felt a rush of heat. Tomaso took my arm. 'Where's that key?'

I handed it to him. The lift doors opened. We got in. I leaned against the back wall. 'Floor three.' My voice sounded little. I knew Tomaso would be studying me with amusement as I fixed my eyes into the top corner, as though checking for spiders. A dull ring announced the third floor. I put my hand out for my key. He dangled it out of my reach. When the lift doors opened, one of the organisers was standing there, formal in his bow tie and dinner jacket. Even though my only crime was being in a lift with another guest, I still muttered a good evening and hurried up the corridor. Tomaso was striding behind me. When I reached my room, he wiggled the key in front of me. 'So, are you going to let me in for a brief publicity lesson, my little closed book?'

'No. I'm sure you've had quite enough of my company for one day.' I tried to sound assertive. Inviting strange men into my hotel room would definitely fall into the category of 'things wives should not do'. But then my whole life was a catalogue of things I shouldn't do – or rather, shouldn't have done. I'd just pretend to be that rebellious woman for a moment longer. I'd flirt with a reinvented me, with an imagined past of discarded stilettos, barefoot in a ball dress, laughing in the rain, kissing under archways, a touch Parisian in attitude, a fraction mysterious, carefree as to where the night, or indeed life, might take me.

Footsteps echoed along the corridor. Tomaso opened the door to my room and bundled me inside. 'I thought for one horrible moment you weren't going to invite me in.'

'I didn't invite you in.' Not very Parisian in repartee. More Surrey utilitarian. Getting rid of attractive men didn't seem to feature highly in my current skill set. I stood, awkwardly, caught between knowing he should leave and enjoying the silliness, the flirtation, the ease of being with someone whose expectations you didn't have to live up to. Though I wasn't certain a human being existed whose expectations I didn't feel obliged to meet in some way.

Tomaso laughed. 'I'll just stay for one more drink and then you can boot me out.' He strolled over to the minibar. 'Right. What now? More champagne?'

I didn't even answer before he was popping the cork.

He led me over to the window and I stood, regarding my startled reflection in the glass. 'Lovely romantic view,' he said, pointing to the bins. I was shuffling my thoughts to find the card that had the lines for the dignified 'That's the end of this bit of fun' exit on it.

I must have been still fumbling with the 'Whooaa, this is all a little bit out of control' card when Tomaso pulled me to him and kissed me.

It reminded me of being in the sea in Norfolk on a windy day, jumping the waves crashing onto the shore. One minute, it was the right side of safe. Rough enough for a bit of a thrill, but not really dangerous. Then, suddenly, my feet were whipped from underneath me and the force of the water was tipping me every which way and I wondered if I'd ever find the surface again.

My mind was pulling away, stretching out for safety, for the fleecy comfort of the status quo. But my body was pushing against him in a whirl of desire as though I had some catching up to do. His mouth was cold from the champagne and within no time at all, he had zipped off my dress and pushed me back onto the bed, freeing my breasts from my bra and nuzzling at my nipples.

I fought to locate my inner nun, a little late in the day. 'Tomaso. Tomaso!'

He looked up, but didn't stop his stroking. 'What?' His voice was gentle, teasing.

'I shouldn't be here. *You* shouldn't be here.' My voice still didn't sound like I was trying hard enough. I was surprised how difficult it was to focus on my family, on how shocked and horrified Mark would be. How I just shouldn't bloody well be doing this.

Tomaso shuffled up the bed. He brushed my hair back from my face and kissed me gently. 'Who's going to know? Live a little. But if you want me to, I will tear myself away from your beautiful body and go and sleep in my cold, cold bed, lonely till morning…'

Live a little. Christ, I wanted to live a lot. Stop this pale existence laced with fear, too scared to enjoy the moment in case the lid blew off the past and my life, everyone's life, lay fragmented on the floor. A defiance I didn't recognise gathered inside me. Tonight was big. I'd done well. Yet Mark had showed more of a reaction when I told him I'd looked at Jamie's messages on Facebook. I'd spent too much of my life slipping past unnoticed, like a Wednesday in March.

So when Tomaso freed me from the rest of my clothes and loosened his belt, throwing off his shirt, that barefoot maverick on the streets of Paris took over. This would be my secret. My moment when I could just be me, my shoulds and should nots buried in the tangle of clothes piling up around us like debris at a church jumble sale.

He looked up. 'They always say it's the quiet ones you have to watch. You could be dangerous.'

'Dangerous?' I said, as his mouth covered mine. I was about as dangerous as a pair of plastic scissors. But god, the mere thought that I could be perceived as anything other than the woman you'd trust with the spare key to your house made me feel wanton and daring; a flamenco dancer of a woman, steaming in, skirts swirling, direct and demanding. I was a woman who sipped champagne, who took her clothes off in front of a complete stranger and had sex with him. I was almost aggressive, staring him hard in the eye, challenging him. I'd thought I'd compare Tomaso with Mark, but my brain seemed to have forgotten that Mark ever existed. I was just there, with those exciting sensations and that mocking look in Tomaso's eyes.

He was unfamiliar, but tender. I wasn't the girl he'd won after a series of dates, intrigued by my gratitude that he should choose me. He didn't know I liked a thriller over a rom-com, or Thai over Chinese. He wasn't interested in whether I was a mother who'd fight my kids' corner or a wife who never let the milk run out. He was interested in good sex.

Afterwards, I wondered if the sex could have been rubbish for him if it was good for me. It seemed that it was far more fun when you didn't care what the other person thought. I wasn't sure what was more liberating, the sex or the not caring.

Or both.

CHAPTER FIFTEEN

I was pathetically grateful that Tomaso put on some boxers before he started wandering about the room, so I didn't have to do the eye dance to avoid staring at his bits. I was even more relieved when he didn't disappear with a 'Thanks, see you around,' but got back into bed and cuddled round me. While I resolutely refused to consider what any of this meant, he kissed my back. 'You've got lovely skin.'

'Do you think so?'

'I don't think you see yourself as others see you.'

I rolled over to look at him. 'How do you see me, then?'

He looked serious, then smiled. 'I think you're really bright, attractive and capable but you don't think you are. I bet you think you're shy but actually I think you're just self-contained. I was watching you tonight.'

'Were you?'

'Yes. I was thinking that I would like to know two things.'

'Can't promise to tell you.'

He leaned over and kissed me until I didn't care what he wanted to know. After all these years I'd discovered that the best silencer of the voice grinding away in my head was lust.

Several minutes later, Tomaso rested on his elbow. 'Wow.' He breathed out. 'I wondered whether this cool, composed woman would be hot in bed. Think you've answered that.'

I felt as though I was looking in a comedy mirror and seeing a completely different version of myself.

'Very deep. And the second thing?'

'Your big secret? You promised you'd tell me.'

'I was kidding about that.'

'The existence of it, or that you'd tell me?'

The flattery had gone to my head. I wanted to be interesting with hidden depths.

'That I'd tell you.'

'Come on, that's not fair. I'm betting that you're not a woman who generally hops into bed with other men.' He grinned. 'So there must be something special about me.'

Tomaso lay down with his face so close to me I nearly had to reach for my reading glasses. I wriggled back slightly and brought his eyes into focus. 'Correct on both counts.'

'So. What have you done so bad that it cannot be shared with the world?'

I could feel myself withdrawing. I'd added sex with another man to the secrets that I'd have to bury deep inside. I wrestled to recapture the feeling of freedom, of abandonment that I'd felt a few minutes ago.

'Shall I tell you my very bad thing? But then you have to reciprocate,' he said.

He ran his hand lightly over my breast. Every fibre of me stood to attention. I glanced at the clock. Four am. The effects of the champagne were wearing off. I no longer felt giddy but almost otherworldly, beyond tired but not needing to sleep. His hand moved up my thigh.

'Go on, then. It can't be that dreadful.'

He took a deep breath. 'Here it is. Bald facts coming your way. If you decide to chase me out of the room, please throw my clothes out after me.'

A picture of a dismembered body in a bucket with feet sticking out sprang to mind as I considered what Tomaso's terrible truth might be.

'I married an Italian, Raffaella, in my mid-twenties. She was the daughter of my mum's friend and I knew her from holidays there. We spent long summers together every year as teenagers, then started going out more seriously when we finished university. We lived in Florence.'

For the first time that evening, Tomaso's face lost the little amused sparkle that sat around his eyes.

'When our son, Giacomo, was born a few years later, Raffaella changed completely. She was so protective of him, she wouldn't go out even if her mother was babysitting. We couldn't take him out if it was drizzly, or too hot or the slightest bit windy. We ended up just stuck in the flat all the time, watching crappy Italian TV, hearing the neighbours having sex next door, smelling the fish cooking in the flat below. Then her mum would come round and they'd both be cooing all over the baby, how amazing he was, how clever, how wonderful.'

Tomaso had lost his cheeky schoolboy sheen. He looked away. 'I know. I sound like such a spoilt knob. I kept telling myself it would get better, that I would adjust. I couldn't even feed the baby in the right way. Every time I lifted the spoon, Raffaella or her mother would be there "No, no, NOOO!" Too much. Too hot. Too bloody something.'

I could feel the misery in his body. His brow wrinkled at the memory.

'So?' I reached for his hand.

'One day, when Giacomo was about three, I tried to take him for a walk. Because the pavements are really narrow in Florence, Raffaella wouldn't let me go, didn't trust me to hold his hand tightly enough. I just flipped. I wasn't even allowed to go out for a wander with my own son. I took my passport, got a plane from Pisa and left. I didn't even tell my parents. Just moved in with some friends in London, drank too much, partied.'

I thanked heaven for the condom.

'Of course, it's caused rifts all over the place. My mother's not speaking to me…' He did a great imitation of an Italian mamma dressing him down. 'Raffaella and her family, well, I wouldn't be surprised if they are knitting voodoo dolls of me at this very moment.'

He ran his hand through his hair. 'My mum goes to see Giacomo whenever she can, but it's destroyed her friendship with Raffaella's family. Tarred with the same brush. She'd been friends with Raffaella's mum since they were at school. I've caused such a lot of unhappiness.'

'And you? When do you see him?'

'I don't. I haven't seen him for nine months. Every day I have a little rush of shame that I couldn't bloody hack it. When the going got tough, I cried in a corner. He's probably better off without me.'

He rolled onto his back. I could feel the ache emanating from him. 'Pretty bad, huh? Bet you're feeling like Snow White now.'

I shook my head. 'You probably won't believe me but I'm not very judgmental.'

Despite the current Cold War with Mark over my spying on Jamie, I knew he trusted me with the children. Even in my darkest moments, I'd never thought Izzy and Jamie would be better off without me. I couldn't contemplate not having any contact with them.

'I can't really be excused for deserting my son though, can I?' His voice held a note of hope.

'You have to live with it. That's a huge punishment to carry through life. Is there no way back?'

'Not at the moment.' He sighed, as though the effort of telling me had wrung every last drop of energy from him. 'Your turn.'

It was surprising how easy it was to be honest with a complete stranger.

CHAPTER SIXTEEN

Heaviness laced with guilt settled on me on the drive home. But coming around the corner into my road jerked me out of it. In full view of the neighbours, Jamie and Eleanor were leaning against a hedge, locked in an embrace with such a lot of face-on-face movement that it was a miracle their teeth had managed to stay anchored in their jawbones.

I jammed the brakes on and wound down the window. 'Jamie!'

I swear there was a squelching noise as he unplugged himself from Eleanor. He dragged the back of his hand across his mouth. That bloody girl folded her arms and did not look anywhere *approaching* mortified.

'Mum!'

'For god's sake. What on earth do you think you're doing? Kathy across the street does not want her five-year-old witnessing your shenanigans. Say goodbye to Eleanor and go home.'

'We're going into town.'

Unlike Izzy, who was so hormonal that half the time I couldn't breathe in a way that didn't repel her, Jamie never really challenged me. But on a day when I'd had about two hours' sleep and done things I should never have contemplated, it wasn't a good time to start.

I flung the car door open. 'Get in.'

'No, I'm not. I'm going with Eleanor. We're meeting some friends. It's Saturday. Just chill out, Mum. God.'

I saw his lips taking on the silent but well-worn shape of 'For fuck's sake.'

I turned to Eleanor. 'Do your parents know where you are?'

She put her face in the most bored expression that anyone had ever conjured up in my presence and said, 'Yeah.'

Not a whiff of 'How horrendously embarrassing to be caught in the privet hedge with your son, whose hands were way past where they should be for any decent girl', but a sullen 'yeah'.

I felt all the self-righteousness drain out of me as the lack of sleep muddled my mind. I couldn't think how to discipline Eleanor in a way that wouldn't provoke Sean and Katya, which might provoke god knows what. And I didn't need to be poking any hornets' nests right now.

I almost heard the rungs shaking beneath me as I staged my climb down. 'Well, don't be hanging around making a spectacle of yourself in town. And Jamie, I want you back here by five. No later.'

He shuffled off, hand in hand with that little tart. I started the car. The big tart would now make her way home.

'How's my superstar?' Mark was standing at the door, looking delighted to see me. He'd obviously decided to brush the fact that he'd put down the phone on me under the carpet.

'Glad to be home.' I forced a lightness into my voice.

He came out in his slippers to fetch my overnight bag, but I waved him away. Even though I'd checked it, I didn't want Mark anywhere near the clothes that Tomaso had touched. Removed. In my mind's eye, I saw his brown hands reaching up to unhook my bra.

Mark took me by the shoulders and shook me in a way that made every synapse judder in my poor hung-over brain.

'Yay! You did so well! The star of Surrey. Did you know you were in the running?'

'Not a clue. They just announced it at dinner.'

'You look tired. Did you have a late night?' Mark asked, giving me a hug.

'Not too bad, awards went on a bit long.' I didn't tell him I felt so fragile that if I found a hair in my lunch I'd probably be sick.

'You don't sound very enthusiastic. I thought you'd be on cloud nine.'

'I was. I am. But you know I hate the spotlight.' I thought of Tomaso's business card, tucked in my purse between the kids' baby photos and Boots loyalty card.

I kept avoiding his gaze. Shame was seeping into me like floodwater through a sandbag. Even though I had showered, I could feel Tomaso on my skin in caresses and kisses.

I ducked out of Mark's grasp and buried my face in Mabel's neck.

'The dog missed you. She kept whining at the door.'

'I must go away more often,' I said, grappling to think what a normal reply would be. 'Did absence make the heart grow fonder? Bed too big without me?' I stopped talking. Whenever Mark tried to be romantic, I got all waterproofs and wellies. Nothing would give me away more quickly than an unfamiliar declaration of love.

I left him in the kitchen making proper coffee. I recognised the apology in the gesture. He usually couldn't be bothered to spend the extra half a minute it required to locate the cafetière. I wondered where all those little niceties disappeared to over time. Sucked away in petty niggles over who let the dog sneak upstairs to get mud all over the white duvet. Who forgot to put the recycling bin out. Who didn't bother emptying the dishwasher but just stuck a bowl on the top for the tidying-up fairy to deal with.

Now, I'd obliterated in one huge stroke all the sly and secret ways that married couples mentally balance the who-does-what and I'm-not-if-you-don't.

I'd touched someone else's naked body, stroked that soft skin between his neck and shoulder, listened to a truth he hadn't told anyone.

Told him the secret that my husband didn't know.

I took my case into the utility room. I was desperate to wash away all traces of my betrayal. I was just stuffing my underwear with its invisible imprint of Tomaso's hands into the washing machine when my mobile beeped. Unlike the kids, the noise of a text arriving wasn't an irresistible pull for me but today, I shot into the kitchen and snatched up my handbag.

Mark smiled round, expectantly. 'New customer already?'

The colour flooded to my face as I read: *I keep thinking about you. Phone me when you can. Tx*

I half-sat, half-buckled onto the kitchen chair, casting about for a cover-up. 'Oh, just some bloke who wanted a few money-saving tips for his daughter's wedding. I don't expect he's intending to pay me for anything.'

Mark moved forward to read over my shoulder. I stabbed at the off button, saying, 'I'm going to have a proper rest today. Bloody phone keeps going.'

'So you did get some concrete leads then?'

Tomaso's words and the knowledge that Mark could have easily intercepted them were obstructing my thoughts. With a huge effort, I managed to say, '*Surrey Life* are doing a feature on the awards evening, which will probably lead to something. They're pretty active on Twitter and Facebook.'

Izzy wandered in, still in her onesie, and gave me a big hug. 'Shall I set up a Twitter account for you, then?' she asked.

'No thank you.'

Izzy looked at me as though I was still trying to write with a quill. 'When that business expert came to talk to us about enterprise at school, he said social media was the way forward, that no business could afford to ignore the power of viral marketing.'

'I'm quite tired today, lovey, so let's not get into all that right now. You know I don't want other people intruding on my life without me knowing.'

Izzy rolled her eyes. 'It's not intruding. Can I get Instagram then, just for me? I won't put anything about you on it.'

'No. You're not putting god knows what pictures on there.'

She pushed the chair back. 'Everyone has got it apart from me. Every time there's a sleepover or a party, they forget to invite me because I'm not on there.'

'Why can't they pick up the phone? Or, god forbid, hand out an invitation? They can't really be your friends if they 'forget' to invite you, just because you're not on Instagram.'

For all the enthusiasm that greeted that observation, I might as well have suggested that Izzy spent the evening doing herringbone stitch on a smock. She snatched up her phone and stomped out.

Mark lowered his voice. 'We should maybe think about letting her have Instagram. Most of them do use it.'

'No way. I need you to support me on this. They do not understand that anything they put out there on the internet is there forever. One stupid photo could change her life.'

Mark shrugged. 'It is hard for her, though.'

'Tough. I'm only interested in keeping her safe.'

The conversation petered out as neither of us appeared willing to launch straight back into a row.

I tried to make amends. 'Anyway, let's have a nice Sunday lunch tomorrow. Anything you fancy? Lamb, beef…?'

'What time were you thinking? Sean wants to discuss some kitchen designs with me tomorrow.'

'Why do you have to see him on a Sunday? Why can't he come into the shop like any normal person?'

Mark folded his arms. 'Because most normal people aren't spending £120k plus with me. Anyway, I like the bloke, even if you don't.'

I didn't trust myself to speak. I felt as though my secrets were biding their time in fragile chrysalises from which hairy great moths would emerge, blundering out into the world and smashing open the truth.

But for now, I was just desperate to call that unknown number on my phone to speak to the person who knew the worst thing about me and liked me anyway.

CHAPTER SEVENTEEN

Mark had insisted on phoning my parents and inviting them for Sunday lunch. 'Let's celebrate the good times. I am so proud. When the pictures come out in *Surrey Life*, I'm going to put them in the shop window.'

'Don't do that.'

'Why ever not?'

'I'm not anything to do with the kitchen shop.'

Mark sighed. 'No harm in being associated with success.'

The children clustered round my dad, cupboard-loving for surplus pound coins and his bag of pear drops. Mabel took the opportunity to race out into the garden and do a welcome lap of honour. My mother bustled in, complaining about how cold it had been in church. Mabel charged back in, immediately wiping her muddy snout, fresh from digging up my tulip bulbs, across my mother's skirt.

'Go away! Naughty dog!'

Before I had a dog, I didn't understand that hearing your dog receive a harsh telling-off rankled nearly as much as other people scolding your children. My mother ran to the sink and started scrubbing at her skirt. 'Put that dog away. We don't want her slobbering round us while we have lunch.'

Izzy sent her grandma a look of distilled hate. 'She'll settle down in a minute. If we shut her up, she'll just bark.'

'I don't know why you weren't stricter with that dog from the beginning. You should have shown her who is boss,' my mother said, grabbing Mabel by the collar and dragging her towards the utility room. Mabel tried to wriggle free. She did a high-pitched woof at the back of her throat. Then unmistakably, she growled. Before I could react, my mother belted her. Mabel shot off into her basket in the utility room, a vision of dejected misery.

My mother smiled around at us, as though she'd demonstrated the lesson we'd needed to learn in a timely and succinct fashion. Izzy looked like lava was about to spurt out of her.

I ushered everyone through to the dining room. 'Mark, you sort everyone out with a drink, Izzy, you come and fetch the plates.'

'I hate grandma,' she hissed at me.

'Sshhhh. I know. Let's try and have a nice lunch.'

Izzy snatched up the plates, muttering, 'I'm not bloody sitting next to her.' I'd never have dared swear in front of my parents. A bit more 'shit, bugger, bastard' might have stopped me going for the 'smile for the birdy' option though, so I didn't bother to tell her off.

My dad wandered through. 'Well done, darling. I am so proud of you. I'm glad I've lived long enough to see you make a success of your life.'

I swallowed. Just that morning, I'd hidden in the bathroom responding to Tomaso's texts. I'd answered 'Never' to his final question of 'When can I see you?' but my brain wasn't satisfied, gnawing away for a different reply.

Everything about me felt rotten to the core. If I got run over, I was pretty sure my insides would smell like rancid courgettes festering in the bottom of the fridge. I forced a smile.

'You okay, pet?'

I leaned into him. 'I'm just a bit frazzled at the moment.'

He put his hands on my shoulders. 'I hope you're not working too hard. Take yourself off for a few days. You've always been the same – whatever you put your mind to, bringing up your kids, setting up the business, one hundred and ten per cent. You need a bit of a break.'

I didn't deserve Dad's praise. For a fraction of a second, I considered telling him about Sean reappearing. I was convinced he was stronger than my mother claimed but she was so adamant that he would go into a decline if I ever brought up 'that whole to-do' again.

With my head on Dad's shoulder, I felt as bewildered as I had at thirteen. This time I really was old enough to know better. Even before Tomaso, I had to weigh up who knew what and which story I was presenting before I could open my mouth. It was like forcing my life through a filter, with great chunks of unpalatable reality catching in the bottom so that the pure version of a life well-lived dripped out into the world beyond.

'You can talk to me, you know.'

I pulled away. I wished I could. But my mother's catchphrase of 'Don't bother your dad with that, just in case…' was second nature now.

'Thanks, Dad. I'm all over the place at the moment.' I rubbed my hands over my face. 'Just pass me that bowl for the Yorkshires.'

Dad stood for a second, opened his mouth to speak, then did as I asked. I dug out my strong voice. 'Take the carving knife through to Mark, will you?'

My mother was serving out the roast potatoes with precision division. 'Jamie, pass your plate for some Brussels.'

'No thanks.'

My mother acted as though she hadn't heard and held out her hand.

'I don't like them.'

'Don't be silly. They're a fabulous source of vitamin C.'

'I'll eat an orange afterwards.'

My mother puffed up like a toad in danger. She turned to me. 'Lydia. Are you going to tell this boy to do as he's told?'

'Jamie, just have a couple.' I hated the beseeching tone that had crept in to my voice.

'Mum, Brussels give you terrible wind. I've got to go to training later. I can't be f—, er, parping on the pitch.' My mother did a theatrical wince. Mabel chose that moment to start barking and whining.

My dad, as usual, tried to lighten the mood. 'Lovely piece of beef, Lyddie. Which butcher's did you use?'

Dad's kindness made me want to cry all over again. 'I went to Browns.'

My mother sat flaring her nostrils. 'I always find them so pricey. They even charge for bones to boil up for stock.'

Mark, who usually left it to me to deal with my mother, found his voice. 'We wanted a little splash-out today because we're celebrating Lydia's success. We're all really proud of her, aren't we, kids?'

My mother managed a nose wrinkle at the word 'kids'. Izzy uttered a defiant 'Yep!', whereas Jamie was obviously far too mired in thinking up ways to organise a long painful death for my mother to join in any conversation. 'Plus, I've had some fantastic orders for kitchens, so things are looking up financially.'

Dad smiled. 'Brilliant. What's caused the rush on kitchens? Economy on the turn? Or marketing paying off?'

My mother looked over at me. I froze, fork in hand.

Mark took a sip of wine. 'There's a bloke at the kids' school who's refurbishing a few houses and he wants high-quality kitchens. His daughter is in Jamie's class and we went over to dinner there the other week. They live over on that new Latimer development, a guy called…'

I almost shouted. 'All right, Dad doesn't need every last detail. You've got a bloke buying three kitchens. End of story.'

Mark looked hurt. 'Sorry. Didn't mean to be boring.'

'I did ask the question,' Dad said.

'Sorry, maybe we've just been talking about the business a bit too much lately. Anyway, did you see anyone you knew at church this morning?' I wasn't too proud to fall on religion in times of need.

I pushed my food around my plate while my parents talked us through the gruesome details of the demise of half of the congregation until I thought my head would implode. Jamie had his elbows on the table, shovelling in food like a digger dredging for clay. Izzy was mouthing, 'Can I let the dog out?' as Mabel's whining became more high-pitched.

I nodded. 'Keep her in the kitchen though.'

I got up to fetch the crumble, massaging my neck muscles as I went. My handbag was next to the fridge. My mobile was in there, as enticing as chocolate cake to a dieter. I glanced into the dining room then whipped it out of the side pocket. My heart lifted when I saw the message: *Can't stop thinking about you. Come and tell me more secrets soon.*

I grabbed the cream out of the fridge. I couldn't let myself go down that route. I mustn't let my one-off mistake become a habit. I was just deleting the message when a huge scream rang out in the dining room.

'For goodness sake! You filthy beast.' My mother was on her feet, looking as though a naked man had burst into the room and waved his willy at her. I peered at her legs to see if the dog had laddered her tights.

Then I saw it. The trail of diarrhoea splodged over the cream carpet like brown mini-meringues. Thankfully, the saint of incontinent dogs was lacking in my mother's repertoire. Mark was making faces and gagging sounds but not actually moving a muscle to help. Jamie was screaming with laughter and banging the table in merriment.

On the way to gather up the cleaning gear, I found my mother's best gloves, her 'church' gloves, on the floor of the utility room. The right one was minus the middle finger. Highly appropriate.

Mabel had an uncanny talent for turning difficult situations into out-and-out disasters.

I prepared myself for a good twenty minutes' drama when I would have to say, 'I didn't see you bring your gloves in. Did you leave them in church?'

I flipped up the bin lid, tossed in the gloves and texted Tomaso.

When are you free?

Tomorrow came the reply.

CHAPTER EIGHTEEN

The second I walked downstairs that morning, Izzy sniffed the air like Mabel scenting a squirrel.

'You smell nice, Mum. Is it the body lotion Dad bought you?'

I engrossed myself in whisking the pancakes for breakfast. 'Well done, Inspector Clouseau. My skin's a bit dry.'

I glanced at Mark. He was lost in *Designer Kitchen and Bathroom* magazine, Shreddies and Monday morning gloom.

'Can I put some on?'

'Not now, we need to get going. Have you got your sports kit ready? Anyway, your pancake's ready. Put some blueberries on it.'

'I want golden syrup.'

'Blueberries.' It suddenly seemed essential to achieve a superfood triumph, as though it would atone for today's outing. At my current rate of sinning, the kids would be on black bean brownies and beetroot cake forever.

I had planned this. Sat down and deliberately thought out where I could go to avoid being seen. Vastly different from bumping into Tomaso at an events do. Premeditated. On the angelic side, I'd chosen a café so it was difficult to see how it could escalate into bed this time. This time. Christ.

I planted a kiss on Jamie's head. Through a mouthful of pancake, he said, 'Get off,' then started patting his hair as though I'd disturbed the carefully arranged strands.

I ran back upstairs and finished my make-up. Mark came in, asking for socks.

'They're in the airing cupboard.' When I got back tonight, I would pair them all up. Every single one of them. Traitorous wife penance.

I gave him a hug. 'I'm off, then. Don't know how long it will take me to get to Guildford at this time of day. Bound to be a complete waste of time as the bride is bringing the man as well. In my experience, the bloke never wants to spend the money.' I needed to shut up. I couldn't believe that I was actually laying the ground for being seen with a man. I could imagine myself waving away the mention of it. *It turned out the groom was more interested than the bride. She kept disappearing off to make phone calls...*

Mark tucked his shirt into his trousers. 'You never know. You've got to throw a bit of bread on the water and see what bites.'

'You sound like Sean bloody McAllister.'

'What is it with you and that man?' Mark banged the wardrobe open.

I snatched up my handbag. 'I've got to go.'

Coffee, I'd said. Coffee couldn't go wrong. I'd just see him and then that would be it. Make sure that he realised that I couldn't get involved.

I'd picked Pret. Nowhere snuggly or suggestive. Just sushi and Swedish meatballs. I was early, but Tomaso was earlier. A big bolt of shyness coursed through me as he stood up. He was wearing a blue open-necked shirt that matched his eyes. He kissed me on both cheeks, a waft of something gorgeous reaching me. And making me not want to let go.

'Lydia. Great to see you. I ordered you a very specific Americano with soya milk.'

'Thank you.'

I must have looked surprised.

'It's what you ordered at the dinner.'

Mark still asked me if I wanted tea most mornings, which I hadn't drunk since I was pregnant with Izzy.

'How have you been?'

'Fine. How about you?'

I couldn't take my eyes off his mouth. That perfect mouth, which knew how to do such perfect things. He had one canine turned at a slight angle. With his bedhead hair, it gave him the air of a posh ruffian.

Tomaso smiled. 'Fair to say I don't know much about the working of a woman's mind but I think even my Neanderthal brain recognises "fine" as code for something else.'

'Honestly, it's not code. I am fine,' I said, ignoring a strong urge to cry.

Tomaso leaned forward. 'How did you get on going home, after, er, the awards ceremony?'

I rarely gave a straight-from-the heart answer. I usually formulated the 'correct' response rather than a spontaneous reply. Tomaso had a way of pushing the override button on that particular character trait.

I hurled it all out there, my guilt at having sex with him – though I called it 'sleeping' with him. My fear that my carefully constructed life was about to blow apart like the proverbial straw house. My hopelessness, my fury at my mother for behaving like such a cow and at myself for letting her get away with it. I didn't mention Mark once.

Tomaso didn't say much. Halfway through, when the genie was not only liberated but swooping between the skinny cappuccinos and Earl Greys, his foot nudged mine. Hard to believe how sexy the simple pressure of shoe against shoe could be. In between rafts of truths that I struggled to recognise after living a lie for so long, I had moments of thinking: *Christ, there he was imagining he'd met a no-strings shag.*

I ground to a halt. 'Sorry. I don't suppose this is what you envisaged.'

'I didn't envisage anything. I just wanted to see you.'

Tomaso spooned the froth out of the bottom of his coffee cup. 'For what it's worth – and speaking as an execrable parent myself – the person who let everyone down was your mother. You were a child. Yes, you made a mistake, but she should have offered you a path out, not trapped you in a quagmire of recrimination.'

I fidgeted in my chair. 'Do you really think so? I've taken it for granted that feeling guilty for the rest of my life was just the price I had to pay.'

'Put it this way. If Jamie messed up – say, accidentally ran someone over when he'd first learnt to drive – you would try your best to help him move on from that, not remind him about it every day for the rest of his life.'

I shrank away from the thought, while recognising the accuracy of Tomaso's statement. There was no way, whatever Jamie or Izzy did, that I would want their guilt about the past to prevent them embracing the future.

The waitress collected our cups. I didn't want to go.

'Shall we walk along the river?' Tomaso asked.

I couldn't pretend he was a groom if we were walking along the river. But I couldn't leave now. It was as though I'd been opened up on the operating table and the guy with the needle had gone on a tea break while my heart was spurting into the ether.

I put on my coat. Once we were out, there was no pretence. Movement made our conversation less intense but our bodies more so. We walked, our coat sleeves brushing against each other. Tomaso told me about his latest hotel inspection where the chef kept a box of condoms in the spice cupboard and I realised with regret that laughing had become something I'd grown out of, a bit like listening to Radio 1. The drizzle was turning my hair into an old-fashioned mop but I was too embarrassed to put up my hood in case I rocked my inner gnome.

When we reached the railway arch, Tomaso stopped. He took my hands in his. 'You're cold.'

I didn't want him to suggest going home. 'I'm okay, I always have cold hands.'

'Can I warm you up?' He pulled me to him. That kiss blanked out everything. I was vaguely aware of a train rattling overhead, as Tomaso's kisses moved from gentle and delicate to hungry and urgent. I couldn't remember feeling desired this much, ever. I was leaning against the railway bridge, the damp cold against my back a direct contrast to the heat between us. Through my thick coat, I could feel the pressure of Tomaso's body and I longed to feel skin on skin.

Tomaso broke away, breathing out. He took my face between his hands. 'Did it feel funny going back to your husband?'

I closed my eyes, then stared directly at him, defying him to ask anything else. 'Yes.'

I'd let Mark down. Let the children down. I wasn't going to compound it by discussing Mark with, who? His rival? No. Not his rival. Tomaso could never be part of my life. He would never love the children like Mark did, would never understand my role in the whole family dynamic.

'Lydia, I don't want to be nosy…'

'Don't be, then.'

He ignored me. 'Do you love him?' His fingers were twisting a lock of hair on the back of my neck.

'Yes. I do.' The irony of my answer sat between us.

Tomaso leant forward to kiss me again, murmuring, 'One hundred per cent?' as his lips found mine.

'Well?'

'I don't love anyone one hundred per cent.'

Frustration flashed across his face. 'Are you capable of a straight answer? I'm not about to go and ring him up.'

'It's true. I keep enough back to survive if it all goes wrong.'

Tomaso had somehow made his way into my coat, caressing my breasts through my shirt. 'So you could never love, flat-out, no holds barred?'

'No.'

'You heartbreaker.'

'Just practical.' I tried to silence him with a kiss.

He wasn't going to let it drop that easily. 'But wouldn't you love to give up control, let someone else take the strain and know that they are going to catch you?'

'Too late, Tomaso. I've lived the life I've lived. I don't know how to exist any other way.'

I shivered.

Tomaso cuddled me close. 'I'm not going to lie to you, Lydia. You do something to me. I don't know what it is. On one level, you are so damn vulnerable, on another, it wouldn't surprise me to see you on telly leading a revolution.' He dropped his head and kissed my neck.

Out of the corner of my eye, I saw a woman cycling towards us. I pulled back, turning away to conceal my face. As she cycled past, her face impassive, I felt a fresh wave of embarrassment. Groping under the railway arches, on the wrong side of forty, with a man over a decade younger, who was not my husband.

Sordid. Far, far worse than Jamie. Do as I say with whistles and pompoms on it. I hoped he'd never discover my hypocrisy.

As much as I tried to smother that thought, I couldn't. 'I'd better go.'

Tomaso groaned. 'I'd love to see you again. We don't have to do this,' he said, his tongue finding mine and managing that clever trick of tightening every nerve ending from my breasts to my pelvis. He broke off. 'We can just be friends. You can have the luxury of knowing that I'm here, delighted to see you for an Americano with a drop of soya milk but equally delighted to have lots of lovely sex with you, should the occasion arise.'

That Italian cheek was so appealing. Mark and I never spoke to each other in such an honest way. By the time we met, I was like a cat burying bad feelings in a litter tray and hoping mind-reading would take care of the rest.

I laughed. 'Tomaso, I don't think we can be just friends.'

'Great. I'd prefer to be having sex with you as well.'

We walked back towards the town centre. Now there was no physical contact between us, my body was squealing out for his touch.

As we got to the steps that would take us back to the main street, our pace slowed. He glanced round and gave me a final kiss, so intense that I knew I would feel the sweet pressure of his mouth all the way home.

I could see how teenagers made mistakes. So hard to tell your body that something is wrong when the brain feels so deliriously happy doing it.

'I'll see you again soon, then.'

I gave him a little push. 'I can't. You know that.'

'I think you will.' He sounded cocky, but his eyes were kind. I wondered if he was right.

CHAPTER NINETEEN

Despite a flurry of texts all week from Tomaso, I'd restricted myself to a couple of non-flirtatious replies, weakening just once to put an 'x' at the bottom of one. But out of the guilt and deceit, one positive had emerged. I was slowly coming round to Sean's point of view that telling the truth might be the way forward. If I'd owned up to a stranger and he hadn't fallen on the floor, surely I could trust someone who'd loved me for a long time?

I didn't know when I was going to tackle it, but the conviction that Mark must never know began to feel as outmoded as Polaroid cameras themselves. The more I thought about telling him, the more something loosened and lightened inside me. As we read the papers over breakfast on Sunday, I kept trialling different opening sentences in my mind. *I should have told you this a long time ago… I'm going to tell you something that will shock you…*

Mark was eating his poached eggs, oblivious to the rehearsals in my head. He suddenly looked up. 'God, listen to this.' He then read a story out of the newspaper about parents being all up in arms at a private school in the next town because it had come to light that the headmistress used to run a brothel in Holland.

'How weird is that? There you are looking at this woman, thinking she's dedicated her life to academia and she turns out to be someone who used to dance on the tables swinging her nipple tassels. I don't know how people manage to rewrite history to such an extent that a Board of Governors actually employs them.'

I'd argued, intellectually at first, that people should be allowed a second chance. Mark shrugged. 'I think it's just dishonest not to disclose things in your past that would change people's perception of you.'

My reasoned argument gave way to emotional rage. 'I don't think you have any idea what some people go through. Who are you to say that she should never be able to leave her past behind, just because she made a poor judgment once?'

Mark put his hand up to stop me. 'Calm down. I didn't say that. But it is disingenuous to think that you can spend five years of your life recruiting vulnerable young women to have paid sex, but not see it as relevant when interviewing for a job that involves responsibility for teenage girls.' He laughed. 'Anyway, when did you become such a liberal bleeding heart?'

I ignored him and carried on making toast. My secrets – first Sean, now Tomaso – were encroaching on my ability to interact with Mark, strangling normality like Japanese knotweed. At least I now knew his stance on revelations a few decades too late.

Mark sighed. More and more lately, he was just letting discussions die rather than risk me snapping his head off.

I tried to restore harmony. 'Would you like some toast?'

'No, I'd better get off.'

'Where?'

'I said I'd just pop into Sean's to adjust the sink unit so that I can get on with installing the worktops tomorrow.'

'So that leaves me with rugby and swimming then? You knew I needed this morning to finish working on the plans for that Italian wedding in a couple of weeks. And I'm not leaving Jamie on his own at rugby. Someone needs to be there in case he breaks his neck.'

As she'd been doing more and more lately whenever Mark and I argued, Izzy jumped in quickly. 'Just drop me, Mum. I can get a lift back with Rhianna. It's only training today.'

'Can you work this afternoon when you get back? It's just that Sean told me Katya's getting a bit irritable living in a mess and I really need to keep them on side,' Mark said.

'God, that woman is a princess sometimes.'

Mark scooted out of the door without finishing his coffee. The old nice me felt a bit sorry for him. The nasty new me wanted to rampage through the house with a crowbar.

I dropped Izzy and drove Jamie to rugby. I spotted Sean taking photos on the other side of the pitch and chose a spot well away from him. I stood by myself, cringing every time the great bulldozers on the other team hurled Jamie to the ground. They all looked as though they'd been eating a kilo of steak for breakfast and lifting beer barrels with one arm instead of watching *Waterloo Road* and eating crisps.

At one point, I had to anchor my heels into the mud to stop myself running onto the pitch and slapping at the tangle of bodies to get off my son. Half of the time I couldn't look. It seemed such a contradiction that I'd spent my life saying, 'Eat your apple and cross at the zebra crossing,' yet made no attempt to stop him doing something where it was highly likely he'd get injured. I tried to think of anything else I'd let him do that might lead to a broken neck, paralysis, certain bruising, mashed nose. Nope. Nothing sprang to mind. Then I saw the game stop and the first-aid man run on. Most of the other parents carried on sipping their lattes. One guy said, 'That was a nasty tackle – the fly half, I think. I expect he'll be coming off.'

Fly half. Jamie was a fly half. Or scrum half? I didn't bloody get rugby. It looked like middle-class mud wrestling to me. I walked along the pitch, telling myself it could be any of the boys. Then I saw Jamie sitting propped up on a bag of rugby balls, blood pouring down his face. I ran over, but he put up his hand.

'I'm fine, Mum,' he said, in a voice that meant 'Go away'. The first-aider was searching through his bag. I assumed it was to find something to clean up Jamie but he produced some disposable plastic gloves, which were stuck together and required a lot of rubbing and blowing before the first-aider, who was not the one bleeding to death, could force his hands into them. Jamie, in the meantime, looked as though he'd have a severe haemoglobin deficit before health and safety had been satisfied.

One of the dads stepped in. 'Come on, let's get this boy something to mop up with.'

The first-aider put his hand up. 'Yes, sir, if you'll just be patient, I need to fill in a form.'

I couldn't bear it. Social death or no social death, Kleenex were coming out of my bag. As the rain mixed with all the mucus and blood, Jamie looked like something out of the video games he was not allowed to play. I was all ready with my 'You've done really well but we need to get you home now,' when the first-aider pronounced Jamie okay to carry on after a quick dab with a wet wipe.

I stepped forward to argue but he'd already disappeared back into the fray. I didn't care whether they won or lost, only that the whistle went while his head was still on the right way round.

After another twenty minutes of clock-watching, my ordeal ended for another week and I walked over to meet Jamie. Eleanor flew past me. Completely disregarding the mud that covered Jamie from top to toe, she threw one arm around his neck, slipped her other hand onto his stomach under his sodden rugby shirt and shouted over to Sean to take a picture. I imagined leaping in front of them, blocking the photo like a bodyguard at a rock concert, but instead I snapped at Jamie to hurry up. He pulled a face that suggested I shouldn't be allowed out on my own.

'I'm going to have a shower. See if you can get me a bacon butty at the clubhouse,' he said, over his shoulder.

Eleanor walked off with him, clinging to his arm.

It shocked me that I was capable of hating a fifteen-year-old girl. Even the way she shook out her long mane and laughed as though Jamie was the funniest person she'd ever met in her life annoyed me. Everything about her was designed to suck the attention out of the rest of the room and deposit it, glittering and spangly, in a little aura around her.

Sean strode over. 'Glad I've seen you. Just wanted to let you know that Mum was down last week and Katya was grilling her about my past girlfriends. She's become so much worse since we moved back to England. It's like she knows something is not right but can't put her finger on it. She's fixated on it, thinks there's some big mystery there, some love of my life I'm not telling her about.'

If I didn't know him better, I would have sworn he looked a bit shy.

I pulled up my collar against the wind. 'I hope you're not blaming me for egging her on. I do everything I can to encourage her to concentrate on the present, believe you me.'

'When Mum told her to enjoy her life now and stop worrying about the past, she turned really nasty and started shouting about people keeping secrets from her. It will be so much worse if she does find out later on. I do wonder whether we should just come clean.'

Rain was seeping down my neck and mingling with the chill that engulfed my entire body at his words. Mark's distaste for the brothel woman, his tone of disbelief, reverberated in my mind. 'No! You can't do that. Please don't tell her anything. I'll talk to her, try and make her see that she has nothing to worry about.'

Sean ran his hand through his hair, scattering raindrops. 'I'm not sure how long I can cope with repeating the same things over and over again. It's like being stuck in Groundhog Day.'

'Welcome to my world, Sean. I've had thirty bloody years of having to think before I speak. And not just to Mark, to everyone. I can't even talk about where I grew up in case people put two and two together. So excuse me if I'm not falling on the floor with sympathy.'

I remembered, just, to bring my voice down to a level that wouldn't have other parents crowding around to gawk at the sideshow. I was stuck between a hiss and a restrained roar.

Sean put his hand up. 'Whoa. I'm sorry. I thought we were on the same side now, friends even. Just trying to do our best in pretty shitty circumstances.'

I turned to face him, hands on hips. 'Sean. *I* will never be your friend. Your behaviour changed *my whole life*. You're just having to deal with a few uncomfortable questions.' I paused. 'And by the way, I don't want your bloody daughter hanging round my son.'

For the second time in five minutes, someone looked at me as though a straitjacket might come in handy.

I snatched up my bag, marched towards the clubhouse and yelled up the stairs for Jamie.

He came thundering down, trainers in one hand, rugby kit hanging out of his bag.

'All right, take it easy. What's the big hurry?'

'I need to get home and cook lunch. You need to get some ice on your nose.'

'Jesus, Mum, my face is fine, just a bit of a nosebleed. Why are you making such a drama out of a roast chicken? I'll just get a bacon butty here.'

'No. We are going to sit down in a civilised manner and have Sunday lunch as a family.'

'I don't want Sunday lunch. I'm going down the park with the others. I'll walk home.' He stabbed at something on his phone, my glare wasted on the top of his head.

I was aware of Melanie walking past, with Victor asking if he could get tickets to the new opera if he did his piano practice. Piano practice! I couldn't even get Jamie to sit at a lunch table with me. Melanie gave me one of those wan little smiles, parenting code for 'See what happens if you're not strict enough when they're little.'

Eleanor came sashaying down the stairs, completely ignoring me. She put a proprietorial hand on Jamie's shoulder. 'Are you coming to the park, then? We're stopping at Domino's Pizza on the way.'

Jamie nodded. 'Yep. Just taking my bag out to the car. Wait for me.' He looked at me in a way that was both defiant and beseeching.

I'd never understood women who bellowed at their kids in public. I'd always thought it was a resounding lack of self-control but now I could see the appeal of pulling the ripcord. Jamie marched off towards the car park and I followed, not knowing where to direct my anger – at Sean, or at Jamie for being taken in by a pair of big boobs and a wiggly walk.

Jamie threw his muddy kit in the boot. 'Mum. Don't be all angry. I just want to have a bit of fun with my mates.'

'With that girl, you mean. You'd better not be getting up to no good with her.'

'Chill out. You always think the worst of me. None of my friends' parents are as strict as you. You've no idea what it's like to be sixteen.'

He slammed the boot and stormed off.

Mark was home when I got back. I sailed in, regaling him with the blood bath, Jamie's rudeness, my dislike for Eleanor. If he'd have said something like, 'Poor you' and given me a hug, I would have probably got the sweetcorn out of the freezer and busied myself with a cheese sauce. As it was, he went for the 'Do you think you're overreacting?' approach, which made the bread knife look increasingly less like a tool for slicing the walnut loaf.

I stuck the chicken in the oven and grabbed Mabel, who looked delighted that discord had led to the second walk of the day. As I was pulling on my walking boots to go out, ranting about the bloody McAllisters, Mark stood there like someone who was watching a Pinter play and couldn't make head or tail of it. It took all of my restraint not to elbow him out of the way.

I drove up to the hill. Something about the view soothed me. All those little ant people running around. I squinted down towards the park. Jamie was somewhere down there, hopefully not behind a tree exploring Eleanor's bra. I wouldn't accept that relationship. But how could Mark possibly understand the strength of my feelings? He must feel as though he was navigating life with a road atlas that had the vital pages 24-27 missing. If Sean spilled the beans to Katya, Mark would get the pages connecting Norfolk to Surrey back again. But where would that leave us?

I sat down on a bench overlooking the South Downs, wondering whether life would ever go back to normal. As normal as it got for me, anyway. Mabel ran around hoovering up sandwich crumbs. She spotted a model aeroplane dodging and diving in the sky and took off to chase up and down below it. I hoped the owner would be sensible enough not to bring it in to land.

This ball of discontent lodged in my chest was becoming familiar. I couldn't remember what it felt like to get up in the morning with nothing more pressing than booking a wedding breakfast for twenty with 'an exceptional view' over Florence.

I strode on. I was just feeling calmer, the weak sun warming my face, when I heard a shout. Mabel was careering across the hill with a huge pink plane in her mouth. It was too big for her and the wings were taking it in turns to bash down into the mud as she bounded away from the owner. His feet were sliding all over the place. I jumped up and started whistling Mabel, who glanced in my direction, then did a 'talk to the tail'. The owner looked as though he might burst into tears, but decided that screaming at me would be far more effective.

'That plane's worth the best part of a grand. You should keep her on a lead if you can't control her.'

I waved my little bag of chicken at Mabel, which had the effect of making her twirl round and smash a bit of the wing into an oak tree before eyeing up the corridor of escape between me and Shouty. She did a rugby dodge through the middle of us, with me making a grab for her collar, Shouty pouncing for the plane and both of us feeling the whoosh of air as she cantered by. In desperation, I scattered chicken in a circle. She stopped and looked at us. Then edged a bit closer. Shouty made to move towards her. 'No! Let her come to us, otherwise she'll just run off. Let's sit down. It's chasing her that's making her think it's a game.'

So there I sat, in an uncomfortable silence, wondering how much it was going to cost me. I looked at Shouty, his little rodent face all pink and anguished.

'I'm so sorry.'

He didn't answer.

Mabel was shuffling towards us. As soon as she got close enough, I launched myself from a sitting position in a move that should feature in the next gymnastic Olympics. The 'tail grab, simultaneous body immerse in mud' trick. Damp was seeping through the front of my shirt.

'Get her collar.'

Shouty hesitated. I could feel her tail slipping through my grasp.

'Will she bite me?'

'No.' But I would, if he didn't get hold of her before we had to go through all these shenanigans again. Once Shouty had got her in a firm grip, I started to wriggle the plane free. 'Drop! Mabel! Drop!' I swear the damn dog would have laughed if it hadn't meant that she would have had to let go. Eventually, I prised the plane out of her mouth, wincing as her teeth scored deep grooves into the shiny pink fibreglass.

Shouty snatched it up, tutting and huffing, clutching it to him like a vulnerable kitten. I wanted to tell him to grow up, that my son had spurned remote-controlled everything by the time he was eleven and he should do the same. He stomped off, shouting over his shoulder, 'I'm going to report you to the National Trust, I am. Shouldn't be allowed.'

'You do that, mate. I bet they've got all the time in the world to come after me over a toy plane.' Mate? I hated that word. I barely recognised myself. And judging by Mark's puzzlement every time I spoke, neither did he.

My fingers curled around my phone as I thought about Tomaso and the luxury of just being myself, imperfect and honest.

I couldn't go where that thought threatened to take me.

CHAPTER TWENTY

My mother's favourite saying was 'Where there's a will, there's a war,' leaping on stories in the newspaper of siblings using up their entire inheritance fighting over who got what. In our family, however, it appeared that 'Where there's a wedding, there's a war' would be far more accurate. The news that my brother's daughter, Tara, was getting married acted like fertiliser on my mother's ability to radiate disapproval.

'I don't know what Michael is thinking of, letting her get married at twenty-one. I don't know what the big rush is. She's got it in her head she wants to get married two days before Christmas.'

'I was only twenty-four when I married Mark.'

My mother pulled the face she wheeled out whenever a proper fact got in the way of her spurious arguments. She waved a hand. 'Completely different, darling. You couldn't keep Mark waiting in case he changed his mind and you fell at the final hurdle.'

It was always so gratifying that my mother spoke as though she'd been standing on the edge of a showjumping ring, fingers crossed, counting down through the water jump, the hogsback and the combination – hopefully no time penalties – before she could hustle me down the aisle and wash her hands of me.

'And there was me thinking Mark couldn't bear the thought of another minute without my hand in marriage.'

My mother glared down at the invitation. 'According to Michael, they're all over the place with the planning. They've left it to the last minute and there's so much to do.'

'They probably need some professional help to make sure all the basics are in place.'

My mother paused. 'I did suggest you helping out, but Michael thought that the budgets and ideas might be more sophisticated than you're used to dealing with.'

There she went, beating about the bush again. I slammed the bin shut. 'How does he know what sort of budgets I work with? I haven't seen him for five years. I won bloody Surrey Business Star of the Year. Just because I can't look into someone's brain and assess the likelihood of them locking themselves in the pantry to eat glacé cherries when they're eighty-five, it doesn't mean that I am thick.'

'Darling. I do wish you wouldn't swear.'

I loved the way my mother always focused on the way I said things, rather than the compelling, superior content of my argument.

'Anyway, they've not given us much notice. I need a new frock. Your father's coming up with all sorts of reasons why he can't take me shopping, so I was wondering if you had any free days?' There went another order, slinking about, disguised as a question.

With my mother in tow, shopping catapulted itself into an entirely different category of hate. Inspecting Mabel's bottom for threadworm was a positive joy compared with my mother picking up every frilly collared blouse with a droopy bow and saying, 'Just try it. Everything looks different on a hanger. It's perfect for you.' Sometimes I gave in, just to keep the peace and then had to suffer my mother peering round the curtain: 'How are you getting on?' It was only a matter of time before I came home with something suitable for a night out at the whist drive.

My dad gave me a little wink when he dropped my mother off for our shopping trip later that week. 'She needs some shoes as well.'

Jesus. It was tempting to join Mabel sulking in her basket. She'd turned her head away when I offered her a chew to ease my guilt at leaving her for the whole day.

We drove to Guildford where my mother offered helpful advice about the perfect parking spot, pausing only to grab the door handle, squeak 'Careful, careful, you're ever so close to the car next to us,' and exhale loudly.

First stop was the shoe shop. My mother asked the assistant to check the fit because her fallen arches were playing her up and causing 'untold agony'. She received the unhelpful reply that they were only allowed to do that for children, not adults. In the rambling diatribe that followed about the 'problems with Britain today', the poor girl had a potted tour of my mother's various soap boxes from the Chinese economy, hard-working Polish immigrants, the lack of backbone in the young today and inexplicably, the fact that we were only now realising that it was sugar and not fat that was making us all obese.

It wasn't until a queue was snaking round the whole department that I managed to guide my mother away from the shoes and into Debenhams. She started gathering up every dress with a frill or a flounce. When we reached the fitting room, she handed half to me. 'I picked these out for you. My treat. Try them on.'

'I don't think they're really me, thank you.'

Sure enough, the 'you don't know till you try it on' speech cranked into action.

'No. Sorry. Very nice offer but you go in and I'll pop these back.'

Instead of backing down, my mother then waved over the shop assistant. 'Can you just help my daughter with these? She wears such masculine clothes. She's always had big legs, but some of these skirts might be quite flattering.'

While I wondered, not for the first time, whether my mother had always been a bitch or whether 'the event' had turned her into one, the shop assistant hovered in embarrassment. 'If you wanted to just see…' she said, gesturing to a fitting room.

'No. I really don't.' I stuck them on the nearest rail and shouted back to my mother that I would wait for her outside. She came out a few moments later in a pink diaphanous number that reminded me of a crocheted toilet roll cover. Successive outfits bore an increasing resemblance to net curtains, which, even my mother with her wisp of a figure, couldn't turn into a triumph.

'I don't know why you're so negative about everything.' The pot-kettleness of that statement left me goldfishing for a reply. My mother was so negative, it was astonishing she didn't show up as a silhouette in photos.

Fortunately, the shop assistant picked out a beautiful sapphire suit that fitted her perfectly. I could tell she loved it by the way she did a little shimmy in front of the mirror. 'How do I look?'

The shop assistant smiled and said, 'You look fabulous. Not many women your age have such a wonderful figure.'

My mother sighed. 'Lots of women my age let themselves go. Mind you, it's not just women my age, is it?' She turned to me. 'I saw that Terri outside school the other day. Gracious. She's piled on a bit of weight, hasn't she? She needs to be careful with that.'

I headed to the till. 'She is a bit chubby, but her figure isn't her selling point. Everyone loves her because she is so warm and friendly.'

'Do they? I always find her a bit loud. And her language!'

I almost staged a full-on swearing fest right there and then for the sheer delight of seeing the look on my mother's face.

'She's a character. I really like her.'

My mother pursed her lips but fortunately, before we could fall out over something that mattered so much less than the other huge things we managed not to fall out over, she had to pay.

My mother suggested coffee. 'Let's pop into the Rose Hotel. I can't bear these dreadful American cafés. Even the smallest coffee is enormous. And those clumpy mugs they serve it all in. Honestly, no wonder everyone is so fat. Is it necessary to have coconut syrup in a pint of coffee? I blame the Americans, really I do.'

We settled ourselves down in the lounge at the Rose Hotel. My mother was nodding her approval at the dainty cups and cafetières. I was just pouring the milk when a member of the hotel staff walked past, ushering a man in a suit over to the table with the cakes and patisserie.

Tomaso. I couldn't remember my body ever reacting to Mark's presence with the same burst of desire. Maybe eighteen years of marriage had blurred that memory.

He didn't notice me at first. The hotel guy was busy explaining how the cakes were freshly made every day. Tomaso was scribbling on a clipboard behind me, so I started glancing about, making noises about needing the loo, soaking up glimpses of his dark hands, his cufflinks. The wave of longing was blotting out my mother who was complaining – among other random rants – that she couldn't persuade Dad to book a holiday.

A light touch on my shoulder made me jump.

'Lydia! What are you doing here?'

Tomaso turned back to the man from the hotel and said, 'I think I've got everything I need. I'll pop into the office and get the fire safety certificates on the way out.'

I introduced my mother, expecting her to send out stranger-repelling waves like a startled skunk, but Tomaso's charm offensive – a load of old guff about not looking old enough to have a daughter my age – soon had her patting her pearls.

'Tomosi. Is that a Spanish name?' she said.

'No, my parents are Italian,' Tomaso said, politely refraining from correcting her.

'Do you speak Italian?' my mother asked.

'Yes, I do a bit of freelance interpreting work now and then. Keeps my hand in now I don't live there anymore.'

'Where did you live?'

I'd never seen my mother so chatty. We obviously had a shared genetic weakness for dark-skinned, blond-haired men.

'Florence. Have you been?'

'No, but I'd love to go. Have you been to the Convent of San Marco? There are supposed to be some marvellous frescoes by Father Angelico.'

I expected Tomaso to make a flippant comment but he managed real – or excellent fake – enthusiasm. 'There are indeed. Wonderful. You should go sometime,' he said.

'My husband doesn't really like churches. Or even cities. He prefers the countryside. Or anywhere there is a golf course.' My mother shuddered. 'I hate being out in the sticks. Too many animals. And the flies!'

Tomaso grinned, his perfect white teeth giving him the air of someone who should be sipping Martinis on a yacht off the Amalfi Coast.

Then my mother piped up with an invitation to take coffee with us.

Tomaso hesitated. He glanced at me. Something shifted in my stomach. I held his gaze long enough to remind myself how blue his eyes were. I nodded. 'Of course, please do.'

After a polite enquiry about not encroaching on mother and daughter time, Tomaso lounged on the sofa next to me, chatting about Italy, explaining to my mother how we knew each other while I focused on a teaspoon. I barely said a word. I held my coffee cup with both hands to prevent myself reaching out to touch him. At one point, I escaped to the loo to have a break from feeling that I might give myself away.

Eventually, Tomaso swigged down the last of his coffee. 'I'd better be going. Lovely to meet you.' He raised my mother's hand to his lips. Usually she would cotter on about all this European kissing nonsense, but not this time. He pressed a business card into her hand. 'If you do ever make it to Florence, give me a ring and I'll recommend some restaurants.'

I'd never seen my mother flirt. She giggled. Dorothy Southport actually let loose a spontaneous and joyful sound, twittering her thanks. Maybe I'd come round to my mother's belief in St Anthony, performer of miracles, after all.

I stood up and put my hand out. Tomaso shook it, gently caressing my skin with his thumb. He kissed me on both cheeks, taking the opportunity to whisper, 'Shall we get a room?' in my ear, which sent a bolt of lust through me.

I backed away, my heart surging.

Tomaso helped my mother on with her coat and took her arm as he showed us out. Normally she would have shaken him off – 'I'm not an invalid' – but clearly, falling under Tomaso's spell was a family failing.

On the way home, she chattered on about Tomaso, more complimentary than I'd ever heard her about anyone. My usual tactic was to say as little as possible about people I liked so that she couldn't find anything to criticise.

'I didn't realise winning that award was such an accolade. I don't know why you don't tell me these things. When you went to the lavatory, Tomosi said that there were over two hundred entries. He also told me you were organising another wedding in Italy. I didn't know you were going there again.' My mother managed to make the most banal conversation into accusations, as though I'd been hiding round corners, giggling behind my hand at the triumph of withholding work secrets from her.

'I don't really like organising weddings abroad, but it is better paid. I hate leaving Mark to juggle the kids. And I always get a bit nervous about how I'll cope with the language. I'll have an interpreter there on the actual day, of course.'

'Well, it's a blessing you found a husband like Mark. Not every man would step in and mop up the slack while his wife swans around Europe.'

I clutched the steering wheel. Swanning had nothing to do with it, cheeky cow. Paying the bloody school fees did. I stamped on the accelerator, not caring that my mother's little bird neck jerked forward.

'Everyone drives so aggressively these days, don't they?'

CHAPTER TWENTY-ONE

The bureaucracy of the Italian wedding sucked up so much time that I'd managed to avoid Katya without trying – or lying – citing truthfully that I was buried in paperwork. Until the Wednesday before half-term when the school held an A-level options evening. I'd obviously been living in Surrey for far too long because fleetingly, I wished I was on Facebook so I could tell the whole world that every teacher was begging Jamie to do their subject for A level – *#GeniusForASon.*

Katya cornered me in the politics session while our offspring sat holding hands under the cover of Eleanor's jumper, absorbed in their world of two. Katya ranted away. 'Sean's mother went very quiet when I told her that he was adamant about us not going to the reunion for his senior school's centenary. I'm sure Sean's hiding something from me.'

I whispered platitudes, dread spreading through my limbs. People kept turning round to glare until I was squirming in my seat with embarrassment.

When we finally got out, I made some excuse about having to rush back for Izzy. Katya shouted after us, 'See you on Friday then, Jamie. Have a good time in Italy, Lydia. Let's catch up when you get back.'

As soon as we got into the car, I turned to Jamie. 'Friday? What's that about?'

'Oh yeah, Mum, I was going to tell you. Eleanor's having a party and Dad said it's all right for me to stay the night.'

I crunched the gears. 'And when exactly was this all agreed?'

'I don't know. Yesterday. Because you're in Italy, he thought it would be easier. He won't have to wake up Izzy to come and fetch me at midnight.'

'And neither of you thought you should discuss it with me?'

Jamie didn't feel the need to answer that query.

I screeched into our drive and yanked up the handbrake. Then I noticed my dad's car tucked in the corner. He didn't generally pop in unannounced: 'You don't want us oldies hanging about.' I searched my memory, to see if I'd somehow forgotten that he was coming but drew a blank. My adrenaline ratcheted up another notch in preparation for a disaster I hadn't foreseen. My showdown with Mark over 'partygate' would have to wait. I pushed the front door open. 'Hel-lo? Is everything okay?'

Thankfully, my dad was watching the *News at Ten* with Mark, a cup of coffee in hand. He pushed himself up to give me a hug, but despite the grunt of effort, he was all sparkly-eyed as though he was holding onto a secret. Of the good sort.

'To what do I owe this pleasure?' I asked, relief coursing through me that his visit was apparently unrelated to Sean McAllister. I'd been braced for a glum hello that heralded an uphill battle to get him back to the doctor.

He clapped his hands together as though he was about to embark on a longwinded story. I brushed away the urge to hurry him along so that I could release the full force of fury festering deep in my stomach against Mark.

'Have a seat, darling. I've got a little favour to ask you.'

'Whatever it is, it's a yes.'

He smiled and put his hand up to stop me. 'You'd better hear what it is first. As you know, your mother keeps wanting to drag me around cities looking at dreary churches. She's all keen to book a break in Florence because she'd been talking to that friend of yours the other week, the foreign chap.'

'He's not foreign, his parents are Italian, but anyway, carry on.' I avoided looking at Mark, though I felt his curiosity.

'As it happens, my golf club have a team going up to Scotland to play against St Andrews this weekend. Someone's dropped out and they've asked me to fill in but I don't want to leave your mother on her own. She says she'll be fine but I wouldn't feel right. So I was wondering if you could take her to Florence with you this weekend? She wouldn't need to come to the wedding or anything, but she could see some of the frescoes she wants to look at…' He winked. 'Save me the trouble. I'll see you right for the flights and hotel room.'

He looked so hopeful. Frankly, I couldn't imagine anything worse than a couple of days of undiluted matriarchal wisdom.

Mark was pulling a 'How are you going to answer that?' face behind my dad's back. But how could I refuse? The poor bloke had sat in prison because of me. I tried to give myself a moment to think.

'What does Mum say?'

'I haven't told her. I want to surprise her.'

Despite the evil prospect of spending 24/7 times two with my mother, the tenderness that my dad still conjured up for her softened my heart. 'Go on then. You'd better bring back the trophy.'

His old face lit up with joy, which kept my anger with Mark trapped in its box long enough for me to wave my dad off.

I was just about to give Mark both barrels of my outrage, when he said, 'Before I forget, there was a message for you about someone called Giuseppe Bardo on the answerphone. Who's he?'

'He's the translator for the wedding. What did he want?'

Mark's face fell. 'He's in hospital with pneumonia.'

CHAPTER TWENTY-TWO

The next morning, the terrifying reality of having two days to find an alternative translator or call off the glamorous Palazzo Vecchio wedding chiselled an extra dimension into my argument with Mark over Jamie staying at the McAllisters.

'How could you be so stupid? They're already all over each other, right under the teachers' noses. At this rate, we'll be lucky if we're not grandparents by the time Jamie's seventeen.'

Mark resolutely refused to back down. 'Katya and Sean are sensible. They'll keep an eye on the bedroom situation. Give the boy a break.'

I tried to remember if I knew anything about the layout of the upstairs of the McAllister house. I imagined Eleanor waiting until Katya and Sean were in bed, whispering down the landing to Jamie, muffling her laughter in the sleeve of her dressing gown. Actually, I bet she didn't even own a dressing gown. Just flimsy shorts and strappy T-shirts. Did Jamie even possess a packet of condoms? That boy who not so long ago would spend hours building cranes from Lego?

My dreams of motherhood had never included an image of my son walking into Boots and flicking along the row of ribbed, cherry-flavoured or extra-sensitive Durex.

'No. I'm not having it. I'll phone Katya and tell her he can't come.'

Mark put up his hand. 'Sorry, but you are not going to embarrass Jamie like that. Or us, because the McAllisters thought they were doing us a favour. We'd just look rude.'

Mark never put his foot down. I didn't know where to push to get my own way because he normally conceded where the children were concerned. With time ticking away, the phone ringing into the ether at the Palazzo Vecchio and my frantic emails as yet unanswered, I had to let it go and start firefighting on the Italian front. If Mark was suddenly the expert on child rearing, he'd have three days to showcase his talents without my intervention – if I managed to find an interpreter.

I couldn't let the bride down now. I briefly imagined making the phone call: 'Really sorry but you won't be needing that tiara…' No. I couldn't let that happen. I combed through every possible solution. My thoughts flickered towards Tomaso, then away again. Since I'd bumped into him in Guildford, I'd forced myself not to respond to his texts. Deliberately going away with him to a foreign city would put me firmly back on the slippery slope.

My mother, with her disregard for anyone's convenience other than her own, was on my doorstep before I'd had my second cup of coffee. She whirled through to the kitchen, grabbing my arm, which, in her book, was positively tactile. 'Your father's told me that we're off on a little trip. I've made a list of all the churches I want to visit. Can you book me tickets for the Uffizi? I've read there are awful queues. I wonder whether I'll be able to climb up all those steps in the Duomo? I think there are four hundred and sixty-three…'

Before she could go any further, I put my hand up. 'At the moment, I'm not sure it's all going to happen.' I filled her in on Giuseppe Bardo choosing right now to do his dying duck.

My mother concertinaed her face as though I was deliberately placing obstacles between her and the reliquary housing St John the Baptist's index finger. 'Get that friend of yours to do it. The one from the hotel. Tomosi! He speaks Italian. Said he did interpreting.'

'I can't ask him.'

'Why ever not?' my mother asked.

'He won't be able to do it at such late notice. He probably wouldn't want to trek over to Italy for such a short time. Anyway, I don't know him well enough to ask for favours.'

I busied myself bleaching the sink as though E.coli was threatening to wipe us all out.

'Nonsense. It's not a favour, it's business.'

'I've left messages with the Italian tourist board in Florence and London to see if they can suggest anyone. I'm just about to call the Institute of Translation and Interpreting. I've still got a few options to try.' I tried to corral some conviction into my voice.

My mother unzipped her handbag. 'You always were such a defeatist. If you don't ask, you don't get. I'll phone Tomosi for you.'

'Don't be silly. You can't start phoning people you've met once and asking them to come to Italy with us. And he's called Tomaso, not Tomosi.'

'Tomaso, Tomosi, same thing,' said the person who became incandescent when people called her Dot, or worse still, Dottie. 'You're the one who's being silly.' She was foraging in her bag, drawing out Tomaso's business card with a flourish of triumph. 'Now, where are my glasses?'

I slammed the bleach bottle down. 'All right. I'll ring him but it won't do any good.' I tried to find a reason to make the phone call from the other room, but my mother stood there, hands on her hips to underline that any hesitation from me would lead to her direct dialling Tomaso.

'Tomaso, it's Lydia. I'm here with my mother.' I hoped he heard the warning in my voice, because if my mother got any closer, we could share a bra. I pressed the phone hard into my ear.

I explained my predicament, trying to ignore my mother, who was semaphoring and mouthing all manner of instructions as though her presence in Florence was actually a selling point.

I prepared myself for a snort of disbelief that I'd wasted my free minutes on seeing if Tomaso could help. Instead he said, 'Serendipity. I've just finished inspecting a major hotel chain. I'd planned to have a few days off anyway, but for you, darling Lydia, I will fly to Italy tomorrow.'

I had my mobile pressed so hard against my head that I was in danger of cutting off the call with my chin. I walked away from my mother on the pretence of digging out a notepad from the drawer in the hallway.

I reiterated that 'both *my mother* and I' would be arriving on the Friday and staying in the Hotel Bonini if he wanted me to book him a room there.

'Won't I be sharing with you? Spoilsport.'

My mother was hovering in the doorway. I adopted my most professional, 'just tying up the loose ends' tone. 'That would be extremely difficult and I don't think it would be appropriate for this particular wedding.'

Tomaso laughed and made some comment about my sexy schoolteacher voice, until fear that his words would reach my mother's bionic ears made me close down the conversation with a promise to email the final details.

I salved my conscience by telling myself that there wasn't much danger of being led astray with my mother in attendance. She could yet prove a cash cow if someone could find a way to market her unique periscope/telescope talents.

Her endorsement of Tomaso and my half-truth – that I'd found someone from Surrey Business Stars – barely caused a blip on Mark's 'fishy coincidences' radar.

He raised his eyebrows briefly. 'How old is this bloke? How come he can speak Italian?'

'He's really young. His parents are Italian.' I hoped I managed to make him sound about twenty-three. 'I was really lucky to find someone who could drop everything and come straight away.'

Mark grinned. 'Thank god for that. It's not even a particularly mainstream language. Poor bloke, having to put up with your mother for more than an afternoon.'

My face burned at Mark's naïve trust in me.

I tried not to think about the fact that I was going to spend almost three days in close proximity to Tomaso. But I couldn't ignore it. Even when I was packing, I'd come over all *Room With A View* and was attempting the 'In my small way, I'm a woman of the world' vibe. I'd squashed everything into a little bag rather than our cumbersome family case, as though I was a seasoned traveller for whom a hop over to Italy was no more challenging than a bus ride to Brighton.

My mother arrived with a case big enough to travel in herself. She frowned at my compact bag and dedicated a large part of the journey to the airport to asking me if I'd got enough warm clothes. Once she'd exhausted that concern, she turned her attention to whether I'd be smart enough for the wedding. The sooner she trotted off on a tour of the churches, the better we were going to get along.

Tomaso had flown out the day before to complete all the legal formalities. By the time we arrived at the Hotel Bonini, having negotiated endless 'Are you sure this is the right direction/train/ cab?' queries from my mother, I barely had the energy for any emotion – excitement, guilt or otherwise. On the upside, I had learnt some marvellously rude hand gestures during the taxi ride to the hotel that I was itching to share with Jamie.

But Tomaso strolling into reception acted like a shot of caffeine on every female in the room. I bet he hadn't had to try to attract the receptionist's attention while she finished polishing her desk.

Tomaso cemented his position in my mother's affections with compliments and cheek kissing. '*Bella Dorothea*, I said Italy would suit you.'

I shook his hand rather formally and tried not to think about the way Mark waved us off into the cab, with an innocent 'No running off with any Italian gigolos.' Nothing would happen anyway. Tomaso and I were just two friends, with honesty between us. Plus one night of sex and a couple of hours of kissing. Which, Tomaso had assured me, against eighteen years of marriage, was such a tiny percentage as to barely count.

Tomaso led the way up to our rooms, more alpha than I'd noticed before, barking out orders to the lad who helped us with the luggage. It was so relaxing not to have to scrabble about wondering whether a one-euro tip was an insult or five would mark me out as an overgenerous fool against a background of the kids arguing over who was having which (identical) bed.

The bellboy stopped outside a room at the end of the corridor. Tomaso grabbed hold of my mother's case and handed it to him. He turned to my mother. 'Dorothea…I asked for a room right at the end for you, where it's quiet. Florence is beautiful but quite noisy. You get settled in, then we'll all go to my favourite restaurant for lunch, if that suits.'

She patted his hand. 'You are a treasure, Tomosi. Lydia is lucky to have found you.'

I left my mother to unpack. Tomaso winked at me and whispered, 'I swapped the rooms round. You're opposite me.'

CHAPTER TWENTY-THREE

I arrived at reception before my mother, who was no doubt still scaring her bathroom toiletries into straight lines.

Tomaso was already there and jumped to his feet.

'Lydia! How is everything?' He gave me a hug, pressing his body into me in a way that made having a hotel room just a few hundred metres away incredibly dangerous. I caught the receptionist's eye over his shoulder and wriggled free.

He looked more Italian than usual, something to do with the way he was wearing his scarf. Handsome as hell. God, if karma did exist, I'd be reincarnated as an earwig for my impure thoughts. Style had to be in Italian DNA. I pushed back my disloyal comparison with Mark in his Meatloaf T-shirt. I hoped Tomaso wasn't thinking, *God, Lydia looks so English and frumpy*.

He spoke quickly. 'Listen, before your mother arrives, I just wanted to let you know that I've arranged to meet Raffaella later this afternoon. She's going to bring Giacomo to see me.' He exhaled loudly. 'I'm not sure whether it's a good idea. What if he doesn't even recognise me?'

'You've got to do it, though. You couldn't come to Florence and not contact them. What time?'

'Not until about five. I thought it would give us time to eat first.'

'Perfect. I've got to go to Hotel Cesare at six to meet the catering manager for tomorrow's reception.'

I couldn't help thinking that if I hadn't seen Izzy and Jamie for nine months, I wouldn't have waited until after lunch. In fact, my heart was constricting at the mere thought of it. And just as I was mulling over the phrase, 'Nowt so queer as folk', my mother arrived. Her beady eyes focused my mind on the fact that two acquaintances don't usually stand so close that the hairs on their arms touch. I shot over to the desk to pick up a map, reminding myself just how much I had to lose if Detective Dorothy got suspicious.

Tomaso took the hint and morphed into tourist guide extraordinaire. 'Dorothea? Are you ready for this? *Andiamo*, let's go.'

We walked along the river towards the Ponte Vecchio. I trailed behind the other two as the narrow pavements didn't lend themselves to group conversations. Now and again, I'd hear my mother clinging obstinately to her version of the facts of the Florentine Renaissance in direct contradiction to Tomaso's informed account. If nothing else, she would be an excellent rehearsal for dealing with his difficult wife later on.

As we headed over the bridge, I took a moment to admire the gold in the jewellery shops. Unlike Mark, who would have wandered off to look at the view down the river, Tomaso came to stand next to me, pointing out a blue sapphire necklace he thought would bring out the colour of my eyes. 'Let's see,' he said, staring directly into my eyes for way longer than a simple 'blue, brown or green?' inquiry. I felt the odd sensation of having one discussion while another silent conversation was taking place. My mother thrusting her guidebook under my nose ended all conversation – mute or otherwise.

Just over the other side of the bridge, Tomaso led us into a little square. 'Here. My son's favourite restaurant.'

My mother did an exaggerated recoil of surprise as though Tomaso had announced he was the owner of a couple of albino llamas that he was preparing for space travel.

'I didn't know you had a son,' she said, in a tone that was approaching affronted.

Tomaso, who was turning out to be quite the feather-smoothing expert, laughed and said, 'There's such a lot you don't know about me, Dorothea. You can do twenty questions over lunch if you like.' He indicated an outside table. 'Let's make the most of the sunshine.'

His fingers rested briefly on my neck as he tucked my chair in for me. I jerked away, blushing and glancing around the square to find something to distract my mother from the physical tension enveloping me every time Tomaso came within touching distance. In desperation, I pointed out the row of Vespas lined up against one wall. That, of course, led to the 'I hope you're not going to let Jamie get a motorbike' rant, but did allow my face to resume its normal colour.

'So, a little wine, ladies?'

I blanked out my mother, who was making 'drinking at lunchtime is for the debauched and depraved' faces. 'Yes please.'

But Tomaso was insistent. 'Go on, Dorothea, you must try the Vernaccia. It comes from San Gimignano, a little medieval town in the Tuscan countryside.'

'Twist my arm, then, Tomosi. Just a drop. You're turning out to be a bad influence,' my mother said.

I wondered if she realised her favourite saying, 'Many a true word is spoken in jest' was racing along behind her, ready to bite her on the backside.

While Tomaso ordered some local specialities for us, I watched the world go by. The thing that struck me most was that the old people didn't just give up. No one was wearing ugly shoes or trousers flapping around their ankles because there was no point in buying a new pair as they'd be dead soon. Instead, there was a neatness, a sense of grooming about them, as though it was a civic duty to put on lipstick or to press a shirt. My mother would have fitted in well. I, on the other hand, would need a completely new wardrobe.

As Tomaso poured the wine and debated over the best, the freshest, the most authentically Tuscan dishes with the waiter, a family walked in – the grandparents, a mother and a son, who was sitting on his father's shoulders. They looked like something from a cereal advert, where everyone was running barefoot with a kite on a hill. My mother usually hampered my own three-generational enjoyment by glaring at the kids for bad language, not picking their feet up, forgetting to use their napkins, elbows anywhere – in fact, the thousands of little details that would bring on a 'youth of today' diatribe. I dreaded the day she copped the spectacle of Izzy and her friends taking selfies, pouting into their phones like adverts for a dodgy massage parlour.

The father swung the boy down, who squealed and ran into the restaurant, shouting, '*Gelato!*', which even my stunted linguistic abilities recognised as ice cream. They all trooped in behind him.

When the waiter bustled off, I waited for Tomaso to lean in with some more anecdotes about Florence. But he was looking beyond me, at the family who'd come into the square. 'That's my wife.' The words, 'And my son,' came out as though they were burning up his throat.

The distress in his face made me want to lead him away from the table and bundle him round the corner, where he could organise his emotions.

'Do you want to go? Do you want us to go?'

The tiny glass of wine had affected my mother's empathising ability, which probably resided on a pinhead even in normal circumstances. 'Go? But we haven't eaten yet. Why would we go? Surely Tomosi can be civil to his wife. I thought you young ones took all that sort of thing in your stride.'

We both ignored her. Tomaso looked glazed. 'My son was on that bloke's shoulders.'

I risked putting my hand on his arm. 'He could be just a friend. He won't replace you anyway.'

'Giacomo probably doesn't even remember me.'

'We should leave.' Crostini and family showdown were just moments away.

'No, I'm not running away from my own son.'

I tried again. 'It might be better to wait until the time you'd arranged with Raffaella, rather than catch her on the hop in front of the whole family.'

Just at that moment the waiter came out with little plates of bruschetta, mushroom polenta and a platter of cold meats and cheese. I had the fleeting thought that it would be a tragedy to leave all this sitting on the table. Then I felt horrible for even considering those garlicky mushrooms when Tomaso's life was falling apart in front of him.

Through the restaurant window, I could make out the family standing at the bar. Given the Desperate Dan amount of food Tomaso had ordered, there was no chance that we'd roll out before them.

Tomaso pushed his chair back. 'I'm going in. Excuse me.'

If my mother hadn't been sitting there, I would have flung myself on him and held him back. 'Tomaso, don't do that. Wait till they come out.'

As it was, his wife and the man appeared first. There was something regal about her. I bet she never had to stop ladders in her tights with nail varnish.

I froze. It was like watching a huge umbrella catch the wind at the beach and failing to grab it before it went spinning off across the sand, spearing toddlers and wreaking havoc among the picnics.

The woman turned her amber gaze towards us. Her hands flew to her face. 'Tomaso!'

Then a long torrent of Italian poured out so fast that I wondered if Tomaso's brain could compute quickly enough to absorb it. I couldn't make out the words but the emotion was painful to watch.

Suddenly her attention turned to me and my mother. It didn't take much imagination to grasp the gist of 'You don't bother seeing Giacomo for nine months and think you're going to introduce him to your bit on the side? And even your new mother-in-law? Sod right off.'

I was doing that international hands-in-the-air thing of 'You've got it all wrong.' I managed to say, 'We're here for work, *lavoro*.'

Raffaella, however, wasn't in Esperanto mode. Raffaella's boyfriend put his arm round her shoulders to steer her away. I did worry for a split second that Tomaso was going to launch into a Hugh Grant/Colin Firth-style fisticuffs that would end up in the square's fountain. I jumped up. I was going to have to appeal to the boyfriend.

'Do you speak English?'

His eyes flicked over me. Clearly I didn't make the grade owing to my lack of Chanel sunglasses, but he nodded.

'We are here for work, I'm organising an English wedding. Tomaso is my interpreter. He needs to talk to his wife. For Giacomo's sake.'

Before he could answer, the wife swung round. Her eyes drilled into me. 'Do not, do NOT say the name of my son.'

Out of the corner of my eye, I could see my mother folding and unfolding her arms in a gesture that signalled the beginning of a tirade about manners, but luckily Raffaella's rising decibels were holding everyone's attention.

'Okay, I'm sorry. I just think you two should move away before G—, I mean, your son, comes out. Why don't you go for a coffee? Your boyfriend can tell your parents where you are.'

Raffaella marched over to Tomaso, jerking her head in the direction of the street.

'Sorry about this. I'll see you later at the hotel.' Tomaso pulled out his wallet but I waved him away.

I sat back down, my heart racing. Through a mouthful of salami, my mother was shaking her head and muttering, 'What a to-do. I don't know why they think you're his girlfriend'. The boyfriend came over and stood in front of our table, making me aware of every last grey hair on my head, every pore that I hadn't massaged with miracle shrinking cream.

'Good luck with Tomaso. He won't be a very nice boyfriend.'

'He's not my boyfriend. Work colleague.' I didn't dare look at my mother in case she picked up on the tiny notch below complete conviction in my voice. Outrage was always trickier to pull off when it was struggling to make itself heard through a cover-up.

The boyfriend gave me a knowing look and pulled the skin down under one eye. I gathered that was the Italian equivalent of 'Yep, my foot'.

I turned away and stuffed a whole *crostino* in my mouth, a kind of Italian up-yours. This might have been more effective if I hadn't inhaled a breadcrumb and coughed small particles of mushroom everywhere.

I didn't bother looking at the disgust on his face. Or my mother's – her idea of filling her mouth too full was eating a whole grape in one go. I was just wondering how we could possibly eat enough cheese and cured meats so that the waiter wouldn't be offended, when Raffaella's mother flurried over and practically jabbed her finger up my nose. I wasn't sure what she said, but from her Michelin-Man mime, I think she was suggesting that I could do with losing a few kilos. Crikey. I'd never been to a country where being a size 14 got you ridiculed in public. But I supposed she was only defending her daughter. When Izzy's friends left her out, posting pictures of the whole gang having 'the best time ever' without her, I wanted to get in there and have a go, too.

Without language on my side to communicate, I went for a peace offering with the cheese plate. Raffaella's mother smashed it out of my hand. It arced up into the air, sending Tuscany's finest produce crashing down onto the cobblestones.

My mother recovered herself the fastest. She leapt to her feet, slamming her fists on the table and making the wine bottle wobble dangerously. She drew up her five-foot frame like a goalie trying to intimidate the opposition and shouted, 'Go away! Go away and leave us alone, you horrible little woman.' She started pushing her backwards. The grandmother slipped on a piece of rogue mozzarella and did a cartoon dance as though she was trying to run on a pile of ball bearings. My mother tucked her hands behind her back, making no attempt to stop her breaking her coccyx. Thankfully, the boyfriend came in useful for something other than sowing doubts about my fidelity in my mother's mind and grabbed her. But my mother was not finished. Not by a long way. Her bellows of 'My daughter has *nothing* to be sorry for!' bounced off the arches, lanterns and medieval doorways, rattling the shutters for show time in every apartment surrounding the square.

I wished that she'd been right.

CHAPTER TWENTY-FOUR

As we walked away from the restaurant, my mother seemed energised by the British grandma versus Italian *nonna* argy-bargy. 'I'm not going to be made a fool of by a bunch of cowardly Itais. In the war, they were the first ones running for the hills.' I did wonder whether my mother actually held a view that didn't have the *Daily Mail* as its source.

Dad would have been horrified at her behaviour. And if he ever came to know about it, mine too. In an urgent need to atone, I opened my map and pointed to a trio of churches within walking distance. My mother was barely able to contain her excitement that the first church, Santo Spirito, had *thirty-eight* chapels. Oh goody. But even I had to admit that the square itself was soothing to the soul, lined with cafés and trattorias, with an elaborate fountain in the centre where old ladies – hopefully non-cheese-plate-smashing pacifists – sat chatting, with an indulgent eye on their grandchildren. As far as I could see, no one minded if kids screamed, kicked or pushed each other over as long as they a) didn't get dirty and b) didn't take their coats off.

For the first time that afternoon, I was able to appreciate my surroundings, spying into the imposing courtyards beyond huge wooden doors, running my fingers over chunky ceramic tiles. I was just admiring a little shrine to the Madonna when a movement in an alleyway caught my eye. With a lurch of recognition, I saw Tomaso, his hands holding Raffaella's wrists, speaking to her with an urgency, an intensity that suggested there was still a story to unfold rather than just a couple of loose ends to snip off. The fight had gone out of her. A little softness had crept into her face. She had her head on one side, very Sophia Loren coquette. She reached up and took his face in her hands. I turned away. He wasn't mine to intrude upon, though there was no mistaking the dull ache of jealousy that I would have to deceive myself about.

I trained my mother's gaze in the opposite direction by pointing out the simplicity of the church façade and scurried past. The next couple of hours shuffling around Santa Maria del Carmine, San Frediano in Cestello and a myriad of saints in various stages of suffering seemed a small price to pay for arriving back at the hotel without any more hand-to-hand combat.

I dispatched my mother to her room to rest and headed out for my meeting with the hotel's catering manager. Now I was alone, I could stop lying to myself: I'd expected Tomaso to text me to let me know when he'd be back.

If he'd be back.

I hated the idea of him taking Raffaella home for good old-fashioned make-up sex.

Even though I couldn't possibly have sex with him myself.

By the time I'd liaised with the sort of chef you could imagine throwing tiramisu in a tantrum, the prospect of a jolly dinner à deux with my mother made me want to hole up in my room. I hoped the waiters were polishing their shoes and their 'right away, madams' – we'd been in Florence less than a day and Anglo-Italian relations were already under fire.

I rounded the corner back to my hotel, depressed rather than uplifted by the streets bustling with people living life to the full instead of just marking time. A teenage boy pushed his bike, leaning over the crossbar to kiss his girlfriend, oblivious to the human traffic jam behind him. A dark-haired girl pulled at her friend's sleeve to make a point, followed by laughter, a great burst of unconstrained joy. No one looked as though their lives were a jumble of last year's Christmas lights they couldn't quite unravel.

I pulled out my phone for the umpteenth time. No word from Tomaso. And why should there be? Because he'd made me feel special? Because for the first time in years I could speak openly without being judged? I grouched into the hotel. The receptionist called to me, '*Signora*. Your mother is in the dining room already, with your – boyfriend?'

I didn't know which emotion to nail down first. The shock that this woman on reception was shouting about Tomaso being my boyfriend for all to hear? Joy that he was back? Relief that I wouldn't have my mother spotlighting on me for the next two hours? Or puzzlement that my mother, who ate less than Izzy's gerbil, hadn't been able to wait until seven-thirty for me?

Tomaso was leaning back in his chair, expansive and relaxed. I searched my mother's face for clues that he'd been too open and aroused her suspicions. Nothing. She waved when she saw me. 'Coo-ee, darling! I heard Tomosi come back and I didn't know how long you'd be, so we thought we'd come down and have some *antipasti*.' My irritation subsided. My mother was clearly proud of her new Italian word. And Dad would be so thrilled she'd had a nice time.

I shouldn't be angry with her just because I wanted Tomaso to myself.

Throughout the meal, it became obvious that was never going to happen. I was dying for a few minutes alone with Tomaso to find out how he'd got on with Raffaella but my mother was like a jukebox that never runs out of money. As soon as one topic of conversation came to an end, she'd pop up with another 'must-know' question about Italy. Now and again, Tomaso's hand would brush mine as we reached for the menus, as he poured me water, as he picked up my fallen napkin. I had to make a concerted effort to keep my voice steady and meet my mother's eye, focusing on her 'plans for tomorrow' against a great surge of lust that made my breathing uneven. I kept asking her if she was tired, if she wanted me to take her upstairs but she developed a sudden desire for coffee – which she never drank late at night – until I couldn't find a reason to stay up any longer myself.

'Right. Better get up to bed then. Big day tomorrow.'

All three of us wandered along the corridor. Tomaso and I said an awkward goodnight outside our rooms, with my mother still rattling on about a lovely evening, 'So much to tell Arthur.'

Tomaso disappeared into his room, bidding me 'Sleep tight' with a look that suggested he'd hoped sleeping would have been the last thing on the agenda. I stood with my door open until my mother was safely ensconced in her room, not sure whether I was hoping or dreading that Tomaso might reappear.

I could hear him moving about in his room opposite, then water running. The shower? Cleaning his teeth? Either of those could mean anything. Then my mother suddenly popped out again. 'Lydia? Aren't you in bed yet?'

I stuttered, floundering for an explanation. 'I thought I heard you knock. Must have imagined it. Goodnight, Mum.' I spoke loudly in case Sod's law sent Tomaso sneaking out into the corridor and the whole Florentine adventure descended into a Benny Hill farce.

I slammed the door shut. Then lay in bed awake until the early hours, both resentful and grateful for my mother's chaperoning skills.

CHAPTER TWENTY-FIVE

'Home' ringing my mobile broke into my slumber. I glanced at the pillow next to me.

Phew.

Jamie's voice came on the line. 'Mum, it's me.'

'How are you? Are you surviving without me?'

'Yeah. Izzy's being a dickhead but otherwise it's all right.'

I overlooked the language. I was grateful that he wanted to talk to me at all.

'What was the party like?' Open-ended question. Get me on the parenting skills.

It didn't produce a pay off. His response of 'fine' held the impatience of a rigmarole to get through until he could nail the purpose of his call.

'Is Dad okay?'

'Yeah. He told me to phone you.'

'Did he? Is there something I need to know?'

'The McAllisters have booked a last-minute holiday to Suffolk for half-term and they've invited me to go with them. They're leaving this afternoon.'

I pulled myself into a sitting position. 'Where are they staying?'

'They've rented a cottage.'

'How many bedrooms has it got?'

'Mum! I dunno. But they're not going to let me share with Eleanor, are they?' I could hear the telltale tapping of the computer, with Jamie probably scrolling down his Facebook feed doing stupid quizzes about what his ideal job would be, his hippie name, his true nationality.

'I'd rather you didn't go. What does Dad say?'

'He says it's up to you. He doesn't have a problem with it but he knows you don't like the McAllisters.'

Nicely passed, Mark. I'll be the bad guy then, shall I? I wondered when we'd stopped working as a team.

Jamie's voice was pleading. We hadn't been able to afford a holiday this year. He'd watched while his friends went off to Greece, St Lucia, Boston and not said a word. Given that I'd become quite friendly with Katya, it was the height of hypocrisy to have a problem with Jamie hanging out with Eleanor. Was it so bad if he went?

My gut said a definite 'terrible'. Even taking Sean out of the equation and the possibility of family secrets leaching out into the atmosphere, there was still Eleanor, temptress of teenage boys, to worry about.

'I'm sorry, lovey. I don't think it's appropriate.'

'Why not?' He kept his voice low but I heard the angry resignation. I was the mother who said 'No'. No to him taking the computer out of the kitchen, no to 18-rated video games, no to buying cider to take to parties and a definite no to holidaying with slapperish fifteen-year-old girls.

'I have a fundamental problem with you going away with girlfriends at your age. You're too young. Your hormones are all over the place and I don't want you to get into a situation you're not ready for.'

I knew his face would be a mask of disgust.

'What situation? Sex? Don't be stupid.'

'I'm trying to keep you safe.'

'No, you're not. You're just being difficult, like you always are. You've always got a "fundamental problem" with something.'

'Jamie, don't be cross with me, love. I'm trying to do what I think is right.'

'Bye.' Astonishing how a single word could neatly encapsulate resentment, despair and 'you've got no bloody idea'. I hoped hate wasn't in the mix. The line went dead.

I dragged myself towards the shower. If I could have bottled it, the lowness of my mood would have been an excellent weapon in warfare to wipe out the morale of invading armies. The pointlessness of motherhood. I'd spent all that time saying, 'Look both ways', 'Don't go off with anyone' and 'Here's a Haliborange and Omega-3' and all that my kids would remember about me was my ability to ruin their lives.

I grizzled through the morning, with none of the anticipation and enthusiasm I usually felt in the lead-up to a wedding ceremony. I tugged on my go-to dress for weddings – light grey wool for maximum fade-into-the-background effect – and knocked at my mother's door. We'd agreed that while Tomaso and I were at the wedding, she'd take herself off to the Uffizi, then to the Duomo to climb the steps up to the cupola. As she opened the door, she looked me up and down. There was no doubt that she could slot right into Florentine life.

'You're dreadfully pale. Here, let me put some blusher on you.'

'No, I'm fine, Mum. See you later.'

She tutted and mumbled, 'Just trying to help.' I marched down the corridor to fetch Tomaso, the prospect of freedom already loosening the tension in my shoulders. Something went weak in my legs as Tomaso appeared in a lilac shirt and dark suit, like some demi-god from an aftershave advert.

He waved to my mother, who was still beaking round her door. 'See you later, Dorothea. Have a wonderful day.'

I felt her eyes on my back as we walked away.

We didn't speak until we left the hotel. I was fighting my urge to skip, twirl and sing.

Tomaso said, 'You look beautiful. *Bellissima*.'

'So do you.'

So easy to be honest.

We walked along the Via de' Calzaiuoli dodging in and out of the Saturday shoppers. I began to understand how Jamie felt when he was with Eleanor, sealed in a private bubble, the power of raw emotion isolating them in a crowd.

'Thank you for putting up with my mother.'

'It's my Italian blood. We're much better at the older generational stuff. She's quite a character. I heard her checking up on you last night.'

I didn't want to give the impression I'd been peering hopefully through the spy hole, so I murmured something non-committal and changed the subject.

'Are you ready to tell me about Giacomo? You don't have to.'

'Raffaella eventually calmed down enough to take me to him. I didn't even know whether Giacomo would remember me. Raffaella was probably hoping he wouldn't and she could prove her new boyfriend would be a better father figure.'

I was conscious of our footsteps keeping perfect time as I waited, braced for his hurt. I shifted closer to him, wanting to absorb some of his pain. 'So…?'

'We met at the lake at the Fortezza da Basso. He just ran straight over to me and said, "*Babbo*", which is Tuscan for 'Daddy'. And then he took my hand to show me the ducks.'

I heard the words shrivelling in his throat, like cling film too close to the hotplate.

Tomaso ran his hand through his hair. 'I've spent all this time thinking that I was a terrible father, that I couldn't cope with the responsibility, that I deserved for Giacomo to reject me.'

He looked so wretched that I wanted to comfort him. The other part of me, the bit that mainlined my mother, was thinking, *Poor old Raffaella. She's done all the heavy lifting through the toddler years, the broken nights, the sheer relentlessness of having to be there, and you pop up because circumstances bring you to Florence and expect to reclaim your role.*

Tomaso must have read my thoughts. 'I guess it's far more than I deserve.'

I could be a serious contender for *Britain's Got Talent* with my award-winning sidestepping skills. 'How was Raffaella?'

'She said she still loves me. She was ridiculously jealous of you.'

Our arrival at the hotel prevented me from having to answer that. But not before registering a mean-spirited jolt of pleasure that a stunning Italian woman, fifteen years my junior, could find something to envy about me.

As I pushed open the door to the hotel, I clicked into professional mode. The bride and groom were London-sophisticated, no family, just friends, and had vetoed the idea of arriving separately. I dispatched Tomaso to walk the twenty guests up to the Palazzo Vecchio, while I helped the couple into the waiting horse and carriage. I set off before them in a cab so I could video their arrival in the Piazza della Signoria, a square of such beauty that it even housed an open-air sculpture gallery in an exquisite arched *loggia*.

Katya would have loved it, particularly the gruesome statue of Perseus holding up Medusa's severed head. Despite everything, I felt a rush of affection for her quirky ways.

Very soon, there was no time for any more introspection. The arrival of the horse-drawn carriage, the photos in front of the replica of Michelangelo's David, the obligatory guest jokes about the size of the statue's penis kept me fully focused on directing everyone to be seated and settled by two-thirty. Tomaso came into his own dealing with the impatient registrar, who herded us into the Red Hall as though the mere frippery of lifelong commitment was standing between him and his next espresso.

And then we were off, a new story of hope, promise and unity unfolding before us, their words echoing around the ornate room.

I loved the certainty in their voices. I'd felt nervous all the way through the ceremony when I married Mark, in case someone suddenly shouted out, 'Do you know what sort of family you're marrying into?' When the vicar pronounced us man and wife, relief made me giddy, as though I'd just shoplifted a bracelet without getting caught. And then within a matter of moments, I'd felt safe.

I should have known it couldn't last.

Tomaso hit just the right note of warmth and solemnity with his translation of the vows. The groom looked so ferociously protective of his bride that every other wedding I'd seen resembled two people promising no more than to take into account their spouse's TV-watching preferences. The registrar unfurled slightly at the sheer force of feeling displayed before her.

A few times Tomaso caught my glance, unleashing a bucket of emotions that was threatening to spill over. When the registrar got to the part about 'forsaking all others', I stared at the floor. The solidity of the pair in front of me contrasted so strongly with the life I'd built out of sand, just waiting to be washed away in a storm.

Then they were kissing. And another couple cast away on the matrimonial sea, blissfully oblivious to how many life rafts they might need.

CHAPTER TWENTY-SIX

By the time the reception was safely underway and Tomaso and I had taken leave of the wedding party, it was gone six-thirty. We were both exhilarated at the success of the day and burst into the hotel foyer, giggling and flirtatious. Yet again the receptionist appeared to be taking a forensic interest in our arrival. She gabbled something to Tomaso, who pulled a face and turned to me. 'Your mother's through there. She's had a fall.'

I rushed through to the area the hotel described as a lounge, though you'd have been hard pressed to find a comfy seat to snuggle up with a book. Perched on one of the über-stylish chairs was my mother, her foot raised on a stool.

'Mum! Are you okay? What happened?'

My mother launched into her tale of woe, involving the steps at the Duomo, the unexpected drizzle making them a bit slippery, the 'unruly' children charging past with 'no parental control'. The net result was a sprained ankle.

'Poor you. You should have phoned me.'

'I didn't want to disturb you at work. And anyway, all the numbers have disappeared off my phone. I don't think you can have put them in properly.'

I didn't even bother responding to that. My mother and mobile phones were as compatible as a penguin and a piano. She filled me in on how a lovely nurse visiting Florence from Bologna had come to help and brought her back to the hotel.

She carried on, 'The hotel staff have been wonderful at bringing me ice packs and tea. Though Italian tea's not quite PG Tips, is it?'

I loved the way my mother always focused on the big picture.

Having ascertained that there was definitely nothing broken and that she wasn't in agony, I turned to practical issues. 'Going out to dinner will be a bit tricky. Shall we get room service?'

'I shan't want anything. They've been bringing me biscuits, cakes and cheese all afternoon. I've made rather a piglet of myself actually.'

'Tomaso and I need to eat, though. We've been on the go all day without so much as a biscuit. Will you be all right if we pop out for some food?'

My mother frowned as though needing to have some dinner was a fatal character flaw rather than a basic human necessity.

Tomaso stepped in. 'The best thing for that ankle is rest. Would you like us to help you upstairs?'

She looked about to argue. But Tomaso simply draped her arm round his shoulder with a 'Come on, Dorothea', hauled her up to her room and then disappeared while I helped her get undressed.

Owing to my mother's prudishness – 'I'll do this bit, just turn your back' – the whole process took forever but eventually I propped her up in bed with pillows, instructions for the Sky remote, a dose of Ibuprofen and a promise to pop back in on her after a speedy dinner.

I told Tomaso that we couldn't be long and was caught between relief and disappointment when he said, 'Don't worry, we'll just have a quick bite somewhere close by.'

And he kept his word. Just around the corner from the hotel, Tomaso pushed open the door to a bar with barely room to squash in among the bodies. Bursts of laughter and loud voices were careering round the tiny space. I persuaded myself that this was the perfect venue, with no risk of intimate conversations taking us to places we shouldn't go.

Suddenly, the florid-faced man behind the bar gave a shout of recognition, thrust a gnarly hand over the counter and launched into a deafening exchange with Tomaso. He kept looking over at me.

I couldn't make out whether it was in a 'Is this the new girl-friend?' sort of way. Or maybe the Italians simply opted for a full-on gawp whenever anything interesting crossed their vision rather than pretending to be glancing out of the window like the Brits.

Their decibel-filled banter ended with a bottle of red wine being brought down from a shelf that required a ladder. The old man stroked it and drew attention to the gold-bordered label, pointing at the date. He made a big show of opening it and sniffing the cork, selecting two huge goldfish bowls of glasses.

Tomaso picked up a couple of scruffy paper menus and smiled his way through the crowd. Traitorously, my mood lifted as I saw a staircase leading down into a cellar bar, hung with old movie posters, Pinocchio puppets and cast-iron frying pans. Tomaso slipped into a candlelit alcove. I took a seat under a wooden cartwheel on the wall.

'Are you happy to try this red? It's pretty special.'

I nodded and glanced down at the menu. Tomaso said, 'There's an English translation, but I'm not sure that helps.'

I read: '*Lampredotto: Cows entrails (bottom stomach) boiled.*' Yum yum. Next: '*Porchetta: Big slice of roast pig with his crunch skin.*'

I felt Tomaso's eyes on me.

'You should have been an actress, you know. Your face is so expressive.'

I tried to deflect the emotion that was closing in around us. 'So what shall I order? I'm ruling out anything to do with stomachs.'

'I'll get a selection. No guts.'

I sipped my wine. I babbled on about how it was remarkably smooth, how Mark liked heavy reds…

Tomaso put his hand up. 'I know you have a husband. I won't forget, even if you don't keep mentioning him. Are things okay with him?'

I blushed. I hoped he couldn't see my cheeks blaring and flaring in the low light. Speaking about Mark to someone I kept wanting to touch seemed so disloyal. 'Everything's fine, thanks.'

I saw the exasperated sigh that escaped Tomaso's lips even if he tried to stifle it.

I raised my glass. 'Cheers and well done for your wonderful interpreting today. Is it a double-edged sword being back in Florence?'

But before I got the answer to that, my phone rang. I glanced down expecting it to be my mother who'd miraculously located my number in the magical mystery tour of her mobile. But it was 'Home'.

I hesitated. I prayed it was one of the kids with a 'Where are my trainers?' question. 'Sorry, I'll be quick,' I said, getting up.

It was Mark. I headed up the stairs, squeezing through the noisy throng at the bar.

'Just ringing to see how it all went.'

I babbled an apology, citing a late finish and my mother and her ankle as an excuse for not calling.

'Where are you now?'

I finally managed to make my way out into the street. 'I'm just getting something to eat before I go back to the hotel.'

'Are you on your own?'

'No, the interpreter bloke just brought me to a bar to get a quick snack. We hadn't eaten all day.' I forced myself to stop talking, which wasn't difficult as panic was making my voice come out in staccato bursts.

'Out on the town with a young Italian. Not sure I like the sound of that.' But he was laughing. His trust in me, the sort of trust built up over years, was so complete that only a truly despicable person would betray it. As soon as the phone call was over, I'd hoof down my dinner and take myself out of temptation's way.

I tried to steady my voice. 'Are the kids okay?'

'Izzy's watching the *X Factor*. And I haven't heard from Jamie since he went off to Suffolk but I'm assuming no news is good news.'

'Suffolk? What's he doing in Suffolk?' I thought I might start running up and down like Mabel when she thinks someone has said 'Walkies' but then no one makes a move to open the front door.

'He's gone with the McAllisters, remember? You spoke to him about it this morning.'

Frustration and fear united to produce a wave of anger. 'For god's sake! I've been saying for weeks that I didn't want him spending time round there. Why would I suddenly agree to him going off on holiday with that precocious little monkey? Use a bit of common sense.'

'He told me you'd said it was okay.'

'And you didn't think that was slightly out of character? A bit strange that I'd suddenly said yes to Jamie spending five days with the McAllisters when I don't even let him spend an hour round there if I can help it?' I was yelling now, attracting glances from passers-by but unable to stop.

'All right, Lydia, don't blow it out of proportion. Of course, he shouldn't have lied to me but it is only a few days by the seaside with the McAllisters.'

'God, you just don't get it, do you?'

There was a pause. 'No, Lydia, you're right. I don't. And I'm getting pretty fed up with trying.'

I cut the call, so furious I could hear the blood pounding in my ears.

I shoved my way back downstairs to find our table crowded with rosemary potatoes, garlicky calamari and spinach and ricotta cannelloni.

Tomaso pulled out my chair for me. 'I waited for you. Is everything all right?'

I struggled not to cry with the relief at being able to tell someone the entire story, not just a fragment of the whole that would make them hate me. Tomaso held my hand while I burst out with the sorry tale. In-between forkfuls of delicious food, I slugged back great mouthfuls of the ripe berry Chianti, dulling the harsh edges of my conversation with Mark and filling me with a soporific warmth. Just hearing Tomaso's words, 'I can really see where you're coming from,' soothed the sting of Mark's words, which underlined, yet again, how he would never understand what my problem was. How could he?

I glanced at my watch. Nearly nine o'clock. 'I'd better go back.'

'Just stay for coffee.'

I suddenly became very conscious of my hand in his. 'No, I'd better not. My mother might be waiting up for me.'

Tomaso flicked his hands up in frustration. 'You sound like a teenage girl. Just another twenty minutes. You can't go to bed this early on your last night in Florence.'

The 'teenage' barb skewered deep. 'It's all right for you. You've got nothing to lose. My mother's got a sixth sense for anything not quite right.'

He nodded an apology. 'Why don't we pop to the hotel and see if she's okay, then come back out for a coffee?'

I let go of his hand. As soon as air filled the space between us, my whole body strained towards him, like a puppy trapped behind a fence, desperate to get to its owner. 'Go on, then. If she's all right, I'll go wild and have a coffee.'

CHAPTER TWENTY-SEVEN

I pushed the shutters back. The early dawn air curled its freezing mantle around my naked body. I needed a moment. A moment in which I could examine the recklessness that had brought me here. It was as though someone had yanked on the handle of a one-armed bandit the night before and come up with a winning line.

My mother telling me that she was confident she'd be as right as rain in the morning and that we should *all* have an early night. Tomaso and I shouting a loud 'Goodnight!' to each other and opening, then banging shut our bedroom doors, before tip-toeing down the corridor. And the final bunch of cherries to create a jackpot – the sheer joy of being with someone who didn't think I'd be right at home popping out of a cuckoo clock. Ker-ching!

I let my mind meander through the events of the previous evening. Coffee – 'Espresso, not cappuccino! Only foreigners drink that after dinner' – had somehow been followed by *amaro*, a bitter liqueur made from herbs. Despite the fact that it tasted like cough medicine, I'd still drunk it, just to prove that I was capable of going with the flow, rather than the uptight misery Mark made me out to be. Somewhere along the way, I felt unfettered, as though someone had slashed at the moorings tethering me to my old self. So, as Tomaso explained that the dessert wine – *vin santo* – was saint's wine, beloved of priests – I was all devil-may-care, look-at-me-go. As we dipped little almondy biscuits into it, I had a definite toe poking over the border between the homeland of family and the foreign wastelands of freedom. By the time we left the bar, I was heady with rebellion, truth and a desire to obliterate not only Sally Southport but Lydia Rushford and all who were disappointed in her.

And unsaintly behaviour had resulted.

Kissing under the porticoes in the square. Stumbling into the hotel, not even bothering to let go of Tomaso's hand as we ran through reception. Wantonly – yes, that was the word my mother would have used if she'd hopped out and caught me – opening the door to my room, just remembering to click it shut quietly as we charged inside, a tangle of limbs and clothes and forgotten vows.

It wasn't so easy to silence Lydia Rushford this morning though. It was as though the person I used to be, a blurry outline of myself, was beckoning to me from a distant shore, shouting over the wind and the waves, trying to make herself heard. Tomaso called me back to bed and I sat on the edge, shivering as he stroked my back, his hands warm on my cool skin. He pulled me down, stretching me out, his hands everywhere until spirals started to squeeze at my insides again, leading me upwards.

Until thought was forced out of the equation. Until everything was reduced to a glorious physical sensation that argued to be heard above all reason, that took away the need for questioning, for doubting, for anything but acceptance of the here and now.

'You'd better go in case my mother suddenly makes a miraculous recovery.'

'I'll make a move in a minute. I wish we could stay a bit longer,' Tomaso said.

And with those words, the transition began from our selfish little bubble into the wider, unpalatable world, where we couldn't just think about ourselves. Back over the border again.

I propped myself up on one elbow.

'This is all so wrong, though. Especially as you know I can't promise you anything.' I squirmed, thinking how arrogant that sounded. I was quite sure the possibility of ending up with fruitcake me hadn't even figured in his equation.

Tomaso dropped a soft kiss onto my upper arm. 'I know, but I don't want to get back together with Raffaella anyway. She's holding a knife to my throat, though. Realistically, she's not going to let Giacomo come to England with me, ever. If I want to be a proper dad, I've got to be here. That guy, that Simone, will eventually take my place otherwise.'

'What about when he's older? She's bound to let him come to England then.' Said the mother who had tried to impose a travelling embargo on her son going two hours up the road to Suffolk. A queasy feeling washed over me. I was hardly the perfect person to be pontificating about morals to my sixteen-year-old son.

'Not likely, is it?'

We sank back onto the pillows. Advice in hopeless situations didn't appear to be my forte, though I was certain my mother would have been able to suggest a suitable saint.

'I've arranged to come back for a week around Christmas time. We're going to find a strategy for moving forward. I'm pretty positive a reconciliation isn't on the cards but we might be able to work towards some civilised cooperation.'

Strategies were such a man thing. I couldn't help thinking that no woman, half-broken from missing her children, would ever think about a 'strategy' for rectifying the problem.

'Don't you want to stay here now? Try and sort it out?'

'I can't think while I'm here. I need a bit of space to sort through what's best for Giacomo.'

I resisted the temptation to point out that he'd had nine months of air flapping around him freely while Raffaella had been toiling away. I couldn't imagine not seeing Izzy and Jamie for ages, having a quick few hours with them, then deciding I needed a bit more bloody space to work on a plan. And although Mark didn't have a perfect scorecard when it came to sports days, drama awards or recorder concert attendance, he never went to bed without checking on the kids, took great pride in cooking scrambled eggs for Jamie before he went off to rugby – 'Put some hairs on your chest' – and was the last word as far as Izzy was concerned on whether she looked beautiful.

A knock on the door and then 'Lydia! Lydia! Are you up yet?' ended the conversation.

If I'd have sneezed, I'm not sure I could have controlled my bowels. Tomaso was quick to react. He shot into the bathroom, kicking his clothes under a chair as he went.

'Coming.'

I ran to the wardrobe where I'd hidden my stripy pyjamas from Tomaso's view. I pulled the bottoms on, struggling in my panic to get my feet into them. I pulled a T-shirt over my head rather than fiddle about with buttons and rushed to the door. I adopted a groggy, just-opened-my-eyes face.

'Morning. How's the ankle? Did you sleep all right? Not in too much pain? You're able to walk on it then?'

I felt as though Tomaso's kisses were highlighted on my neck in neon yellow. Although I was standing blocking the view into the room, my mother appeared to be practising a little limbo dance of the sort Mabel performed when she got bored in the garden and tried to slither under the gate.

'I'm much better this morning, just a bit sore. Thought I'd make myself useful and give you a hand packing as you're up a bit late.'

I just fielded a scream. 'No!' I cleared my throat and managed to produce a more normal voice. 'It's only eight o'clock. I'm just about to have a shower. There's hardly anything to do, anyway. I didn't bring very much.' Jesus. How did anyone get away with a crime when they were interviewed by the police? My babbling would give me away immediately. It took all my willpower not to look round and see if my knickers or Tomaso's boxers were lying in the middle of the floor.

But my mother wasn't finished yet. She stepped forward to come in. 'I need some more Ibuprofen.'

It was enough to convert me to Catholicism the way the gods had lined up to salute me. I'd taken some Ibuprofen first thing for my hangover, which now, gloriously, was sitting on the bedside table within arm's reach. I handed it to her, saying, 'I'll give you a knock when I'm out of the shower', then banged the door shut.

I sat on the bed, whimpering with relief, shock coursing through my body as though I'd narrowly missed running over someone who'd suddenly stepped out in front of me.

Tomaso poked his head round the bathroom door. 'Did we get away with it?'

'I don't know, I think so. Quick, you'd better get out before she comes back.'

And like something out of a slapstick comedy, a barefoot Tomaso scuttled across the corridor while I kept watch and wondered how, in a matter of months, my safe little life had converted itself into a bomb waiting to detonate.

CHAPTER TWENTY-EIGHT

We landed just before three o'clock.

The second we'd touched down onto British soil, the tense, edgy feeling that resided permanently in my stomach magnified. Tomaso took advantage of the immigration officer distracting my mother by peering closely at her passport to whisper that he didn't think she'd noticed anything. Indeed, when Tomaso took my mother's arm as she hobbled along, she was friendly and charming, all 'Tomosi, you *are* kind.'

As we exited the blue channel, Tomaso asked, 'Are you getting a train home or is someone picking you up?'

It was astonishing how the words I was hearing were about modes of transport but the speech I was reading in his eyes was completely different. I didn't want to leave him without getting a chance to talk. With my mother hawk-eyeing on the plane, I hadn't even dared let my elbow stray onto the same armrest.

I was about to reply that we were getting a cab, when I spotted Mark at the arrivals barrier, a couple of feet from us. With Izzy. What the hell were they doing there? A surprise apology for letting Jamie go off with the McAllisters? Or had Mark discovered one of my many lies and couldn't wait to confront me? The scene fragmented in front of me in a kaleidoscope of details I couldn't process. Tomaso was saying something about the cabs being on the right-hand side of the airport. Mark had that bloody awful T-shirt on, with the frayed sleeve. Izzy hadn't done her hair. Neither of them was smiling or waving.

I darted over to the barrier, away from Tomaso and my mother. 'Hello! What are you doing here? Hello, Izzy darling, did you miss me?' I sounded like someone presenting a TV programme for kids. My heart was hammering, waiting for Mark to accuse me of something that would change our family panorama forever.

He just nodded towards the exit. 'There's a bit of a problem. I'll meet you over there.'

'What problem? Is it Dad?'

'It's Jamie. He's been taken to hospital. They think he's got appendicitis.'

'Is he okay? Where is he?'

Mark paused for a fraction of a second. 'He's in hospital in Suffolk.' He hurried on. 'If we get moving, we might make it before he goes into theatre.'

'I can't leave Mum, she's hurt her ankle.'

'Well, she'll have to come with us then.'

I couldn't let my mother be in the same space as the McAllisters. She'd never be able to pretend she didn't know Sean. Katya would sniff it out straight away. Then Mark would find out.

Oh god. Oh god.

My boy would be so frightened.

I couldn't let Mark meet Tomaso.

Mum wouldn't be able to manage that enormous bloody case on her own, with her ankle like that.

The desire to get to Jamie wiped out any British reserve. I ran back to Tomaso, who was still shuffling through the crowds, my mother leaning on him, as he dragged her suitcase and juggled his own rucksack.

'That's my husband, sorry, my son's in hospital with appendicitis. Could you put Mum in a cab, please? Mum, sorry, we've got to dash up to Suffolk.'

Her hand flew to the cross round her neck. 'Why is he in Suffolk? Why isn't he in East Surrey Hospital?'

'He was on holiday with a friend.'

Thankfully, I didn't have to admit *which* friend. My mother shook her head as though we'd deliberately complicated things before saying, 'What are you waiting for? You'd better get on your way.'

'Will you be okay?'

'I'll have to be. Tomosi will show me where to go, won't you, dear?'

I thrust some money at her, briefly registering Tomaso telling me he'd take her home first then make his way to Guildford. I shouted my grateful thanks and pushed through the crowds, not caring that my case was banging into ankles and threatening to catch the wheels of overladen pushchairs.

I finally erupted out of the flow. Mark grabbed my case.

'Why didn't you phone me?' I asked.

'Sean's only just rung me. I knew you'd be on the plane.'

I ached to be with Jamie. 'Are they going to call you from the hospital?'

'Yes. With a fair wind, it should only take us a couple of hours to get up there.' He reached out to touch my arm. 'Sorry you're coming back to this.'

I shrugged him off. 'Let's go.' As we roared out of the airport, I was vaguely aware of Tomaso standing with my mother at the taxi rank. This was my punishment. While Jamie had been writhing in agony – how long had they waited to take him to hospital? – I'd been closing my eyes on the plane, reliving the previous night, with a little buzz of desire pulsing round my body. My poor boy.

'Anyway, how did it go in Florence?' Mark said.

I knew he was trying to distract me but I could only think about Jamie. 'I can't concentrate on that now.'

Mark patted my knee. 'He will be okay, you know. It's a bit unexpected but it's not the end of the world.'

'But what if it turns into peritonitis? That can be fatal, can't it?'

I was trying to bring to mind what I'd read on the internet every time the kids complained of stomach ache when they were little. I was brutally unsympathetic with Mark when he was ill, ridiculously resentful that he could lie in bed groaning and weakly requesting tea. I never allowed myself to believe that I was ill enough to merit a day in bed, too beset by guilt over unanswered emails, dirty laundry and Mabel's 'When is it walkies?' whimpers. The children were a whole different matter. They'd spent half their childhoods with a thermometer jammed in their mouths. Jamie had been about twelve before I could watch him on a swing without shouting, 'Careful.'

God knows how I'd cope when Jamie started driving. I'd have to stowaway in the boot, a ghostly voice seeping through the backseats: *Slow down for that corner*. I should probably start stockpiling sleep now.

Izzy put her hand on my shoulder. 'He will be all right, won't he, Mum?'

'Of course he will, lovey. He'll be in a bit of pain at the moment but the doctors will sort him out.'

I pulled out my phone and rang Katya.

She sounded so relieved to hear from me. 'Oh my god, Lydia, how terrible for you to come back to this. You must be so worried.'

I couldn't cope with her hysteria when I was only just managing to stop screaming myself. I butted in, way beyond social niceties, with a question that shocked me. 'Is Sean there?'

'He's just been in with the doctor. Hang on, I'll pass you over.'

Sean was clear, calm and reassuring, talking me through the operation Jamie was about to have. Disloyally, I was glad Sean had taken charge – for all his faults I knew that he would have asked the right questions, refused to accept any answer that didn't satisfy him and stayed focused on the facts, not the emotions of the situation. 'Your lad's been a real trooper. You should be proud of him, he's a star.'

It was a day of surprises. I couldn't remember the last time I felt so grateful to anyone.

He promised to call me if anything changed before we arrived. My initial relief that Jamie was in good hands faded the further I got into relaying the conversation to Mark. I stared out of the window. My mother had been right. God did know what was in my heart.

And now he really was going to get me back.

Even Izzy looked as though she would do anything to have Jamie irritating her to death, deliberately humming in her ear when she was trying to do her homework.

At fifteen-minute intervals, Mark kept saying, 'He'll be as right as rain in a couple of days,' as though he were reading the weather forecast.

Katya was waiting outside when we got to the hospital. Mark dropped us at the door and went to park. Katya hugged me but I all but pushed her off. She got the hint and led the way. 'It was Sean who realised it was something serious. I was all for getting out the Rennies and a hot water bottle but he knows Jamie so well. Said he was very stoic on the rugby pitch even when he'd taken a real knock. He was sure he wouldn't make a fuss for nothing. Jamie hadn't wanted any breakfast because he had stomach ache. Then during the morning he'd been in real pain, lying on the sofa groaning. When he started being sick, Sean just bundled us all in the car and drove him straight here.'

I was too grateful to Sean to temper my thoughts with anything other than pure unadulterated thankfulness.

We galloped up the stairs, herding up to the third floor and clattering along the corridors. Sean was waiting on a plastic orange chair, Eleanor next to him, looking younger and more vulnerable than I remembered. Sean leapt to his feet. No pleasantries, for which I was grateful.

'He went down forty minutes ago. Sorry. I did tell him that you were on your way and that you'd be here when he came out.'

'Was he frightened?'

'No, not really. He made a joke about hoping that the knife didn't slip and deprive him of his manhood. To be honest, I think he was in so much pain, that he just wanted to get it over with.'

'How long did they say he'd be?'

'The doctor said he'd probably be back on the ward within two hours.'

He stepped closer and put his hand on my arm. He looked directly into my eyes and dropped his voice in that way he had of making you feel he'd crafted his words for your ears only. 'Sal, he's going to be okay.'

I froze at his use of 'Sal'. Katya was fidgeting on a chair close behind me. I mouthed 'Lydia' to him and backed away, conscious of Katya monitoring Sean even in a situation like this.

Mark hurried along the corridor, shaking hands with Sean and thanking both of them. 'You can disappear now, if you like. Sorry that we've rather messed up your holiday.'

Katya turned to me on the verge of tears. 'I'm so sorry that he's been ill. He's a lovely boy. The son Sean never had.'

I couldn't cope with smoothing Katya's feathers today. She'd hinted before that Sean would have liked a son. I couldn't think about that now: I had no caring about anyone else other than Jamie left in me. Sean's son-wanting, Katya's insecurity about it, Mark's own fear taking refuge behind his 'He's going to be just fine' bulletins.

'Honestly, don't feel you have to wait,' I said. 'I'll text you and let you know when he's out. We might not even be allowed in to see him till tomorrow.'

Without even glancing at me, Eleanor turned to her mother. 'I'm not going home until I've seen him.'

I was expecting Katya to do the big-eyed drill stare that I would have done if Jamie had suddenly decided to tell Eleanor's parents what he found an acceptable course of action. But no.

Katya put her arm round Eleanor and said, 'All right sweetheart, we'll see what we can do.'

Never had I wanted to stand in front of a hospital ward door more and declare, 'Family only.'

I moved away, clamping onto my retort until the nerves throbbed in my teeth.

Time ticked by. Now and again someone would make an effort to speak, but the conversation kept fizzling out. Mark kept pacing up and down, his agitation amplifying my own.

'Izzy, why don't you go with Daddy to find a drink?' Mark was much better if he had a task. I, on the other hand, liked to concentrate all my efforts on worrying as much as possible as a perverse insurance against the horrors of my imagination actually coming to pass. Mark went off with Izzy. My phone bleeped. I waited for someone to whirl out of a medical theatre and tell me that I was interfering with their heart monitors. I sneaked a look. Tomaso. My mother was home safely. I breathed out. For the time being, Mark hadn't paid him any attention beyond a distracted 'Thank god he was there to stick her in a cab'.

I switched the phone off.

Finally, a young doctor, his face mask round his neck, appeared. He looked to Sean, who introduced me. 'It was more complicated than we thought. We caught it just in time.'

'He will be all right?' The air in my lungs felt thin and sparse.

The doctor nodded. 'He's young and fit. We'll keep him under close observation overnight.'

'Can I see him? Can I stay?'

'He's just about to go onto the ward. You'll be able to pop in shortly. Unfortunately we don't have facilities for parents of children over twelve to sleep here. Visiting hours only, I'm afraid.' He was still addressing his comments to Sean, including me as an afterthought.

Sean shook his hand. 'Thank you very much.'

This was all wrong. Thirty years vilified as the person who put my dad in prison and now he was acting in loco parentis to my son, while I had been off like a sow having a last hurrah before the final slaughter.

The doctor was suggesting that we contact the information desk for a list of local accommodation. Sean said, 'We have room for them in our holiday cottage. Thank you.' Before I could react, the doctor told us where to find Jamie and hurried off.

Mark and Izzy appeared clutching various drinks.

'Come on, Jamie's out, we can go in,' I said.

Eleanor got up, her tiny zebra-print skirt out of place in the drab corridor. Sean must have caught the look on my face and stepped in. 'Not you, Ellie. You can see him tomorrow.'

'I'm going now.'

Sean took hold of her wrist. 'No, you're not.'

I barely registered her fury and the tussle with Sean. I was having to stop myself from running through the corridors, shoving trollies out of the way and scattering Zimmer frames. At the door of the teenage ward, I forced myself to smile when I caught sight of Jamie's pale face. I was afraid to hug him in case I hurt him. Still groggy from the anaesthetic, he managed a wan smile and a joke about incorporating the scar into a tattoo. The sister on the ward kept flitting past to tell us that he needed to rest, just stopping short of shooing us out. 'It's only a minor operation. He'll be grand in a couple of days.'

Minor to her, maybe.

I kept stalling until Mark patted Jamie's hand and told him we'd be back first thing the following afternoon. I tried to hold myself together as I kissed his forehead but there was no disguising the tears plopping onto his pillow. Jamie flinched in pain as he tried to reach up to hug me. 'Mum, I'll be okay, don't worry. Is Eleanor coming to see me?'

His voice sounded small and young. I managed to produce a neutral-sounding 'Tomorrow,' before I allowed Mark to lead me away.

Back outside, the McAllisters were waiting. Eleanor kept butting in with questions when I was trying to update Sean. That girl really needed someone to sit her down and explain that what you have to say is not more important than what the person speaking has to say. Where did that confidence come from?

Katya kept hugging me and telling me that it would be 'absolutely no problem' to put us up. I wanted to book myself into a hotel but I had no energy left for that particular fight. The McAllisters tactfully walked on ahead of us, saying they'd wait for us downstairs, while I dithered about, wanting to remind the nurse to call us if there was a problem. Mark steered me gently down the corridor, but although my feet were moving forward, my whole body was braking, aching with every step that I moved away from Jamie.

While we waited for the lift, Mark said, 'Sean's a really good bloke. God knows what would have happened to Jamie if he hadn't been there. Really nice of them to put us up, isn't it? Glad we're not having to trawl round some grotty B&Bs. I'm knackered.'

'Me too.'

For once I didn't end any comment on the McAllisters with a jibe.

CHAPTER TWENTY-NINE

I had my nose pressed on the ward door as soon as visiting time began at two o'clock. Sharing living space with Sean and needing to be thankful to him on many levels made me feel a total traitor to my parents. As 'sleeping with the enemy' as it got. For the first time in many years, I had a fleeting thought about going to confession. It didn't last long.

Jamie was sitting up and looked completely different from the groggy teenager of the previous day. He immediately asked for his phone and when Eleanor was coming to see him. It was embarrassing how my self-flagellating 'I will forever be patient and listen properly to children without one eye on my emails' stance had morphed into an irritation that all Jamie was interested in was the flaming McAllister girl. Any useful information such as what the consultant had said to him, how long it would be before he could play rugby again, even whether he could get the wound wet, provoked a furrowed brow. Clearly the ability to get onto Facebook and plot against me with Eleanor far outweighed any health considerations.

The consultant came to discharge him. My surge of joy that we wouldn't have to spend any more time at the McAllisters' competed with my fear that Jamie wasn't ready to leave yet. While I bombarded the doctor with questions, Jamie was doing 'that' face, the one he did when I asked if his friends had girlfriends, what he looked at on YouTube and how to record on Sky. That, far more than anything the consultant told me, convinced me that he was on the mend.

Once we got back home, Jamie milked his 'near-death experience' for all it was worth. I even relented and let him have his computer in the bedroom for a couple of hours a day, which led to much trotting in and out to see what he was up to. I supplied a never-ending conveyor belt of Innocent smoothies, tomato and mozzarella rolls and god help me, the Dunkin' Donuts that Izzy insisted on buying. I kept sitting on his bed, often failing to resist the temptation to hold his hand. From the way he waited a requisite nanosecond before wriggling free, mine was not the hand he wanted to be holding.

Two days after we got home, Eleanor turned up on the doorstep, in a dress so short that I was pretty sure that the unwelcome knowledge of what sort of underwear she wore would soon be mine.

'I was just wondering if I could see Jamie for a few moments. I brought him this,' she said, waving the latest Lee Child book.

I hesitated. Jamie was upstairs in his bedroom. Bed, teenage girls, McAllisters of any description. Ugh. Plus he wasn't wearing a top because his stitches kept catching on it.

'Um. He's upstairs.' I was thinking out loud rather than giving permission but she walked past me with an intimidating sense of entitlement and headed up. She turned left at the top of the stairs towards Jamie's bedroom in the manner of someone who was all too familiar with the layout of the house. It was amazing that a fifteen-year-old girl could make me feel inadequate in my own home. I marched into the kitchen, grabbed a bottle of lemonade and two glasses and tiptoed upstairs, although in my mind, I was stomping. I hesitated outside the door. No voices. Presumably they weren't poring over Maths homework together. I wondered whether to knock, then decided there should be absolutely no reason why I should need to. With my elbow, I poked the door open and burst in. Then I wished I'd knocked, as Eleanor pulled her face off Jamie's and he yanked the covers over his hips to disguise gruesome things a mother should never need to see.

'Mum!'

Eleanor was looking at me with amused, hooded eyes, a sarcastic half-smile so like Sean's lifting the corner of her mouth. Not so much as a delicate rose blush on her cheeks. I still felt embarrassed if my mother walked in on me when Mark was giving me a hug.

'Sorry, I was just bringing you a drink.' I was determined not to run away, even though the forces of teenage hormones were practically repelling me out of the door. I put down the tray on Jamie's chest of drawers. 'I'm just going to open the windows. It's a bit stuffy in here.' Jamie showered regularly, but his room always smelt vaguely of onions.

There was a lot of eye-talking going on behind me as I rustled about, finding a key to the windows. Jamie turned up the music, the noise of some rapperish racket filling the room. The days of singing along to Adele on the school run seemed as long ago as Nintendos and Warhammer battles.

I shouted above the bass beat. 'So, did you enjoy the rest of your time in Suffolk, Eleanor?'

'No. I hated it. I wanted to come home. I was worried about Jamie.' That slightly posh, breathy confidence again. She was clearly making an effort to leave the 'duh' off the end of her sentence.

I registered a note of surprise that Eleanor had actually replied to my question. There was something powerful about her, some funny ability to make me feel inferior, as though she was doing me a favour by responding in a civilised manner.

I forced myself to face her, to look at her directly. 'Jamie can't have visitors for too long at the moment because he still needs to rest.'

'I'm all right, Mum,' Jamie said, just stopping short of leaping out of bed to push me out of the door. Eleanor didn't even acknowledge that I'd spoken, simply gazed at me blankly as though

I'd suggested they had a game of Ludo or played a few LPs. She was holding Jamie's hand, far too near his crotch for my liking.

I had to gather all my reserves not to slink away. 'Let's say twenty minutes. I'll shout up.'

Eleanor didn't quite roll her eyes, though her sockets must have been aching with the effort of looking straight through me.

I marched out, feeling her stare burning into my back. No doubt she was wondering how I lived with a backside that size. If your own mum was a size 8, I supposed a size 14 looked like a grizzly bear on the move. I felt ridiculously close to pointing out that at her age, I also had boobs that sat pertly without the aid of a bra. Boobs her father had rather liked.

I shut the door before my thoughts could convert themselves into words. I'd barely taken my hand off the handle before Eleanor's laugh rang out.

CHAPTER THIRTY

Jamie keeling over in the care of the McAllisters cemented Katya into our lives. I don't know whether it was because she felt so relieved that he hadn't actually died on her watch but she'd definitely developed a sense of ownership, jokingly asking, 'How's my future son-in-law feeling today?'

I surprised myself by not pushing her away. With her invitations to coffee, art galleries or lunch, she was a welcome distraction from the guilt-ridden navel-gazing that threatened to unhinge me. She was so irreverent, so honest about her shortcomings – and everyone else's – that I often caught myself laughing days later at her observations about people we knew. She had an energy and sense of fun that counterbalanced my introspection. Not for Katya the weighing up of who said what and what was meant by it. Unless it involved Sean, when she would dissect every word with the zeal of someone searching for a diamond earring in the contents of a hoover bag.

'Do you worry when Mark goes out for business meetings with other women?' she asked.

'Mark works in other women's houses all the time. I'd drive myself mad if I worried.'

She stirred her skinny latte. 'I don't know how to be that person.'

'But he's never given you any reason not to trust him, has he?'

'No. But he's so tactile and flirtatious with everyone. I mean, we have a great sex life – he's highly sexed – but how do you know if you're providing enough variety?'

I nearly blew my cappuccino froth across the cafe. I certainly didn't want to know that Sean and Katya thought hanging from the doorframe while dressed as a giraffe was normal. I couldn't look at her.

Katya clapped her hand over her mouth. 'Oh my god. I've embarrassed you. So sorry! I've always thought you were such a woman of the world. You always seem to know what to say and do. I thought you'd be really open about that sort of thing.'

I blushed even more. 'Not really. I blame my mother. She was always praying to St Bridget.'

'St Bridget?'

'Yep. Patron saint of fallen women.'

One of the things I loved about Katya was her ability to laugh about things I'd never realised were funny before.

'That's hilarious. Do you know many fallen women, then?'

Luckily she said it in a way that didn't require me to say, 'You're looking at one.'

I wished I'd never got onto the subject when she asked, 'Do you think Jamie and Eleanor get up to anything? I don't mean sex obviously, but you know, fumbling about?'

The temptation to kick the table over and run hollering into the street was almost too tempting. I wasn't going to fill her in on the upstairs shenanigans when Eleanor had come round. I didn't know whether Eleanor did it as an act of defiance or whether she didn't realise I was standing at the bottom of the stairs but she was blithely adjusting her bra strap as she left. I was quite certain Katya would find that a lot less perturbing than I did.

I mumbled, 'Don't think so,' then scratched around for a change of topic. 'So will you come and help me get everything ready for the hog roast fundraiser this Saturday?'

'Only because you've asked so nicely. I might not feel so shy if I'm there from the beginning. Everyone knows Sean because of the photography and I feel like they're all disappointed when they meet me. Not glamorous or beautiful enough.'

I wondered whether she was winding me up. Whenever I saw her, she was always chatting to someone as though she'd been the fulcrum around which Eastington House's parental population pivoted all her life.

When Saturday rolled around, I thanked the Lord that Katya was coming to help out. Despite organising hundreds of events a year, this felt so much more personal, as though I was giving the entire school an opportunity to judge me.

Mark watched as I got dressed. 'You're talking to yourself.'

I snapped back. 'That's just how I process thoughts. You know that.'

'It wasn't a criticism. I love the way you're so intense about everything. You looked like you were having such a serious discussion. I'd love to be in your brain sometimes.'

That phrase reminded me so much of Tomaso. Every time I was tempted to phone him, guilt stopped me even scrolling down to find his name. I couldn't forgive myself for having sex, laughing as we kept time with the church bells of Orsanmichele while my son, the boy I'd longed for, held close and promised to keep safe, was depending on Sean bloody McAllister to save his life.

I'd texted Tomaso a brief explanation of what had happened with Jamie, thanked him for looking after my mother and had ignored his texts and emails ever since.

Mark put his hands on my shoulders. 'Relax. You'll do a brilliant job.'

I reached for his hand. 'Thank you. How do I look?'

'As though you are about to conquer the world.'

I had to smile at that.

We walked into the marquee, my wedding planner eye screeching over the many things that weren't quite to my liking. I set to work, moving flowers out of the eyeline of the stage, straightening cutlery, readjusting the swagging around the edges. Sean came up to me, camera round his neck, while I was checking in with the caterers.

'Hi there. Looks amazing. Let me take a photo of you in front of the hog roast.'

'No.'

'Come on, don't be such a spoilsport.'

The chef was obediently shuffling over to make room for me.

'No.'

Sean closed his eyes. 'Just come over here a moment.' His voice was gentle.

I don't know why I felt obliged to obey – my mother and her 'You will *not* make a scene', I suppose. I followed him to the corner of the stage.

He bowed his head, talking quietly into my ear. 'Sal. Please. Let's just move on. I thought we'd got through all that, after what happened with Jamie. I hoped you'd gone some way to forgiving me.'

I looked up into his eyes, which were trying to draw me into his web. It was no wonder I'd stripped off first and worried about the consequences later. I gathered my feelings and arranged them around the hard knot of hate I'd sculpted over the last thirty years.

'Do *not* call me Sally. Thanks to you, that person is dead. I am incredibly grateful for what you did with Jamie. But forgive you, no. There's no way you are taking a picture of me. I imagine you know why.'

Sean let out a deep breath. '*Lydia*. I'm sorry. I do understand why you feel like that. Really I do. But it wasn't me who put the photo in your dad's textbook.'

'I know that but if you hadn't been showing off, no one would have known the Polaroids even existed, let alone stolen one from your bag.'

We didn't get any further entrenched in our stalemate because Katya appeared, putting her hand on Sean's arm, her eyes flickering between us. 'Everything okay?'

Sean nodded. 'Yes, we were just discussing photography for the evening.'

I forced a smile. 'Katya, could you give me a hand with moving that table nearer to the side of the stage for the raffle?'

I walked off, with a tense Katya in my wake. She made me so grateful to have a husband who reserved his charm mainly for me. No wonder Katya was so thin. She must burn up a whole cake's worth of calories on the furnace of her jealousy at every social event.

'Were you really talking about photography?'

I added another lie onto the bonfire of all the others and watched as her shoulders came down from around her ears. 'Yes, we were.' I paused. 'I'm not that sort of person, Katya. Sean loves you. He's not interested in other women.' I tried to keep the impatience out of my voice.

I was relieved when people started to filter in and the event gathered momentum, with a queue at the raffle, shouts of laughter and the odd curse from the roulette table. There was a hubbub of voices and appreciative murmurs as the wine worked up appetites and people headed to the hog roast.

The evening flashed past as I instructed the caterers, oversaw the bar staff and averted a coffee machine crisis.

Then it was time for the speeches before the dancing. I'd refused to make one, so Melanie had volunteered. Given how thin she was, she probably needed the spotlight to keep her warm. I did admire her, even if I didn't like her. Her talent for shaming people into buying raffle tickets and coughing up vast sums on the silent auction for wine tasting evenings, villa holidays in the South of France and helicopter rides was immense. Especially when, as far as I could see, the chief motivator behind the new rugby clubhouse was to build somewhere with a balcony where the parents could get quietly sozzled and eat bacon butties while watching their offspring get flattened.

With a final 'Dig deep and support Eastington House!' Melanie snapped her fingers at the DJ and said, 'Music, maestro'. Within minutes, the school's great and good crowded onto the floor.

Katya beckoned to me to dance. 'I love Wham. Come on.'

I shook my head. 'Sorry. You'll have to find someone else. I'm not a dancer. Ask Mark. He loves dancing.'

At that moment, Mark waltzed up to me. 'I suppose I'm dancing on my own again, am I?'

I nudged him towards Katya. 'Go and dance with Katya. She needs a partner.'

Her face was all 'Don't you mind?' Which I didn't, not at all. I felt bad for Mark that he never had anyone to dance with. Besides, I was too busy wrestling my guilt back into its box about the last time I danced at the Surrey Business Stars Awards and how one dance had led to a jig of an entirely different kind.

With Katya and Mark grooving to *Club Tropicana*, I slipped away to sit in the shadows for a minute. I'd just settled myself onto a bench by the stream that ran through the garden, when, as if by night-vision radar, Sean appeared. Internally, I put my head in my hands and screamed.

'Hi. Sorry, we were interrupted. Katya really likes you but I think you tap into her jealous streak because you're so self-contained. She sees that men are really intrigued by you.'

'Sean. Men are not intrigued by me. Men don't notice me.'

'They do.' He scuffed his shoe on the grass. 'I do.'

I shrank back against the wooden arm of the bench. If Katya came out now and saw us tucked away, there'd be big trouble. I'd worked so hard to bury the whole Sean thing, I wasn't intending to exhume as much as a fingernail. I didn't want to ask him what he meant. I'd got through life quite well without needing to get to the bottom of many things. Forensics weren't my thing.

But despite my telepathic barbed wire, Sean was going to have his say. 'I want you to know that back then, I wasn't just fooling around with you. Over the years, I've convinced myself that what happened wasn't a big deal. But seeing you again, seeing what I did, I can't carry on sticking my head in the sand. I know we were young, but for what it's worth, I did love you. I was a stupid, arrogant show-off and I couldn't resist being the big man.'

I'd convinced myself that Sean had just taken what he wanted from me, then thrown me to the wolves. I didn't have the energy for creaking back the boulder of history and reconfiguring my views. After all this time, how was it possible to define our feelings? My concept of love was as blurred as a foggy November morning. I already had the nebulous shape of Tomaso drifting across my vision of Mark. I didn't need anyone else floating up from an era of Kylie and Jason, waving a shrivelled-up carcass of teenage romance and lame excuses for arseholian behaviour.

'Too late, Sean.'

'I was sixteen, for god's sake. The same age as Jamie. I didn't know which way was up. You've still gone on to have a good life. Izzy's great and Jamie, well, I'd have been absolutely made up to have a son like him. Or even another daughter.'

For a second, curiosity got the better of me. 'It's not too late, is it?'

The raw flash of pain over Sean's face shocked me. 'Katya refuses to go through another pregnancy. She was obsessed with how fat she was, thought I'd go and have an affair with someone thinner. It got to the stage where I couldn't even go to the pub for a couple of hours without coming home to a screaming match. I don't think we could survive, to be honest.'

I could have felt sorry for him. I nearly did. But a little part of me felt vindicated that he hadn't been tiptoeing through the roses, carefree as a kite while I'd been hacking a new life out of concrete.

As though my mother had thrown her voice from her sitting room sofa, I said, 'We all have our cross to bear.' Then I asked the question I had no business to know the answer to. 'Do you love her?'

'I did. Still do, I think. I hope. I'm finding it hard to live within a radius of five metres before she starts suspecting I'm up to no good. And she's like a dog with a bone about my past at the moment.' He ran his hands through his hair.

Not the devil-may-care lad I remembered at all.

None of us were.

The night air was damp on my back. I shivered. 'I need to go back in.'

'Wait. Tell me that I didn't ruin your life.' He put his hand on my arm.

I shook him off. 'No.'

'No, I didn't ruin it, or no, you won't tell me?'

I ignored the question and hurried away from him, across the grass, feeling the damp seep into my shoes.

I made it to the marquee just as the music slowed and couples took to the floor. Katya almost leapt away from Mark when she saw me. 'Here, you dance with Mark. Have you seen Sean?'

I wanted to escape Katya and her laser antennae. 'No, sorry,' I said, shocking Mark by pressing myself into him and putting my arms round his neck.

He laughed. 'Mrs Rushford. Am I really having the pleasure of this dance?'

The warmth of his body filtered through my dress. I leaned into him, kissing his neck.

He pulled away slightly. 'Hey you, has someone cloned my wife? Shall we get a room?' He smiled at me, his face surprised but pleased. Even this late in the evening, I could still smell little traces of Issey Miyake on him. The smell of familiarity, of someone on my side.

I wondered if he could smell the deceit on me.

I didn't have too long to ponder that because my attention, everyone's attention, was drawn to the shouting in the corner of the marquee. The music played on but I could see Katya gesticulating, shouting.

'Sugar. That's Katya.' I pulled away from Mark.

'Leave it. Let Sean deal. He's here somewhere. She's absolutely shit-faced. When she was dancing with me, I practically had to hold her up.'

'I can't let her make a show of herself like that.' I felt like an older, wiser sister entrusted with saving her younger, outrageous sibling from herself.

I ran over to her. Sean had her by the wrist while she thrashed about, shouting at Melanie, her hair sticking to her face, which was wet with tears.

'Katya. Katya! Come with me, come on, we're going to get you some coffee.'

'She's after my husband. She was all over him, pressing herself up against him.'

Sean tried to lead her away but she kept pointing her finger at Melanie.

Adopting her no-nonsense headteacher voice, Melanie stepped towards her. 'Katya, listen to me. Sean was just walking past when *Love Is All Around* came on. It was my wedding song but I couldn't see my husband, and I do love it, so I invited Sean to dance with me. There was nothing in it. I mean, we're not teenagers running off with each other's boyfriends, are we?'

Katya broke free of Sean and shoved Melanie backwards. As Melanie stumbled, her heel caught in the matting and she ended up in a heap on the floor.

'Ow, ow, my ankle! I think I've broken it.'

A little posse of people gathered around her, giving conflicting instructions: 'See if you can turn it'; 'Keep it still'; 'Wiggle your toes.' Briefly, I wondered whether we were insured for fisticuffs among the punters.

I grabbed Katya. 'Come on, out now. Sean, go to the caterers and get some ice in a tea towel for Melanie.'

The big man estate agent, the bloke who clapped other men on the shoulder and drew women to him like wasps to a mango just stood there.

'Sean!'

His eyes were glazed, as though he was somewhere else. Like a slow-moving film, an image of him trying to win a huge toy rabbit at the Great Yarmouth funfair sprung to mind. Checked shirt, bulging rugby muscles, white teeth in a huge smile. A surge of pride in me. I'd ignored the other girls, their curious glances about what sort of insipid girl would lay claim to a superstar like him. I mourned who we were.

More softly, I said, 'Sean, fetch some ice. Please.'

He blinked and clicked into action. Mark appeared at the other side of Katya. She wrestled with us but we held firm. Mark shook his head and nearly made me laugh.

That good, reliable man.

CHAPTER THIRTY-ONE

The later I went to bed, the earlier I woke. Mark was curled on his side. I studied him. Really looked at him. His eyelashes were just like Izzy's, long and dark, right down to the tips. We'd shared out the noses in our family. Izzy had my thin, slightly hooky nose, while Jamie had Mark's neat, snubby one. In his features, I could see the patchwork of my children. Little ear-lobes like Izzy. Dimpled chin like Jamie. A dear, familiar face with a thousand expressions and emotions replicated in the kids. I wanted to wake him up and shout, 'You deserve better! You don't know what I've done!'

But as I did most mornings, I gathered up the bad feelings, brushing them into a central heap like dirt on a marble floor, then trapped them tight, pushing them into a corner of my stomach, where they would sit all day, a dull weight of disgust.

I went downstairs to find Mabel in the last few minutes of chewing through Izzy's new pumps. 'Naughty dog!'

She snatched the shoe up and started dancing around the table, flinging it about as though it was a great game, if only I could learn the rules.

To that and many other things.

The shoe was unsalvageable and I didn't have the energy to go through my 'Mabel, here's some sausage' routine. It was as though I'd been given a well of coping, managing and admonishing and now, at the grand age of forty-three, I'd exhausted my reserves. I'd have to manage for the next forty years on 'whatever'.

I made a cup of tea and thought about Katya. Poor thing. I bet she was feeling a little shamefaced this morning. I imagined Sean wouldn't be in the best shape either. He'd picked a handful there. I wondered what had made her like that. Maybe he'd had an affair. My little army of judgments leapt to accuse then slumped back down again.

Infidelity changed so many things.

I texted Katya: *Mabel up for a walk if you need some fresh air.*

She arrived within twenty minutes with a bottle of Vittel, sunglasses and a bag of doughnuts. 'Thank you for still speaking to me.'

'Who am I to judge? We all make mistakes. Do you know if Melanie's okay?'

Katya grimaced. 'She went off to A&E. Sean said she couldn't put pressure on her ankle. It's not great, is it?'

I pulled a face. 'Let's get out on the hill.'

Unlike our normal walks when Katya steamed along, determined not to miss the chance to burn off her carrot stick calories, we ambled, watching Mabel chase after squirrels and bark up trees. 'Do you think anyone will speak to me at school?'

'To be honest, I don't think Melanie is that popular. Anyway, it's nearly Christmas so people are far too busy to worry about a drunken scrap at the hog roast.'

We walked in silence. Katya sipped from her water. I bellowed at Mabel, who was darting in and out of the cows. The last thing I needed this morning was a herd of Belted Galloways thundering after me. Mabel reached a compromise by eating the cowpats, rather than goading the providers.

'What did Sean say?'

'I haven't seen him. I didn't make it upstairs last night. Fell asleep on the sofa. Usually he wakes me up but I guess he'd had enough of me.'

'Did Melanie do something to make you jealous?'

Katya laughed, a sore, mirthless sound. 'Any woman who gets near him makes me jealous. Can I be honest?'

I tried to lighten the moment. 'Please don't tell me anything about your sex life.'

Katya stared into the distance. 'If you weren't such a good friend, I'd have a real problem with you. I know you've only met him a few times but Sean seems to tell you things that he's never mentioned to me.'

I concentrated on whistling Mabel, who for the first time in her life, came immediately, thus depriving me of an excuse to ignore Katya's statement.

'I'm sure he doesn't. He's probably told Mark, who's passed it onto me. I remember all sorts of rubbish that everyone else doesn't bother to retain in the first place.'

Katya looked wretched. 'Over the years, Sean's stopped trusting me with anything because he's afraid I might use it against him at a later date. He tells you things because he knows you don't gossip. And you're so happily married, I bet he hopes it will rub off.' She sighed. 'I'd love the simplicity of your life.'

A little knot of anger contracted in my stomach. Me and my impeccable life. The stalwart of the fundraising committee. The woman who makes a living out of peddling a dream that can't possibly be sustained. The DIY king of a husband. I'd even managed to have one boy and one girl. Except that my life was the family equivalent of Venice: the foundations were rotting and the water levels were rising. Whether I could shore it up in time was anyone's guess.

I flung the ball for Mabel. She ignored it and ran in the opposite direction. My main exercise these days was fetching the ball myself.

'Katya. You've got to stop thinking that everyone, especially me, is so perfect. One, I hardly ever see Sean, so there's no opportunity for him to tell me anything. And two, no marriage is how it appears to everyone else. People make mistakes in their relationships all the time, it's just that most of the time, it's not as obvious as a punch-up at the hog roast.'

I was hoping to make her laugh, but she grabbed my wrist, all hoarse-voiced and madwoman-in-the-corridor eyes. 'Can I tell you something? That you won't judge me for?'

I wanted to back away like Mabel did when I tried to make her eat a piece of cucumber. I didn't want to hear anything that I'd have to keep a secret. I already needed heavy-duty concrete to keep the lid on my own misdemeanours. 'I don't judge anyone, Katya.'

'Years ago, just after Eleanor was born, I had an affair.'

'You had an affair?' I almost heard my preconceptions scraping across the floor of my brain to rearrange themselves and accept that it was Katya, not Sean, who'd been unfaithful. And then a flood of disdain, that she would do that. Maybe I did judge people.

Until I remembered.

My brain still strained to find a way to make me less culpable than all the other dishonest people who decided that it was their right to have some fun regardless of the cost to the people who loved them.

'I did. I felt so unattractive and frumpy. And then this friend of ours started making a play for me, and Sean was out working all hours and it just sort of happened.'

'Does Sean know?'

Katya looked away and nodded. 'It hasn't exactly improved our marriage. Because he's so attractive, I feel I should be grateful that he even looked at me in the first place. I could just about cope before this happened but now I spend my whole life expecting him to get his own back on me.'

'Have you had any counselling?'

'We probably needed it. Sean refused point blank. Said he wasn't dragging up the past and would just concentrate on the future.'

I stayed silent. Selfishly relieved that Sean hadn't gone delving into the past.

Katya laughed, the sort of dry, dull sound I might make if someone told a sexist joke but I didn't want to fall out with them. 'I bet this is so alien to you. I envy you so much, having a clean slate. It's just such a simple way to live – marrying one person, having children with them, staying faithful. No need for any pretence. I guess some people are destined to have straightforward lives. I don't think I was one of them.'

I struggled to find a response. Katya sounding jealous of my life based on erroneous assumptions made me want to lie on the grass and thrash about screaming. I was not someone to admire. Not someone with whom to compare herself and pump up the pain, inflating her own failings under the glory of my glittering excellence.

She scuffed along beside me for a moment, then burst out with, 'I'm thinking of leaving Sean. Not because I'd be happier, but because he would.'

'Don't be silly, Katya. He loves you.'

'How can you know that?'

Her words were straining out, as though the knotting and twisting inside of her had strangled some vital airway. I couldn't let her throw away her life on a whim. They'd weathered the worst. She just needed to forgive herself and move on. Said the woman who'd superglued herself into 1982.

'I know because he told me. Last night, actually.'

'Last night? When? Why were you having that conversation with him? I thought you said you never spoke to him.'

The slumped shoulders had vanished. Her head was up. It was as though I'd pushed her into a bed of nettles and all her nerve endings were quivering as they tried to override the shock. I stopped walking and put my hand on her arm.

'You should be pleased. How many husbands go round telling people they hardly know how much they love their wives?'

She shook me off. 'But how did you come to have the conversation in the first place? You're supposed to be my friend. I don't want you talking to my husband about me behind my back.'

I ignored the stab of injustice and forced my voice into a placatory tone. As Mark would say, this wasn't about me. 'I wasn't talking about you behind your back, silly. I can't remember how the conversation came about. I think we were discussing how lucky we were to have chosen the people we married.'

I breathed out, not daring to look at her in case she saw the truth on my face.

She burst into tears, trying to speak, little bubbles of saliva gathering in the corner of her mouth. 'I must seem pathetic to you. Please don't go home and tell Mark how ridiculous I am. And don't tell him about the affair. He'd be so horrified.' She tried to smile. 'He's so lucky to have such a nice wife who doesn't go round screwing his friends.'

Anger swept across my skin like a sandstorm across a desert. Saint bloody Lydia. And before I could reason, the next sentences rushed out of my mouth, as involuntary as a sneeze. 'For god's sake, Katya. He's not lucky at all. If only he knew just how bloody unlucky he is. I've had an affair. And not years ago, like you.'

I just shot it out there, like a suicidal atoning of my guilt, travelling on a wave of rage. As soon as the words hit the Surrey air, my emotion fragmented. Fear surged through me.

Katya knew one big secret. Sean knew the other.

And Mark's happiness depended on them finding the strength to keep that knowledge to themselves. I would have done anything to suck back in those words, bury them under the sandbags of shame where they belonged.

Katya's face was the stuff of the stupid YouTube videos Jamie loved. I could quite imagine the bug-eyed image of her spreading around the world with the title: 'Middle-class mother hears shocking news from someone she thought was a nun,' followed by a dramatic folding up and slumping to the floor.

'When?'

'At the Surrey Business Stars Awards in September. An Italian guy. It was all a mistake.' Everything in me burned. The alien feeling of confiding in her, anyone, made me want to run away and hide in the dark, somewhere soft and warm.

Mabel saved Katya from having to form words into any kind of sentence by arriving with a baby rabbit in her mouth, its eyes bulging with fright. Jesus. Never mind getting a dog to keep your blood pressure down. I needed to get rid of mine to increase my chances of not having a heart attack.

'Mabel! Off! Off!' She cavorted away, with the poor bunny's back leg scrabbling helplessly in the air. I fumbled for the chicken in my bum bag.

'Mabel, look, here, chicky, chicky-chick-chick.'

I laid a little Hansel and Gretel trail towards her, but she kept dancing away. I couldn't blame her really, since a lifetime of pent-up anger was channelled into yelling her name.

Katya was screaming, 'Oh my god, oh my god!' Not very helpful, but a useful outlet for her shock at the news that I was a right old slapper. I bellowed at Mabel, the rage in my voice so unfamiliar that I almost turned round to see who was shouting. As a woman walking a golden retriever appeared from the tree line, I registered a middle-class moment of embarrassment. Fortunately, Mabel stopped to sniff the other dog's backside. I found my 'mother who plays Scrabble with her children' voice. 'Could you grab her for me, please? I'm having a bit of bunny crisis.'

Life crisis, actually.

Once the woman got hold of Mabel, the tricky task of prising her jaws open began. I kept having visions of the rabbit's eyes popping out of its head and exploding onto the grass in front of me. The more I tried to prise Mabel's mouth open, the more the rabbit's eyes seemed to be clinging into their sockets by the tiniest thread. I belted her rump in desperation but she didn't even flinch, let alone release her jaws.

Eventually the other woman produced a squeaky ball, which had an instant effect. The rabbit was dumped unceremoniously on the hill, while Mabel almost made a pyramid on the golden retriever's back in her efforts to reach the ball. I picked up the rabbit, trying not to squeal myself and popped it under a blackberry bush. I didn't even look to see if it was capable of stumbling off to die somewhere else.

I yanked Mabel away in a scene I should have videoed for Harry Hill. I gave the woman two pounds for her ball rather than waste another moment waving chicken while skidding about in cowpats. Mabel strutted towards home, producing the odd boastful squeak from the ball with an expression of satisfaction for how her morning had turned out. I, on the other hand, staggered forwards, forcing my way through the big cloud of horror that enveloped Katya and me. I needed to be the one to speak but it was as though someone had turned me upside down like a money box and shaken all the words out of me.

Eventually, Katya stopped. 'I'm not going to tell anyone.'

'I shouldn't have put that burden on you. I just couldn't bear you thinking that I was so perfect. It was a mistake. Please don't tell anyone. Mark doesn't know. No one knows. It only happened once.'

Now I was lying again. Only recently I had taken Jamie to task when he lied about going on Snapchat. I couldn't see how the taking of any photo, even if it disappeared after a few seconds, was going to lead to a good outcome. My last words to him were, 'No one likes a liar or a cheat. Don't be that person.'

We reached the car in silence. Mabel did her usual standing there like a lump when the only barrier to her jumping in the boot was her own contrariness. I heaved her in. I'd toed the line for thirty years, filtering out information on a need-to-know basis like sand through an egg timer. For one crazy moment, I had the urge to turn to Katya, pat her knee and say, 'And that's just the beginning. I'm gonna tell you a story. It started with your husband, three decades ago....'

Instead, I turned the key in the ignition and headed towards Katya's house. I hadn't had a close friend in years.

And now I had one who could blow my life apart.

CHAPTER THIRTY-TWO

Tomaso chose my wedding anniversary to phone, exactly a month after we'd come back from Florence. My mother had just bustled in with my anniversary card. Her dogged dedication to reminding me about the date – 'Only three weeks to your anniversary. Anything special planned?' – always seemed more of an accusation than a congratulation. I was just going through the motions of reading the 'special' words in the card, as nothing in my mother's life happened by accident, when I saw 'Italian interpreter' flash up on my mobile.

'Mum, make yourself a cup of tea. I need to take this. It's a work call.'

I knew it would lead to a diatribe about 'pushing yourself too hard' but fear that he might phone back when Mark was there sent me scuttling out into the garden.

I managed to answer as though I had no idea who was calling, feeling a rush of sunshine through me when he spoke my name.

'Lee-dya. Tomaso.'

'You're not supposed to call me.'

'Had to, sweetheart. You won't reply. And you wouldn't want me to end up in the madhouse, would you?'

Those tiny little Italian inflections. The slight trace of a rolled 'r'. I was sure he did it on purpose to sound sexy and exotic rather than the boy from Bermondsey. He succeeded.

I couldn't understand how someone simply asking how I was sent such a burst of excitement coursing through me. Quite different from the mixture of guilt, familiarity and love I'd experienced that morning when Mark brought me a cup of tea in bed and told me that he would marry me 'all over again'. He'd sat on the bed, reached for my hand and said, 'I do love you, you know.'

I couldn't get the reciprocal words out. I'd just smiled and said, 'Thanks.' I did love him. But I couldn't say it. It seemed wrong to claim such lofty emotions, when there was so much buried underground.

Yet with Tomaso, the person who knew the least – and the most – about me, I could be completely honest. I explained, without embarrassment, how hard it was for me to keep ignoring his calls, how desperate I'd been to talk to him but Jamie being ill had been a wake-up call. Adultery and motherhood didn't mix.

'Let me just see you once more. Please. I've got things I want to talk to you about.'

I could see my mother pacing up and down inside. I turned my back on her. Then swivelled round again in case she crept up on me. 'I can't see you, Tomaso.'

'Just once, then I promise I'll go away. You know it makes sense.'

I knew it definitely didn't make sense, but it didn't stop me wondering how I could see him without it being 'wrong'.

There wasn't a way it could be right.

'What do you want to talk to me about?'

'I've been doing a lot of thinking about Giacomo. There are a few things I'd like to run past you.'

Out of the corner of my eye, I could see my mother cleaning the inside of my kitchen windows. She was probably chiselling a bugging device into the glass.

'If you're quick, you can run them past me now.'

'Come on. Don't be like that. Just meet me for one evening.'

I heard the laugh in his voice. That suppressed giggle that made me feel carefree, young and daring.

'I can't. Really I can't.'

'I'm leaving to live in Dubai for a few years.'

'Dubai? I thought you were moving back to Italy. Are you all going?' I braced myself for finding out that he was back with Raffaella, heading off to a new life in the sunshine. I readied myself to be pleased for him.

'No. No, we're not. Just me.'

'But what about Giacomo?'

'I was headhunted for the job, the pay's really good and I thought if I earned decent money for a bit, I'd be able to contribute more to his upbringing, make sure he has everything he needs.'

There was something in his tone I couldn't quite grasp. It reminded me of Jamie when he was listing all the 'unselfish' reasons he should be allowed Call of Duty: 'Then I wouldn't irritate Izzy, then you'd have more time to work, I wouldn't go out as much so I wouldn't be asking you for money all the time…'

I was just trying to get my head round the logic of being a brilliant father by working thousands of miles away when he said, 'And it will be nice to live somewhere warm. It's supposed to be a great place to be an expat. There's a lively social scene.'

I didn't flatter myself that he was trying to make me jealous. And in that moment, jealousy was the last emotion that surged through me. This man was more concerned about the quality of his beach barbecues than the fact that his four-year-old might soon start calling someone else Daddy. There was something repulsive about even mentioning a social life when he was walking away from his own son. I was silent.

'Do you think I'm making a mistake?' Tomaso sounded hurt that I hadn't fallen over myself to congratulate him.

'I'd be worried about being so far away from my son for so long.'

Tomaso sighed. 'I know, but Raffaella would make it hard to see him anyway, so I figured I might as well get on and earn some money, while she sees sense.'

'She might come round more quickly if you went back out to Italy and showed her she could rely on you.' A schoolteacher tone had crept into my voice. I couldn't imagine entertaining any life choice that would keep me from my kids for more than a few days at a time.

Tomaso sounded almost petulant. 'I thought you'd be pleased for me.'

I realised that I was doing to him what Mark had done to me at the Surrey Business Stars Awards – taking a piece of good news and sucking all the energy out of it.

But I couldn't bring myself to say 'well done' when all I could think was, *Mark would never abandon the children like that.* I'd betrayed my husband for this man. Given him a special place in my affections, as the 'one who really got me, with whom I could be totally myself'. Fooled myself that this person, with no backbone or staying power, was something special. Disgust at him, at myself, made me end the call quickly, barely able to articulate, 'Good luck with it all.'

Tonight, I'd definitely tell Mark I loved him.

CHAPTER THIRTY-THREE

When I went back inside, my mother was all sucked in. 'Why don't you go into your office where you can concentrate? Surely you must need to write things down so you don't forget?'

'Sometimes walking about helps me think creatively.' Especially about how deluded I'd been. 'Anyway, I thought I might make a crumble for Mark for tonight.' A total non sequitur but enough to move my mother on.

'Your dad likes a good crumble.'

My mother couldn't have fished for an invitation more if she'd sat there with a jar of maggots and a hook. I couldn't invite her. She'd sit there chipping away at me when it was all I could do to hang together.

'I promised him I wouldn't tell you but he's gone into one of his funny moods again.'

As always, my guilt rose like floodwater.

'He keeps saying he thinks you're ashamed of him because you don't invite him to any of the children's events at school any more,' she said.

'How can I? How can I risk him bumping into Sean? What do you want me to do?'

'If you invited us round here to the house a bit more, he might not notice that you're keeping him away from the school.'

An evening in my company would probably just confirm in Dad's mind that everything really was as bad as he thought. But I had to try.

'Would you like to join us tonight, then?'

'On your anniversary? We wouldn't want to be in the way.'

I hadn't even mustered up a feeble 'Don't be silly, we'd love to have you' before my mother was on the phone, telling my dad to check his striped shirt was ironed, as 'Lydia is very keen for us to join her to celebrate her wedding anniversary.'

When Mark arrived home from the shop, as I'd predicted, he laughed and said, 'Your mother does redefine the meaning of romance. Better go and get a bottle of Harveys Bristol Cream and take the edge off her. Beer or red wine for your dad?'

I loved him for not making a fuss. I guess after eighteen years of marriage, he wasn't expecting to sit there making eyes at me through the candlelight. And at least with my mother to contain, I wouldn't have time to dwell on the fact that a month ago, I'd betrayed him with a man who had the integrity of a loan shark.

Dad's arrival pushed every thought of Tomaso out of my head. He hovered on the doorstep, his hand gripping my arm as though he needed to anchor himself to someone, this jovial man who could sort anything when I was little with a hug and a mint toffee. It made my heart ache. And harden.

'Dad, lovely to see you. Come on in.'

My mother followed behind him with her 'told you so' face on, waggling her eyebrows and jabbing her head in his direction. Mark waved them in, swiftly absorbing the panorama and taking charge by sitting Dad down and finding him a beer. My composure wobbled as Dad shrank into his chair, none of his usual quips about 'I can smell burning' or 'Shall I get a takeaway?' I wondered if he'd stopped taking the medication for what my mother always described as 'his nerves'. She followed me into the kitchen.

'Is Dad okay? He looks terrible.'

She sighed. 'You know how it is. It's cyclical. Always worse at this time of year. It's the autumn term. He still misses launching himself into a new school year.'

When her features softened, she looked so much younger.

'It's been a long time though, since he was doing that,' I said.

'Yes, well, the things you love dearly are hard to leave behind.'

From purr to hiss. In a cartoon my mother would definitely be the cat that tricks you into thinking it's a sweet ball of fluff, then suddenly leaps onto your back and rips half your skin off.

'No children tonight?' she said, as though they'd deliberately scattered for the hills the minute they knew she was coming.

Izzy was getting in touch with her inner thesp in some weird modern production of *Fiddler on the Roof.* Jamie was – of course – at Eleanor's. She was like some big-breasted magnet for him. The more I tried to pull him back and clink him onto something else, the more he strained to be with her. And my Facebook snooping wasn't getting me anywhere. After an initial flurry of Googling all the baffling abbreviations, I decided that discovering BEG meant 'Big evil grin' or DGA was 'Don't go anywhere' was not a good use of my time. However, after reading a newspaper article about social media speak, I'd frantically combed Jamie's interactions with Eleanor for IWSN (I want sex now) and GNOC (Get naked on camera) but there was nothing to suggest they were getting physical. But frankly, how would I know if she was offering him one behind the privet hedge (BTPH perhaps?) on a regular basis?

My mother turned the heat down under the gravy, which made my teeth grind slightly. Though not as much as her peering into the pan with 'I think this needs a sprinkling of cornflour,' then opening my cupboards and causing the caster sugar to cascade onto the floor. Izzy had been baking at the weekend and rarely showed the same enthusiasm for putting things away as she did for getting them out.

'I don't know why you don't keep all your things in tins,' my mother said, tutting away.

I sent up a prayer that she'd never open Jamie's wardrobe and be buried under an avalanche of rotting rugby kit.

While I fetched the dustpan and brush, my mother wrestled with Mabel, who was like a shark circling a bleeding body as she tried to lick up the sugar. Mark had disappeared down to the shed to fetch a bottle of whisky when the doorbell rang.

I shouted through to the sitting room. 'Dad, can you let Jamie in?'

That boy and his flaming keys.

Dad let out a wheeze of effort as he hauled himself out of the chair, then shuffled into the entrance hall. The sounds of ageing.

My mother gave Mabel a sharp belt on her bottom. I saw Mabel's lip curl. For a dog who would happily share a pack of custard creams with a burglar before leading him to my jewellery box, it was proof positive that my mother pushed everyone to their limits.

I was just wondering if I should rescue Mabel from Dorothy the Dog Whisperer, when I heard, 'Good evening. Sorry to disturb you, I was just wondering if Mark was in. I've brought back some samples he left for me.'

I shot out into the hallway, but too late. My dad was waving Sean in. 'Come in, he's just popped down to the shed for a minute. He'll be along in a second.'

I stood behind him, making terrified 'bugger off now' faces. Sean was hovering uncertainly and holding out the bag to me. He had his hand up, 'No, no, it's fine, thanks. I'll get going, just that Mark needed these for tomorrow.'

I never thought I'd see the day when I was grateful for the fact that Dad kept refusing to get his eyes checked, even though every time he drove me, I kept breathing in and braking.

Dad was looking at me expectantly, waiting for me to introduce him. Instead I snatched the samples and said, 'Mark's been doing a kitchen for him.' I moved forward, intending to close the door in Sean's face.

But Dad wasn't going to miss out on a chance to praise Mark, though unlike my mother, he didn't make me feel it was *just* because Mark had rescued his tainted and tarnished daughter. 'Good, good. Bet he's done a great job. Clever with his hands, isn't he? Build anything out of anything.' Dad picked up a walking stick that Mark had carved out of a piece of oak from the umbrella stand behind the door. He held it out to Sean, his veiny hands shaking slightly. 'Look, did he show you this? So detailed.'

'Lovely. He's done an excellent job for me, too,' Sean said, backing away from the front door.

I had to restrain myself from rushing at him and shouting, 'Get lost, get lost, you've done enough damage!'

Over the last couple of months, I'd got used to Sean being around. I no longer experienced a great storm of emotion every time he popped up. But seeing my dad there, so trusting and vulnerable, brought a renewed surge of fury into my heart.

I wanted to scream, 'Look what you did. Are you satisfied now? Do you remember how vibrant my dad was? How he could walk into any room and everyone would just quieten down, without him saying a word?' Grief, raw and tender, wrapped itself around regret for all that Dad was and never would be again.

Dad returned the walking stick to the umbrella stand. He was frowning. I wished I had Izzy's capacity for drama and could faint in a convincing way, anything: fall on the floor, throw up, haemorrhage blood. But instead I stood there like the idiot everyone is pointing behind in a pantomime, paralysed, unable to think of anything that wouldn't draw Dad's attention to the fact that it was *him*.

'Lydia here won the prize at the Surrey Business Stars Awards. Best business in Surrey.'

I took Dad's arm. I tried to make my voice kind, but it came out as a reproach. 'He doesn't need to know all that.'

I felt something withdraw in my dad, a little quiver of hurt. I wanted to stamp my foot and say, 'I'm not ashamed of you, but you really, really don't want to know who this is.'

I grabbed the bag from Sean and was just stepping towards the front door to close it when Mark came in from the garden.

'Sean, hello there. See you've met my father-in-law, Arthur. Did Lydia introduce you? Arthur, this is Sean McAllister, my best customer. Are you coming in for a quick drink, mate? It's actually our wedding anniversary today and we were just going to pop a cork.'

Sean and I stood there like a couple of actors employed for their ability to play lampposts. I didn't look at Dad. There was a pause while Mark waited for Sean's answer and I waited for the sky to fall in.

The toilet cistern gurgled. Mabel's muffled whimpers seeped through into the hallway. Sean backed away. 'Thanks, but I need to get going. See you soon.'

Mark had barely articulated, 'Just a quick one,' when my dad let out a groan. He swayed a little on his feet. The expression on Sean's face hovered midway between concern and horror. Mark swung round to Dad. 'Arthur, are you all right?'

'What's he doing here?' Dad straightened up. He drew himself up, suddenly looking less frail. Something stronger in his voice. He yanked the front door wide open. 'What are you doing here?'

Sean put his arm out. I wasn't sure whether it was to fend my dad off, or to steady him. Mark was doing that 'Who? What? Where?' thing Mabel did when she knew Izzy had hidden a biscuit in the garden for her. His gaze darted from Dad to Sean and finally came to rest on me for an explanation.

Sean opened his mouth but didn't manage to force any words out into the air. Dad, who often looked as though he might struggle to climb the stairs, appeared to claw back a bit of authority. But what none of us had bargained on was my mother. Like a flying squirrel in full flight, she suddenly came out of the kitchen, dustpan brush in hand, and launched herself.

She echoed my father with 'What are you doing here?' but then took it several stages further. 'Get away. Get away! Don't you dare show yourself anywhere near this family. Nowhere!'

She brandished the dustpan brush at Sean, little grains of sugar flicking over the hallway.

He made the mistake of saying, 'I'm sorry. I really am.'

This seemed to ignite my mother like a Bonfire Night rocket that soars upwards and scatters into a hundred little stars. 'Sorry? Sorry? I'll give you sorry. Have you any idea what you did to us? You and your bully-boy father?'

Mark stood there transfixed, as though he'd been rolled down a hill in a barrel and needed a second to get his thoughts flowing in a straight line again.

My dad stepped in. 'You'd best go now, son.'

There was a fragment of his old teacher voice in there, a dusty souvenir of the man who'd believed so passionately that education was the greatest civilising force of mankind.

He clicked the front door shut, but didn't turn round. Just stood there with his hand on the latch.

I touched his back. 'Dad. Come on. Let's go and sit down.'

Mark pulled himself out of his stupor. 'Arthur, come with me.' He did a 'What the heck?' face in my direction but I was pretty certain my expression hadn't yet found one single emotion to settle into. He took Dad's arm and helped him through to the closest seat, in the dining room, which now looked ridiculous with the neat little vase of roses and the sideboard with the happy family photos. How easy it was to live a lie. How difficult it was to ensure it lasted forever.

My mother skittered through, still pulsing with adrenaline, her lips moving with all the vitriol she hadn't found an outlet for. She parked herself next to Dad, with a warning to 'Keep it brief'. I saw an understanding pass between them and hoped to god we were all on the same page.

The smell of gravy burning reached me. I dashed out into the kitchen and snatched it off the stove. It was tempting to start checking on the lamb, stab a knife into the carrots, shake the roast potatoes to guarantee maximum crispiness. Anything to maintain the status quo for half a minute more.

Anything rather than meet Mark's questions.

He was used to excruciating scenes with my mother. The many times when she'd felt obliged to educate a waiter in customer service. Imparted her knowledge on how to run an airline on one memorable holiday to Bordeaux. Singlehandedly attempted an explanation of how Marks & Spencer could reverse their fortunes if they'd just stock 'the sort of clothes that people want to buy, rather than all this modern tat'.

I knew he wouldn't yet have connected me to the latest debacle. Of course, he'd be dying to know how my mother could have encountered Sean to an extent that would merit her witch-on-a-broom scenario. But he wouldn't have guessed that I was centre point around which all the hate revolved.

I switched off the oven and prepared myself for the past to catch up with the present.

CHAPTER THIRTY-FOUR

Hearing my dad explain 'the unfortunate incident with Sean McAllister' all those years ago, not making any attempt to gloss over his part in it, unleashed a sadness in me that I didn't know I was still capable of. The tears kept coming. Not the great wrenching sobs of the emotionally incontinent, but the quiet tears of the defeated.

Reliving the cataclysmic events put into action by a silly teenage girl who wanted to fit in nearly sheared me in two. I kept looking at Mark but his face was impassive. Would he want to stay with me now that we'd laid out not only our family history, but also our family lies in all their sordid glory?

In between glancing at Dad to see whether he was becoming too distraught, I kept putting myself in Mark's position. However we tried to adorn the facts, they were ugly and not easily smoothed over. The woman he married hadn't bothered to enlighten him that she'd bared her breasts – and her bum – for his best customer, who hadn't held back on getting his tackle out either. The nice respectable family he'd married into had a criminal record. Plus the little matter of my mother masterminding a fresh start with a new name for me, like something out of *Gone Girl*. And most tellingly of all, despite the fact that he'd seen a baby, twice, pop out of her body, his wife had never trusted him enough to tell the truth.

So now, all the truths we had shared, the truths that were real, appeared bent out of shape by the omissions.

I tried to catch Mark's eye but he was looking away from me in a manner that I couldn't describe as casual. It was as though he was sitting in the optician's chair having various lenses slotted in front of him until what he thought was an F revealed itself to be a P. Similar, but completely different.

Dad finally ground to a halt. He spread his hands out on the table in front of him. 'I don't come out of this well. In the end, he was a young lad who'd made a mistake, but I took it so much further and ruined everyone's life. Dorothy's, Lydia's, even my own, though that matters the least.'

And as though something was wrenching and twisting inside me, the memory of going away with my dad, three months before his trial, barged in. We'd rented a cottage in Somerset, just the two of us. It was the last time we'd talked openly, when I still saw him as someone to rely on, not someone to protect. In between games of Yahtzee, we discussed what had happened, how we'd cope. He spent the week instilling in me that I was strong, that I could survive, that this was just a bump in the road. That we'd go on to lead good lives after all of this was over.

For years I thought he'd been right.

I put my hand out to cover his. 'Dad. *You* didn't ruin anyone's life. I did that myself. If anything, it was the other way round.'

He gripped my fingers. 'No, darling. I picked you up five minutes after you were born and promised I'd never let bad things happen to you. What happened that day was the result of my fury at myself that I hadn't protected you. But it's not an excuse. I was the grown-up with a duty of care, even to Sean McAllister. You were just a teenager trying to find her way in life. That's a huge difference.'

My mother had remained quiet. Every time she shifted in her seat as though she was about to have an opinion – which was approximately every thirty seconds – my father put his hand up to silence her. Scenes I'd long deleted from my memory stirred within me, a bit like a dog drying out after heavy rain and taking on a different shape all together.

Despite considering my mother a dictator for the last thirty years, Dad hadn't always capitulated when my mother strode through the family, delivering her rules and regulations in a no-prisoners-here way. They'd clashed swords, my mother in a shrill, coming-through-now bulldozer fashion, my father in a far lighter but determined manner. I did recall, seeing him now, that he'd often diverted her with a joke or a compliment. All her hackles would settle down again until the next time she had a diktat she wanted us to follow. In the middle of all my panic about whether Mark would demand a divorce and what would happen to Izzy and Jamie, I kept feeling slivers of joy at the glimpses of my dad, as he was, years ago, confident and capable.

My mother was the first one to ask Mark a direct question. 'Are you terribly shocked by all of this?'

When he replied, 'Yes,' it still surprised me. I was so used to Mark having a liberal view of everything – of Jamie's vodka-swigging at parties, his fumbling in the bedroom with Eleanor, Izzy's predilection for watching wall-to-wall *TOWIE* on TV. My brain struggled to comprehend that this man, the one who indulged my need to have a particular mug for my tea, who accepted that I couldn't sleep unless the curtains were completely closed, did have a tipping point of shock. He'd always been the one to take everything in his stride, allowing me the luxury of going off the deep end.

My mother did her usual delicate beating about the bush. 'So, Mark, where does this leave you with Lydia?'

'With all due respect, Dorothy, it's none of your business. It's something Lydia and I will discuss without you sitting there ready to tell her what to think. What I will say, is quite a lot is falling into place for me. I'm a bit stunned that Lydia's had to live a lie for so long.'

My dad stretched out his other hand and took my mother's. She didn't bat him away like she normally did. She clutched it, her knuckles white against his craggy old fingers. I waited for my mother to launch into Mark but she said, with the sort of gentleness that I'd associated with other people's mums, 'I only wanted the best for her, you know.'

She sounded so desolate. I tried to smother my resentment. How could putting down Tripod be the best for me? Incubating my shame at the perfect temperature all my life? Making sure there was never a chance to forget?

My dad squeezed her hand. 'I know you did, love, I know you did.' She leaned against him.

My dad got up. 'Come on, Dorothy. We need to leave them to it. That's enough for one night.'

My mother made no move to get up. 'You won't do anything silly, Mark, will you? Don't make any decisions, you know, well…'

She walked stiffly round the table. Briefly, she stroked my hair. Her touch was lighter than I remembered. 'I did what I thought was right, Sally. I did it all for you. So you wouldn't be, you know, so you wouldn't, for the rest of your life, be *that* girl.'

My dad put his arm around her shoulders. I wanted to see them out but I was afraid to go to the front door in case Mark followed me and pushed past us, out into the night. I couldn't let him leave without trying to explain, though the only real explanation was that we'd all lied to him.

And in my case, laid new lies like frosted icing on top.

CHAPTER THIRTY-FIVE

Mark was always the one who came in search of cuddles. I accepted them rather than sought them out. That night, once Jamie had returned, ten minutes past his curfew with his shirt hanging out, and Izzy had danced in, singing a couple of lines of *If I Were a Rich Man*, I'd yearned to be held. Longed for the solid feel of Mark's body, the way he tucked his pillow down so our faces could be close together. Mark settled Izzy into bed, who even at thirteen still liked to be officially snuggled in. I went through the motions of responding to where Jamie might find a shirt for the morning or whether I'd bought any biscuits for break. It was as though the elements of my life had fragmented, like a windscreen that shatters but remains in place, without anyone knowing for how long.

We got ready for bed, not speaking at all, just orbiting around each other in an unnatural way. I kept looking at the things that usually grated on my need for order: Mark's whiskers round the sink, the dirty socks balled up rather than shaken out, the light left on in the hallway. Suddenly, if not endearing, they seemed representative of certainty, of a life shared.

In bed, I stretched my hand out towards his. For a moment, his fingers didn't flicker, then they gripped mine.

'I'm sorry,' I said. It wasn't a sorry dashed out to keep the peace, dominated by resentment, a sense of apologising to move forward, without really acknowledging being at fault. This sorry came deep from the core of me. A recognition that I'd let this man down by not confiding in him.

Mark shifted next to me. 'I can't process it all.'

'I know. Will you tell the children?'

He took his hand away. I felt him rub his face.

'I don't know. It's not just our family, is it? Jamie will tell Eleanor. But if we don't say anything, we're infecting another generation with secrets and lies. Jesus. You could have got it all out on the table right at the start, then they'd have grown up knowing and it wouldn't have been a big deal.'

'I couldn't tell you. My mother was adamant I was never to speak about it again.'

'But you're forty-three now. There must have been some point over the last decade when we could have had the conversation.'

Normally I'd have got angry. But I could feel the hurt blistering out of him. His voice was hoarse, as though the words were scraping past the pain in his throat.

'When would there have been a good time to sit down and say, "By the way, darling…"? A few weeks ago, you were going on about that head teacher who used to run a brothel, all shocked about how she'd covered up her past. Never mind you telling everyone at Katya's dinner party that you wouldn't want anyone you knew seeing me naked. Every time I was on the cusp of blurting out the truth, I felt this dreadful terror that you would walk out on me. A bit like I do tonight, actually.'

I'd never let Mark know how vulnerable I felt before.

Mark turned on his side and took my face in his hands. 'That's completely different. She was abusing young people. You just did something stupid as a teenager. I don't know what more I could have done to convince you that you could trust me. I wouldn't have gone anywhere then and I'm not going anywhere now. In some ways, a lot of things have fallen into place: your funny little way of withdrawing, of creating this self-contained aura.' He rolled over onto his side. 'I'm not sure how I feel about knowing Sean went out with you. Though I suppose it would have been worse if you'd actually slept with him,' he said, gently moving on top of me. 'You didn't, did you?'

I closed my eyes. It was an obvious question. And the time had come to stop lying about the answer.

CHAPTER THIRTY-SIX

The next couple of days passed in a backwards and forwards of: 'But you were only thirteen!'; 'The same age as Izzy!'; 'Weren't you worried about getting pregnant?'; interspersed with 'I feel a right bloody idiot, working away in Sean's house all this time, not knowing he's had sex with my wife.'

I wanted to argue that it wasn't as sordid as it sounded. That when Sean and I were in bed together, everything that was wrong with my teenage life receded into a haze of closeness and connection. We couldn't wait to steam out of lessons and race back to his, our feet echoing down the lanes, the smell of the spring hedgerows in the air. When he was making love to me, the world changed into a landscape of intensity and colour that I wanted to trap in a jar and inhale when I was away from him.

But reminiscing about how good another man made me feel didn't seem like a solid situation-rescue strategy. I didn't know what to say to absorb the hurt. And really, what had I been thinking? When I looked at Izzy, with her rainbow array of nail varnishes, her collection of snow globes and posters of puppies on her wall, I couldn't imagine her kissing a boy, let alone having sex. She was just so young. And although I'd thought I was so grown-up, going out with the mighty Sean McAllister, I'd been no more than a child myself.

Thankfully, my mother kept out of our way, letting Mark and I relax back down into some semblance of normality. The heat of accusation gradually faded away, moving towards a genuine desire on his part to process and accept. His questions were considered but not overwhelming. I felt more understood in those few days than in thirty years. Living life without a filter, however, took some adjusting to. I had to concentrate to make myself speak freely, to allow memories and thoughts to make their way out into the world, unchecked and unsanitised, at least when the children weren't around.

With typical generosity of spirit, Mark insisted we should take our time to work out how to tell the kids because of the domino effect on Sean's family. His view was there was no rush, given that 'all that business' hadn't been spoken about for so long, that letting little bits of information slowly trickle out would reduce the shock value when the whole truth came to light. 'Anyway, Jamie can't see beyond Eleanor's tight T-shirts and Izzy's too busy being in love with that bloke off the *X Factor* to give much of a hoot about what their mother got up to in the '80s – too last century, darling!'

I loved him for his measured approach, for having a plan to keep us on an even keel when terra firma was shifting. I deliberately didn't answer calls from my mother. From now on, I was going to make my own judgments without the drip-feed of my mother's warnings: 'I shouldn't…'; 'I wouldn't…'; 'It's probably best if you don't…'

My mother, however, wasn't the sort to be defeated by caller I.D. When I suspected my dad had been unable to restrain her any longer, she turned up when she knew Mark was at work. I'd only just filled the kettle when she skewered straight in. 'Mark's not going to leave you, is he?'

I shook my head, pathetically grateful that I didn't have to face her reaction to a 'yes' answer.

I saw the tramline wrinkles down her forehead ease and fade with the relief that the family wasn't going to suffer a second humiliation: the saviour son-in-law leaving the prodigal daughter.

With a crunch of a chocolate digestive, she banged down the lid on that particular Pandora's box and turned her attention to the state of my flowerbeds at the front of the house. From divorce to dandelions in five seconds flat. A hidden camera, the Rushford/ Southport family and a reality TV show could bring new meaning to the word 'surreal'. Yet the idea of confronting my mother, digging back in time to excavate a huge mountain of rubble to expose real feelings was just too exhausting to contemplate.

After she'd tottered off down the drive, throwing in a warning about threadworm after Mabel had chosen the moment of her departure to drag her backside from one side of the hall to the other, I wished I'd taken her to task.

I was still sifting through the various home truths I'd like to have shared with her when I picked up the kids. It took me a while to realise they were talking to each other in the back of the car. Usually they preferred to bicker over whose rucksack was taking up the most room or who was bagsying the TV – for rugby in Jamie's case or *Strictly* in Izzy's. But today they were whispering. Izzy was casting anxious glances in my direction. Jamie had his finger on his lips. My maternal antennae were waving about like treetops in the wind. I smiled into the rear-view mirror. 'Everything all right?'

The over-bright 'Yeah, yeah, all fine, Mum' from Jamie alerted me to imminent disaster. The last time they behaved like this, Jamie had received a detention for imitating the Geography teacher when a wasp flew up her skirt.

As soon as we got through the door, they both scattered upstairs bypassing the biscuit tin in the kitchen. In my experience, Izzy would crack first. Sure enough, light little footsteps pattered · down the stairs.

'Mum?'

I stopped chopping carrots and turned round. 'Darling?'

'It's Jamie, Mum. He's in real trouble.'

Izzy's idea of real trouble and Jamie's were diametrically opposed. Izzy's dramas tended to revolve around microscopic rebellions such as writing in black ink instead of blue, but latterly, Jamie didn't class anything as trouble unless it escalated as far as Head of Year and even then, he saw it as a chance to enhance his standing as a cool dude. I blamed bloody Eleanor. I couldn't remember him even being told off until he met *her*, with her sassy madam ways.

'He hasn't been imitating Mrs Randle again, has he?' I laughed.

'Mum, it's not funny.'

I put the vegetable peeler down. Izzy was pulling her jumper over her hands. 'You'll stretch your sleeves doing that.'

She rubbed her hands over her face. 'Promise me you won't start shouting.'

'I'll do my best. Do you need a cuddle?'

She raced to me and hugged me tightly. Most of the time, she shook me off if I went anywhere near her, flouncing out of the room if I so much as stroked her hair. She had my attention now.

'Don't be cross. Jamie said I can't tell on him.'

'Sweetheart, if he's in trouble, I have to know what's going on.'

I could feel the tension in her bony shoulders.

'Eleanor sent a photo to Jamie on her phone,' Izzy mumbled into my chest.

I lifted her face up. 'What sort of photo?' Fronds of fear were beginning to quiver.

'You know, one of her, um, fanny. Her vagina.'

Given the actual message, it surprised me that I still managed to recoil from Izzy's casual use of 'fanny'. And in other circumstances, I would have suppressed a smile that she felt the need to translate for her closeted mother.

'How do you know?'

'She sent it while he was at rugby practice. He'd left his phone on the bench in the changing rooms and one of the boys picked it up and started looking at his messages.'

'Just a minute, love. I need to get Jamie down. He needs to delete that photo, right now.'

'But Mum, it's too late. They sent it to everyone. Even Freya's sister saw it and she's in the first year.'

I shot upstairs, shouting for Jamie. Dread was compressing my voice. All the horrible stories I'd ever read about teenagers hanging themselves after stupid arguments with their parents, B grades instead of A*s, cyber-bullying, raced through my mind. I could barely look as I rounded the corner on the landing. I barged into his bedroom, not bothering to knock. He was face down on the bed, head in his pillow.

I put my hand on his back. 'Jamie, love. I gather there's been a bit of trouble at school.'

He raised himself onto one elbow. 'I've really let you down, Mum.'

I sat on his bed and pulled him into my arms. 'Darling, we all make mistakes. But you're going to have to tell me everything so I can help you. I know about the photo.'

His shoulders slumped. 'Do you know what sort of photo it was, though?'

'Yes, I do.'

'I thought you'd go mad.'

'I don't think it's a time for that. How did they get into your phone? Didn't you have a password on it?'

'I kept doing those stupid passwords where you draw a pattern with your finger and getting locked out because I'd forgotten what I'd done, so I just left it off in the end.' The distress in his voice was fanning my own fright.

This was not a moment for a lecture about the perils of disorganisation but honestly, I would have to pencil in a day to wring his neck at a later date. For god's sake.

'Right, so who picked up your phone?'

'Just some bloke in the lower sixth.'

'Who?'

'You don't even know him. What does it matter? The photo's gone out and they'll all think it was me.'

'No, they won't, darling, because I'm going to get down to the school and sort this out.'

'No! You can't do that. Everyone will think I've told on them. They'll think I'm a right sneak.'

'What about Eleanor, though? Does she know?'

Jamie's face crumpled. 'I tried to talk to her after school but she told me she hated me and ran away in tears.'

'It was her fault for sending such a stupid photo in the first place. What was she thinking of?' Out it came: 'Little trollop.'

Jamie pulled himself away from me. 'She's not a trollop. I knew you wouldn't understand. I wanted that photo. I asked her for it. It was supposed to be private. You've no idea what it feels like to be young. I don't suppose you and dad even have sex any more!'

He swiped at the tears that were leaking down his face.

The temptation to say, 'Last night, actually,' was buried under the realisation that this was my occasion to be a grown-up. I gritted my teeth against the memory of my mother's slow articulation of exactly 'how disappointed' she was in me. She'd hard-wired my brain to believe I could never make a success of anything ever again. I was about to set the template for Jamie's ability to handle his mistakes for the rest of his life.

I pulled him to me again, feeling the damp heat of his face through my shirt. 'Jamie, I remember exactly what it felt like to be a teenager and to mess up. Now you'll think it's the end of the world, but I promise you it's not. One day, I'll tell you some of the mistakes I made. I think you should go and see Eleanor's parents.'

Jamie pushed me away again. 'I can't do that.'

'I'll come with you.'

'Will I get into trouble at school?'

'We'll probably have to have a word with the headmaster.' I wasn't sure what was worse, being the pupil who'd cocked up or the mother who'd let it happen.

'Do you think Sean will find out? He'll be really angry. He was always joking about me being the son he never had.'

'Of course, he'll have to know but he might understand more than you think, darling. Though dads can get a bit protective over their daughters. I need to phone Daddy.'

Jamie sagged against me. 'Do you have to tell him?'

I marvelled at the naïvety of teenagers. In some ways, my kids knew so much more about life than me. I was quite positive that Jamie could name a variety of dodgy sexual practices with household items I would never view in the same way again – but he still showed a remarkable lack of understanding about what was in the 'serious shit' category.

I was beginning see the advantage of packing kids off to a single-sex boarding school aged seven. 'Is Eleanor sixteen yet?'

'No.'

'You don't have to answer the question I'm about to ask you, lovey, but I think it's going to come up.'

Jamie looked at the floor. 'Mum! This is just embarrassing.' He slumped back down and curled up in a ball, facing the wall.

I touched his shoulder and felt him tense away from me. I screwed up my eyes and scrabbled about for my 'this is a perfectly normal conversation to be having with my sixteen-year-old son' voice. 'Have you slept with Eleanor?'

'For god's sake. We haven't actually had "intercourse", just you know...'

'So technically Eleanor is still a virgin?' I was glad he couldn't see my face.

'Ye-es.'

'You're sure?'

'Yes. Go away.'

I hoped, more than I'd ever hoped for anything in my life, that he was telling the truth. The trouble with kids was that it wasn't that they grew out of lying, they just got better at it so you didn't realise how often they did it. I picked up an array of water glasses from his chest of drawers, the sheer quantity going some way to explaining why we were down to three glasses between the rest of us.

Though water glass scarcity wasn't the most pressing problem to tackle right now.

CHAPTER THIRTY-SEVEN

My hopes that my friendship with Katya would ease our discussion were not so much dashed as ground into dust when she opened the door. She emitted a chilliness that made me want to keep my coat on. She led us into the kitchen that Mark had grafted on for so long. If I totted up all the hours he'd spent on it, I swear he'd have been earning minus thirty pence an hour. We'd stopped discussing it in the end.

Sean was sitting at the big oak table with Eleanor. She was braless under a thin vest top, the outline of her nipples clearly visible. If she was my daughter, I'd have strapped her up in a hessian sack by now.

I was glad Mark had persuaded me to leave Jamie at home. 'I think he's more focused on the fact that Eleanor won't answer his calls than what deep trouble he's in. Still thinking with his willy rather than his brain. Plus if it does turn nasty, I'd like to respond without Jamie listening.'

My relief that I could just hand over the lead to someone who loved Jamie as much as me made me realise – again – how deranged I'd been to entertain the idea of Tomaso. The man who missed his child so much, but couldn't quite be bothered to get a job in the same country.

Sean stood up and shook hands with Mark. I put my hand up in greeting.

'Hi there. What can I get you to drink?' Sean's voice was deflated and strained, but not accusatory.

'We're fine, thanks,' Mark said, pulling out a chair at the table for me. He sat next to me, while Katya parked herself opposite with Eleanor.

Katya took a large gulp of wine. She already looked a bit flushed. She was worrying at some fine hair near her temple with her thumb and index finger. 'I'm really disappointed in Jamie. I thought he was such a good boy.'

Sean put his hand out. 'Katya,' he said, 'this is not all down to Jamie.'

'It is as far as I'm concerned. Eleanor would never have sent a picture like that to him unless he'd forced her to.'

All my good intentions of not getting dragged into apportioning blame took turbo-charged flight. 'Hang on a minute, Katya. I don't think Jamie "forced" her to do anything she didn't want to do.' It was only the fact that Eleanor was sitting opposite me that stopped me adding, 'In fact, I think Eleanor has been quite an eye-opener for Jamie, if anything.'

I turned to Eleanor. She still had that lick of defiance about her, as though I was just slightly too stupid to be sharing the same air as her. I would have to resist the whole 'blame and shame' malarkey that my mother had rolled out with such aplomb. I reminded myself that she was only fifteen and had to be feeling terrible. Her way of dealing with it was just different from mine.

'I am sorry, Eleanor, though I hope you know that it wasn't Jamie who sent the picture around the school.' I forced myself to soften my voice.

Katya made a harrumphing sound that I decided to ignore.

Eleanor shrugged, though I saw her eyes glisten.

Mark stepped in. 'Clearly, we need to contact the school to explain what's happened.'

Katya flicked her hand in a gesture of impatience. 'Christ, I should think it will be on the fucking *Ten O'Clock News* tonight. They won't need to wait to hear it from us.'

Mark coloured slightly but pressed on. 'What I meant was I think we should present a united front, talk to the head and try to work out a damage limitation plan.'

Sean was nodding opposite me. For a man who usually ran the show, he was displaying as much verve as an under-inflated balloon. His burly, blokey manner had slipped into something distressed and uncertain. After all these years of wishing curses upon him, I was astonished to find that I found no pleasure in his discomfort.

Katya folded her arms. 'I can't see what the school can do. I mean, the photo is out there for all to see. It's probably on the internet right now, with all sorts of weirdos perving over it. How is the school going to legislate for that? Bit late to suggest Jamie takes better care of his phone, don't you think?'

I started to understand what Sean had lived with all these years. Katya in heat-seeking missile mode, determined to sear the blame into someone, regardless of the facts. I glanced at Eleanor, who looked as though she was just beginning to realise what a massive deal this was. She edged closer to Sean, who put his arm round her shoulders.

With the breath that I'd been holding in case a great jet of dragon's fire came out of my mouth, I released a light, gentle-sounding sentence. 'Come on, Katya, it's probably not that bad. It'll be the talking point for a couple of days and then they'll all move onto someone else. What's done is done. We just need to help them through it.'

I tried to catch Eleanor's eye but her head was down.

Katya jumped up and pointed at me. 'It's all right for you. Your son comes out of this quite well – the cool kid whose girlfriend is putting her foofoo on display for him. You've no idea what it's like for Eleanor. She's going to have to walk in there tomorrow and face everyone. They'll all be thinking she's a right little tart. "Eleanor McAllister, wasn't she the one who…?"'

Somewhere in the far corner of my brain, I knew that Mark would make a joke about 'foofoo' at a later date. But more immediately, I recognised my mother's words from a couple of decades ago, delivered in the same withering tones. Eleanor cried quietly, all her earlier bravado crumpling under Katya's prophecies of doom.

Sean and Mark both rushed to answer. I all but shouted them down with the force of my maternal urge to protect, rumbling through the room with the power of a tank towards its target.

'Actually, Katya, I did have a bit of a similar experience when I was younger, so I do understand what it's like for Eleanor.'

Mark jerked round and shook his head imperceptibly. But I wasn't going to be derailed by anyone.

Mark leapt up and took Eleanor's arm. 'Come on, love. The adults might need to have a bit of a private discussion. Can you give us five?' As she followed him out with no resistance, I recognised the numbness in her. I remembered that feeling of wading through crushed ice, where my body had shut down to a level where it could still function but not feel. For all her bravado, she was still a child.

There was a moment of silence, while Katya and I out-glared each other. Mark hurried back in, clicking the sitting room door shut behind him. He sat down and squeezed my knee.

'Thirty years ago, my boyfriend took a picture of me naked. A teacher found it at school and it created a right old hoo-ha. It really wasn't "all right" for me. Obviously, what's happened now isn't ideal but I do know that Eleanor – and Jamie – are going to need us to help them, not cause more problems by falling out with each other.'

I didn't look at Sean but I was aware of him staring at me. Mark's hand relaxed and he breathed out. I realised he'd been expecting me to blurt out the whole story.

Katya looked at me as though she hated me, a far cry from the complex, funny woman who giggled on our walks together.

'The internet wasn't even invented then. How many people saw the photo? Five? Ten? Whoop whoop. You can't compare the two.'

'I wasn't trying to make out that what happened to me was worse, just that I understand what this situation feels like. I'd be really happy to have a chat with Eleanor to help her appreciate that she'll get through it.'

Katya pointed a finger at me. 'You? You think you're going to have a nice little tête-à-tête with my daughter when we wouldn't even be in this situation if it wasn't for your son? Jamie hasn't even had the decency to come round and apologise. He's just let Mummy and Daddy do the talking for him.'

'That's not true,' I said. 'We were the ones who wouldn't bring him.'

Sean put up his hand for silence. 'Katya.' His voice held reproach. 'I think tempers are running high enough, without putting all the blame on Jamie. I know you're upset, but Eleanor did take and send the photo. Jamie didn't push the button to distribute it to everyone.'

'Trust you to side with everyone else. Maybe one day you'll actually stick up for your own family rather than turning on the charm for Joe Bloggs down the road. I suppose you're feeling sorry for Lydia with her pathetic little sob story rather than your daughter, who's a total laughing stock.'

Katya topped up her glass and took a big slug of wine. 'If Eleanor fails her GCSEs because of this, I'm going to sue you two for the money to repeat the year.'

The looks I'd always envied – Katya's little elfin features, the sort of face that could carry a short crop, a contemporary version of Twiggy – twisted into something hard and vicious.

Sean frowned. 'She won't fail her GCSEs. Anyway, they're a good six months away.'

'How do you know? You can have a delayed reaction to these things. If she loses focus for a few weeks, that'll be the end of eleven

A*s.' Katya made it sound as though she was coming to terms with a terminal disease, not the prospect of a C in Geography.

'Let's not panic. All I meant was that Lydia's well-placed to help Eleanor because she's been through it herself.' Sean tried to reach for her hand but she snatched it away.

'I knew you'd think she'd handle it better than me. Perhaps if I ran my own business conning people with the happy-ever-after bullshit so they'd pay me a fortune to organise the big day, you'd have a bit more respect for me. I'm clearly doing a crap job bringing up my own daughter.'

Katya was twisting her gold bangle round and round on her little bird wrists.

Sean scraped his chair back, stood up and put his hands on her shoulders. He said, very gently, 'Katya, this isn't about you. For the record, I think you are very good mum to Eleanor and this is just a mistake – quite a public one, I grant you – but it's only going to become insurmountable if we let it. Of course you're going to be Eleanor's main support but I'm just suggesting that we use all the resources available to us.'

But Katya refused to be placated. 'She's *my* daughter for god's sake. What could Lydia do for her that I can't?'

Something changed in Sean's face. I'd seen it before. That switch into reckless, tearaway mode. It was what had made him the 'McLegend' on the rugby field at school.

I felt like a goalie on the wrong side of the pitch. It wouldn't matter how fast I ran or how high I jumped, I wouldn't be able to save the day.

I put out a warning hand to Sean but he was locked in, towering over Katya.

'What Lydia is kindly not telling you is that the boy who took the Polaroid was me. And it wasn't just of her, it was of both of us, completely naked and pretty compromising, much worse than the one of Eleanor. Her dad was the deputy head, he got really upset – a bit like you are now – and we ended up in a fight. The net result of that was that he finished up in prison and Lydia had to move away to a completely new area. So I think, yes, she does know what she is talking about.'

I couldn't believe the casual way that information flopped out into the world. This huge secret that had been residing in its own mausoleum with pillars and porticoes had suddenly been wheelbarrowed out into the world with no more pomp and ceremony than the dumping of Cheerios into a cereal bowl in the morning.

Wine had dulled Katya's reactions for a moment. Her eyebrows knitted together while her thoughts kayaked through the alcohol. 'You knew Lydia from before? She's the one your mother was going about, who broke your heart? The reason you don't like talking about your schooldays?'

Her eyes darted from Sean to me, and back again. A pause, as though coins were registering in a parking meter. And then, like a machine gun swivelling on a pivot, she turned to face me. I tried not to shrink back in my chair as Katya's wrath, bubbling and molten, poured out of her. 'You bitch. You absolute bitch. There you were pretending to be my friend, the listening ear. Was it just so you could get close to Sean? Some kind of bizarre unfinished love affair that you wanted to have another bash at, thirty years later?'

I leaned closer to Mark, reassured by his solid presence as the bitterness spewed out of Katya.

'I wanted to tell you. Of course I did. For the record, I wasn't pretending to be your friend. I really enjoy your company. I had a new identity and Sean had never talked about what happened, so it was just easier to forget that we'd ever known each other.'

Katya turned towards Mark. 'You knew this, did you? That my husband and your wife had "history" together? That they'd seen each other naked?'

Mark's calm voice was a complete contrast to the hysterical pitch of Katya's. 'I didn't know anything about it until this week, either. But it's so long ago now I'm not going to get worked up about something that happened years before I met Lydia. What matters, Katya, is the here and now, our families.'

'So you all knew, except me? "Poor old Katya, she'd be so upset, best not tell her so she doesn't have to worry her little head about it." You're pathetic, all of you, creeping about with your sordid secrets.' She swung round towards Mark. 'So like me, you've been living a lie all these years? Being made a fool of?'

Mark ran his fingers through his hair. 'I did feel a bit like that when I first found out. But they had their reasons, Katya. They didn't set out to hurt us. More like protect us, actually.'

Katya paused. She glanced at Sean, then at me. 'You've slept together, haven't you?'

The venom in her voice frightened me. We both hesitated. Silence filled the room, though if brains made a noise, we'd all have been deafened by the collective whirring and assessing of who knew what.

Sean made the first stab at an explanation. 'We were young and silly, Katya. It was thirty years ago. We didn't want to rake it all up and upset everyone for no good reason.' His voice was weary, defeated rather than defensive.

Katya, on the other hand, was generating enough rage to annihilate us all. She glowered at Mark, with a mixture of accusation and pity. 'You have no idea who you're married to, do you? What she's really like?'

I jumped up. Fear flashed through me in a way that threatened to fold my legs underneath me. 'That's enough, Katya. We're here to sort out the kids, not attack each other.'

She stared at me. 'At least my husband knows the truth about me and has decided to stay anyway. Unlike Mark, he's had the opportunity to make an informed choice.'

'Don't. Don't do this, Katya.' I was begging, I could hear it. I couldn't marry up the woman in front of me, burning up with resentment and spite, with the one who laughed about the mothers at school racing their worn-out offspring from Mandarin to karate to trampolining.

'Why shouldn't I? It's a bit of a day for telling the truth. Why should I be the only one left out, again?'

I felt as though I was leaning on my front door, trying to force an intruder out, to keep my family safe, but ceding tiny increments of space, little by little until inevitably, I'd be slammed into the hall wall, flattened under the weight of superior strength.

Sean stood up. 'Katya. That's enough. I don't know what you're talking about but let's stick to the topic in hand, which is what we are going to do about Jamie and Eleanor.'

He sounded so reasonable, so rational that for a tiny moment, I hoped – rather than believed – that we could forget Katya and her insinuations and move into the comparatively more stable area of teenage disaster management.

Katya turned on Sean. 'You'd love that, wouldn't you? You'd love me to toe the bloody line, just as I always do, terrified of rocking the boat in case you do actually leave me. Well, do you know what? I don't give a shit about that any more. Yes, I had an affair. But maybe you should think a bit about why that was. Or was that 'all so long ago' that it doesn't bloody matter any more?'

She turned to me. 'For you, though, Lydia, it wasn't that long ago, was it? September, wasn't it, some Italian from that Surrey Business Stars thing?'

I'd never really believed that people gasped before. I thought it was something invented in books to denote surprise. But gasp was what Mark did. A strangled, shocked, intake of breath.

I grabbed his arm. 'Mark, let me explain, it's not as bad as it sounds.' I wanted to claim that Katya had made it up, just to be spiteful but how could I? The big lie I'd been living since I was thirteen had spawned a thousand little lies, scattering about like poppy seeds and colonising great tracts of landscape, encroaching a little more on the truth as every year passed.

He shook me off and stood up. He was blinking, as though the scene in front of him was a figment of his imagination and he just needed to refocus. His face was pale, mottled with horror and surprise.

'I'll talk to you when we get home, Lydia.'

He marched towards the door.

I grabbed my bag to dash out after him with an explanation, to make the horrible thing nowhere near as bad as it sounded. But in reality, it was worse because Katya didn't know the half of it, didn't know that when Jamie was ill, I was oblivious, naked in my hotel room in Florence, thinking only about my own selfish pleasure. It wouldn't take Mark long to put it all together, though.

Katya put her hands on her hips, her eyes huge in her face as though she'd taken some mind-altering drugs. 'Before you go, Mark – and you, Lydia – I just want you both to know that if I do find out that Jamie has had sex with my daughter – my *fifteen-year-old* daughter – I will go to the police and press charges.'

I caught Sean's eye and hesitated for a fraction of a second. He was watchful, as though he was ready to be ambushed from behind.

I faced Katya head-on. 'Sean slept with me when I was *thirteen*, so we can all play that game.'

I enjoyed a fleeting moment of satisfaction as her mouth gaped open. But she was quick to rally, gathering up her ammunition and flinging her next assault across the room. 'How are you going to prove that after three decades?'

I really hoped I wouldn't have to.

CHAPTER THIRTY-EIGHT

The next morning, I cooked scrambled eggs for Jamie. I made toast without the crusts for Izzy. And I held myself together, pulling desperately on the fraying threads of my life to stay upright. In the end, we didn't need to contact the school because I'd had a call from the headmaster at seven-thirty that morning, asking me to bring Jamie to his office for nine-thirty.

'Will the McAllisters be there?'

'You'll be spoken to separately.'

My eyes were prickly through lack of sleep. I hadn't seen Mark that morning but I was conscious of him moving about, getting in the shower, the airing cupboard door opening and closing.

Mark hadn't said a single thing to me when we got home. He'd driven, extra-carefully, threading the steering wheel through his hands like a seventeen-year-old out in his parents' Volvo for the first time. With his eyes fixed on the road, he refused to acknowledge that I was pleading with him. He went upstairs as soon as we got through the door, leaving me to check on a subdued Jamie.

'Is Sean furious, Mum?'

'I think Katya's more upset than Sean. But it will all seem different in the morning.'

'Where's Dad?'

'He's already gone to bed – his stomach was hurting.'

'Does he hate me, Mum?'

'Of course he doesn't. We're both a bit shocked but we don't hate you. Quite the opposite.' Jamie's misdemeanour was looking negligible compared with my lifetime of messing up. 'Off to sleep now. Love you.'

I couldn't hug him. Any human contact would unravel me. I couldn't wait to get out of his bedroom before someone else realised I wasn't who they thought I was. He was looking to me to be strong, right at the moment when the entire foundations of my life were juddering like the final cycle of a washing machine.

I crept down the landing and peered round our bedroom door. The light was off and Mark was huddled in a heap under the duvet. I put my hand on his shoulder. 'Can we talk?'

'Not now. Tomorrow.' He sounded croaky, as though he was having trouble getting enough air into his lungs.

'Please.'

'No. Piss off, Lydia. Just fuck off. I can't talk to you now.' There was something in his voice, something so hard and unforgiving, that I didn't argue. I shuffled off to the spare room, lying flat on my back on the unfamiliar mattress without the slight dip to one side where Mark's body usually resided. My mind was a labyrinth of self-loathing, flitting between then and now, burrowing among the secrets, the wrong turns, the lies. Regret burnt through me, searing through my body with the familiarity of a well-trodden pathway: lightly covered with brambles and bracken but easily navigated if you knew where to look.

And now, when our marriage was more fragile, more vulnerable than it had ever been, we needed to be united for Jamie.

I was used to getting through things, to finding a face and squeezing my real feelings down to nothing, like spinach wrung dry. But today, over breakfast, with both of my children looking to me to make it right, I was having to remind myself how to move. Giving a semblance of capability for Jamie required so much energy that it was taking me all my time to propel myself between the fridge and kettle. Mark came in, shifting the atmosphere in the kitchen. Whatever there was to play out between us had to wait.

If it could.

I hoped his love for Jamie would surpass his disdain for me. I glanced round. A rush of affection and gratitude stung my eyes, making it harder to seal in my tears. He'd automatically put on a suit and tie without even knowing that we'd been officially summoned. Mark hated formality, 'poncing about all tuckered up' and I loved him for doing his best to look like a responsible parent without me having to prompt him.

He didn't acknowledge me at all. He walked over to Jamie, who was pushing scrambled egg about his plate, put his hand on his shoulder and said, 'You all right?'

'Do you think they'll expel me?'

Jamie stared up at Mark with such trust that I had to look away.

'I don't know, but Mum and I will do what we can.'

Only the strongest effort of will stopped me crying at hearing Mark presenting us as a team.

I filled him in on the phone call, hearing the nerves jangling in my voice as I spoke. He nodded. I put a coffee down in front of him. The kids disappeared to clean their teeth. 'Mark.'

'Not now, Lydia.' He pushed his mug away. 'I'll wait in the car.'

I'd completely forgotten that there was a fundraising committee powwow that morning. As Mark and I got out of the car with Jamie, Terri and Melanie were just heading into the 'abomination of a meeting centre' as Melanie liked to call it, owing to the fact that the only coffee available came out of a jar rather than a grinder. It was a measure of the speed of bad news that Melanie contented herself with a sucked-in 'Under the circumstances, I thought I'd chair in your absence.' For all I cared at that moment she could cover herself in golden syrup and roll butt-naked in a basket of raffle tickets.

Terri smiled sympathetically and boomed, 'Bloody bad luck, Jamie. If Eleanor had stuck a picture of her fandango in a frame and hung it in the Tate on the end of a fairy wand, no one would have batted an eyelid.'

She'd always have a special place in my heart for that spectacularly un-PC comment.

On the other hand, Sonia, the headmaster's secretary, would no longer be safe on the streets when I was out on a dark night. She was one of those women who smiled and acted all deferential but couldn't quite stop her face quirking out a judgment. So although she was doing that whole soft-voiced 'If you'd like to go through, Mr and Mrs Rushford, and you, Jamie,' her eyebrows were up in her hairline delivering their 'Well, I never' message.

The headmaster leaned over his desk to shake hands. He indicated that we should sit. I felt as though I'd time-travelled backwards. I could picture the red and green of the swirly carpet in my headmaster's office. The slight squeak of the chair as I fidgeted about. My mother, refusing to accept that I'd been to blame and hissing about 'that delinquent Sean McAllister' while the headmaster explained that he had no option but to expel me.

I reached out for Jamie's hand. I didn't care that he was sixteen and the headmaster, and Mark too, would probably think he was way too old to hold hands with his mum. He was not going to feel alone, ashamed or isolated as long as I was still sucking in air.

The headmaster waffled on about hormones, adolescence, the dangers of the internet – which if I was totally honest, was just a more monotone version of the sort of thing I said to Jamie every time I saw him on Facebook. I wanted to speed him up and shout, 'Just get on with it!' I liked my bad news delivered quickly, not strung out for maximum suffering for all.

'However, we pride ourselves at Eastington House on not having knee-jerk reactions to incidents inside, or indeed, outside the school. Therefore, we've decided to talk to the whole of the fifth year about this topic but not to take any further action regarding

Jamie. Or indeed Eleanor. So, Jamie, the best thing is that you get off to your lessons straight after this meeting.'

Jamie let go of my hand and wiped his palm on his trousers.

The headmaster couldn't quite let us escape without some pompous little dig. 'I would advise, however, as parents, that perhaps you monitor your children's technology more closely. Although I do understand that it is difficult to police, especially when you both work.'

Relief mingled with the urge to say, 'If you didn't keep putting up your fees, I might be able to work a bit less and devote my whole bloody day to spying on my son.'

I tried to catch Mark's eye for a complicit 'what a twit' smile, but the way he marched out into the corridor rather than standing back to let me through first reminded me that complicity might well be a thing of the past.

CHAPTER THIRTY-NINE

Mark turned on the car radio after a silence so thick, I opened the window just to breathe, to hear the noise of other people with normal, uncomplicated lives. A woman with a buggy stopped on the pavement as we drove past, pecked the man she'd been walking with on the lips and pushed on as he waved, smiled and headed off in a different direction. The ordinary moments that make up an ordinary life of togetherness.

I couldn't work out what Mark was thinking. I didn't know whether he was estimating how many suitcases and car journeys it would take to move out all of his stuff – or mine – or whether he was calculating how many strands of dishonesty we would have to unplait and brush out before there'd be any hope of recovery.

I tried to engage with him, to ask him what he thought about the meeting.

His eyes didn't waver from the road. 'I think he's been lucky. Hopefully he'll buck his ideas up a bit now.'

It was on the tip of my tongue to say, 'And now we've got through that, what about us?' But I couldn't. I shied away from asking a question I really did not want to know the answer to.

When we got home, Mark went straight upstairs. Part of me wanted to go up after him, force him to talk to me. The prospect of what I might hear filled me such sick-making dread that instead, I hovered downstairs, wiping the work surfaces, putting the milk away, tucking the cereal bag back into the box and listening, listening all the time for the telltale sound of the attic door squeaking open and the rumble of suitcase wheels. At every creak, a big chill engulfed me.

The doorbell rang. Just when I thought my day had reached rock bottom, my mother stood there, handbag in the crook of her elbow. 'Are you ready?'

'What for?'

She clicked her tongue. 'To come with me to buy shoes for Tara's wedding.'

'Oh god. I'd forgotten all about that. I've had a bit of a morning.' I stopped speaking before my voice crumbled away.

'You really do need to organise yourself, Lydia. Where's that diary I bought you for Christmas? If you wrote everything down, you'd keep on top of it all a bit better.'

I nodded, the quickest way to cut off the oxygen to that conversation.

'Go and get ready then.'

'This might not be a good day for looking for shoes. I've got quite a lot of things going on.'

I wasn't sure what was worse, hanging around the house with this awful paralysing fright squeezing my vital organs until I felt as though my intestines might suddenly shoot out of my mouth, or holding myself together under my mother's scrutiny.

'You've always got a lot going on. You will insist on stretching yourself so thinly, taking on too much work. Now Mark's kitchen business is doing better, you need to take a bit of a backseat and prioritise the family.'

I couldn't seem to organise the words, 'No. Sorry. Today is definitely not a day for debates about kitten heels and wide fittings,' into a sentence. Instead, I finished putting the Weetabix back in the cupboard, surreptitiously scraping the crumbs off the worktop into the palm of my hand, conscious of my mother's eyes sweeping round in a *How Clean Is Your House?* judgment.

'I'll get my bag.'

As I walked upstairs, Mark was coming down. 'I'm just popping out with my mother.' The words stuttered out of me, wholly inadequate. I couldn't bring myself to finish it off with 'She wants to buy a pair of shoes.' I did, however, want to throw my arms around him and beg him not to pack his pants while I was away. Images of wire coat hangers jangling in an empty wardrobe flashed through my mind.

'Nice to see you've got your priorities right.'

Little bits of my heart were scattering about all over the place.

'What do you want me to do? Tell her the truth? Because if that is what you want, I'm on my way. Just tell me what I can do to make it better.'

He leaned towards me. 'I want you never to have done what you did.' He pushed past me, and I heard the front door slam.

It was hard to believe that three months ago, Sally Southport had been dead and buried and my mum was twittering with delight because I'd finally proved to her I was respectable, the pillar of society, chair of the fundraising committee. Now Sally Southport had screwed up again for a second time.

I could hear my mother moving things around on the work surface downstairs. God forbid a bottle of olive oil should loiter randomly in the middle rather standing to attention against the wall. Life couldn't always be lined up. I grabbed my things and raced back downstairs. She bustled out to the car with me. 'Mark was in a bit of hurry this morning. Barely said hello. Busy, is he?'

I grunted out a non-committal 'Hmm.' I'd spent my whole life managing her reactions, protecting my dad, never feeling that I had a right to be upset about anything myself. Today, I could only take responsibility for my own feelings. For once, everyone else would have to be accountable for their own happiness. Or misery, if necessary.

My mother adjusted the seat. She liked to sit completely upright as though her collar was caught on a coat peg. She'd probably combust if she ever caught sight of Jamie slouching so low over his computer, it was a wonder that he didn't have QWERTY stamped on his forehead.

I concentrated on the traffic. I was having to think about how to get to the car park, a route I'd taken so many times before.

My mother kept tutting as I hesitated at the roundabouts, tapping her nails on the car window to indicate which turning I should take.

'Are you going to buy some new shoes as well? A bit of heel would suit you.'

I ignored her. She didn't require an answer anyway: it wasn't a question, it was a criticism. While I negotiated the tiny spaces in the car park, she opened her purse and counted out the exact change for ticket machine. Enough for one hour. Good. She obviously wasn't intending to have lunch with me. I couldn't have eaten anything anyway. My stomach felt sour, as though I'd feasted on crab apples.

Once we were in the shoe shop, my mother kept picking up silly little pointy-heeled things and poking them at me. I managed a calm 'I'm already sorted. You concentrate on finding a pair for the wedding.'

'Darling, I think you're letting Mark down by taking such a pragmatic approach to dressing. Every man likes a bit of femininity in his wife.'

I drifted off to look at the winter boots, acutely aware of the shop assistants giving me the once-over to see this great butch failure of a wife. Forty-three. Forty-bloody-three-years-old. Here I was, being talked down to by my mother while my husband was probably zipping up his holdall and working out what would be a fair amount to take out of the joint bank account. The boots blurred before my eyes, the domain of people who had headspace to think about what might stop them getting chilblains during a cold snap, people whose lives weren't about to go skidding down the hill like an overturned jar of marbles.

But there was no escaping my mother on a mission. She jabbed a shoe with a ridiculous peep toe in my direction. 'These. They'd go well with that suit you're wearing to Tara's wedding.'

She'd blame me for wearing them when I was sporting a bunion three months down the line. In a supreme attempt to keep the peace, I said, 'Izzy would love them. I like something a bit sturdier.'

My mother, instead of receiving the peacekeeping gesture and whipping out her own white dove, produced a little hand grenade to liven up the proceedings. 'I was just thinking the other day that she's looked a bit tarty lately. All that eyeshadow and mascara. You need to keep an eye on that.'

My lethargy honed itself into something sharp enough to etch the finest diamond. I didn't let her get as far as 'We don't want history repeating itself'.

'Don't you dare. Don't you dare.' All the adrenaline that I'd been suppressing, the pent-up terror squeezing my stomach, the self-loathing jolting into my thoughts burst out from their hiding places and into the bright lights that had been designed to showcase the sparkly sandals, not illuminate the raw and bleeding beasts of family history. To the astonishment of the clientele weighing up the pros and cons of Hush Puppies, I snatched the shoe from my mother's bony little hand and began prodding her with it. She looked like an affronted goose to start with, all swively-necked and pecky, until I really got going.

'Don't even think about criticising Izzy. She's brilliant. As far as I'm concerned, she can speak back to me, be rude if she wants to, without wondering – *ever* – whether I would have been happier if she'd never been born. She won't need to ask herself whether it's okay to be her, just as she is. When she makes mistakes, I won't talk about them for the next thirty years. I'll open my arms, suck her in and tell her that sometimes we all fuck up and that I will always, always love her, whatever she does. Even if she screws the entire rugby A, B and C team at Eastington House and hangs her knickers from the flagpole.'

Swearing at my mother was as liberating as flinging off an underwired bra that's been digging into your ribcage all day. I was aware of faces turning towards me and away from me as though I'd wandered in from under the railway bridge waving my can of Strongbow cider and shouting about how I used to be a famous ballet dancer.

My mum was goggle-eyed. She'd probably have looked less surprised if her vacuum cleaner had suddenly come to life and started attacking her. A tiny corner of my mind registered the little lines around her mouth, the eyeshadow creasing into her crêpey lids, the grey that had changed the texture of her hair. But the hard kernel in me had split open, the poisonous triffid inside bursting forth: selfish, entitled and oblivious.

Out of the corner of my eye, I saw all the teenage shop assistants scattering to the stairs leading to the stock room. Their mothers would be grateful to me for the rest of their lives. They would never even reach the lower echelons of the ranks of 'so embarrassing' again. One of them shouted up the stairs, 'Sheila! Sheila!'

I didn't wait to see poor Sheila emerge, trying to grasp how a day cataloguing brogues and boat shoes had turned into this. With a brief glance around the shop to see if I actually knew anyone, I marched out, head held high, feeling my euphoria seep away before I reached the first corner.

CHAPTER FORTY

I replayed my shoe shop diatribe as I drove home, closing my eyes in a cringe. My dad would be so upset that I'd left my mother stranded.

'In this family, we look out for each other.'

I'd always wanted to argue that my mother never seemed to be looking out for me, though she had an eagle eye on what the neighbours thought. Then I'd remind myself what Dad had suffered on my behalf and vow never to bring it up.

My stomach fizzed with acidity, which brought to mind my Gaviscon days when I was pregnant with Izzy. My naïvety back then was astounding. I'd actually allowed myself several moments of smug relief that the girl 'who'd done bad' had managed to end up married with two children. The perfect family.

As I parked on the drive, I released my grip on the steering wheel. I realised I'd been braced for an empty space where Mark's car had been. What if he just hadn't got round to leaving yet? I turned the key in the door and pushed it, feeling resistance on the other side. My face crumpled, great whirls of desperation surging through me. Were they suitcases blocking the door? My god, Mark really was going. But the resistance suddenly gave and I fell inside to be greeted by Mabel, sniffing and wagging, yawning in a cartoon manner that suggested she'd been on a twenty-mile rabbit hunt rather than an extended sleep as a door stop.

Mark wasn't in the kitchen but the house didn't have that wallowy feel, the gaping emptiness of absence. I walked quietly upstairs, not sure whether I wanted him to know I was home or not. He was in the study, sitting at the desk, head bent over something. Typical Mark. Start with the practicalities like the bank statements and deal with the emotions later. I leaned against the doorjamb.

'Any word from Jamie?'

He swivelled round in the chair. 'No, all quiet.' There was nothing inviting about his tone.

I squinted to see what he had in his hand.

He indicated a pile of photos: Izzy with her white-blonde hair as a toddler, Jamie with his goofy front teeth. 'Just trying to work out where I messed up. When the moment was that you decided that your vows didn't mean anything anymore.'

I couldn't hold on then. I ran over and kneeled on the floor in front of him. 'You didn't make it go wrong. I did. Too many lies. Or too many omissions. I couldn't keep the lid on it anymore. I couldn't tell you. I could only tell a stranger.'

Mark flinched. 'You could have had counselling. You didn't need to go and shag someone else, for god's sake. You went to Italy with him. And I was happy that you'd found him. Thought he'd take care of you and your mother. So bloody naïve.'

The anguish in his voice sliced through me like a hundred tiny paper cuts. I'd hardly ever heard Mark use bad language. It was one of the many things that made him acceptable to my mother.

He picked up some photos of him and the kids at Winkworth Arboretum a few autumns ago, before the children had blurred into teenagers. I wasn't in any of them, always behind the camera. He pointed to Jamie. 'Do you remember that squirrel falling out of the tree and scaring him half to death? We were happy that day. Or were you just going through the motions, even then?'

I had been happy. Of course I had. But it had always felt like happiness with an expiry date, a smudged 'best before' stamp that no one could read. I looked down at Jamie's face, flushed with cold air and excitement. What if Jamie had had sex with Eleanor? What if Katya carried out her threat to go to the police? I might be hovering on the fruitcake margins myself but Katya was as unhinged as a barn door in a hurricane.

Mark looked down at me, his eyes serious. 'Tell me it wasn't all a lie. That some of it was real.'

'It was *all* real! My love for the kids, for you, it was *all* real. It's just that in the beginning, you know, back then, my mother forbade me to breathe a word about it, and over time, I really thought I'd begun a new life; I believed that I could put that shame and upset behind me. Then Sean turned up and I was just so frightened the whole time.'

Mark shook his head. 'You must have felt so alone. It makes me feel really horrible that you didn't trust me.' His voice dropped. 'And now it's too late.'

I grabbed his knee. 'No. Don't say that. I should have trusted you. I should never have done what I did. Never. But don't let that overshadow what we still have.'

Leaps of terror were bounding through me as though my heart was free-falling into an uncertain future.

'Don't do anything now. Please don't. Don't stay for me but stay for the children, just until we get through all this Eleanor/ Jamie stuff. Then you can make your mind up.'

I wanted to cling to him, stop him getting up from his chair even though he was showing no signs of moving.

'I'm not going anywhere.'

I felt something steady, the tipping and shuttling inside me easing into something horizontal. 'Ever?'

'That I don't know.'

Mark didn't meet my eye, as though he couldn't quite believe that the wife he thought was so ordinary, had turned out to be such a bag of trouble. 'I won't do anything until I know Jamie's okay.'

The contrast between Mark and Tomaso, the man I'd kidded myself I could be so open with, was so huge that I'd never be able to trust my judgment on anything ever again.

'Thank you.' I opened my mouth to try to find an explanation when there wasn't one. Or at least, not one that could ever come close to justifying what I'd done to this man, this man who loved his children as much as I did. That alone was an incredibly good reason to ring fence the whole family with pitchers of boiling oil against weaselly imitations and their promises of excitement and adventure.

'I'm so, so sorry.'

I don't think I'd ever managed to gather such intense regret and sentiment into an apology. It was as though I'd herded my words into a test tube then distilled them over a Bunsen burner into the one sentence that defined my emotions.

Mark studied me, acknowledging he'd heard with the slightest nod.

I wanted him to forgive me. My mother's favourite phrase, 'No harm in wanting' rang in my ears. But forgiveness seemed far from his agenda. The way he shrank away from me every time I leaned towards him chilled me. He'd always been the tactile one, not me. Now I craved his touch so absolutely that my skin felt as though it was lifting up and stretching towards him. My mother's second comforting mantra hustled into my misery: 'You reap what you sow.'

I glanced at my watch, defeated. 'I'll go and pick the kids up.'

Mark got to his feet. 'I'm coming with you, just in case there's any trouble from Katya.'

Anger-laden car silence was so much better than will-I-won't-I-come-home-to-an-empty-house fear.

CHAPTER FORTY-ONE

I'd always imagined that the unravelling of life would be a sudden storm of events, followed by quick decisions and swift, sharp ultimatums. Instead, over the next few weeks, my marriage turned into a slow puncture: a wheezing out of energy, a scraping along with less commitment to going in the right direction but not quite buggered enough to merit a full call-out of the RAC.

We still sat down to eat as a family. Mark carried on with the Groundhog Day of telling Izzy to stop picking at her vegetables and just 'get on with it'. I continued to nag Jamie about getting to bed at a decent hour. We both pulled our weight on the homework front, Mark with Maths and Science, me with languages and Art. Jamie seemed to have settled back into school. I see-sawed between a detailed investigation about whether he was still going out with Eleanor and sticking my head into the deepest sandpit I could find. Certainly, he was still spending a lifetime with the hairdryer and gel every morning, in a cloud of deodorant that enveloped the bathroom like a spring mist.

Unlike my mother, who would have accepted 'I'm fine' if my leg had been hanging off as long as I didn't bleed on the rug, I did try and keep those elusive channels of communication open. Most of the time, I felt as though I was talking to everyone through an empty cardboard tube, muffled and distorted.

Worst of all was when I'd put out my hand to touch Mark when we were in bed at night and he'd just lie there like a phone mast, not shrugging me off but not relaxing into me either.

One thing that we had agreed on very quickly, in a super-polite, 'No, no, you speak first' discussion was that, before Katya put her own spin on it, we had to tell the children about my own history so it didn't reach them via Eleanor and Chinese whispers. But of course, it wasn't as simple as me just cracking open the secrets over spaghetti bolognese. The story wound its way like ivy round Dad and Sean.

We decided to invite Dad over for the great unveiling of 'the thing that must never be spoken of'. My mother was still waiting for an apology for my behaviour, which worked to my advantage in a way she couldn't possibly imagine. Without the drip-feed of her criticism eroding me, I was able to think without examining my actions through my mother's looking glass. Cracked and broken though I might have been, my reactions were just that – spontaneous responses rather than a consideration of how to act. In fact, despite everything, small suggestions of self-belief were pushing through, so much so that I toyed with the idea of inviting Sean – who, given the *entente uncordiale* in my house, was starting to look like less of an enemy and more of an ally.

Sean would have helped the children see that this person they called Mum, the person without any feelings, who was just there, roboting through life, producing food, clean clothes and homework help, was human, with an ability to make hideous mistakes and hopefully, a capacity to repair them.

But when a long list of 'snagging issues' in the kitchens Mark had fitted arrived by recorded delivery, purporting to be from Sean but with the hallmarks of Katya all over it, I knew better than to suggest it.

On the day, Dad came to dinner so much more like his old self, with his stinky beef sticks for Mabel in one pocket and a clutch of pound coins for the kids in the other. I got as far as explaining to the kids we had something important to tell them before Dad put out his hand and said, 'Lydia, if you don't mind, I'd like to tell the story.'

And tell the story he did, slightly airbrushing the truth about me, while, if not darkening, certainly pulling no punches when it came to claiming responsibility for his part in the proceedings. As he spoke, I could see that putting the whole sorry tale out there for judgment was giving him strength rather than feeding his fear.

Izzy's face was a picture – a whirlpool of emotions shifting across her features like the reflections in a fast-flowing stream. Her granddad, the jovial toffee-giver, was taking on a different dimension before her eyes. Jamie's lips twitched with amusement when Dad cleared his throat and said, 'I really did go a bit overboard in teaching the poor chap a lesson. I'd never hit anyone before and I don't think I knew my own strength.' The more the details of the past made contact with air rather than being sealed away in the dungeons of family history, the less huge and traumatic it sounded.

All of them appeared to be understanding things about me, which seemed odd, given that I wasn't any different from the person I'd been the day before. Jamie said, 'That's why you'll never get in the photo.' He almost laughed, then decided against it. We weren't anywhere near finding the latest photo-related debacle funny. He did pull a bit of a face when it dawned on him that Eleanor's dad had seen me naked.

'So you showed your bits to Sean?'

'Well, not in the same way that people of your generation take photos of each other, no.' I blushed. I hoped I'd made it sound arty rather than sordid. I wasn't the sort of mother who left the bathroom door unlocked. I looked away, avoiding everyone's eye, but especially Mark's. A quick glance at his face told me that he wasn't thinking about Sean, but about Tomaso.

Jamie seemed quite fascinated by the naked element of the story. 'Does Katya know?'

I nodded, trying not to think about her little face twisted with rage. Or the threats she'd made to Jamie.

'Can I tell Eleanor?'

'I think that's up to her mum and dad really.' I detested the idea that the little madam would be all agog at my own lack of propriety – with her father. Some part of my brain was managing to store away the confirmation that Jamie and Eleanor were still speaking. 'Has Eleanor mentioned anything about how her parents are?'

'What do you mean?'

'Whether they're getting on all right?'

Jamie shrugged. 'She did say her mum was always shouting at her dad.'

'Do you know what over?' I still woke up in the night and top of the list of worries barking for attention was whether Jamie had slept with Eleanor and whether Katya would involve the police if he had.

Jamie wrinkled his nose, indicating that interest in other people beyond a passing curiosity in whether they were still alive or not was for losers. I couldn't sit there one moment longer. There wasn't one single thread of my life that didn't have complications hanging off it like a litter of suckling puppies.

'Right, I'm shattered. I think it's an early night for everyone.' I got up, mustering my last dregs of energy to shoo the kids upstairs.

I stood with my dad in the hallway. I hugged him, feeling the sharp edges of his shoulder blades through his shirt. He stood back, holding me by the arms. 'Are you okay? I suppose this has stirred up a lot of bad memories for you.'

My eyes stung with suppressed tears. 'There are lots of things going on, Dad. Mark and I aren't in a good place right now.'

Panic shot through me as though I might have delivered some knowledge Dad wouldn't be able to handle, that would send him spiralling off into that vacant world of staring into space and time-delay responses.

But he looked me straight in the eye. 'Lydia. He's a good man. You're a great wife and brilliant mother. Find a way through this. Talk to each other. We should all have done more of that.'

I nodded.

'You need to make it up with your mother. She did what she thought was best, you know. They were different times back then. Nowadays anything goes – you've only got to look at the telly, no one's shocked by anything anymore.

I shook my head. 'I don't think it's that different, Dad.'

He raised an eyebrow but I had no appetite left for explanations.

CHAPTER FORTY-TWO

As the autumn term drew to an end, with Christmas a couple of weeks away, it dawned on me that Mark was probably just staying until the festivities were over, clinging on for one last family tableau of togetherness. One day soon, I'd have to pose the question. I'd tried to be open, to make it easy for him to ask me anything. But he'd turned in on himself. Apart from occasional bursts of rage over Mabel licking plates in the dishwasher, the kids finishing the bread without bothering to get any more out of the freezer and an uncharacteristic bellow at a delivery boy who chucked a package over our wall, it was like living with a grudge-harbouring ghost.

'Is there anything you want to know that might help us work through this?' The words sounded all wrong, so alien for our marriage. Working through had never been a strategy for our relationship in the same way that ignoring or brushing under the carpet had. We'd managed pretty well for eighteen years. But there was no more ignoring to be done. The issues were out there, raw and exposed, like jagged wounds that could squeal under a dose of TCP and stand half a chance of healing or be left untreated to fester into further infection.

One morning, with Mark dressing with his back to me, a retracted image of unhappiness, I could stand it no longer. 'Mark. We can't go on like this. I can't bear to see you so unhappy, knowing that I've caused it. I know the kids haven't picked up on anything yet but they're not stupid. If you really can't stand to stay with me, then we need to make plans.'

As an ultimatum, it would have been quite effective if I hadn't stood there with a torrent of tears pouring out of me.

Mark put his hand on my shoulder. 'Lyddie. Lyddie. Don't cry. Please don't cry. I'm sorry. I wish I could just let it go, get over it, move on or whatever I should be doing. But I can't. Every time I even hear the word 'Italy', I feel sick. I keep thinking about you with that bloke. I'm not sure I can get past that. I just feel so ridiculous, so stupid that our entire life has been one big farce.'

'No, that's just not true.'

His response, 'That's not what it feels like to me,' slipped out into the bedroom and curled, coldly, around my heart.

The day the kids broke up from school for Christmas, Mark popped home from the shop just before pickup. There was something decisive about him. Hope flared in me. He looked lighter of spirit, younger than the careworn man who'd been moving round the house as though he wanted to disappear into the walls.

'It's really quiet in the shop so I'm going to close early for Christmas and head off for a few days.'

'Where?'

'I don't know yet.'

Alarm roared through me. 'Are you coming back for Christmas? What about Tara's wedding on the twenty-third?'

'I don't know whether I can stomach a wedding.' He laughed, a sound that seemed to call into question the idea that laughter was something joyful and spontaneous.

I wanted to insist, to tell him that he had to come, that I couldn't face everyone on my own. Not my brother, mother or anyone at all. But I had no right to insist on anything. 'The kids will be devastated if you're not here for Christmas.'

I heard myself keeping my voice neutral, non-accusatory, sticking to the facts like a proper grown-up. I wanted to fly at him, snatch up my brush from the dressing table and batter him about the head with it, spike some sense into us, into our marriage.

'I will be here for Christmas.' Mark's measured tone matched mine, cocooning within its words the unspoken threat that he might not stay beyond that.

Was this what a marriage falling apart looked like? Clipped, calm sentences batting about a bedroom while the whole family edifice was tumbling off a cliff, chunks of unity shearing off in all directions and plunging down a jagged rock face into a swell of oblivion?

I stood. I watched. The careful folding up of the T-shirts. The tucking of socks into shoes. The packing got quicker, more slapdash, as though he just needed to be gone. I heard the squeak of the bathroom cabinet opening and closing. The rustle of the razor packet. The snap of the toothbrush charger coming out of the socket. The sounds of leaving.

He stood opposite me with a holdall over his shoulder. 'Tell Jamie and Izzy I've had to go away for work.'

I nodded.

Feeding that lie into Izzy at pickup proved to be a doddle as she was far more distraught about not being invited to a party that *everyone* was going to than Mark's whereabouts.

Jamie, on the other hand, sat morosely in the front seat.

'Aren't you happy it's the holidays? I thought you were desperate to break up.'

He turned to me. 'Katya wants to go to the police. She's told Eleanor she'll get me arrested for having sex with a minor.'

'What?'

I swerved round an old man on his bike, who almost met his maker prematurely. Maybe Jamie and I could share a lawyer.

Jamie muttered, 'For fuck's sake,' under his breath. For fuck's sake indeed.

'When we get home, you can start by telling me the truth and we'll take it from there.'

I looked in the rear-view mirror to see if Izzy was listening but she'd taken refuge in her phone, Instagramming or Snapchatting or some other hideous thing that Mark had argued she should be allowed to have because that was how children communicated these days. I'd fought him over it, never telling him why I felt so strongly. I'd trotted out all the arguments about damaging a developing brain, the kids not having the maturity to understand that pictures were somewhere on the internet forever, peer pressure to post stupid things.

Now he knew.

But back then, it had been three against one, a trendy little team taking on the pterodactyl and in the end, they'd worn me down. As it happened, I'd been proved right.

Now, all the hate I'd once felt for Sean had transferred itself to Katya. But the anger I'd aimed at Sean looked like watered-down orange squash versus the surging one-hundred-per-cent-proof absinthe of evil I harboured towards Katya. She wanted to have a pop at my son.

She would regret that.

When we got home, Izzy dashed upstairs to FaceTime the girls she'd been sitting next to all day at school. I managed to stop myself shouting at Jamie to 'sit down right now and tell me what's bloody well been going on', when he insisted on getting changed first. Instead, I made myself a cup of tea, feeling my emotions ratcheting up cog by cog. One thing I was crystal clear about was that Katya was not going to get my son a police record to blight his life.

Before his life had even started.

I washed up the pan I'd used for scrambled eggs that morning, cursing myself. I'd had my eye on the wrong things. A bit less worry about whether Jamie was getting enough protein and fibre and a bit more about his girlfriend hovering over a smart phone with her pants down would have been a more productive use of my time. There was so much fury pulsing through my body, I half-expected to look down and see the washing-up water bubbling up like a witch's cauldron. But it was just me, in my Marigolds, figuring out how I was going to stop Katya before another McAllister-related disaster blew my family apart.

I'd defended Sean all those years ago. A memory of a policewoman sitting opposite me, all soft-voiced and 'you can tell me anything' speared into my mind, as sharp as glass. I'd sat there, silent. Even when she'd asked me if there was anything at all she should know that could help my dad, I bound my knowledge to me, swaddling it in layers of obstinacy. I wasn't sorry Sean had a photo of us naked. I was sorry we'd been found out; mortified that Dad, the police, a whole array of people had seen me on a bed with everything on display. But I still knew, clung onto the fact, that Sean loved me.

He made my ordinary life extraordinary.

When I was with him, I wasn't the girl whose mother wouldn't let her wear high heels, who had to leave parties at eleven-fifteen instead of midnight, who had to scrub her black eyeliner off before she went home. I was a girl to be envied. Someone, who, under the umbrella of Sean's attention, had become fascinating and intriguing – and capable of snaring the boy every girl wanted. Sean loved quirky old me. When he could have had any one of those girls with their flicky hair and ready smiles. I wasn't going to get him in trouble by telling that policewoman I'd had sex with him.

And I certainly couldn't risk my mother finding out.

I glanced up as Jamie came in. 'Sit down, lovey.'

He slumped in a chair and immediately started scratching at something on the table – probably a lump of dried-on porridge. Currently, it was as much as I could do to ensure no one had to wear the same pants and socks for two days in a row.

I put my hand on his shoulder. 'Truth time. Did you have sex with Eleanor?'

No hesitation. 'Yes.'

My stomach felt as though it was on a ferry in the Bay of Biscay in a gale. I steadied myself on the back of the chair.

'How does Katya know?'

'She went through Eleanor's school bag and found her pills.'

'How did Eleanor get the pill? She's only fifteen.'

Jamie wrestled to take the 'Don't be an idiot' look off his face. 'We ordered them on the internet.' He put his head in his hands. 'I didn't want her to get pregnant. We tried to be really careful.'

I wished their care had extended to flushing the pills down the loo the second the shit had hit the fan.

Jamie looked up. 'Do you think I'll go to prison like granddad?'

'No. No!' I took a deep breath to get my voice into something more solid than a scream. 'No, of course you won't. I won't let that happen.'

I still wanted to pretend I could make everything all right. My kids weren't going to sit in their rooms staring into the mirror, wondering whether running away would be an option, what it would be like to have their faces on a 'Missing' poster.

I dragged myself back to the present.

Jamie stood up. 'Can I have a hug?' he said.

I held him close, marvelling at how that little boy who'd lain on the rug lining up his cars with absolute precision, was now so much taller than me. 'I'll talk to Katya.'

Jamie pulled away. 'Do you think that will help, Mum? Only Eleanor says she hates you.'

'I think Katya is probably one of those people who exaggerates for effect. I doubt that she really wants to go to the police. It would be a real ordeal for Eleanor, too. Perhaps I'll have a chat with Sean. He seems a bit more reasonable.'

Sean McAllister. The boy who hadn't even bothered to say goodbye when I moved away was now the man who could help me save my son.

CHAPTER FORTY-THREE

I spent the evening and the early hours of the morning calling Mark. Repeatedly. I imagined him holed up in a hotel some- where, watching my number flash up on his phone. I pictured him turning away, realising that he didn't care whether he ever spoke to me again. But this wasn't about us. This was about keeping Jamie out of trouble with the police. I cursed the fact that Jamie had already had his sixteenth birthday in September. I looked at the class list to see when Eleanor was sixteen. Of course she was an August baby, one of the youngest in the year. Two bloody weeks later, she would have been in the year below, not even on Jamie's radar.

In between trying to contact Mark, I Googled laws governing sex and the under-sixteens. I'd started off thinking sex between two consenting teenagers might somehow be more permissible these days but in the end, it was like Googling a headache and convincing yourself that you had a brain tumour. The more I read, the more frightened I became that Jamie was looking at five years in a young offenders' institution. What if Eleanor turned against Jamie and said she hadn't consented?

As much as my brain picked away, scouring for alternative ways to protect Jamie against Katya's accusations, I kept returning to a single unpalatable option. I went back to Google and began to type, screwing up my eyes before pressing return, bracing myself for what I hoped and dreaded I'd find.

I tried Mark again. I left yet another message on his voicemail, not even bothering to contain my distress, which fear was turning to anger: 'I know you're pissed off with me and you have every right to be but you can't just walk out of the kids' lives when they need you,' accompanied by a desperate sob.

At three in the morning, I took myself off to bed.

I lay there in the dark, my eyes flicking over the shadows and shapes in the room, seeing bogeymen in every dressing gown and armchair. My mind darted between possibilities. Was it better to talk to Sean first, or just present Katya with a *fait accompli*? I needed to move quickly before she involved the police. I was going to have to make this big decision, carry out this undoable act without speaking to Mark. It couldn't wait.

I pushed my face into his pillow, breathing in the smell of his hair and the slight fragrance of Issey Miyake that lingered there. Now it came to it, I didn't want revenge on Sean. But I'd promised Jamie I'd make it right.

I wished I didn't have to make it wrong for someone else.

On Saturday morning, when Mabel dived Scooby Doo-like onto the bed, I had to work hard to wake up. She jumped about madly, straining to lick me as I took refuge under the duvet. I tried to stop thoughts bouncing round my brain – veering from Jamie going to prison, to where Mark was, round to Sean, Katya and the next instalment of this particular horror story.

Mabel was quite a good distraction. It was impossible to focus on anything when her great raspy tongue was flapping towards its target. She picked up my bra and scarpered off down the landing, shaking it like a rabbit whose neck she wanted to snap. I ran after her, which thrilled her. She stood at the top of the stairs, ready to bound in either direction, depending on whether she thought a telling-off or a cuddle might be coming her way.

In the end, she chose a dash down the stairs in a manner which I could only describe as foolhardy, smashing right into Jamie who was carrying a huge bowl of Rice Krispies up to his room, now splattered all over his bare chest and pyjama bottoms.

'Shitting hell, Mabel, you bloody dog!'

I raised my eyebrows at the swearing but really, I couldn't have agreed more.

'What?' Jamie was all aggressive. I recognised the way his fear worked. Like mine, it ran in tandem with anger.

'Language, Jamie.' For all I gave a hoot about his swearing right now, I could have said, 'Go and have a shower,' with more conviction.

'Shit isn't swearing. Fuck is swearing.'

My mother would have disagreed, but shit, fuck or otherwise, a few swear words weren't going to change my world. In fact, there was a strong possibility I was going to hear more of them shortly.

My voicemails to Mark's phone oscillated between anger and worry. I didn't want to alert the children to my suspicions that he'd just walked out on us completely, so I pretended my mobile wasn't working. 'Have you heard from Dad? I can't seem to receive messages on my mobile at the moment.'

Izzy rolled her eyes and said, 'Have you switched it on?'

Jamie just shook his head and lay back down on the sofa, watching reruns of *Friends* in his dressing gown. I paced up and down, wondering how long Katya would wait before she went to the police if she decided to go. I spent the day clearing things out. Baking tins I never used. Old gloves and slippers. The single socks that sat in a basket in the airing cupboard in the hope that their mate would turn up from the corner of a sports bag. I found it oddly comforting.

By Sunday morning, I couldn't sleep or eat. I couldn't risk waiting any longer. There was every chance this final act could finish off my marriage completely. The last part of the puzzle that I'd prayed I'd never have to slot in. God, I really hoped Mark would understand.

No point in roaring round to the McAllisters' at the crack of dawn though. Not much traction to be gained in standing on the doorstep with Sean faintly embarrassed by his pyjamas or Katya worrying about being braless under her nightie. I needed attention that wasn't diluted by them trying not breathe on me because they hadn't cleaned their teeth yet.

I decided that eleven-thirty would be perfect timing. That left me with three hours to fill. I decided to start on my tax return, that guaranteed mood enhancer. Businesswoman of the Year. That was a joke. My work had dwindled over the last month. I'd taken my time to follow up on enquiries, been a little less prompt about calling people back. And a damn sight less patient with the ones who phoned, picked my brains for half an hour and then decided that their mum knew how to arrange flowers and Great Aunt Nellie knew a man with a Costco card.

The tributes on my website of 'patience of a saint' would soon become 'bad-tempered old harridan' if I didn't get a grip. If Mark left me, I'd need the business more than ever. Just letting that idea waltz through my brain triggered a rush of despair so deep that it transported me back to the turbulent days following Dad's dismissal from school.

I put the radio on, forcing myself to sing to every song until the shaky feeling passed. The irony of *I Won't Let The Sun Go Down On Me* wasn't lost on me. I sang it at top volume until Mabel leapt up excitedly, catching one of her paws in the pocket of my cardigan and laddering the fine knit with her claw. I didn't have the heart to shout at her. Mabel didn't understand about living life in moderation.

I walked round the kitchen, using Mabel as my audience for what I was going to say to Katya and Sean. Her floppy ears kept twitching up in puzzlement, her eyes widening then hooding over every time I said a word beginning with 'w' that didn't translate into 'walk'. My whispered speech sounded mean-spirited, petty and vindictive. I had the sense that instead of raising myself up, I'd sunk down to someone I despised.

I tried Mark again. That slight South-West accent in his answerphone message. That voice I trusted. That man I should have told everything to.

I marched out to the car. I couldn't think about my dad's words – 'Two wrongs don't make a right' – the mantra that he'd repeated to me so often whenever I'd told him I'd get my own back on the McAllisters one day. He'd be really sad that his daughter could stoop so low. But Katya wasn't going to ruin my son's life. She wanted to fight dirty.

She had no idea how filthy I was prepared to get. Whatever the cost.

I drove carefully, talking myself through the directions to Sean's house. I noticed more and more that the things that I used to do automatically – drive, make a cup of tea, feed the dog – required me to concentrate.

I edged round the corner into the cul-de-sac where Katya and Sean lived. My eyes were stinging as though sheer will was holding back the water in my tear ducts. It took me a moment to realise that Mark's car was outside their house. A surge of relief that he was all right and still in the area made me tremble. The unpleasant feeling that they were all in there, talking about my despicable behaviour followed. Maybe Mark had decided to interrogate Katya about my affair.

My rational mind knew that Mark would be focused on Jamie, if he knew what Katya was planning, if he'd listened to my messages – any one of the five hundred that would be clogging up his voicemail by now. But I still wanted to burst in and say, 'We've all bloody well made mistakes. I've done some good things, too!'

I turned the car round at the end of the cul-de-sac so I'd be able to zoom straight off once I'd said my piece. I looked in the rear-view mirror, a last glance at the person I was before everyone's opinion of me shifted forever. I was just getting out when the front door flung open with a crash and Mark appeared. Katya followed, screaming at him and lashing out. 'You bastard, you bloody bastard. Don't you ever come near us again. Just fuck off. Fuck off.'

Sean was behind her, trying to grab her wrists, barking, 'Katya! Katya! That's enough! Stop it!'

Then she turned on Sean. 'This is all your bloody mother's fault. Stupid cow. What was she thinking of? Protecting someone else instead of her own son.'

Sean clocked me first but didn't react. Mark was too busy dodging Katya. He didn't retaliate, just did that thing he did so well – stayed completely calm, backing down the drive at his own pace, not rushed, not chased out, just resolute. 'Think on what I've said. And be very clear that I'm not making idle threats. I have no interest in carrying them out, none at all, but I will if you leave me no option.'

I was looking from one to the other, seeing anguish everywhere. I felt as though I had been handed the impossible task of piecing together the fragments of a delicate vase that had just smashed to the ground, without ever having seen it whole.

And then Katya saw me, broke free from Sean and flew at me like a Jack Russell intent on devouring the postman. 'You bitch! You absolute bitch! You put him up to this.'

Mark wasn't quick enough. She managed to claw my face before he grabbed her by the shoulders and restrained her. For the first time ever, I heard him shout, a great deep baritone that reverberated round the cul-de-sac: 'Enough! That is enough! Go inside and get your own house in order before I call the police.'

I froze like my life depended on winning Grandmother's Footsteps. Katya wavered – my god, did she waver. Her desire to give me a good thumping almost triumphed. I sensed the energy surge in her body subside, before Sean reached her and she collapsed, sobbing, against him.

He nodded at me. 'Mark will explain.' He paused. 'I'm so sorry, Lydia. I don't know what to say.'

I tried to understand why he was apologising to me. His face was full of emotions I couldn't decipher. I grappled for a moment, feeling as though everyone was talking a language I was powerless to comprehend.

Mark put his hand on my back and propelled me down the drive. For a moment, we felt like a unit again. Then the McAllisters' door slammed shut, Mark moved away from me and I slithered down a couple of rows on the family snakes and ladders board.

CHAPTER FORTY-FOUR

I stood by my car. Mark moved to touch my face, then stopped mid-air and put his hand in his pocket. He nodded at my cheek instead. 'That's nasty. Let me fetch the first-aid kit out of the car.'

If I hadn't been trying to redirect the adrenaline of my unused speech, I would have smiled at Mark's capacity for having the right thing at the right time.

He handed me a wipe. 'Just under your eye.'

Eventually he took it from me and did it himself, dabbing gently.

I shook him off. 'What the hell happened in there?'

'Let's go and get a coffee and I'll fill you in.'

'Why don't we just go home?' I paused. 'Or do I take it you're not coming back?' A big sob was sitting at the bottom of my throat, stretching my vocal chords until my voice sounded as though it was trying to squeeze out of a space too small for all the huge emotions contained within it.

Mark scratched at the stubble on his chin. I'd never seen him unshaven before. His voice was soft but determined. 'Every time I think I've come to terms with a new discovery about you, something else pops up. I've loved you for such a long time, Lydia, and what hurts so much is that you've never been honest with me. Truths offered up freely feel so bloody different to truths that come out because you're cornered in a lie.'

'There aren't any more truths.'

'You've just proved my point.'

'You know everything there is to know now.'

But Mark carried on shaking his head. He couldn't have discovered the last thing I hadn't told him. There were only two other people who knew and I was positive they wouldn't have revealed it. I glanced at the windows of Sean's house. I didn't want them to be watching this conversation. They wouldn't have to hear the words to see that this was a marriage struggling to stay upright in a full-scale storm.

'Let's sit in your car,' Mark said, as I shivered in the December drizzle.

The concentrated space gave our conversation a 'do or die' feel.

'Do I take it that you've somehow found a way to stop Katya calling the police on Jamie?' I asked.

'You could have done the same,' he said.

'How?'

He looked out of the window. 'You know how.'

Of course, I knew how. I'd come here with the express purpose of wielding that particular weapon. But how the hell did Mark know?

'Is this to do with Sean?' It was a tricky business trying to keep a secret *and* find out whether someone else knows the truth, without discovering you've dug yourself a turd moat to drown in.

Mark turned to me. 'You could say that.'

I felt something in me throw itself onto the funeral pyre. Mark had already left me. What happened thirty years ago didn't matter now except in terms of how it could save Jamie.

'What did you tell them?'

'That you'd had an abortion. That, if necessary, we'd contact the clinic to get the records. Wouldn't actually prove it was Sean you'd had sex with, but I thought it might be enough of a bargaining tool to make them think twice.'

Even though I'd been prepared to shout it at them myself, hearing it come out of Mark's mouth made my whole body go weak with regret. I knew he'd be thinking about the excruciating two years it had taken for me to fall pregnant with Jamie. The times we'd sat discussing intimate details of our lives with doctors who could find nothing wrong. And all the time I'd cradled my guilt, wondering whether my abortion was responsible, shame oozing through me like a weeping sore until I thought I would suffocate beneath it.

And still I said nothing.

I stared at the floor, forcing some volume into my voice.

'How did you find out?'

Mark leaned back in the seat. 'I went to Norfolk.'

'Norfolk?'

'Yes. I wanted to understand, to go back to the beginning. I thought it might help me if I saw where you lived, where you'd come from, the school where your dad worked.'

A visceral sense of longing for those open skies flooded through me. 'It's beautiful, isn't it?'

'Gorgeous. I went to Thornham. Stayed at The Lifeboat Inn. Walked the coastal path to the nature reserve at Holme-next-the-Sea.'

Memories of drinking dandelion and burdock in the pub garden and throwing sticks into the sea for Tripod wriggled in next to the cold reality of today's conversation.

I made myself look at Mark, still waiting to discover how he knew.

'I went to see Sean's mother,' he said, as though he had clarified everything.

But I was still in the dark. Margie couldn't have told him, though she was probably one of the few people who would have understood. I'd loved Margie. She'd made me feel that it was okay to be me. She teased me all the time but not in the way the girls at school did. She teased me *because* I belonged.

'How did you find her?'

'Come on, Lyddie. It's a tiny village. God knows what it was like for you after your dad got the sack. I asked at the shop.'

'Why did you want to see her?'

'I wanted another view of what happened back then. I didn't have to press her too hard.'

'Is she okay? She was very kind to me. It was Sean's dad who pressed the charges. I don't think she wanted to.'

'She didn't. In fact, she begged her husband not to get your dad prosecuted. She was delighted that you'd married and had children. She burst into tears when I showed her a picture of you and the kids, really sobbing.'

I wanted to hurry Mark along, but I could see that in the telling, he was still processing his own feelings about what he'd heard.

'Then she just came out with it. "Thank god she's gone on to be happy. I felt guilty for years after that abortion, thinking about how frightened she must have been. I often wondered if she'd managed to have kids later on."'

'Oh my god. I didn't know she knew. Did she realise I hadn't told you?'

'She didn't when she said it. She was shocked when she saw my reaction, but she didn't try and take it back.'

I shifted in my seat. 'How did she find out, anyway? I never even told Sean.'

'She came round to talk to your mother, to apologise for her husband refusing to drop the charges. Unfortunately, it was the day you'd gone to Somerset for the abortion.'

Mark kept pausing on that word, as though he wasn't quite sure how to pronounce it, as though it couldn't belong in the same context as me. The shame I felt, the strength of it in the face of Mark's bewilderment, made me want to curl up into the smallest, tightest ball.

It almost matched the intensity of that awful day, three months after Dad was first arrested. We were just beginning to adjust to our new reality, coming to terms with the fact that Dad might go to prison. As soon as I heard my mother leave for church, I'd stood at the door of the sitting room, waiting until Dad looked up from his paper. Then I'd thrown myself onto his lap, burying my face in his shoulder, sobbing out that I was pregnant with Sean's baby.

After weeks of repeating that we'd just been messing about in those photos, that 'of course we didn't have sex'.

I forced my attention back to Mark. As he was speaking, his face carried an expression of disbelief, as though he was expecting me to contradict him, to say, 'No, no, of course not, that never happened.'

'Apparently your mother completely lost it with Margie, started screaming at her, told Margie she should feel responsible for killing a baby for the rest of her life,' he said.

'I think she might have been projecting her own guilt there. You know what a staunch Catholic she is. But my dad was absolutely adamant. There was no way he was going to let me have a baby at thirteen. And I think Mum saw the sense in that too. But she really struggled with it.' I forced myself not to cry. 'Margie would probably have come with me to the clinic. My mother couldn't bring herself to. Dad and I pretended to everyone we'd gone away for a little break, just the two of us. When I came back, my mother would never let us talk about it again.'

I tried not to think about Dad steadying himself on the banister at the bottom of the clinic steps, before grabbing my arm and pulling me up them.

'I wish Margie had taken me. Dad found it so traumatic. He kept saying, "You're just a child yourself." Margie wasn't shocked by anything. She made everything I felt, all the big emotions I couldn't tame, seem normal. She always told me that when I grew up, I'd understand them. I'm not convinced she was completely right about that.'

I shivered. I turned the key in the ignition and switched on the heating. 'Why didn't she tell Sean though?' I asked.

Mark shrugged. 'She was protecting him, I suppose. She didn't want to risk her husband finding out. According to her, "He'd have killed Sean himself."'

Mark rubbed his hands together. 'I don't understand why you didn't come straight round here though. You could have shut Katya up yourself.'

'That's why I'm here now. I wanted to discuss it with you first but in the end, I was so terrified that Katya would report Jamie I couldn't wait any longer. I did leave you about nine hundred messages.'

'No signal in that part of Norfolk. The handset nearly blew up when I got to King's Lynn. I was already on my way back when I got your message about Katya wanting to go to the police, so I just drove straight here.'

'Why didn't you ring me when you got in range?'

Mark leaned away from me, huddled up to the door. 'You'd been protecting Sean all this time. I wasn't sure you'd agree to threatening them with that. For me, the priority was Jamie.'

I felt the breath leave my lungs. I stared at Mark as though some random stranger had been walking along the street and decided to hop in and rest his legs in my car. 'You honestly thought I would protect Sean over Jamie?' The unfairness of the accusation had shredded my voice into a tinny thread.

'Forgive me if my trust was a bit shaky. I couldn't allow some bizarre sense of loyalty to Sean to stop me getting them off our backs.'

I thumped the steering wheel. 'How could you ever think that I would let anything happen to Jamie that was in my power to prevent? I've spent the weekend Googling the bloody clinic, trying to find out if it's still there and how long they keep the records for.'

'How could I ever think that you would change your name? That you'd keep it from me that your poor old dad had been in prison? That you'd had underage sex with someone I've grown to consider a friend and top it off with a little Italian affair that I was never supposed to know about? Let alone not breathing a word about the abortion the whole time we were struggling to conceive?'

He threw open the car door. 'I'll be in touch about Christmas. Tell the kids I'm still working away.'

CHAPTER FORTY-FIVE

The days leading up to my niece's wedding were agony. If there had been a medical emergency requiring the opening up of my chest cavity, they would have discovered a congealed lump of tangled matter, haemorrhaging wildly with veins and arteries waving about like wisteria on a windy day, desperate for something to cling onto.

Which made a visit from my mother, whom I had resolutely refused to see since the shoe shop debacle, the least welcome experience I could have imagined beyond the aftermath of Mabel eating a maggoty hedgehog. Dad had popped by to take the kids golfing. I was so delighted to see him full of motivation again, that I was slow to register that as the kids leapt into the car with him, my mother tottered out.

She looked old in the sunlight, despite her make-up. 'Could I come in?' she asked, as Dad's car reversed off the drive. I nodded and stood aside. Mabel came galloping out to greet my mother, who, for once, stroked her – albeit with a flat, rigid hand rather than the proper ruffling and squidging of a dog-lover. But as an olive branch, it was a good start.

'I've got a lot going on at the moment,' I said, as a preamble to telling her she couldn't stay.

My mother frightened me by patting my arm – the closest we ever got to hugging – and saying, 'I know, dear. I do know. I'll make coffee.'

She put a cup down in front of me, with a couple of slices of toast, as if she knew I hadn't had any breakfast. Then she sat down, pursed her lips and said, 'Daddy tells me Mark hasn't been around much.'

Her pale eyes watched me carefully.

I surprised myself. 'He's left me.'

My mother didn't miss a beat. 'Of course he hasn't,' she said, as though I'd told her he'd taken up macramé or hang-gliding. She'd now become the walk-on-water wonder of marriage guidance. She'd always struggled to accept things that didn't concord with her world view.

I looked at her. For once, I didn't care about her disapproval. 'Please do save me from any lectures. I have as much on my plate as one human being can reasonably be expected to deal with.'

'I knew that McAllister boy would end up bringing trouble.'

I felt oddly defensive of Sean. 'It was such a long time ago. I want it to stop now. I'm not going to let 'all that business' affect the next generation too. We were both as bad as each other. I'm just sorry Dad got caught in the middle of it.'

As the words left my mouth, I realised that I didn't want to pursue Sean, even if Katya did go to the police. I hoped that the threat was enough but if not, I'd save my energies for helping Jamie, not for exacting revenge on the McAllisters. I wasn't going to turn on the boy – man – I'd loved so long ago, even if I'd trained myself to hate him over the years. I'd been a willing participant. I couldn't lie about it now.

My mother reached for my hand. My instinct was to withdraw it but I kept it there. 'All men are very proud. It will have hurt Mark to find out our secrets after all this time. He'll just be needing some time away. He's a good man. He wouldn't leave the children.'

My mother sounded as though she was convincing herself.

'It's not about that anymore.'

My mother's eyes narrowed. 'What is it about, then?'

All the years of weighing up whether my thoughts were acceptable enough to be allowed to sully the air my mother breathed ground to a halt. The truth flowed out of me like slurry from a gravel pit.

Jamie, Eleanor, Katya. And god help me, sex with Tomaso as well.

As the multiple horrors came to light, her eyes grew rounder and rounder until she looked like a bush baby. The rest of her was inert, slumped into her seat. She withdrew her hand from mine. I saw the weariness in her bones as she instructed herself to sit up straight and mount a fight back. She pursed her lips. 'I wondered about that Tomosi. Far too charming for his own good. Good job I kept an eye out in Florence. And to think I'd encouraged you to take him…'

I didn't disabuse her of the idea that it had been a Surrey-based one-off. I knew she'd be racing through her mental list of patron saints to call upon in these extreme circumstances. But even St Gregory the Wonderworker wouldn't be able to make this one right.

I held up my hand. 'Don't say anything.'

She didn't. Just leant forward, covered her face with her hands and sobbed.

I watched her tears drop onto her silk blouse. I sat there, immobile as shock spread through me. 'Don't cry!' I could hear the panic in my voice. I wanted to put my arm round her but ended up sitting next to her, afraid to touch her in case she brushed me off. My skin prickled with the desire to comfort her. A long-buried image of my mother refusing to look back at our house as we drove away from Norfolk for the last time came to me so vividly that I could smell the sea air. Little flashes of my mother wrapping up her best china and gently laying the photo of her and Dad on top followed. And later, when he came home from prison: her begging him to eat a spoonful of soup, leading him by the hand to the shower, putting his chair outside in the sunshine 'to get a bit of air'.

She interrupted the parade of memories by grabbing my wrist. Her fingers were strong and cold. It took me a while to understand what she was saying.

'I'm so sorry. I wanted to protect you but I got it wrong. So wrong.'

But unlike me, she'd done her best.

CHAPTER FORTY-SIX

By the morning of Tara's wedding, there'd been no sign of Mark. I hadn't phoned him. I didn't want to hear what he was going to say. I just had to get through the wedding, avoid Michael's questions about Mark's absence and get home again without becoming the 'one' that everyone remembered for the wrong reasons. I almost refused to go, but my dad kept talking about how lovely it would be to have the whole family all together again – if we overlooked the Mark-shaped hole in the photos – and I couldn't let him down. The kids were keen to see their cousins, even though Jamie pronounced Michael's youngest son, William, a 'total knob'. Izzy kept humming, 'Here comes the bride, all fat and wide,' wondering out loud if Tara had gone on a diet, causing me to add 'hopeless mother on correct attitude to body image' to my long list of failures.

Standing in front of the mirror in a beige dress that hung off me, I reflected on all the times that I'd longed for a few hours to myself, the evenings I'd been secretly glad Mark had to work, just to have one less person to think about, to cook for, to pick up after. That was the trouble with marriage. It became so comfortable that the brain attacked itself in search of novelty. Like my dress, everywhere in the house had a flapping, draughty feel as though the space around us had ballooned.

Just the night before, Izzy had scuffed into my bedroom and asked where Mark was.

I looked at her and said, 'We've been under a bit of strain recently. Dad's just taking a bit of time out to sort out his feelings.'

'You won't divorce though, will you?'

'I hope not.'

Izzy's face dropped. More proof, as if I needed it, that I could no longer fix everything for my children, though thankfully Jamie seemed to have accepted my version of the truth that Katya wouldn't want to subject Eleanor to the ordeal of going to the police. Every time the doorbell rang, my heart still jumped in case a policeman wanting to arrest Jamie was on the other side.

I tried to feel positive about a day away from home, where the focus wouldn't be on any of us. Hopefully, we'd be able to sail under the radar at the reception and leave before I had an urge to stand on the table with a megaphone and share the reality of 'marriage according to Lydia'. It wouldn't be a day for burying myself in a bottle of wine when I felt as though the tripwire of my sanity could be triggered by sneeze.

My mother had obviously reported back to my dad. He had decided that relentlessly jovial was the way forward. Jamie, on the other hand, was the human equivalent of storm clouds gathering. 'I'm not wearing a bloody suit! Who gives a shit about Tara and her wedding?' accompanied by plenty of random 'Jesus Christs' and door-banging.

I ushered Izzy out to the car.

'Jamie, come here, love.'

I tried to grab him by his shoulders and make him look at me but he dodged out of my reach.

'What?'

'Don't spoil the day, darling. It's so long since the whole family were together and it means a lot to Granddad.'

'Why should we have to play happy families when – duh – Dad isn't even living with us anymore?'

I tried to imagine a crappier day to have a discussion about our problems when we were about to watch two dewy-eyed hopefuls declare 'for better, for worse'.

'Jamie, Dad and I have a lot going on now but we haven't made any definitive decisions yet. Just for today, can we focus on something else?' My voice crumbled slightly.

Jamie shook his head. 'Isn't that what did it in the first place? Sticking your head in the sand?' He looked at me as if he hated me. The non-maternal bit of me wanted to point out that his girlfriend sharing her front bottom with the world hadn't exactly enhanced our lives either.

I grappled for the high moral ground. Mark would never have let Jamie get away with talking to me like that. I manage to find a fragment of parenting ability. I held out Jamie's jacket. 'That is enough. Put this on, raise your game and say to yourself that sometimes people mess up – you should know that – and sometimes they can never put that right no matter how hard they try, but it doesn't mean they should be punished for the rest of their lives.'

I didn't have any energy left for further oratory, so I grabbed my bag and marched out of the front door. I willed Jamie to follow so that my dad could carry on sunny-side up and my mother wouldn't have to witness a teenage tussle that would impress her – not in a good way – even after everything she'd seen lately.

Thankfully, Jamie squiggled into the back of the car next to me, taking care to keep his entire body a regimented two centimetres away from me. Dad popped on his Carpenters CD as though we were off for a day at the seaside.

Izzy whispered, 'Can we put Capital on?' but frankly, I thought we needed as much *Top of the World* as we could find. I wanted to put my head back and disappear into sleep but couldn't escape the feeling that if I let a single muscle relax, my whole being might empty out all over the seat, swamping everyone in folds of fear and frustration. So I sat rigidly for an hour and a half, imagining my brother's resigned look as he shuffled round the table settings that had been months in the planning.

As we drew into the church car park on the outskirts of Oxford, I ached all over from resisting intervening every time my mother turned round to frown at Jamie and Izzy for playing on their phones. Her newfound niceness didn't extend to putting a sock in it over 'breeding a generation of children with no social skills'.

The kids hopped out as soon as my dad pulled up the handbrake but I didn't even take my seatbelt off. I'd been into so many churches because of my job – I'd even stood persuading a bride with cold feet that she really did want to hurry down the aisle before the vicar gave up on her. But now, the idea of walking through that arched door and shuffling in next to my children, breathing in musty hymn-booky emptiness in the space where Mark should be standing, floored me.

Dad opened the car door. 'Lydia?'

My mother poked her head round him like an impatient penguin waiting for her chick to waddle down to the water. 'Darling. Come on. You have to do this,' she said. But her harshness had receded. It was almost as though if push came to shove, she'd let me lie on the back seat and sleep through the service rather than attempt to force her will on me.

Dad held his hand out. I grabbed onto him, surprised by his strength.

'Let's go. The kids need you.'

A short and simple motivator. He always found the right words.

I got out of the car and he tucked his arm through mine. My mother marched ahead with the children, who were pretending not to notice her and walking a bit faster than she could manage. Dad leaned into me and said, 'Your mum told me what's happened.'

My arm tensed in his. I had hoped I would never make another mistake that I'd have to explain to Dad after 'the big one'. Disappointingly, it seemed that I wasn't a one-screw-up wonder. I opened my mouth to speak but he shook his head.

'I'm not judging you, Lydia. I've no doubt some of your behaviour is rooted in how your mum and I have handled things. It's going to be hard but you can get through it, you've survived a lot worse.'

I nodded, but didn't speak in case I cried. My mother strutted through the door and down to the front, only to be rebuffed by Michael's wife, Olivia, and shooed back a pew or two. Dad ushered me in next to my mother, but I asked to sit on the outside. If the cauldron of unhappiness at the bottom of my stomach suddenly boiled over, I needed to be able to make a quick exit.

Unlike the kids, who were gawking around whispering about people's clothes, I stared straight ahead. I tried to concentrate on the professional aspects of the wedding – the arrangement of the silver-sprayed teasels, the pews crammed with the groom's friends and family versus the sparsely populated ones on our side. I didn't even look round when the music started up and everyone's head craned towards the back of the church.

I couldn't stop thinking about how I'd felt the day I married Mark. I remembered how the sense of isolation I'd carried with me throughout my teens and into my twenties dissolved as he put the ring on my finger. His eyes held mine, all the way through the service, crinkled up in the corners with delight. As we made our vows, I heard the smiles in our voices and felt as though, at long last, someone was firmly on my side.

Michael walked past with Tara on his arm and I tried not to notice my mother light up and glance across the aisle to make sure that the groom's family were paying appropriate homage to her doctor son. 'He's a neurologist, you know.' Michael parked Tara next to her fiancé and stepped back, shoulders straight, head up.

Then the ceremony started. As the vicar's voice rang out round the church, I tried to steer my thoughts away from my own wedding day. But the memories were too strong. I'd stood there with my hand in Mark's, the registrar clipped and to the point. I'd never wavered in my belief that I'd made the right choice: I'd found a steady platform on which to build the rest of my life. Back then, I'd been absolutely certain that we'd be able to weather anything.

I wriggled my toes in my shoes. The December draughts rattling in under the door were more than a match for the church's ancient heating.

I could feel the vows building to 'for better, for worse'. I held my breath. Keeping absolutely still seemed the only way to stop something ripping inside me. My loneliness reached up to the rafters, threading itself through the words of *Give Me Joy in My Heart*. My mother sang with righteousness and operatic gusto. We would definitely be having the 'At least they chose hymns we all know' conversation on the way to the reception. The children didn't sing at all. I did hope it was because singing, especially in church, wasn't cool, not because their spirits were so low they couldn't find it within themselves to participate in anything jolly.

During the prayers, there was a line about forgiveness, which acted as a Stanley knife through the last little stitch holding my heart in place. The tears that followed wouldn't adhere to the slipping out quietly rule. I stifled one sob, and half-muffled another. I scrabbled for a tissue, but the delay between pocket and face allowed a huge, wild wail to echo round the church. The rustle of heads turning round from the pew in front, my mother's eyebrows shooting skywards, Izzy mouthing, 'Mum?', the groundswell of other people becoming involved in the Rushford family fiasco was too much for me. I picked up my bag and blundered down the aisle, head bowed, avoiding all the intrigued faces lining my route.

The church door banged behind me but I didn't care. Let everyone talk about Michael's weird sister. It was the crap wife and mother moniker that bothered me. I shivered in my dress, my winter stole ineffectual against the wind. I realised too late that Dad had the car keys. It wouldn't be long before everyone came out. I needed to make myself scarce or rein in the great hiccupping sobs in time to get my confetti-throwing face on. A disappearing act looked like the best option. I hurried across the graveyard.

The rain was pelting down from a leaden sky, threatening to add see-through dress to my list of my niece's wedding day highlights. I ran as fast as I could on the uneven path towards a thatched shelter next to some of the grander tombstones. I stumbled in, swiping my soaking hair off my face, then bit back a scream as I clocked a man in the corner with his coat pulled up round his ears. Parallel thoughts flashed through my head: *Perfect hide out for a tramp. It doesn't smell of wee in here. Mark's got a coat like that.*

Jesus Christ, that is *Mark.*

CHAPTER FORTY-SEVEN

Oddly, the whole bursting in on a tramp/husband/graveyard scenario plus general unhappiness translated itself into shouting laced with some snotty sobs.

'What are you doing hiding in here? Why would you do that? Leaving me to explain to Michael's whole perfect family why you aren't there?'

Any romantic reunion I might have dreamed of imploded right away.

Mark had his hands up. 'Lydia. Calm down. Here, have this, you're soaking.' He stood up and took his coat off.

'No. I'm fine.' I was thankful to have a tissue so I could level the playing field just a fraction by having a clean nose.

Mark ignored me and placed his coat round my shoulders. He hesitated, then faffed about untucking my hair from the collar.

Something in his face stopped me doing the deranged wife routine. 'What?'

He looked away. 'I've been trying to get my head around leaving you.'

I couldn't look him in the face. I stared at the empty beer can under the bench. My stomach lurched and the sick feeling I'd been fighting all morning became a real possibility.

He stepped towards me. 'But I can't. I just can't imagine a life without you in it.'

Mark pulled me to him by the lapels of the coat and put his arms around me. 'I've really missed you, you madwoman.'

Our cold lips touched, giving way to the warmth of our tongues. Slowly, the sensation of being wound in the opposite direction, loosening the tension in my thoughts and feelings, took over.

'Are you sure?' I whispered, as he slipped his arms inside the coat.

'I've told myself I should leave. But every time I try and imagine it, I feel so empty. I don't want to be without you, Lydia. I just don't. There was so much I didn't understand about you when we met but I still loved you.' He tried to make a joke. 'Now I do understand, maybe I can love you a bit more.'

I didn't know how to respond.

He dropped his head onto my shoulder. 'I know what people will say if they find out about, the – you know, the other guy.' I was grateful he didn't mention his name. 'But I don't care if they think I'm weak. As long as you are certain it's over and you definitely want to be with me.'

'I couldn't be more sure.'

He didn't answer. Just held me.

The church bells started ringing.

'They're coming out. I'd better go and find them all.'

Mark took my hand. 'We're not going to the reception.'

'We have to. I can't just not turn up. Michael's seen me. And the kids wanted to spend time with their cousins.'

'You have done what you should, rather than what you've wanted, forever. Today, Mrs Rushford, you're not doing it. We are not going to sit there while your pompous brother pontificates on his A* daughter who's going to live in some bloody eco-mansion in the New Forest. I'm taking you away.'

'But what about the kids?'

'They can stay in the hotel with your parents for one night, can't they?'

I was shocked that Mark could even think about sneaking off. But planning something naughty *together* cheered me in a way that doing the right thing could never have done.

'The kids are a bit all over the place. They think we're going to get divorced. We can't leave without telling them.'

'I've no intention of disappearing without talking to them first. I've been desperate to see them but we just need an opportunity to talk without worrying about the flapster ears getting the wrong end of the stick. Staying together is probably the best Christmas present they can have. Though I guess for Jamie that would be a close run thing with a PlayStation 4.'

I smiled, recognising a grain of truth in his words.

Mark waved me away. 'You go and get in the car.'

'But it's Christmas Eve tomorrow.'

'We'll be back for that. Wouldn't miss putting out sustenance for Santa for anything.' Mark laughed. The kids reiterated every year that they were *waaa-aay* too old to believe in Father Christmas but still wanted to leave carrots for Rudolph.

'Where will we go? My case is in Dad's car.'

'I'll fetch it. We're going to lay a few ghosts.'

'What do you mean?'

'We're going back to Norfolk. You're going to talk me through the missing bits.'

I sat down on the bench. 'I don't know if I'm ready for that.'

'You have to do it, Lydia. You can't run away any more. I'll hold your hand.'

The big rush of fright carried with it a fine thread of something else I struggled to identify. Yet again, the English language didn't quite provide a word to describe my feelings. Hope mixed with rebellion? Equal measures of reluctance and desire? Belief in a good outcome because someone you loved was with you?

Today was not my day to call the shots. Today was my day to be beyond grateful for the husband I had and his hugeness of spirit. And if that meant I had to walk those beaches, shine a light on those dark places in my mind, I'd do it. I felt almost excited at the prospect.

'One other thing. Sean phoned me.'

I braced myself.

'He wants to leave Katya.'

That didn't surprise me, but it wasn't the thing that interested me. 'Is she going to the police?'

Mark ran his hands through his hair. 'I'm not sure how I feel about this.'

'What?' My heart was speeding up.

'She's promised that she won't go to the police about Jamie if Sean doesn't walk out on her.'

'And is he going to stay?' I felt as though I was shouting, but Mark was leaning in, as though he couldn't hear me.

'He said he owes you. His turn to live the lie.'

I'd dreamed of getting my own back on Sean McAllister for years and all I felt now was a deep sadness for someone trapped in the wrong life. And selfishly, relief. Relief that made my body loose and weak.

'I'd already decided I wouldn't take him down if Katya reported Jamie.'

Mark touched my cheek. 'I never thought you would. I wouldn't have done either, but Katya doesn't need to know that.'

I wondered out loud whether Katya and Sean would find a way to be happy. Mark kissed me on the lips. 'Sometimes, there isn't a happy ending for everyone, Lyddie. We owe it to him not to squander the opportunity for ours. On that note, just hang on here a minute.'

Mark thrust the keys at me and strode off towards the church, his shirt sticking to his back in the rain. He was right. Too much toeing the line made for a crushed spirit and a wasted half-life. Anyway, I had no doubt my brother would be delighted I wasn't there, spoiling the photos with my drowned ratness.

I peered out from my hiding place, to see Jamie smiling and shaking hands with Michael. Then I watched Izzy throw herself on Mark, my dad scoop him into a bear hug, my mother offer a cheek to be pecked.

My mother frowned. My dad looked round, puzzled, then smiled and spoke forcefully to my mother. She quickly rearranged her face into acquiescence. Jamie hugged his dad really tightly, then stepped back and listened to him with a look of concentration. A wash of relief passed over his face, his shoulders relaxing. A small darkness crept back in as he received the news of parental absence from the rest of the proceedings. Izzy obviously decided to be the grown-up. She tapped Jamie on the arm, gesticulating first to my mother and Dad, and then to Mark, followed by a wider, vaguer wave out into the graveyard, which I guessed meant, 'That feckless mother of ours, screwing everything up. We'd better let her disappear with Dad and sort things out, otherwise we'll be left alone with her at the rudder and we'll all be up a gum tree.' Jamie shrugged and nodded as Mark turned to leave.

I walked to the car, texting *Thank you* to Sean.

THE END

LETTER FROM KERRY

Hello there,

Thank you so much for reading *After the Lie* – I really hope you enjoyed it – it's always nerve-racking, sending a book out into the world where people who are not related to me are going to be reading it. On the other hand, escaping family verdicts can sometimes be a huge plus. My mother: 'I always tell my friends the language is a bit spicy, but explain that, at your age, I can't stop you swearing.'

One of the things that sparked off the idea for this novel was talking to my friends about how glad we are to have grown up in a pre-internet age, without our adolescent mistakes being plastered all over Facebook. I have two teenagers and am acutely aware that they know so much more than I do about social media – at least, how to use it, if not the pitfalls. It's one of the areas of parenting that frightens me most because I feel so ill-equipped to protect them. Though my son learning to drive this year comes a close second. Like Lydia, I'm going to start stockpiling sleep now…

Family relationships fascinate me and I enjoyed putting a mother-daughter relationship under the microscope in *After the Lie*. Unlike Lydia's mother, Dorothy, my own mother always made me feel that whatever I did, she would still be proud of me – despite my spicy language. Weirdly, I find it easier to imagine the complete opposite of my own experiences rather than attempting to fictionalise real life. I'd be interested to know if you had any sympathy for Lydia's mother in the end. In my mind, she tried to do her best in very difficult circumstances.

Finally, I wanted to explore the idea that small secrets grow more toxic as they pass down the generations, until the original secret is nowhere near as dramatic as the betrayal of being lied to for so long. I cannot imagine living in a family where nothing is discussed – even the dog has far too many opinions in our house. Which brings me to my Lab/Giant Schnauzer cross, Poppy. She was the inspiration for Mabel and has done all the naughty things in this novel and more. I decided that it was time she earned her keep.

Anyway, if you have enjoyed *After the Lie*, I'd be really grateful if you could leave me a short review on Amazon – I always feel ridiculously embarrassed mentioning this, but reviews are so important to authors in getting the word out about our books. I cannot tell you how much it brightens my day when readers get in touch, so I'd be delighted to hear from you on Facebook or Twitter .

Messages from readers are motivational gold when you're staring down the barrel of 300 blank pages and wondering, 'How exactly did I do this before?'

If you'd like to be kept up-to-date with news of my next book, please sign up to the link below. We won't bombard you with anything else.

www.bookouture.com/kerry-fisher

All the very best,

Kerry xx

www.facebook.com/kerryfisherauthor
www.twitter.com/KerryFSwayne

312

ACKNOWLEDGMENTS

From a half-baked idea scribbled on the top of a newspaper over breakfast, there are so many people involved in the process of delivering a finished novel. I'm always terrified that I'll miss someone out, but here goes. I have to start with my agent, Clare Wallace. I'd be all over the place without her support and good judgment. I am so grateful to have her on my side, as well as the rest of the team at Darley Anderson. I'm also indebted to my editor, Lydia Vassar-Smith at Bookouture, for her enthusiasm and her ability to coax the book into the best shape possible.

Without a doubt, my big band of writing friends push and pull me to the finish line with their listening and support. In particular, the cheerleading and suggestions of my writing buddy, author Jenny Ashcroft, have made the writing/publishing process so much easier.

My husband, Steve, deserves a huge cheer for always believing in me. As do my children, Cameron and Michaela, for helping me understand how teenagers communicate and for making technology work before I completely lose the plot.

For this book in particular, I'm sending a trolley-load of thank you biscuits to my dog, Poppy, who brings her own special brand of joy to my life and a level of picnic destruction previously unseen on the Surrey Hills to everyone else's.

I'm thankful once again to the long-suffering Gary McDade – as well as Mandy Bewicke, Ellie Ludlam and Julie Fisher – who answered my questions about court cases and police procedure. Any inaccuracies are entirely down to me.

Thanks to the lovely book bloggers whose level of commitment to promoting books fills me with awe. And also to all the wonderful people who make the effort to leave a review on Amazon, champion my novels in book club forums (Alexina Golding is a phenomenon) or send me messages on Facebook and Twitter.

But most of all, a loud and long hurrah for all my readers – it's such a privilege to have you spend your precious free time reading my books.

Thank you.

Made in United States
North Haven, CT
13 January 2022

14713658R00172